A NEW BEGINNING

Crossing the crest of the hill, David glanced around, then suddenly stopped. He gazed out over the landscape, gripped by a sense of wonder. While traveling about on his work in England, he had seen the moors and the great fertile plain of Yorkshire, but they would be lost here.

Somewhere west of the Bathurst plain was the outback, a gigantic, mysterious region that remained unexplored. He had heard that some people had been there, but very few. On maps, it was a blank with an extent like that of the seas.

When he had heard about the outback, it had meant little to him. But now, as he looked out across the landscape, its significance was vital. Standing on Prospect Hill and gazing to the west, he had come to a crossroads in his life.

In the outback, he could build himself a new life, cutting himself off from all that had happened to him and leaving his agony of sorrow behind.

Exuberant happiness swelled within him, too much for him to contain. In a boyish impulse, he lifted his arms over his head, whooping at the top of his voice and shouting his joy to the world.

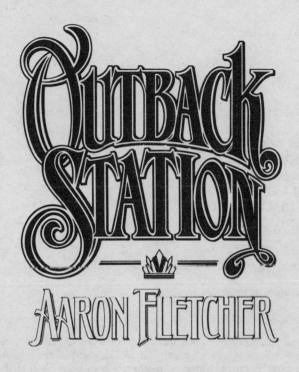

OUTBACK STATION

AARON FLETCHER

LEISURE BOOKS　　NEW YORK CITY

A LEISURE BOOK®

June 2000

Published by

Dorchester Publishing Co., Inc.
276 Fifth Avenue
New York, NY 10001

ISBN 0-8439-4730-6

Does the road wind uphill all the way?
Yes, to the very end.
Will the day's journey take the whole long day?
From morn to night, my friend.

Christina Georgina Rossetti, 1830-1894

Part I

Chapter One

When he heard the first loud crack of a thick beam in the mine ceiling behind him, David Kerrick reacted instinctively. Dropping the heavy hammer he was using to pound a steel drill into the coal to break loose slabs of it, he picked up the lantern at his feet. "Follow me!" he shouted at the two convicts who were shoveling up the loose coal, then he stepped quickly to the side of the mine.

The two men were slow-witted, as well as lethargic from the grueling labor. Remaining where they were, one of them called out in surprise as they were left in darkness, "What the bloody hell . . ."

His voice and the metallic clatter of other convicts' picks were suddenly drowned in the deafening roar of supporting timbers splintering and huge rocks falling. The cave-in, some forty feet away, was at the junction of the main tunnel and the branch where David and the others were working. He stood beside the framework of supporting beams at the side of the mine, holding the smoky oil lantern close and sheltering its flame with his body.

The dark, low cavern quaked violently as its roof at the junction with the main tunnel collapsed, and swirling air currents from the tons of falling rock snuffed out the other lanterns. In the total, oppressive darkness, the air was thick with choking coal dust. The supports beside David groaned and sagged under the stress, but they held. Nothing larger than pebbles rained down on him.

As the rumble of falling rocks faded away, two men, pinned under the debris, screamed in agony. The other convicts, terror-stricken, stumbled about in the darkness, shrieking that they were doomed. In contrast to their panic, David had a detached, impassive attitude. Having escaped the near-brush with instant death, he saw that his life—such as it was—would continue.

Turning away from the side of the tunnel, he lifted the lantern, its light reaching only a few feet through the thick dust in the air. One of the men charging wildly about in the darkness rushed to the light, clawing frantically at the lantern. "Give that here!" he bellowed. "I'm going to find a way out of—"

He broke off as David hit him, driving a fist solidly into his face. As he reeled back and fell, Kerrick turned to the dim shadows of the others in the darkness. "Get yourselves in hand!" he shouted. "We'll never get out of here unless you keep your wits about you!"

"We won't in any event!" a man wailed in fright. "We're trapped like bloody rats, and we'll meet our end in this bloody coal pit!"

The man started to continue, then fell silent and cringed, when David lifted a fist and moved toward him. As another convict brushed past him, David seized the man and hurled him toward the others who were still rushing about. He collided with several of the men who in turn stumbled against those near them, sprawling in a tangle of flailing limbs.

"Now settle yourselves," David ordered, walking toward them as they climbed to their feet. "The more you move about, the sooner you'll use up the air in here." He pointed to one of the men. "You, find another lantern and a pick. The rest of you sit down. I'll have a look and see how we can get out, and I'll call you if you're needed."

The man David had pointed to disappeared into the darkness toward the coal seam, and the others quietly sat down. Well over six feet and two hundred pounds, David towered above most of them, and he had the assurance of an intelligent, well-educated man. Through painful experience, some of the men knew it was unwise to cross him, and they were wary of him for yet another reason. While they had been transported to Australia for minor crimes, David Kerrick had been sent to the penal colony for having committed murder.

David lifted the lantern higher, moving toward the cave-in. Two men, now moaning and whimpering in pain, had been carrying out full hods of coal when the ceiling had collapsed. They were partially buried in the pile of rocks and dirt that blocked the front of the tunnel, and three other men pulled at rocks near them.

"Leave that," David told the men. "Get the rocks off those two there and pull them back with the others."

"You look after them," one of the men replied. "I'm getting my arse out of here, and everyone else can go to . . ."

His voice faded into a yelp of surprise and pain as David seized his shirt and flung him back from the debris. "Get the rocks off those two," David repeated quietly, "and take them over to the others."

The man grumbled resentfully, climbing to his feet,

then joined the other two in moving the debris off the buried men. The dust started to settle, but David still saw very little in the weak light from his lantern. Then the man who had gone to the other end of the tunnel stepped up beside him with a lantern and a pick. David lit the wick in the lantern with his, then held up both of them.

In the brighter light, he saw that the situation was perilous. The crossbeams supporting the ceiling were cracked and sagging, the ceiling itself bulging downward. The stones blocking the tunnel were too large to move, and the rest of the ceiling would collapse if they were. David looked at the smaller stones near the ceiling on one side of the pile, then extinguished a lantern. He climbed up on the debris with the pick and began cautiously moving the stones.

The other man followed him, holding the lantern and pushing rocks on down the pile as David pried them loose. "I heard you tell Boggs that the shoring here wasn't safe," the man muttered. "If he'd had to keep his arse in here with ours, he might have listened to you."

Making no reply to the reference to Cyrus Boggs, the superintendent of the mine, David levered another stone free. An emancipist—a former convict who had served his time—Boggs was a gruff, stubborn man who was slow to grasp that conditions here were different from the mines he had worked in England. When Boggs had shrugged off the warning, David had dismissed the subject himself. Having nothing to look forward to but endless misery, David merely did what was necessary from day to day, with little concern about when or how it would end.

Pushing rocks and dirt toward the man behind him, David lay on his stomach and dug a narrow passage into the debris, just under the ceiling. The air became thin as the minutes passed, and the dust that he raised in the confined space compounded his difficulty in breathing. The man behind him began panting heavily, his lungs laboring for air.

At first, it appeared that the path was blocked when David came to two larger stones wedged under the end of a crossbeam. He prised at one of them, levering on one side of it and then on the other with the pick. It finally pulled loose as the thick timber settled an inch, and the exertion of pushing the stone to the man behind him almost exhausted David.

The light from the lantern was dimmer, its flame tiny in the thin air as David worked at the second stone. The man behind him, having moved the first stone, collapsed and gasped hoarsely. The other convicts, alarmed, complained that they were smothering. Some of them stirred and then sat back down, the effort to move too overwhelming.

Loosening the stone was almost too much for David, and his lungs burned as he panted breathlessly. His own life purposeless, he was willing to accept fate, but he had an ingrained sense of responsibility toward the other men. Despite his low regard for most of the convicts, he had to do whatever he could to save them.

The stone shifted as the heavy crossbeam groaned and sagged another inch, but it held. Summoning his strength, David pulled the rock and pushed it to the man at his back. The convict pulled at it feebly, while David slid under the crossbeam and moved loose debris out of the way. Then he stopped, listening closely.

Over the ringing in his ears and his ragged breathing, he heard tools clanging against the rocks on the other side of the debris. Convicts from other parts of the mine were working hurriedly to clear a path through the rocks and dirt, but they were at the center of the cave-in.

David rapped the point of his pick against a rock in front of him, stopped to listen, then hammered the rock again. When he paused once more, there was silence on the other side. He struck the rock harder, and a moment later, he heard digging noises straight in front of him. Dropping the pick, he waited as numbness stole over him.

From what seemed to be a long distance, David heard voices as the scraping of tools and the rumbling of rocks being moved grew louder. At last, the rock in front of him shifted. Fresh air flooded around the stone. David drew in deep breaths, and the light of the lantern brightened. The rock was pulled aside, and lanterns shone through the hole.

Men with shaggy hair and beards, their eyes wide and staring in their coal-blackened faces, peered at David. One of the convicts turned and shouted over his shoulder, "We've cleared a way through to the men, Mr. Boggs. One of them is right here."

"Then get out of the way so I can talk to him," Boggs replied brusquely. "Come on, make room there."

The men moved aside for the irascible Boggs, who was in his forties and had a red, bulbous nose above his thick mustache and beard. Responsible for mine safety and for meeting the coal-production quota, he was worried. "Did anyone in there get killed?" he asked David.

"No, but two men are injured. I'll have them brought out first."

"Aye, very well," Boggs said morosely, then turned away and spoke to the other men, "you there, go fetch the surgeon. You four stay and help get the injured men outside, and the rest of you get back to work. This is no reason to stop work and loiter about for the rest of the day."

The superintendent shouted more orders as David moved back through the narrow passage. The other convicts had gathered at the end of it, eager to get out. "Bring the injured men here," David told them. "The first ones to leave can take those men with them."

"Somebody else can take them," a man muttered,

pushing past David. "I want out of here before the rest of it falls in."

David pulled the man back, then shoved him onto the pile of rocks and dirt. "Bring the injured men," he repeated impassively.

Turning away and clambering down the debris, the convicts muttered resentfully among themselves. Moments later they climbed back up, the first ones carrying the two helpless, moaning men. David held up the lantern as two men backed into the passage and pulled the injured men into it. Then the others filed into the opening after them.

When they were gone, David sat for a few minutes in the silence, needing the privacy. The most tormenting time of his life had been the months of close confinement with hundreds of men in the filth and disease on the ship that had brought him to Australia, and he always took advantage of every opportunity to be alone. Finally, he crawled into the passage.

At the mouth of the mine, amid a litter of coal hods, jute bags, and sledges used to haul the coal to the wharf, the surgeon worked over the two injured men. The grimy convicts sat a few feet away while Boggs talked with the commandant, Lieutenant Oliver Bethune. In his early thirties, the lieutenant was a meticulously neat man of average build, a stern, but fair, professional soldier. Frowning in annoyance, he listened as Boggs anxiously tried to explain away the accident.

David stepped to one side of the mine, which was on a low hill set back from the village of Newcastle. He surveyed the hamlet that was some eighty miles north of Sydney, with its wharfs and main streets on a peninsula flanked by the Hunter River on one side and the ocean on the other. Established in 1804 as an isolated penal outstation for incorrigible convicts, and called Coal Harbor at the time, the village had grown and changed over the years.

Now in June of 1820, with the crisp chill of late

autumn changing into winter, the barracks, cook-house, and other buildings for convicts were only a small cluster of structures at one side of the thriving village. During the past years, emancipists and free immigrants had cleared the dense acacia and eucalyptus trees from the fertile river valley reaching back from the peninsula. Now tidy stone cottages were scattered among pastures dotted with livestock and fields where crops had been gathered.

Along with coal, Newcastle was a source of wood for furniture and moldings in government buildings, the cedar growing in vast stands far up the Hunter River. As David looked at the village and outlying farms, a raft moved down the river toward Newcastle. The raft was made up of cedar tree trunks some forty feet long and six to eight feet thick, with a hut on it where the convict work party and their military guards had lived during the long trip down the river.

Bethune walked toward David with Boggs following him. "I understand that you were responsible for getting the men out of there safely," the lieutenant commented. "That was very well done."

"I can't take full credit, sir," David replied. "The men who dug through the cave-in from the outside did as much or more."

"Even so," Lieutenant Bethune insisted, "you kept your presence of mind and prevented a cock-up from becoming a disaster. That was highly commendable. Did you happen to observe what caused the cave-in? Mr. Boggs tells me that he's had trouble getting enough suitable timber for shoring, so I suppose the cave-in occurred where it was insufficient."

The superintendent eyed David worriedly, fearing he would mention his warning about the shoring, then relaxed at David's reply. "There was sufficient timber, but too much of it was used for transverse supports and not enough for bracing. The construction of the shoring is more suitable for the mines in England, where the coal seams are much smaller than they are here."

Lieutenant Bethune pursed his lips thoughtfully as he took a snuffbox from his waistcoat pocket. He inhaled a pinch of it, then brushed his nose with a handkerchief. "That's right, I remember from your records that you're an engineer," he mused. "From now on, you'll work as a foreman. Your first task is to clean up the cave-in and put that part of the mine back into operation, then you're to inspect and make all necessary improvements to the shoring throughout the mine." He turned to the superintendent. "Assign him a work crew and see to the other details, Mr. Boggs."

Boggs nodded and replied, touching his hat as the lieutenant walked away. When the officer was out of earshot, Boggs cleared his throat uncomfortably. "I'm grateful that you didn't tell the commandant what you said to me about the shoring a few days ago," he muttered awkwardly.

"It wouldn't have changed what happened," David replied, shrugging.

"Aye, that's true," Boggs agreed cheerfully. "Anyway, all's well that ends well, and you're a foreman now."

The lieutenant and surgeon went down the path to the village, and the convicts followed them with the injured men on stretchers. David pointed to them. "What did the surgeon say about the men who were hurt?"

"He said they should recover soon enough. One may be a bit gimpy from now on, but it could have been much worse. Now that you're a foreman, you can go to the storeroom and draw new clothes to replace those canaries you're wearing. Also, a couple of the foremen's huts are empty, so you can move your swag into one of them." He turned away. "You can do that now, and I'll assign you a work crew the first thing tomorrow morning."

The superintendent went into the mine, and David headed for the village. He saw that the cedar raft had reached the sawmill at the upper end of the hamlet. When it was tied up at the bank in front of the mill, the work crew straggled toward the convict compound, while the guards went into a tavern. Under the present governor, convicts were not guarded constantly and were permitted some latitude when not working.

But David knew it was latitude only in comparison with the stricter policies of other governors, and the treatment of convicts depended more upon the mood and personality of their overseers than official policies. And for those who tried to flee or rebelled in other ways, there was Norfolk Island with its brutal labor, harsh living conditions, and savage lashings—a cruel, precarious life that few survived.

Joseph Lycett, a small, sallow man, came out of the village church as David passed it. An artist convicted of forgery, he was an example of the governor's leniency gone awry. He had a frail constitution and had been given a sinecure as a post-office clerk in Sydney. There, with access to a printing press, he had promptly flooded the town with bogus five shilling notes. As punishment, he had been banished to Newcastle, where he was painting a triptych for the church altar.

At the storeroom, the clerk, an aged convict, issued David sets of brown wool trousers, coats, and rough cotton shirts. Carrying the clothes, David went to the barracks, a sprawling, gloomy structure of slab lumber that quartered some three hundred convicts. A number of men were loitering in the barracks when David went inside, and they watched in silence as he gathered up his belongings and left, knowing from experience that the wisest course was to leave the tall, muscular man completely alone.

The foremen's huts near the barracks were scarcely less dingy than the main building, but David was more than satisfied as he stepped into an empty one and looked around. It offered solitude as well as escape from the filth and stench of the barracks. He put his things on the cot, then went to the bathhouse.

After washing off the coal dust and grime, he lathered his face and shaved, as he did daily. Returning to the hut, he looked at the new clothes in satisfaction and put on a set. Wearing yellow woolens that identified convicts as far as the eye could see had never particularly bothered him, but his had become shabby, while the new clothes were neat and clean.

When he finished dressing, David walked to the cookhouse as others straggled toward it from the barracks. At a workbench beside the building, one of the convict women scrubbed the kettles. Young and pretty, she drew whistles and ribald comments as well as polite greetings from convicts, which she disregarded.

Glancing up at David, however, she smiled warmly. "Wearing browns now, are we?" she remarked gaily. "When I first saw you, I knew you wouldn't be wearing canaries very long." Her voice became softer, her smile inviting. "If you asked me, I'd go walking beside the river with you."

David made no reply, ignoring her as he passed. She flushed with embarrassment and anger, then tossed her head and dismissed him with a shrug as she bent over the kettles again.

In the noisy cookhouse, David stood in line for a bowl of tepid, watery fish soup and a slice of coarse bread. Taking it to the end of one of the long, puncheon tables where no one else was sitting, he sat down and ate. Amid the hubbub of conversation, many of the convicts complained loudly about the unappetizing meal, but David ate without distaste or enjoyment, but simply satisfied his need for food.

When he left the cookhouse, he walked past the village and down the peninsula between the river and the ocean. It was a deserted wasteland where he often came. The crests of the sandy dunes were covered with gorse and tussocks of hardy grass, thickets of wiry boxbush filling the hollows, and clusters of tall eucalyptus trees. The trees were still in full foliage even at the end of autumn, the eucalyptuses shedding bark instead of their leaves.

Gulls and terns circled overhead in the sunset, and the trees were alive with a variety of noisy parrots finding roosts for the night. A flock of galahs, small cockatoos with gray backs and pink breasts, passed overhead against a cloud touched with crimson by the setting sun. The birds seemed to change color when they swerved, showing gray then pink and then gray once more.

At the foot of the cliffs flanking the mouth of the river, the blending fresh and salt water swirled around stumps of petrified trees, remnants of a forest from eons ago. Across from Hobby's Head, the southern point of the river entrance, the peninsula rose to a knoll overlooking the shoreline. On the knoll was a solitary gum tree, gnarled from the buffeting of ocean storms, but still tenaciously sturdy and robust. Sitting under the tree in the fading daylight, David pulled out his watch.

Twice during the voyage on the convict transport ship that had brought him to Australia, David had savagely beaten men who had tried to steal the watch. While it was not a particularly expensive timepiece, to him it was priceless, worth immeasurably more than the few guineas it would cost in a shop. But it was also a source of constant torture, an agony that haunted him with every breath he took.

Inside the lid of the watch was a miniature of a young, beautiful woman. As he looked at it, David writhed inwardly with yearning love that was bitterly caustic from a sense of betrayal. It was a searing, consuming torment that had become more intense rather than fading with time.

Chapter Two

Aboard the *Phoebe,* a sloop that plied between Sydney, Newcastle, and ports in Van Diemen's Land, Lieutenant Oliver Bethune stepped down into the companionway to the crew cabin as he took out his snuffbox. He opened it and inhaled a pinch of the powder, then stifled a sneeze. Sighing in satisfaction, he put the box away and brushed his nose with his handkerchief as he went back up into the cold, winter wind sweeping the deck.

The sloop was low in the water, its hold full of coal and stacks of thick cedar slabs lashed down on the deck. Pulling up his collar against the wind, Bethune sat on a stack of the aromatic wood. He looked at the coast several miles off the starboard beam and contemplated the possibility of his being transferred to a regiment in India or Africa.

It appeared favorable because he had solicited the help of his family and friends in London who had influence in military assignments. His chances of promotion would be better in India or Africa, but far more important, he would be a soldier again instead of a jailer. He hoped he would find mail with encouraging news on the subject waiting for him in Sydney.

As he scanned the horizon, he saw that the trip from Newcastle was nearing an end. In the far distance to the south, the sails of two ships out at sea from Sydney came into view. A few minutes later, Jackson Heads, the entrance to the harbor, rose above the tops of the waves.

At the bow of the sloop, two crewmen were relaxing during the run down the coast ahead of a favorable wind. One of them stood up, looking back at the man at the helm. "Jackson Heads off the starboard bow, Captain Barnes," he called. "Shall we make ready to put about?"

"Wait your hurry, jocko," the captain replied. "I'm the boss cockie here, and I'll tell you when to get ready."

The master and owner of the vessel, a tall, well-built man in his early twenties, had the accent of those born in Australia. It was completely unlike any that the lieutenant had ever heard. While it had overtones of Cockney and Irish accents, it was neither of those nor any other regional accent from Great Britain. Twangy, sharp, and nasal, it divided some words and crowded them into adjoining words. It was unique and unmistakable, as distinctive as the land of its origin.

His efforts to be transferred gave him a transient's attitude of detachment, making him an observer of the Australian people and their customs. Social barriers existed, principally between free immigrants and emancipists. However, among the free immigrants was a wealthy, landed group called "exclusives," who kept aloof from everyone. The groups were divided by social distinctions and not by wealth, because some of the emancipists were as wealthy as many of the exclusives.

The activities of the exclusives were the subject of

much amused commentary among other free immigrants and emancipists, who often referred to them as the "bunyip aristocracy." It was a term that always provoked great hilarity, because the bunyip was a part of Aborigine mythology. Supposedly, it was a hideous creature that inhabited ponds and streams, leaping out to devour the unwary who came to drink.

Social distinctions had done nothing to inhibit progress in the colony, Oliver thought, noticing the numerous vessels as the sloop drew closer to the port. A major transshipment point of sandalwood, pearlshell, beche-de-mer, and spar timber from all over the South Pacific, Sydney carried on a lively trade with ports in England, Ireland, India, China, and the United States. In addition, scores of whaling ships from various nations called at Sydney frequently, many of them using it as a base of operation.

When the port was almost straight southwest from the sloop, Captain Barnes shouted to the crewmen, "Look alive there, mates! Check the lashings on the deck cargo to make certain it won't shift when we come about, then we'll go in with the wind off the quarter."

"No need to bother with the deck cargo, Captain," a crewmen replied. "We drew up those lashings tighter than a nun's knees."

"You'd best shut your tucker hole and take a look at those lashings," the captain retorted. "Ahead of a quartering wind, we'll have a rail awash, and that wood mustn't wobble about. If it shifts as much as a hair's breadth, I'll batten down this wheel and use your talleywhacker as a pinch bar to snub up those lashings."

The crewmen laughed, going to the stacks of cedar and examining the ropes securing them to the deck. Finding some that had stretched slightly during the run from Newcastle, they used a boat hook as a lever to tighten the ropes and retie the knots. "Stand ready to let go the boom," Captain Barnes ordered when the crewmen finished. "Lieutenant Bethune, have a care that the boom doesn't take you over the side when it comes abaft."

Oliver returned to the companionway and went down into it, taking out his snuffbox. As the rudder gear rumbled and the sloop began turning, the captain shouted at the crewmen to release the lines on the boom. Pulleys chattered, ropes whipping through them, and heavy timbers groaned as the vessel swung to the southwest. The dark shadow of the thick boom and sail crossed the companionway hatch to the port side of the deck.

As Captain Barnes shouted orders, the crewmen scrambled about, securing the boom and trimming the foresail. Oliver brushed his nose with his handkerchief as he went back up to the deck. Ahead of the wind off the starboard quarter, the sloop was heeled over sharply to port, the tops of the waves splashing over the rail on that side. Moving carefully across the slanted deck, Bethune returned to the stack of wood and sat down.

As it sailed toward the harbor entrance, the sloop passed within a hundred yards of a dozen Aborigine men, women, and children in three bark canoes. They were fishing, as well as cooking and eating the fish, the smoke rising from fires on clay in the center of the canoes. The captain shouted something to them in their language, and they laughed happily as they replied in a chorus of voices, holding up several large fish for him to see.

A few minutes later, sandstone cliffs, soaring two hundred and fifty feet, flanked the harbor entrance and towered over the sloop. At the waterline was a jumble of boulders the size of houses. The sea was more turbulent near the coast. The long swells that had run unimpeded across seven thousand miles from South America slammed into the boulders. They exploded, turning into a maelstrom of boiling foam and hurling shimmering spray a hundred feet into the air.

The spray drifted across the deck of the *Phoebe* as it smoothly rounded North Head into the harbor. In the shelter of the cliffs, the vessel slowed as it started up the vast expanse of water. Captain Barnes shouted orders, and the crewmen raced about, trimming the sails to the lighter wind. As the sloop glided on up the harbor, past a reef and outlying rocks called the Sow and Pigs, the heights of the cliffs were lower and the breeze freshened again.

Ahead of the sloop, a cargo ship moved slowly, its sails patched and ragged from a long, stormy voyage. Peering at it closely, Oliver made out its name, the *Harmony* out of Bristol. The sloop was catching up with the ship, and one of the crewmen pointed to it as he called, "We're overtaking her smartly, Captain."

"Of course we are!" the young captain replied impatiently. "That old scow has a bottom as foul as yours and rags for sails, while *Phoebe* can make good headway in a heavy dew ahead of a lamb's fart of wind. We'll be unloading cargo before she wets her anchors."

The distance between the two vessels continued to close. Only two hundred feet from the ship, the sloop began nosing past it. At the rail of the ship were some fifteen men and women, with several children. Evidently free immigrants from England, and showing the effects of their months at sea, they were exuberantly relieved that their voyage was ending. They waved happily and shouted greetings to the sloop, and one man's voice rang out over the rest as he asked how much farther it was to Sydney.

"Sydney, did you say?" Captain Barnes exclaimed in pretended astonishment. "You're a bloody long way from there, jocko. Sydney is in Australia, you know, and this is the Bay of Islands in New Zealand."

The people fell silent, all of them motionless for a

long second. Then, turning as one, they rushed toward
the quarterdeck in a bedlam of angry voices. The
captain of the ship came into view as he stepped to the
edge of the quarterdeck and looked down at the
people. Shaking his head vigorously and replying to
them, he motioned up the harbor. The people disagreed in a babble of voices, pointing to the sloop.

The captain looked at the sloop, then stormed down
the steps to the main deck. Leaning over the rail, he
shook his fist and bellowed in rage, calling Captain
Barnes a lying scoundrel. The captain and the
crewmen howled with laughter as the sloop drew away
from the ship. Oliver smiled, both amused and sympathetic toward the travel-weary voyagers.

Up the harbor, the cliffs diminished into ledges
between numerous inlets. The coves were densely
forested, the underbrush striving for sunlight under
the canopies of huge eucalyptuses. Occasionally Oliver spotted a tree with a large oval scar where Aborigines had chopped off a slab of bark that was shaped to
fit over a skeleton of sticks for the hull of a canoe.

Where streams had carved gullies in the sandstone,
paving it with beds of colorful algae, giant cabbage
palms spread their fronds and provided damp shade
for a variety of ferns and mosses. Along the shore tons
of shell had accumulated at the entrance of caves
where countless generations of Aborigines had eaten
oysters and discarded the shells.

At the largest of the shell middens, boats were
drawn up on the shore. There, convicts worked
around smoking stone kilns, burning the shell for lime
to make construction mortar. In some of the coves,
crews of convicts were felling trees, trimming them,
and assembling the logs into rafts at the edge of the
water to tow up the harbor to Sydney.

Pinchgut, Goat, and Cockatoo Islands, and other
islands rose out of the harbor, some only bare knobs
of stone. The shore dipped back into larger, sheltered
bights, including Parsley Bay and Farm Cove. Whalers

and other vessels were at anchor in some of them, their crews making repairs.

The harbor extended on to the west, narrowing into the mouth of the Parramatta River, and the sloop turned in at Sydney Cove. On a rocky point at the west side of the anchorage, ramshackle huts were set along narrow, winding alleys. This thieves' kitchen of the colony was where some female ex-convicts worked as whores. Officially designated the Rocks, it was more popularly called the Pissmire.

Vessels of all descriptions were at anchor in the wide, sheltered bay, as lighters ferried cargo between them and the piers. Others were docked at the wharfs. Warehouses, storage yards, refitting docks, and a shipyard lined the waterfront, and the town spread up the slopes back from the cove. It was neat and pleasant, with streets of shops and small manufactures. Farther back, half-timbered houses and tidy cottages built of freestone were fronted by well-tended yards enclosed in hedges and paling fences.

When the sails were furled and the anchors set, a crewman rowed the lieutenant to the piers. From a distance, the town always reminded Oliver of English port towns and seaside communities, but his sense of familiarity faded at close range. There were acacia bushes instead of ivy and privet hedges, noisy, colorful parrots took the place of wrens and finches, and he heard the distinctive Australian accent on every side.

Most of all, it was different because of the canary woolens of convicts. Scores of them were working or filing down the streets to tasks, some followed by guards. Oliver passed a group repairing holes in a street, wearing leg irons that identified them as either new arrivals or convicts being punished for minor offenses.

Farther back in the town were large, luxurious private homes, and the homes of government officials. Government House was a two-story stone building in the Regency style, set back on landscaped grounds from a wide, shady street. A church and other large structures were being built on the street, evidence of the governor's large-scale construction program.

Inside Government House, Oliver crossed the lofty, expansive foyer and ascended the wide staircase to an anteroom outside the governor's office. He took a seat and waited. Soon after, the colonial judge advocate exited the governor's office, then an aide showed the lieutenant into the large, well-furnished room.

At fifty-nine, Governor Lachlan Macquarie was a tall, lean man with a military bearing from a lifetime as a professional soldier. Pausing inside the door, the lieutenant bowed. "Good day, Excellency, and thank you for receiving me so soon."

"I've been looking forward to seeing you, Lieutenant Bethune," Governor Macquarie replied as he returned the bow, a slight Scottish burr in his deep voice. "Please sit down. I was reading your last report on activities at Newcastle again this morning, and I'm very pleased with it."

The lieutenant sat on a chair in front of the desk and took out papers he had brought to present to the governor. The aide helped Governor Macquarie find the report on Newcastle among the papers on his desk, then left. The governor put the report aside for the moment and sat back in his chair. "Now, what do you have that you'd like to discuss, Lieutenant?"

Handing the governor a paper, Oliver explained that it was a list of convicts he was recommending for a ticket-of-leave which would set aside the remainder of the men's sentences so they could find work in the colony or do whatever else they wished. However, it could be revoked for any offense. The governor put on his spectacles, looked at the list, and discussed each of the convicts with Oliver. Satisfied, he nodded in approval and put the list aside for his clerks to prepare the documents.

The other paper the lieutenant presented was more controversial, a recommendation for a pardon. As the

governor frowned musingly and studied the paper,
Oliver understood his reasons for hesitation. Many of
the landowners in the colony, having influential
friends in London, had brought pressure to bear on
the governor through official channels because of the
number of tickets-of-leave and especially pardons he
had granted.

Those disapproving property owners objected on
the basis that convicts should serve full terms in the
interests of justice, but Oliver knew their real motives.
Landowners were authorized to have convict workers.
In return for the labor, the owners provided room,
board, and clothing for the convicts. But between
those convicts the governor employed on public construction and the number granted tickets-of-leave and
pardons, some landowners rarely had as many convict
workers as they wanted.

"Hiram Baxter has been a foreman for a year,"
Bethune said, justifying the recommendation. "He's
been very diligent in his duties, and there isn't a mark
against him on his record. In addition, I think it
would be in the best interests of the colony to grant
him a pardon."

"The best interests of the colony?"

"Yes, Excellency. Baxter is a skilled, experienced
shipwright. He's been in contact with James Underwood, the emancipist who owns the shipyard here in
Sydney, and Underwood has offered to hire him.
Baxter would make a much greater contribution to the
economy of the colony by working in his craft than he
does as a foreman at Newcastle."

The governor pursed his lips, pondering a moment
longer, then nodded and put the paper aside. "Very
well, I'll grant the pardon. It'll be another log on the
fire that's cooking my goose in London, but one more
won't make that much difference. Even though Baxter
has a good record, I give much more weight to your
recommendation, Lieutenant Bethune."

"I'm very gratified by your confidence, Excellency."

"You've more than earned my confidence," the governor replied, reaching for the report on activities at Newcastle. "In every respect, you've done much better than your predecessor. Also, you haven't had any workers killed in accidents. I had a very difficult time convincing the officer who was there before you that our task is to reform convicts, not kill them."

"I very narrowly avoided having several men killed two weeks ago," Oliver admitted candidly. "There was a cave-in at the mine that trapped several men and almost smothered them, but one of the convicts kept his wits about him and got the men out. The shoring was faulty, and as it turned out, the man who saved the others is an engineer. His name is David Kerrick, and he's seeing to the shoring throughout the mine now."

"An engineer?" the governor mused, interested. "What is his offense and term of sentence?"

"He was sentenced to hang for murder, then it was commuted to transportation for life. However," Oliver added as the governor frowned, "in Kerrick's records, I found some basis for what he did. It seems that a man named Wesley Hammond was making free with Kerrick's wife while Kerrick was away on a construction project. When he came home, Kerrick caught Hammond with his wife."

Governor Macquarie sighed, nodding in understanding. "Yes, that puts it in a different light, doesn't it? Kerrick must have had the help of many friends to get a sentence for murder commuted to transportation."

"Judging from the records, there was influence on both sides. Hammond's father, Sir Leland Hammond, is a Yorkshire squire and apparently did his best to see that Kerrick was hanged. On the other hand, Kerrick had been the principal engineer on several projects in York, and he had recommendations for clemency from the aldermen and the mayor."

The governor nodded, stroking his chin. "That

must have been a close inning, but it turned out well. There is a Nevil Hammond here in Sydney, a lawyer. I wonder if he's related to the Yorkshire Hammonds."

"I've no idea, Excellency, because I'm not acquainted with the man. The name isn't all that common, though, so it seems likely."

"Yes, that's true. What sort of man is Kerrick?"

"Not one to trifle with, because he's knocked heads among the convicts from time to time. However, he bothers no one when he's left alone, and he's more considerate of the men who work for him than most. All in all, I regard him as the best foreman at Newcastle."

"Well, that sounds very favorable, and I could make good use of that man here, Lieutenant. I have ample laborers and sufficient craftsmen for construction work, but only one man more or less qualified to oversee an entire project. That's my architect, who isn't the best of supervisors, and we have several works in progress. An experienced engineer should be able to oversee the construction of a building."

The lieutenant smiled wryly. "I'm sure he could, but it appears that I've talked myself out of a good foreman, Excellency."

"No more than you did with Baxter," the governor pointed out. "Kerrick will be of greater advantage to the colony if he can get a building completed here, and in a better position to help himself. I reward good work, and I might consider a ticket-of-leave or a conditional pardon for him. He can never leave Australia, but he could make the best of his situation here."

"It isn't my concern, of course," Oliver said hesitantly, "but if that lawyer in Sydney is related to the Yorkshire Hammonds, he would undoubtedly hear about it and be very angry if Kerrick were given his freedom. And if Hammond has friends in London, he could cause trouble."

"I'm sure he has friends in London, because he's

from there, and he moved here with his family only some months ago. However, my duty is to administer justice, not to provide people with revenge. I can look forward to having Kerrick here very shortly, then?"

"Yes, Excellency. When I return to Newcastle, I'll send him on the next vessel."

The governor nodded in satisfaction, the discussion moving on to other subjects. As they talked, Oliver's thoughts were divided between the conversation and wondering if he would find letters from his family and friends waiting for him when he went to the postal office. He wistfully hoped he would, and that they would contain encouraging news about his chances of being transferred to a regiment in India or Africa.

On a rainy, windy afternoon a week later, David Kerrick arrived in Sydney on a trading barque that shuttled between ports in New Zealand and Australia. While other convicts at outlying locations tried to get sent to the capitol, it didn't matter to him. One place was the same as any other. But from what he had been told, he would be kept busy here, which was what he wanted. Work occupied his mind and made him weary so he could sleep through the long, lonely nights.

His belongings rolled in his blanket and slung over his back, he went ashore in a boat with part of the crew, who talked in eager anticipation about going to the Pissmire. With rain dripping from eaves and the streets muddy, only a few people moved about the town. Having spent a few weeks in a chain gang immediately after his arrival, he was familiar with Sydney. So ignoring the rain soaking into his clothes, David made his way toward the convict compound.

At the dingy, cluttered compound office, the illiterate guard on duty passed David's travel authorization to the convict clerk. The clerk read it, smiling ironically. "Not only is he in browns, but he's here at the governor's personal command, Corporal Atkins," the man commented. "Perhaps we have a peer of the realm amongst us now."

"Aye, I noticed the fine carriage he came here in," the guard grunted sourly. "What's his name, and what's he to do?"

"David Kerrick, and there's an order from the commandant on him," the clerk replied, rummaging through papers on a table. He separated one, looking at it. "Here it is. He's to go to Parramatta and work for Francis Greenway. That's the one who got a pardon from the governor as soon as he came here because he knows how to build churches and such."

The guard nodded and motioned impatiently. "I know who Greenway is. Write him out a pass to Parramatta and be quick about it."

Taking a piece of paper and a pen, the clerk wrote out the travel credential in an awkward scrawl, then handed it to the guard. As the guard examined it closely, exercising his petty authority, the clerk stood out of his line of view and grimaced at him derisively.

"Go eat in the cookhouse," the guard told David, handing him the paper, "then find a cot in the barracks. Tomorrow, take the road up the river, and you'll come to Parramatta. Show this to somebody in the cookhouse before you leave, and they'll give you some tucker to carry along. It'll take you a good part of the day to get there on foot."

"The assembly," the clerk reminded the guard as David turned away and started to leave the office.

"Aye, that's right," the guard said. "All convicts are to assemble in the courtyard at sunrise tomorrow. We probably won't have a sunrise because of the weather, but be there anyway."

"What's the purpose of the assembly?" David asked.

"You'll find out soon enough," the guard replied brusquely as the clerk grinned knowingly. "Just be there."

David left the office and went through the wind and rain to join the convicts crowding into the noisy, dirty cookhouse. Receiving a slice of stale bread and a piece of boiled, unsalted fish, he sat down at a table. While eating, he heard others talking about the assembly. Two convicts who had fled into the wilderness had become bushrangers, preying on travelers and isolated farms. Having been captured, they were to be hanged the next morning, and all convicts in Sydney were to observe the hanging as a warning to any who might be tempted to try the same thing.

In one of the littered, grimy wings of the decrepit barracks, David found an empty cot, a rough board attached to the wall. During his few weeks of living in the hut at Newcastle, he had become gratefully accustomed to solitude in a place he had kept clean which made the stench and congestion of these barracks seem even worse. After sleeping fitfully through the night, he was awakened by guards who entered the barracks before dawn, shouting for everyone to assemble in the courtyard.

Light rain was still falling as David went out into the darkness and toward the courtyard at the side of the compound with the other men. Away from the shelter of the buildings, the drizzle swept across the courtyard ahead of the gusty, icy wind, and the convicts shivered and cursed resentfully. As a gray, gloomy dawn broke, the guards moved about and shouted, arranging the convicts in ranks and ordering them to be silent.

Across the courtyard was a wooden triangle, its apex turned down, where convicts were tied to be lashed. Near it was a gallows, the two nooses hanging from the crossbeam swaying in the wind. As he waited, David reflected that as an object lesson, the assembly utterly failed its intended purpose as many of the convicts looked forward to the hanging as entertainment.

A few minutes later, a procession came from the

guardhouse, led by two drummers beating a marching tattoo, followed by the commandant and a clergyman. Behind them were the two prisoners and guards. One of the prisoners was sullenly defiant, trying to shrug away from the guards gripping his arms, while the other one wept and sagged on his feet as the guards dragged him.

At the gallows, the drums fell silent as the guards escorted the convicts up the steps. The guards centered the men on the trap doors under the nooses, and the weeping prisoner flinched from the rope as the wind brushed it against him. The clergyman mounted the steps and took out his prayer book as he stood beside the sobbing man. He put a hand on the man's shoulder, his voice inaudible to David as he read from the book.

As the clergyman moved toward the other convict, the man turned and spat at him. Pocketing his prayer book, the clergyman descended the steps. Standing at the foot of the gallows, the commandant spoke to the convict who was weeping, and the man shook his head as he sobbed. The commandant then spoke to the other convict.

"Aye, I have some last words," the man snarled. "To bloody hell with all of you, with the bleeding governor leading the flaming parade and you bringing up the arse of it, where you bloody belong."

With the wind ruffling the tassels on his epaulettes, the commandant turned away and motioned to the guards. They fitted cloth bags over the convicts' heads, tying them around the neck, then put the nooses in place and filed down the steps. One of the guards stood at the lever on the side of the gallows, his hand on it as he looked at the commandant.

The drums boomed into a steady roll, the sound rising and falling in the eddying wind. As the commandant motioned, the drums abruptly fell silent and the guard jerked the lever down. The two convicts plummeted, the trap doors opening under them. The

ropes snapped taut, and the two men bounced as their
necks broke with loud cracks that sounded like wood
breaking. They wriggled and jerked convulsively, then
became motionless.

As he left the courtyard in the crowd of convicts,
David heard some of the men laughing and discussing
other hangings they had seen that had been more
entertaining, the hanged men having taken longer to
die. Others were silent, their mood matching his.

After he ate in the cookhouse, he showed his travel
authorization to a convict cook who brought him a
piece of bread and two boiled potatoes.

When he reached the road to Parramatta at the edge
of town, the wind and rain diminished. A few minutes
later, the rain stopped entirely, the wind dying away to
a breeze, and by the time David was a mile from the
town, the clouds were breaking up. It became a bright,
cheerful winter day, the sun warm enough to dry his
clothes.

During the first hour of his walk, David noticed that
houses were scattered along the road which teemed
with people on foot, riders, and carts taking produce
to Sydney. Then the houses were left behind, replaced
by farms set back in the fields, and the traffic thinned
out. After a while, David was the only one on the road
as it wound through open forest near the Parramatta
River.

At noon, he stopped in a grove beside the river to
eat. It was a pleasant, rustic scene among the ancient
eucalyptuses with mounds of bark at their bases and
strings of half-shed bark hanging from them. Overhead, the cries of parrots darting through the trees
blended with the chatter of pipits and swallows. A few
yards away through the silvery boles of the trees, the
river was wide and placid, mirroring overhanging
branches.

After he ate, David sat and rested for a few minutes.
In the solitude of the grove, he felt almost content, at
peace with himself and the world. It was an unusual

mood for him, but his sorrow and troubles seemed to be very distant for once.

The feeling ended as he took out his watch. Looking at his former wife's portrait, he yearned to cast the watch into the river and banish her from his life, but cutting off one of his arms would have been easier. His love for her remained a vital part of him, even though it was like a devouring cancer. He put away the watch and picked up his blanket roll, then returned to the road, resuming his trek.

With farms and small sheep stations scattered around it, Parramatta was a bustling hamlet of several hundred people with shady avenues of tidy houses set around a cobblestone street of shops. The buildings in the convict compound on the north side of the village were characteristically drab and shabby. As he went toward them, he saw a very large, two-story stone building in the early stages of construction a short distance from the compound.

Between the barracks and cookhouse was a long, low building, divided into individual rooms, which the guard at the compound office pointed out as the foreman's quarters. He told David to take the end room and then report to Francis Greenway at the building under construction. David left his belongings in the room and went to the construction site.

The frame of the immense building had been completed, along with part of the roof, and masons were laying lower courses of stone. David looked around as he went through the gaping entrance, seeing that some flooring was in place, as well as beams for partitions. With the roof still incomplete, the rain of the past few days had drenched the interior.

As saws rasped and hammers resounded, David made his way past carpenters and their helpers to a ladder serving as a staircase. Francis Greenway was on the second floor, his suit and cravat standing out among the men in canary woolens as he pored over the building plans on a workbench. In his early forties, the architect was a short, portly man with thinning hair and a sparse, stringy beard and mustache.

He had a nervous, artistic temperament, his normal expression an anxious frown. As they exchanged greetings, Francis appeared to be relieved that David had arrived, but impatient because of the interruption of his work. While he eagerly wanted help, Francis seemed reluctant to entrust part of the work to anyone else. He showed David the building plans, questioning him closely about the work he had done before.

"Several bridges," David told the architect, "with spans up to a hundred feet. I built breakwaters and stone piers at Hull and aqueducts at Leeds. I also did several projects in York, including a new waterworks, but I didn't see the waterworks through to completion."

"But no large public buildings?" Francis mused doubtfully.

"No, but this seems straightforward enough," David replied, looking at the plans. "Apparently it's going to be a barracks."

The architect nodded, explaining that it would house six hundred convicts. He told David that the number of variously skilled craftsmen working on the building was more than adequate. In addition, a large number of the convicts at the Parramatta compound had been allocated to the project as laborers.

"However," he added, "it's supposed to be finished by next summer, but it's far behind schedule. In addition to this, I have other buildings under construction and I'm constantly shuttling back and forth between here and Sydney. But most of my problems are with this building."

"There's much to be done before it'll be finished," David commented, looking around, "and work always proceeds more slowly during winter."

"Indeed," Francis agreed. "The rain during the past few days has been dreadful, and I'm very concerned about these beams."

"Well, they're seasoned hardwood, and they haven't come to any harm yet. If the roof is finished before more rain comes, the beams should dry without warping or cracking."

"I hope so," Francis sighed worriedly, putting the plans into a portfolio. "If the completion of this building is delayed even more, the governor will be very dissatisfied. I'll go around the site with you and point out the particulars."

As they walked, the architect explained details of the work, as well as talked about himself. He said he had been falsely accused of forging a signature on a building contract in Bath, then had suffered the additional misfortune of having a perfidious judge at his trial. Upon receiving a pardon after arriving in Australia, he had brought his wife and children and lived in a comfortable house in Sydney.

It was similar to what David had heard from others of professional status, many of whom claimed innocence of any wrongdoing. In contrast, petty criminals often attempted to portray themselves as worse than they were, trying to impress others. In both instances, he believed the truth usually lay somewhere in the middle with very few cases of misplaced justice and the truly innocent convicted.

The convicts were the flotsam of teeming, over-crowded cities and of a society racked by the upheavals of transitioning from cottage industries to factory production. Discarded as human refuse, they had been sent to an unknown, raw land, making a complete break with their past and given a new beginning in life. As for himself, David acknowledged that his sentence had been more than fair in comparison with the usual penalty for murder. But instead of a fresh start, he foresaw only a grim, dreary ending to what had gone before.

During the tour of the site, David saw the main reason why the work was behind schedule. The various craftsmen and their helpers were working hard, but some of the laborers were loitering, slow in taking materials to where they were needed. That resulted in delays, confusion, and frayed tempers. The fault lay with Francis Greenway who was more expert in designing buildings than in supervising the work to complete them.

The day was ending and the men were leaving when Francis finished showing David the site. The architect untied his horse from a grassy verge at one side of the site, commenting morosely about the distance he had to ride to get home, then having to return the following morning. "Let me have the roster of the men, and I'll attend to the muster tomorrow morning," David offered. "Then you won't have to be here quite as early."

"I don't think that would be wise, at least not yet," Francis objected cautiously. "I'd like to know more about you."

"You already know that I've dealt with working crews," David replied impatiently. "If I'm to be a laborer here, I'll join them tomorrow. If I'm to be an overseer, then give me the roster."

The short, stout man frowned reluctantly as he handed it over and rode away.

David cleaned up, ate, then returned to his room in the winter twilight to clean it. When he finished, he lay down on the cot, in a way relieved that it was too dark for him to look at the miniature of his former wife in his watch.

The next morning when the workers gathered at the site, David studied them as he called the roll. As a group, they were better than the average crew at Newcastle. None appeared to have been brutalized into stubborn resistance by sadistic guards or overseers, which sometimes happened.

The craftsmen, having committed some crime when drunk, or among the wrong companions, or unemployed and penniless, made the most of the situation. Their skills in demand throughout the colony, they worked hard and avoided any infractions, looking forward to when they would be free to seek employment and send for their families.

Most of the laborers were from the crime-infested districts of large cities. Away from that environment, and with quarters and food better than many of them had ever known, they had a new opportunity. Some would do well, others well enough, and a few would end up at Norfolk Island.

Among the laborers, David saw some he had not seen the previous day. He knew the men had sneaked away and that the others had loitered, too frightened to leave yet disinclined to work. Of equal importance with the work to David were several of the laborers who were barely more than boys. They would be tempted to follow bad examples that would eventually result in their being sent to Norfolk Island.

One of the men who had been missing the previous afternoon was easy to identify and would be impossible for David to forget. A crimson birthmark covered one side of his face, and his eyes were an exceptionally pale shade of blue—cold, merciless eyes that looked like pieces of glass. His thick, coarse features matched his eyes, and his lank hair and beard were blond.

Of medium stature, Enos Hinton was heavily-muscled, and appeared evil, as though he had no redeeming, human qualities at all about him. At his side was a taller, muscular man, Daniel Crowley, who had also been absent the previous afternoon. They made quiet, sarcastic comments to each other as David called the roll, Hinton the instigator of the remarks.

After dismissing the craftsmen and their helpers, David assigned crews of laborers by name to the various tasks. They scattered and began working, but David expected trouble at some point. It came within a matter of minutes, when Hinton deliberately dropped his end of several boards he and another man were carrying to a carpenter.

As the lumber crashed to the ground, Hinton laughed sardonically. "Well, fancy that," he sneered. "I suppose it was too heavy for me."

A few men laughed, but most of them were silent, waiting for David's reaction, as was Hinton. Not expecting a physical challenge, the smirk faded from his ugly face, and he looked startled as David walked toward him with long strides. Then Hinton grinned derisively and lifted his fists, apparently enjoying brawls and confident that he had enough experience fighting to overcome David's advantage in height.

David had another advantage in that he detested fights and threw himself into them with a relentless fury to finish them as quickly as possible. He jabbed at Hinton's face, and Hinton lifted his fists, leaving his stomach unprotected. David slammed a right into his midriff that rocked Hinton on his feet. Hinton flailed with his fists as David drove through the blows and hit him solidly in the face. Hinton went down.

Bouncing back up, Hinton roared in rage as he charged, his head lowered to butt. David lifted his hands, tensing his stomach muscles and bracing himself to take the blow. As Hinton's head drove into his stomach, David slammed his palms against the man's ears. Hinton howled in pain, holding his ears as he stumbled backward, bent over.

David followed him, gripping his tangle of greasy blond hair, and drove his knee into the man's face. His legs weakening, Hinton began sagging toward the ground. David snapped his knee into Hinton's face again, the force of the blow jerking the man's hair out of his grasp. Blood gushing from his nose and mouth, Hinton collapsed on the ground.

It was over quickly, mere seconds after the lumber had fallen. Men gazed in astonishment, then hurriedly resumed working when David glanced around. The man who had been helping Hinton carry the boards started to restack them, but David motioned him away from them. "Leave that and work with those men," he said, pointing.

The man moved away from the lumber, and David approached Hinton, standing over him. "You're going to carry boards by yourself today," he said quietly, "and from now on, you're going to work. If you crack a board from throwing them around, I'll break it over your head. Do you understand?"

Making no reply, Hinton began lifting himself to his hands and knees. David kicked him in the stomach, and Hinton yelped in pain as he rolled toward the boards. Following him, David loomed over him again. "I asked you if you understand," he said in the same quiet tone.

Blood streaming down the crimson birthmark on his face, the man's coarse features were transfixed with rage and humiliation, his pale blue eyes glaring. "Aye, I hear you," he croaked, his voice shaking.

Almost sobbing in fury, Hinton began stacking the boards. Francis had just arrived, looking on in concern, and David briefly explained what had happened. The architect shook his head, doubtful about the wisdom of David's actions. "The commandant is the best one to deal with disciplinary problems," he told David, "but you do as you wish. I daresay, though, that you'd be well advised to keep an eye on your back."

Having thought of that already, David nodded and turned away as Francis went inside. The laborers moved about briskly and David worked with them to show them that he was willing to do anything he expected of them.

Carrying slate up the tall, rickety ladders to the roof was grueling and dangerous, a task all the laborers tried to avoid. David toted the loads of the flat, heavy stone on his shoulder, and each time he came back down the ladder, he looked around to make certain the other craftsmen had ample materials immediately at hand. When the roofers had all the slate they could use that day, he began dragging logs to the saw pit.

The hours passed swiftly, David keeping an eye on all of the work in progress as he helped out. The next problem arose during the afternoon when he heard an argument at one side of the building and went to investigate. Crowley, who had been assigned to mix mortar, was confronting a mason who insisted that a bucket of mortar was too thin.

Irate from the unfamiliar experience of working for hours, the muscular Crowley shook his fist in the small, graying man's face. "Then mix it yourself, you old swine!" he snarled. "If I hear another bloody word out of you about it, I'll give you a taste of this fist!"

The mason backed away apprehensively, then relaxed as he looked past Crowley and saw David approaching. Crowley started to turn and look himself when David seized one of Crowley's wrists and twisted his arm behind his back with a quick jerk. The man bellowed in pain and lifted to his toes, trying to ease the pressure on his shoulder joint.

As Crowley teetered, David kicked his feet from under him, and he fell to his knees in front of the mortar bucket. David twisted the man's arm higher, gripping the back of his neck, then plunged his head into the mortar. Crowley thrashed frantically, almost overturning the bucket as large bubbles surfaced in the mortar and popped.

Glancing at the mason's helper, David nodded toward a bucket of water. As the man moved the bucket closer, David pulled Crowley's head out of the mortar and pushed it into the water. Crowley spluttered and choked, splashing the water on his face and washing the mortar out of his eyes. Then he leaped to his feet with his fists cocked, his matted hair full of mortar and the cement trickling down his enraged face.

David beckoned. "All right, come on, Crowley," he

said quietly. "If you want to fight, let's get it over with."

His eyes wild with fury, Crowley almost charged, then he thought again and turned away, grinding his teeth. David pointed to the mortar. "You've been doing that all day, so you know how to do it right. Get that thickened before it starts setting. And if you're wise, Crowley, from now on you'll do your work and not cause any more trouble."

Crowley snatched up the bucket and stamped away, and the mason and his helper smiled gratefully at David. The other men who had been watching resumed working and Hinton, who was among them, twisted his ugly, disfigured face in hatred.

Francis, looking out a window opening, shook his head morosely in warning as he turned and moved away from the window.

David knew that the architect had been right about referring disciplinary problems to the commandant, and that was what most overseers did. But Kerrick had seen the ground in front of whipping frames soaked in blood mixed with flecks of flesh. He could kill, but in committing other men to that punishment, even men like Hinton and Crowley, he would be doing something that he could not live with.

Going to the other side of the scrap wood near the saw pit, out of view of the men, David stirred the pieces of wood with his foot and glanced over them. He saw a short, heavy billet shaped like a club, thick at one end and tapering at the other. Small enough to hide under his coat, he picked it up and tucked it under his coat, reasonably certain that eventually he would need it some dark night.

Chapter Three

Lying on the floor across the room from his cot, David slept fitfully with his hand on the club, ready to awaken at any sound. But as the hours passed and dawn came, the door of his room remained tightly closed.

When the convicts mustered that morning, they were more orderly than the previous day. None of the other workers wanted to hear Hinton and Crowley's sarcastic mutterings, nor were the two men inclined to make any comments. They merely glowered in silent, seething hatred that was a warning.

The following night, hours after the convict compound had become quiet, David lay in the same place on the floor, sleeping lightly, when a squeak from the leather hinges on his door awakened him. He gripped his club, lifted his head, and looked toward the door.

It opened, and Hinton and Crowley were silhouetted against the dim light outside. As they tiptoed silently into the room, David saw their clubs. He drew up his legs and held his club tightly, poised to get to his feet. "Now!" Hinton snarled gleefully.

Crowley laughed scornfully as the two men charged the cot. David silently rose, moving sidewards to keep the men silhouetted against the doorway. As their clubs thumped on the empty cot, Hinton and Crowley cursed and exclaimed in surprise. Then David swung his club rapidly.

The heavy wood struck the men with meaty thuds, their outbursts of perplexity changing to howls of pain, and they flailed back. David ducked and dodged, staying in the darkness and keeping the men in view against the doorway. A club glanced off his shoulder, then one hit his side harder. But each time he swung his club, it struck with a solid, hammer-like blow that opened a wide gash in the skin, making a deep, painful bruise.

Crowley gave up first, dropping his club and fleeing out the door. Then, as Hinton started to run, David kicked his stool in front of the man and tripped him. Hinton sprawled and scrambled about, frantically trying to reach the door as David pounded his back and shoulders with the club. Hinton got to the door and ran out as David hit him a last time.

As the two men raced away into the darkness, the door of the adjacent room opened and the occupant looked out. "What the bloody hell is happening over there?" he demanded sleepily.

"I was disposing of vermin," David replied.

"Disposing of vermin?" the man snorted. "It sounded more like whipping day at the triangle." Grumbling, he closed his door.

David shut his own door, then went to the side of the room and picked up his blanket. Lying on the cot, he pulled it around himself, then fell into a sound sleep.

The next morning, after scrubbing the spatters of blood in his room, he ate breakfast, and did not see either Hinton or Crowley in the cookhouse. But when he went to the construction site, they were present for the morning muster.

Hinton appeared scarcely human with the birthmarked side of his face massively swollen, and dark bruises on the other side. Crowley looked little better. His forehead bulged around a cut and a purple bruise that reached his eyes and turned them into puffy slits. Both of the men, stiffly hunched from other bruises on their bodies, grimly endured their pain, while the other men glanced between them and David in understanding.

After the roll call, David dismissed the craftsmen and their helpers, and assigned tasks to all of the laborers except the two battered men. As the men moved away, David went over to Hinton and Crowley. "By now," he said quietly, "it should be clear to you that whatever you try, I'll be waiting for it. But what you don't know is what I'll do to you if you cause me any more trouble, so I'll tell you. I'm going to kill both of you. Now do you understand that?"

Seething hatred burned in their eyes, but it was mixed with fear. As they muttered and nodded in reply, David knew that the trouble with them was at an end, at least for now. He led them over to the saw pit where the sawyer in charge was organizing his work for the day.

Logs rested across the deep, large hole in the ground where men used long whipsaws to slice the timber into boards. It was exhausting labor, and working down in the pit, where clouds of choking sawdust spilled down, was the most despised task on the construction site. David told the sawyer that Hinton and Crowley would work in the pit until further notice. "If you have any trouble at all with them," he added, "let me know immediately."

The man nodded and motioned the two convicts down into the pit as David walked away. Francis Greenway had still not arrived, and David inspected both floors of the building to see if any problems were developing. When he completed his tour and all the work proceeded satisfactorily, he went outside and joined the laborers who were carrying slate up to the roof.

It was late morning when the architect finally showed up, looking even more nervous than usual. "Difficulties have arisen at the church under construction in Sydney," he told David, "and the governor is displeased about it. And with this building behind schedule, he's very dissatisfied indeed. You've apparently taken a better grasp on things here than I expected, so I intend to leave you in charge of this site."

"Very well, I don't think I'll have any problems."

"I hope not. When the roof is finished, obtain a travel authorization for the roofers and send them to Sydney, because I urgently need them there. I'll come here every few days to see how you are managing, and do try to keep from falling further behind schedule."

The architect left, and David returned to his work. Far from falling further behind schedule, he was confident that the work pace would increase enough to meet the original date of completion for the building, and possibly even better it. The results of fully organizing the workers was becoming evident. The confusion and delays now eliminated, the rate of the work was gradually improving.

The immediate problem was the threat of rain. The heavy beams and the portions of flooring that had been finished inside the building were still slowly drying from the last drenching. A section of the roof still remained to be completed, and during the day, gray clouds tumbled across the sky ahead of a chill winter wind. That night, David was awakened by the drumming of wind-driven rain against the wall beside his cot.

The temperature dropped below freezing during the night, and the next morning was raw and frigidly cold.

The muddy ground was covered with icy slush from sleet mixed with rain. On top of the building, even the rough boards that remained to be covered with slate were slippery, and the rest of the roof was glazed with ice which was perilously dangerous for the roofers. Inside, rain water streamed down beams and puddled on the sections of flooring.

David provided the roofers and their helpers with safety ropes, and had fires of scrap wood kindled around the building. The laborers paused at the fires to warm themselves, and craftsmen came out to the fires with their assistants after completing parts of a task. Occasionally, the roofers and their helpers came down the ladders from the full blast of the wind on top of the building and huddled beside fires, shaking with cold.

While the fires lifted the men's spirits, David's consideration for their comfort made them even more cheerful, and work progressed despite the miserable weather. During the day, when finishing touches on portions of the roof that had been covered with slate were done, all of the roofers began working on the last section.

The following day, the cold, wet weather continued, but the last courses of slate were laid. With boards covering the window and door openings on the windward side of the building, the interior was finally protected from the rain.

After muster the next morning, David sent the roofers and their helpers for their belongings and took a list of their names to the convict compound office to get a travel authorization for them. In addition to the guard on duty and a clerk, the commandant and a civilian were in the room, poring over old convict records.

Captain Barrett, the commandant, was an outgoing man who had spoken cordially when he and David had passed each other in the compound. He nodded affably to David in contrast to the civilian's reaction.

A short, pudgy man in his thirties wearing a stylish suit, he glanced at David in contempt, then continued talking quietly with Captain Barrett as the two of them sat at a table and looked through the records.

From their conversation, David learned that the man was a lawyer from Sydney named John Fitzroy, and had been contacted by a family in England about the settlement of an estate that involved a convict who had been at Parramatta. When their discussion ranged off the subject of their search in the records, the commandant mentioned a name that immediately drew David's attention.

"I understand you've been keeping company with a young lady named Hammond," the captain said. "She's a lawyer's daughter, isn't she?"

"Yes, that's correct," John Fitzroy replied in satisfaction. "Her name is Alexandra, and her father is Nevil Hammond. The Hammonds are a very well-connected family who immigrated from London some months ago."

"So you might improve your situation by marrying the young lady and forming a partnership with her father," Captain Barrett suggested.

The lawyer lifted his eyebrows archly and shrugged. "My present situation isn't unsatisfactory, and while Mistress Hammond and I are keeping company quite regularly, a partnership with her father is another matter entirely. His clientele and mine are completely different."

"You mean he doesn't limit himself to dealing with exclusives," the captain interpreted bluntly. "Well, many of the emancipists are wealthy, and they're not as slow as some of the bunyip aristocracy in opening their purse strings for what they want. Besides that," he added with a laugh, pointing to the records, "whom are you dealing with now?"

"With a client in England," Fitzroy replied frostily.

The captain laughed cheerfully over the lawyer's chagrin, as they resumed their perusal of the records.

David outwardly controlled his reaction to the conversation, waiting for the clerk to finish writing out the travel authorization. The name that had been mentioned was more than familiar to him, because the man he had caught with his wife was Wesley Hammond. During his trial, David had heard that the Yorkshire Hammonds had relatives in London, one of them a lawyer.

The clerk finally completed the paper and handed it to David, then he left. Hearing about the Hammond family had resurrected the galling sequence of events in his mind, the cataclysm that had destroyed his life. The bitter memories were revived with renewed force, along with crushing sorrow and his twisted, agonizing love for his former wife.

David took the document to the roofers and sent them and their helpers off into the rain toward Sydney. Then he returned to the construction site where he threw himself into his work. After going through the building to see that were no problems, he dragged logs to the saw pit, smothering his memories by straining at the heavy timbers until his body ached and his mind was numb with fatigue.

The next day was Sunday, which David always dreaded because the governor had designated it as a day when all public works ceased. Sundays provided opportunities for solitude, but while David found that deeply satisfying, work to occupy his mind and to make him sleep soundly was more important to him. Spending the day at the construction site, he carried lumber and dressed out stone blocks, maintaining a grueling pace until evening.

The other convicts spent the day in various ways. Those who were craftsmen often worked in the village for wages on Sundays and at night, which was officially sanctioned, and many of the laborers pursued pleasure. The Female Factory, where women serving their sentences lived and made clothing, was in Parramatta. Despite the weather, virtually every clump of brush that David passed as he went back to his room that evening was occupied by a convict and a woman from the factory.

Female convicts of better character lived with villagers, working as maids or earning their keep by making homespuns. At the end of a street adjacent to the compound, David passed a young woman who might be one of them, or possibly a member of a village family. She smiled at him tentatively in greeting, then frowned resentfully when he ignored her.

Although his former wife had divorced him after the trial, and the memory of her was still painful, David wanted no other woman in his life. In a sense, he knew that he was guilty of judging all women by his former wife, which was unfair and illogical. She had been self-centered and fickle, and he had overlooked that partly because she had also been gay, spirited, and beautiful, bringing color to his life. But mainly he had disregarded her faults simply because he had loved her, and in a grotesquely warped and poisoned way, he still did.

The following day, David gratefully settled back into the routine of work. With the departure of the roofers, he had an excess of laborers, and they were apprehensive at the morning muster. For the most part, they wanted to stay at the site and continue working for David.

It was an opportunity to get rid of Hinton and Crowley, but David knew he would have to give up more than two men if he broached the subject with Captain Barrett. He found tasks for all of them, explaining that he would have to release several if he received an order from the commandant. By Tuesday, however, he had heard nothing about it from the officer, and he knew that the extra laborers would be allowed to stay.

On Wednesday, another miserably cold, wet winter day, Francis came to see what progress had been made on the building. Rain streaming down his oilskins, the architect shivered with cold as he dismounted his horse and greeted David, who met him outside. Francis was distraught, explaining that the governor was displeased about the construction of the church in Sydney.

"That's one of the reasons I'm here," Francis confided. "I certainly don't enjoy riding about in this weather, but his excellency has been coming to the church daily and berating me, so I came here today."

"What's wrong at the church?" David asked.

"The work is simply going more slowly than the governor wishes," Francis replied morosely. "Although he has a reputation for leniency, he can be very caustic. He actually told me that he'd never met an infantry corporal who didn't know more than I about organizing work. I'm a professional man, and I'm not accustomed to enduring such insults."

As they went inside, the architect immediately became more cheerful, looking around in surprise. "Why, the joists have been completed, as well as many of the studs for the inside partitions!" he exclaimed.

"Yes, I'll soon start some of the carpenters on the rest of the flooring and the others on finishing off the doorways."

"Finishing off the doorways? Before the inside partitions are completed? That's putting the cart before the horse."

"Partitions are usually completed before doorways, but there's no reason why they must be. From what you've said about the other construction, you aren't using joiners now, and you must have some. While they aren't doing anything else, they can make and hang the doors."

The short, heavy-set man stroked his thin beard, pondering, then acknowledged that the idea had merit. They went upstairs, where Francis looked at the construction schedule, again commenting in pleasure on the amount of work that had been done.

David explained that part of the progress was due to the extra laborers he had kept. He also told the architect that many of the younger ones were working for craftsmen as additional helpers, getting the opportunity to learn a trade so they could better themselves.

Francis nodded absently, thinking of something else. "I try to avoid having the governor visit buildings under construction," he mused, "because his excellency is usually satisfied with what he sees only when they're completed. But this building will soon be on schedule, which is such a favorable development that I think I'll ask him to visit it."

Indifferent toward a visit by the governor, David shrugged and made a noncommittal reply. Francis continued ruminating about the idea as they went back downstairs, looking around. Soon after, the architect rode off into the rain as David returned to his work.

The following day, the wintry weather continued as sleet mixed with the rain and a frigid, gusty wind keened around the building. Near noon, while David was checking the alignment of partition supports with the carpenters, workers outside called to him. As he exited the building, an official coach was moving down the street toward the construction site.

The driver, bundled in a greatcoat and oilskins, stopped the coach beside the building and then scrambled down to open the door. Francis Greenway stepped out, followed by the governor. His manner betraying concern that Governor Macquarie would find something wrong, the architect introduced David to him.

"Ah, yes, the engineer," the governor said, touching his hat as David bowed. "Lieutenant Bethune recommended you highly, Mr. Kerrick."

"I'm very grateful that he did, Excellency, because I enjoy the work here. I trust that the lieutenant is well."

"So do I," Governor Macquarie replied wryly. "He left here only a few days ago for a regiment in India, and I already miss him sorely."

The architect anxiously escorted the governor into the building, and David followed them. Governor Macquarie stopped inside, looking around at the workers. "There seems to be many helpers with the carpenters," he mused. "Why are there more here than at other buildings under construction?"

Francis frowned in alarm, glancing around. "They'll be sent back to the convict compound immediately, Excellency."

"I didn't tell you to do that," the governor said impatiently. "I merely asked why there are more here than elsewhere."

While the architect fumbled for words, David explained, "The carpenters can work faster if they have additional helpers. Also, the extra helpers are learning a trade, which will enable them to better themselves and be of more value to the community."

"That's quite true," the governor agreed heartily. "I fully endorse the idea because it benefits everyone." He turned to Greenway. "We should look into doing this at all of the projects."

"Yes, immediately, Excellency," the architect replied absently, the governor's reaction to the building his sole concern. He pointed to a partition framework. "Ordinarily, the partitions are completely finished before the doors are made and hung. However, we have joiners at Sydney who are working as carpenters for the lack of anything else to do, so I've decided to send them here to work on the interior doors."

"Good, good," Governor Macquarie commented in approval. "That will be making the best use of your workers, which is a point I've been stressing with you. That's a very good idea." He paused, glancing from Francis to David musingly, and apparently realized the origin of the notion. "It's an uncommonly good idea, in fact," he added dryly, then pointed to a section of flooring. "What sort of wood is that?"

The architect replied as he and the governor walked through the building toward the ladder to the second floor. David accompanied them upstairs as Francis pointed out and explained details of the construction. After touring the second floor, they filed back down the ladder. Governor Macquarie looked around again and left the building.

Returning to the coach, the governor commented favorably about the progress on the building. "Occasionally," he told David, "we provide a stipend to overseers of exceptional merit. Accordingly, I'll have the commandant tell his paymaster to put you on wages of seven shillings a week. And in due time, if the work continues in the same fashion, I'll take your sentence under review. Those convicted of capital offenses can never leave the colony, but within that limitation, I can reward the deserving."

David thanked the governor, and Francis radiated with pleasure over Governor Macquarie's satisfaction with the building. Then the two men disappeared into the coach and David returned to his work as the vehicle moved away.

He was pleased about the money, a generous amount that would buy oilskins, candles for his room, and other things he wanted. But he was completely indifferent about the prospect of a ticket-of-leave or pardon, neither wanting nor needing more liberty. His only confinement was to his past, and his only escape from it was his work.

That afternoon, the rain and sleet diminished, and the wind died away as the temperature fell. By that evening, the clouds were starting to break up. Dawn the next morning brought clear skies and a bright, cold winter day. The ground began drying, and a period of more moderate weather set in, making the work easier.

Late one morning, a guard told David to bring all of his workers to the compound courtyard at noon for an assembly. Assuming it was for a public lashing of a convict, David commented to that effect, but the guard shook his head.

"No, it's for an announcement," he said. "The commandant received a message by courier this morning from Sydney, and he hasn't told anyone what it's about. He just ordered us to assemble all of the work gangs for an announcement. The villagers and farmers are also being summoned to hear it. Make certain that all of your men are there."

David replied that he would, and the guard left. In the penal colony, unusual developments were usually unpleasant ones, and David speculated about the message as he resumed working. The most likely possibility that occurred to him was that Governor Macquarie was being replaced, which would be extremely bad news for convicts. Life in Australia was a grim ordeal for some convicts even now, but under the rule of a few governors, it had been a wretched existence.

That afternoon, David led his workers to the compound courtyard. Families from nearby farms were gathering around carts and horses they had ridden, while villagers left their houses and shops to join them. Crews of convicts who had been working on roads and other projects were also present, one chain gang among them.

The weak winter sun cast thin shadows across the courtyard, and other convicts arrived as the number of village and farm families grew. The entire force of guards filed into the courtyard, then the women from the Female Factory arrived in a roar of bawdy exchanges between them and the convicts. The guards moved about, bellowing and restoring order.

A few minutes later, silence fell as Captain Barrett came into the courtyard. He stepped onto a stand and unfolded a paper. "Your attention, please," he called. "I've been ordered by the governor to assemble everyone in my area of jurisdiction and read aloud the proclamation issued by his excellency after receiving the grievously sad tidings of the death of his Royal Majesty, King George III."

The commandant began reading the proclamation, the first sentences a formal statement of sorrow and respectful condolences to the royal family. The news not what he had feared, David relaxed, and the reaction of other convicts was widely at odds with the tone of the proclamation.

"It's past time that daft old codger got his deep six," a man behind David muttered. "His face ain't been seen, and he ain't attended to affairs for years. All that time, he was cosseted in the greatest luxury one can imagine, and he could have been in an almshouse for all he knew. He didn't have enough brains to crowd a sparrow's head."

"The last one was no better," another man added. "He died on his thunder mug, it's said, from a heart seizure brought on by straining too hard. He ruled the realm, but didn't know enough to take a tonic."

Other men grumbled as the commandant read on. Then he reached the formalities of mourning that would be observed in the colony. The next Sunday, the governor would lead a procession of officials, clergy, and others who wished to participate from Government House to a church for a memorial service. Further, from Saturday until Tuesday, all businesses in the colony would close and public works would cease.

The muttering around David stopped as the convicts reacted to the last part of the proclamation with poorly-concealed glee. The captain dismissed the assembly, and David returned to the building, his workers following him. They talked and laughed in happy anticipation about the upcoming free time, but David's mood was the opposite of theirs. Instead of having only a Sunday to while away, he would have three full days without work.

The following Saturday, the period of cold, clear weather still lingered as the sun shone brightly but without warmth. And at the very beginning of his long, dreaded period of idleness, David looked over the entire construction site, but was unable to find anything to do.

Some of the laborers had finally discovered that hard work made time pass quickly, and had toiled busily the previous afternoon to fill the hours until their free days began. Large amounts of lumber and stone were stacked in place for the carpenters and masons, and the bins were filled with lime and sand for mixing mortar.

Unable to think of anything else to do, David went to the edge of the village and set out down the road to the west. With everything in the colony at a standstill, the road was deserted. Bordered by open forest and small farms set back from it, the road wound up a long slope that David had heard about, a rise called Prospect Hill.

Crossing the crest of the hill, David glanced around, then he suddenly stopped. He gazed over the landscape, gripped by a sense of wonder. While traveling about on his work in England, he had seen the moors and the great fertile plain of Yorkshire, but they would be lost here. In an immense, panoramic sweep, the rolling hills unfolded ahead to the Nepean River and its wide, verdant valley was set against the backdrop of the hazy Blue Mountains that rose on the horizon miles in the distance.

With isolated farms and flocks of sheep scattered over the hills, the landscape was a vast expanse. Although it was almost overwhelming in size, David knew it was only a promise of what lay beyond the Blue Mountains. He had heard about Bathurst, a village west of the mountains in an enormous grasslands plain, much of which remained unused even with sheep stations encompassing tens of thousands of acres scattered across it.

And even the far reaches of the Bathurst plain were only an indication of the land beyond. West of Bathurst was the outback, a gigantic, mysterious region that remained unexplored. He had heard some people had been there, but very few. On maps, it was a blank with an extent like that of the seas. Information about it was scarce and unreliable, a web of hearsay facts mixed with a large amount of supposition and fanciful tales.

One absolutely certain fact, however, was the concrete reality that it was there. When he had heard about the outback, it had meant little to him. He had been disinterested, burdened with sorrow and his energies centered entirely on his work. But now, as he looked out across the landscape, its significance to him was vital. Standing on Prospect Hill and gazing to the west, he had come to a crossroads in his life.

A feeling unlike anything he had ever known gripped him. On the day he had walked to Parramatta, he had experienced a premonition of it in his deep contentment while sitting beside the river, but he had failed to realize what had created that mood. Now he understood completely, and it was a revelation as intense and profound as a religious awakening.

In the forested glade beside the river, with no indication that others were within miles, he had found contentment in peaceful solitude. It had lasted only a few minutes, but a lifetime of it lay beyond the mountains. In the outback, he could build himself a new life, cutting himself off from all that had happened to him and leaving his agony of sorrow behind.

Exuberant happiness swelled within him, too much for him to contain. In a boyish impulse, he lifted his arms over his head, whooping at the top of his voice and shouting his joy to the world. For the first time since the bitter day when he had discovered his wife's

infidelity, he was able to think about what lay beyond
the present moment.

He had a future once again, bright with promise. A
new, fresh world seemed to have opened up around
him as he walked on down the road, almost running.
The sun looked brighter on the wintry July day, the
chatter of the birds more lively and cheerful. Gazing
from side to side, he drank in the scene as he hurried
toward the river.

After he passed the last farm, he had the sense of
peaceful solitude once again. The wide, fertile river
valley was taken up in sheep stations, the nearest
houses and flocks miles away. A track, a narrow trail,
branched off the road to the south, weaving in and out
of the thick trees beside the river.

Although the track was evidence that people were
within a few miles, the place felt much like a wilderness to David as he walked. Wildlife he had never seen
before was abundant. Wallabies and kangaroos
bounded away ahead of him, and a wombat scurried
through the brush. Small animals similar to flying
squirrels glided between the trees, and other animals
stirred the foliage.

Green clouds of budgerigars whirled overhead, so
thick they cast shadows on the ground. A gum tree
with a flock of white cockatoos on its branches looked
like it was covered with chalky blossoms. Yellow
crests on the birds' heads stood erect as David walked
toward them, then they burst from the tree in a
bedlam of hoarse cries. A seemingly endless variety of
other colorful birds chattered and swooped between
the trees.

At sunset, David entered a thicket of trees and
brush near the road. The chill of evening settling in,
he picked up sticks and slabs of eucalyptus bark to
build a small shelter, then found dry, decayed bark for
tinder and used his flint and steel to kindle a fire.

With the fire blazing in front of it, the shelter
became comfortably warm. At nightfall, David was

hungry, but his contentment was infinitely more satisfying than any amount of the most delicious food.
And the fire, holding back the cold night with its
warm, cheerful glow, gave him a sense of comfort at a
deep, primal level.

Gazing into the fire, David thought about what he
had to do. The governor had stopped just short of
promising him his freedom, which had now become
of paramount importance. The only means of a
livelihood in the solitude west of the mountains was as
a grazier, so he had to learn how to care for sheep and
other livestock. Then he would have to work and save
to buy a flock and other necessities. All of that would
take time, but at twenty-six years old, he had his life
ahead of him once again.

Finally, David settled himself comfortably and
went to sleep. When the fire burned to ashes near
dawn, the penetrating cold woke him. He left the
shelter and went up the road, walking briskly to warm
himself. When the village came into view, he had a
sense of returning to a grim, dreary prison.

The convict compound was quiet, smoke from the
cookhouse chimney the only sign of life. David went
to the bathhouse then on to the cookhouse. In contrast
to its usual uproar, it was virtually deserted. The
convict cook who should have been doling out food
was sitting at a table with his head on his arms,
haggard from a hangover. He pointed to the pans of
food, telling David to help himself.

Having eaten nothing since breakfast the day be-
fore, David took several pieces of bread and salt pork.
He sat at a table and ate, then went back to the cook.
"Do you have any potatoes?"

"Back there," the man groaned, motioning toward
the kitchen without lifting his head. "Take whatever
the bloody hell you want."

David went into the grimy, cluttered kitchen. A
wide shelf was filled with baskets of potatoes, in a
corner were casks of salt pork and beef, and loaves of

bread were piled on a table. Finding a small basket, David put pieces of pork and beef into it, then he filled his pockets with potatoes and took a loaf of bread.

Returning to his room, he rolled his soap, razor, and mirror in his blanket, then he set out for the road leading west. After he passed the outskirts of the village, his feeling of confinement faded, and his exuberantly cheerful mood of the day before returned. He walked down the road with a long, swinging stride, happily whistling a tune.

With a gusty wind blowing, it was colder than the previous day, but David felt an inner warmth when he reached his shelter. In some vital way, the small, crude structure seemed like home to him. He put his things inside, then piled wood and kindled a fire.

Work had made time pass rapidly for him, but never as swiftly as did the solitude near the river. The hours fled like minutes in his enjoyment as he explored the forest, watched the birds and animals, and cooked over the fire. He remained there Monday night, rising well before dawn the next morning, and returned to the convict compound in time to put his things in his room and go to the cookhouse for breakfast.

As he resumed his routine, instead of dreading Sunday and looking forward to the work week, his priorities had been reversed. At the same time, the building project had taken on a crucial importance as his passport to the new life he wanted. With that burning ambition driving him, David threw himself into his work with concentrated energy.

The days passed quickly, and the work inched ever closer to the completion schedule the governor had set for the building. On Friday, David received his first wages, pay for two weeks' work, and bought oilskins and supplies.

The following day, activities proceeded smoothly at the construction site until noon, when an incident threatened a work stoppage. At the saw pit, a long, steel lever with toothed jaws attached to one end was used to turn logs while they were being squared off and sawed up into boards and support beams. While a log was being turned, one of the jaws broke off the lever. The sawyer told David that the logs could be turned with crowbars, but it was difficult and time consuming, too slow to provide the carpenters with the amount of lumber they were using.

David gathered the pieces of the lever and carried them to the blacksmith shop on the outskirts of the village. He explained the situation to the burly owner of the shop, telling him that he would arrange payment through Greenway if the man could repair the lever. The blacksmith examined the pieces, then nodded and told David that the lever would be ready for him to pick up on Monday morning.

The problem resolved, David went back toward the building in a cheerful mood, looking forward to spending the next day at the river. The houses were scattered on the north side of the village, where lanes between farms were in the process of becoming residential streets. As he turned a corner at a distance from the nearest house, he saw a man and woman beside a buggy that had broken down, a wheel having come off. Then, recognizing John Fitzroy, David immediately knew who the woman was.

"You, there," John Fitzroy called brusquely, beckoning David. "Fetch someone who can put this wheel back on the—"

"Don't be so utterly boorish, John," Alexandra Hammond interrupted him impatiently, then she turned to David. "Could I prevail upon you for your assistance? If you could either put the wheel back on the buggy or tell me the whereabouts of a wheelwright, I'd be most grateful."

Walking toward them, David silently stared at Fitzroy until he looked away, but his anger over the man's attitude was almost lost in his mixture of contrasting reactions to the woman. A relative of the man who had destroyed his life, she brought back his grief and rage of that time in full force. However, he saw that her cordial manner was completely natural, not a pose to solicit help. Fitzroy was peevishly ill-tempered over the accident with the buggy, while she was taking it in stride.

She was also the most exquisitely beautiful creature he had ever seen. Appearing to be about nineteen years old, she had long, thick brown hair tucked up under her wide hat and large blue eyes set in finely-modeled features that were far more lovely than the most perfect image a master sculptor could fashion. With ample reason to be vain, instead her eyes and face reflected a sunny good nature along with a spirited, independent personality.

While he urgently wanted to ignore her and walk on by, a more compelling impulse made him stop. As he looked at the wheel and axle, seeing that they were undamaged, she pointed to the threads on the end of the axle. "Apparently something came off there," she suggested.

"Yes, it's called a wheel nut," he replied. He turned away from the buggy and began searching along the street. "It came off a short distance away, because the wheel won't stay on very long without it."

Lifting the hem of her dress and long winter coat to keep them out of the mud, Alexandra helped him look for the nut. A few yards from the buggy, he found it in weeds at the edge of the road and picked it up. "Well done!" she exclaimed happily. "Is it harmed in any way?"

David shook his head, approaching the buggy. "No, wheel nuts are made of steel, and they're difficult to damage."

Taking a firm grip on the axle, David lifted the side of the small, light vehicle to slide the wheel back into place. Obviously wellborn, the young woman was totally unpretentious and had an industrious, restless energy. Unable to remain idle, she gripped the spokes on the wheel, helping David push it onto the axle.

"Alexandra, what are you doing?" John asked indignantly.

"I am helping with a task at hand," she replied evenly, "whilst you stand there and sulk. So we are both doing what we do best, John."

The lawyer sighed in exasperation, turning away. Alexandra glanced at David with a twinkling smile that was both a silent, humorous comment on John Fitzroy's childish petulance and an apology for his rude behavior. With the smile wreathing her lovely features, her beauty was dazzling, like gazing into a brilliant sunrise after a cold, dark night.

As they slid the wheel onto the axle, David was acutely aware of how near she was. The alluring scent of her perfume wafted around him, and her shoulder brushed his. She remained close when the wheel was on, watching as he put the nut on the axle to hold the wheel in place. Then he pointed out the small hole in the nut where a cotter pin was needed.

"A nail or a piece of wire will suffice," he told her. "But if something isn't there to hold it, the wheel will come off again."

Alexandra smiled, nodding. "I'm sure something adequate can be found at the farm where I'm going. I might not have reached there today but for your capable assistance, though. I'm most grateful indeed."

As he answered appropriately, David knew that she was going to introduce herself in a moment, necessitating the same from him. Certain she would recognize his name, he dreaded the thought of the horror on her beautiful face if she found out who he was. He quickly made a brief farewell, lifting his hat and bowing. Alexandra replied, smiling as he turned away.

Torn by diametrically opposed emotions, David continued walking toward the construction site. In one way, his reaction to Alexandra had shaken his belief that there could never be another woman in his life. At the same time, the sorrow and anger she had resurrected from his past had reinforced that belief into an absolute conviction.

David tried to dismiss his turmoil and concentrate on going to the river the next day, where he would have peace. He was only partly successful, looking forward to the next day, but unable to force the mental image of Alexandra's lovely, smiling face out of his thoughts.

As the buggy moved down the street which gradually turned into a rural road, Alexandra waited for John to make a disapproving remark about what she had done, knowing that he would. When he did, she turned on him. "Are you venturing to chastise me, John?" she demanded.

"No, no, of course not," he assured her hastily. "However, I feel that your father would have considered it unseemly. After all, the man was a perfect stranger, and perhaps a convict. I believe I've seen him among convicts somewhere or other, so he's either that or an emancipist."

"My father's attitudes toward what I do don't concern you. That man may be a convict, emancipist, or a free settler, but he is also a gentleman. And a gentleman who knew how to repair the buggy."

"Well, I don't profess to be a mechanic," John said resentfully. "I'm an attorney at law, and I can't understand why you've taken such umbrage over a passing comment about what you did, Alexandra."

"I've told you before that I won't listen to reprimands from you, John. My brother isn't a mechanic, but I daresay that Creighton could manage to put a wheel back on a buggy if he had to."

John lapsed into offended silence. Alexandra knew that her response to what he had said had been indeed too heated. She also candidly admitted to herself that it had been because she was defensive. While she always felt compelled to lend a hand where it was needed, in that particular instance it had been inappropriate. She had crossed over the line from being cordial and had been forward with the man.

In part, it had been to atone for John's usual discourtesy toward those he considered beneath him, but it had also been because the man had intrigued her. A large, strikingly handsome man, clean-shaven and meticulously neat, he had been very reserved but polite. His speech and manner had indicated he was well-educated and from a good family, but his clothing had revealed that he was either a convict or so financially hardpressed that he had to buy clothes from government stores.

None of that, she reflected, touched upon why she had been so curious about him. She decided that it had been his eyes, which had been the source of some vaguely mysterious quality about him. He appeared to have suffered an agonizing ordeal, the aftermath of it lingering, but she had also seen in his blue eyes an undeniable interest in her that had overshadowed everything else. She wished she knew more about him, at least his name.

Stirring from her reverie, Alexandra pointed to a lane ahead. "Turn in there, please," she said.

John pulled back on the reins, slowing the horse, then turned onto the lane. "It would have been enjoyable to attend the social gathering at the Montague home today," he mused regretfully.

"I did say that I was perfectly willing to come here alone today," Alexandra reminded him firmly. "You could have gone to the Montagues while I came here to see my friend and deliver the baby clothes."

"Friend?" John echoed disdainfully. "Alexandra, the woman worked as a maid in your father's household."

"From when I was a small girl," Alexandra added, annoyed. "Lavinia came here with the family as a maid, met a good man, and has a happy marriage. I consider her a friend, and I'll ask you to act accordingly."

Sighing in resignation, John nodded. As the buggy moved down the lane into the small farm, the wheel on Alexandra's side bumped through a rut. It was the one that had come off, and she remembered what the tall man had said about the need for the nut to be secured. Leaning out, she looked at the wheel to make certain it was still firmly on the axle.

Sitting back in the seat, she continued thinking about him, recalling the few things he had said and done. When he had put the nut on the axle, his hands had drawn her attention. Very large and strong, but not those of a laborer, they had also looked gentle.

At the small, neat, freestone cottage, John started to draw up the buggy in front of it. Alexandra pointed to the rear, knowing that Lavinia would be in the kitchen. His pained expression conveying what he thought about going to the back door of a house, John drove on and stopped the buggy in the yard between the cottage and outbuildings.

A stout, rosy-cheeked woman in her thirties came out of the cottage as Alexandra stepped down from the buggy. "Mistress Alexandra!" she cried in delight, rushing to her. "How very good it is to see you again!"

"And you, Lavinia," Alexandra replied as they embraced. "I was ever so pleased to hear about the baby, and I've brought some clothes for her. You've met Mr. Fitzroy, I believe."

The woman nodded, her smile fading as she bobbed in a curtsy, and John bowed stiffly in response. Alexandra took the bundle of baby clothes out of the buggy and handed them to the woman, whose warm smile returned. "You shouldn't have, Mistress Alexandra," she said, "but I'm most grateful. I'm even more grateful to see you again. Come on in, then."

"I can stay only long enough to see the baby, Lavinia," Alexandra explained apologetically. "We had a mishap with the buggy that delayed me, and

Mother will be worried if I tarry too long. Where is Tom?"

"He was seeing to the cow a short time ago," Lavinia replied, looking toward the barns. "Aye, there he is now. He must have heard the buggy."

A tall, lanky man in baggy homespuns came toward the house, a wide smile on his sun-browned face as he took off his cap. "G'day, Mistress Hammond," he said. "I'm mightily pleased to see you again."

"It's a pleasure to see you again, Tom. I don't believe you've met my escort, John Fitzroy. John, this is Thomas Delaney."

The men greeted each other, John straining to be civil, then Alexandra told Tom about the need for a retaining device in the wheel nut on the buggy. "Aye, it's a cotter pin you want, Mistress Hammond," he replied, "and I have plenty in my tool shed. I'll put one in for you."

"Thank you, Tom. John, I'll be out presently."

He nodded, getting back into the buggy to sit and wait as Alexandra followed Lavinia into the cottage. In the warm, spotless kitchen, the baby was sleeping in a cradle beside the homemade table. Alexandra smiled in delight, leaning over the cradle to touch the small face tenderly.

Lavinia ladled water from a bucket into a teakettle, then placed it on the fireplace hob to heat. "You can stay long enough to have a cup of tea, my dear," she announced firmly. "Let me take your coat, or you won't have the benefit of it when you go back outside. I see that you're still keeping company with that one out there to pacify your father."

Taking off her coat, Alexandra smiled wryly and nodded. At best, her relationship with her father was an uneasy one, her need to be involved in productive activity clashing with his desire for her to be much less independent. He had gone to lengths to encourage a relationship between her and John, and she cooperated to an extent in order to avoid arguments.

"John is under no illusions about my feelings," she told Lavinia, handing her the coat. "We are social companions, no more."

"He's trying to wear you down, my dear," Lavinia warned her somberly, hanging the coat in a corner. "You must keep your wits about yourself and not let him, because you can do much better than that. I trust that your mother and grandmother are still in good health?"

Alexandra sat down at the table, replying that they were. Then she told Lavinia what the members of her family had been doing recently, the woman bustling about the kitchen and preparing the tea. As they talked, the baby began whimpering, and Alexandra rocked the cradle gently.

Glancing out the window, Alexandra saw Tom kneeling beside the buggy wheel, putting in the cotter pin. Thoughts of the man she had met on the road immediately raced through her mind, and it occurred to her that anything even remotely associated with him made her think of him. Once she did, it was difficult for her to dismiss those thoughts.

A vague memory from years before surfaced in her mind, and she mentioned it to Lavinia. "Didn't one of the cooks we used to have in England have some sort of saying about strangers and not being able to forget them?" she asked. "I think it was the Corliss woman."

"No, it was Darcy Hubble, my dear," Lavinia replied, placing a cup on the table. "Let's see now, how did that go? Aye, it's, 'If you meet a stranger whom you can't get out of mind, he'll no longer be a stranger if you'll only bide your time.' That's what she used to say."

Alexandra nodded, looking down at the baby as she rocked the cradle. "Yes, that's right," she agreed musingly. "That's what she used to say."

Chapter Four

"G'day. I'm Frank Williamson."

David stopped on the road, returning the greeting and introducing himself. Ever since he had started going to the river, he had passed the man in his horse-drawn cart every Sunday morning. Wearing heavy work clothes and a stockman's hat with the wide brim turned up on one side, Frank Williamson had once been a burly man. Now he sagged with age, his flowing beard and mustache snowy white, but his eyes were still alert and youthful.

"I'm not one to try to mind another's flock," Frank said, "but I appreciate a word of caution myself when I have mine on pastures I don't know well. You could encounter trouble whilst camping at the river."

"Am I trespassing there? From the look of the land, I thought it was property held by the colonial authorities."

"The verge along the river is, with the edge of my property reaching down to it, but that isn't what I meant. Bushrangers use this road, and some of them could notice your fire sometime. If you've as much as tuppence in your pockets, that's what your life is worth to them."

The warning well taken, David thanked the man. "I've seen no one about down there," he continued, "and I didn't realize I had drawn anyone's attention. How did you know I was camping near the river?"

"It wasn't hard to unravel," Frank replied, amused. "When I began passing you on my way to visit my family in Sydney every Sunday, I began noticing smoke in the trees down there when I came back on Sunday evening. I thought that it had to be you."

"Yes, I suppose that follows," David agreed, laughing. "So you own the station bordering the river on the south side of the road?"

The aged man smiled sadly, shrugging. "Such as it is. I used to be a grazier, just as I used to ride a horse. Now I graze a few thousand head on that patch of land and I go about in a cart most of the time."

"It looks like very good property to me, as it would to most. Did you have one of the large stations over at Bathurst?"

"No, those are mere patches as well, David," Frank replied, gazing reminiscently into the distance. "I used to have a real sheep station and as much land as a man could want, in the outback."

"The outback?" David exclaimed, fascinated and pleased to have at last met someone who had actually been to the distant region. "I've heard talk about it, but very few have been there."

"Aye, only a few," Frank agreed. "A good friend of mine is there now on what used to be my station. A drayage company in Sydney sends him supplies every year and brings out his wool, and I hear that the drivers are always glad to get back, liking the clatter and crowds." He lifted his reins. "If you're going to be down near the river, I'll stop on my way back from Sydney this evening and talk with you."

"I'd like that very much indeed," David replied emphatically.

Frank nodded, touching his hat and snapping the reins, and his cart moved away. Walking on down the road, David was elated at having met the likable, friendly man with firsthand information about the outback, and he looked forward to talking with Frank at length.

It was the middle of August, the weather cold and unsettled, with a scum of ice covering the puddles on the road. Gusty wind shredded the smoke rising from the farms' chimneys, and the people were bundled against the chill as they went about their tasks. A mile beyond the last farm on the road, David identified the track leading into Frank's station. A narrow, muddy trail, it stretched to the south across rolling hills covered with acacia, grass, and open forest.

Reaching the track that branched off the road at the river, David went down it and into the trees to his camp. During the past Sundays, he had enlarged the first crude shelter into a bark hut with a frame of sturdy limbs. He kindled a fire in the ring of stones in front of the hut, then unrolled his blanket and took out food and cooking utensils he had bought in the village.

With his wages, he could afford tea and other luxuries. Following the stockman's practice, he brewed it in a billycan, a tall, slender pint container with a bail. He filled the billy and a small pan at the river, then set them on the fire and sliced up vegetables into the pan. When the billy boiled, he took it off the fire and put a piece of mutton on a spit.

The food he bought was so much better than convict fare that his meal was one thing he looked forward to on Sundays. However, his main pleasure by far remained the quiet solitude and reflecting on when he could begin a new life. After eating, he passed the hours in walking along the river, thinking of when he might have his own sheep station.

During late afternoon, he returned to the hut. Soon, he heard the rattle of harness chains and rumble of wheels as Frank turned off the road onto the track. David moved through the trees, exchanging greetings with the grazier as he clambered stiffly down from the cart, then they unhitched the horse so it could graze.

The trip to Sydney was a considerable distance, and David commented that the old man had spent only a short time there. "No, not long," Frank agreed. "I don't like being in towns. Also, my wife and sons don't enjoy my visiting them any more than I enjoy doing it."

"I wonder why you do, then."

"Because they're my wife and sons, and I think that I should visit them," Frank replied, taking a fire-blackened billy and tea from a bag in the cart. "I'm a man who does what he thinks he should."

David commented that it was a good rule to follow, as he and Frank went into the copse. After filling their billys at the river, they made tea and smoked their pipes. David talked briefly about himself, telling the grazier that he was an engineer and the overseer of the building in Parramatta.

Frank made no attempt to find out more, avoiding asking personal questions for many men had reason to resent prying into their background. "Well, when you get a ticket-of-leave or pardon," he observed, "you shouldn't have trouble finding work that pays well."

"Perhaps, but I want to be a grazier."

Frank puffed on his pipe, studying David, then nodded. "Aye, you have the look of a man who can stand to be alone, and moreover who would prefer it. Getting started as a grazier can be hard, though. Land is very expensive here but considerably more reasonable at Bathurst."

"And more reasonable still in the outback."

"Indeed, because the use of it is free. You can simply get a grazing license and squat on as much land as you need. The license costs only a guinea, but the land won't belong to you, and not everyone can live in the outback. People either love it or hate it, nothing in between."

Taking a drink of his tea, David asked, "Is it anything similar to the land here?"

Frank shook his head, replying that it was more arid, with different vegetation than the coastal region. Fewer sheep could be grazed per acre, and water was very scarce. Grass fires, floods, and droughts were a menace, along with dingoes, the wild dogs of Australia. However, if those difficulties could be overcome, he said, it was an excellent region for grazing, and flocks multiplied rapidly.

He described the outback and related his experiences there. Dusk had gathered when he fell silent for a moment, musing. Then, the firelight flickering on his wrinkled face and white beard, he began talking again and tried to convey a more abstract impression of the outback. Not a particularly articulate man, he searched for words to describe its beauty, vastness, and the effects it had on people who went there.

"In one way or another," he continued reflectively, gazing into the fire, "it gets into one's blood and bones. As for me, I wanted to stay there for eternity, finishing out my years and being buried there. It took my wife the other way, because she went a bit daft, and it took my sons the same way. They were only boys when we brought them back, but they still don't like to venture away from the streets of Sydney."

"The loneliness?" David suggested.

"That, as well as being all alone, and there's a great difference between the two. Also, it seems that people who like it there have to be able to look at themselves squarely and be satisfied with what they see. Whatever it was, my family couldn't stand it there, and I felt that I had a responsibility to bring them back. So that's what I did."

"And you sold the station to a friend."

Frank drank his tea, nodding. "I sold it to Pat

Garrity, who worked for me from when he was a lad. The sons of my body are in Sydney, but Pat is the son of my soul. He calls the place Wayamba Station, and it's by far the largest in Australia. He has a wife and children, and a good number of stockmen who like life in the outback."

"His wife and children apparently like it there, then."

"Aye, and little wonder," Frank replied, amused. "His wife, Mayrah, is an Aborigine and has been a big help to Pat. Together, they can deal with bushrangers or any other problem that comes along."

"There are bushrangers in the outback?"

"They don't loiter because the brigands like to stay near whores and rum, and they're not the sort who would like the outback. But they've been known to go there, shoot stockmen, and make off with the flocks. Some have also got lost out there and either died of thirst and starvation, or become so daft that they didn't know up from down."

"Where does the outback begin, Frank?"

"That depends on who you ask. Most people will say west of Bathurst, but in my opinion, it begins well to the west of that. There's a great river out there that the Aborigines call Cobdogla, which means land of plenty or something of the sort. I'd say when you get to the Cobdogla River, you're well into the outback, because you're out where things are different. For instance, that must be the only river that flows upside down."

"Upside down?" David echoed, laughing.

Frank laughed, nodding. "If you ever see it, you'll know what I mean. It must be the muddiest river in the world."

The conversation continued, and David became more and more fascinated with the immense land to the west. The isolation and other characteristics that some regarded as drawbacks were advantages to him. As the aged grazier talked, his voice had a note of wistful longing to return there, and it was a feeling that David could understand. Most of all, David became certain that it was indeed a place where he could shape a new future for himself, leaving his past behind him.

It was late when the two men fell silent for a few minutes. David stirred the fire's ashes and tossed sticks on them. The wood crackled as it began burning, driving the darkness back with a circle of light. "I'd like to have a sheep station there, Frank," David commented quietly. "I want that more than anything I've ever wanted in my life."

"Aye, I gathered you wanted to go there." The grazier chuckled, then he sobered as he looked at the young man reflectively. "Well, you're the kind of man who'd like it there, David. And I daresay you'll have a sheep station in the outback one day, because you're also the kind of man who does something when he sets his mind to it." He sighed, picking up his billy and stiffly climbing to his feet. "It's time these old bones were in a blanket."

"I'll help you with the horse," David offered, standing up.

"I appreciate it. That horse can be tetchy and we'll need a light to keep from getting kicked, but I have a lantern in the cart."

They went through the trees to the cart. David took the lantern, bringing it to the fire to light it, then returned to the cart and helped the grazier hitch up the horse. As they were fastening the harness chains, David expressed the hope that they could talk again soon.

"Aye, we'll have plenty of chin wags," Frank assured him. "While we were talking, I thought of something that would help both of us. If you'd like to work at my station on Sundays, I'll pay you three shillings and found for the day. How does that sound?"

"It sounds too generous by far, Frank. I don't know

enough about sheep to earn three farthings a day, much less three shillings."

"You'll learn, and if I don't miss my guess, you'll learn much faster than anyone else. Also, you'll be learning what you'll need to know if you're going to be a grazier. Lambing time will come soon, and it's most important that you know how to attend ewes when they're lambing. Further, you would be of considerable help then, because many of the ewes lamb at the same time, and every available hand is valuable."

"I'd like to do it, but I don't see how I can. By the time I reached your station, part of the day would be gone. And I'd have to be back in Parramatta in time to muster my workers on Monday morning."

"That's easily cured. For some time, I've been thinking about seeing my wife and sons on Saturday instead of Sunday, which would be better for everyone concerned. I'll start doing that, and as I come back through Parramatta on Saturday evening, you can meet me and ride to the station. On Sunday night, you can use a horse from the station to return to Parramatta, and one of my stockmen can go with you to bring it back."

David fastened the last harness chain, then turned to the aged man in the dim, yellow light of the lantern. While they had talked beside the fire, the beginnings of a very warm friendship had developed between them, but he felt that the grazier was being too obliging. "Your offer is more than kind, Frank," he said, "but that would be an unreasonable amount of trouble to have someone work at your station for one day a week."

"That depends on who the someone is, David," Frank replied firmly. "This will be of help to both of us, and it's something I want to do. I've reached the time in life where I should be able to do as I wish about some things, and beyond that . . ." He paused, his voice fading, then he laughed. "It's strange, because you and Pat Garrity are entirely different, but at the same time, you're very much alike. Pat gives me credit for helping him get started, and I'd like to do the same for you."

David hesitated, then agreed. "Very well, Frank. Needless to say, I'm very grateful, because this will be of great help to me."

"To both of us," Frank corrected him. "I'll meet you in Parramatta next Saturday evening, then."

The two men shook hands, then Frank climbed heavily into the cart with the lantern. The vehicle moved away, and David watched the spot of yellow light grow smaller. In a physical sense, he reflected, he remained where he had spent the past Sundays, but in another way and as a result of having met the grazier, he had taken a giant step toward the outback.

The next Saturday, as early dusk fell at the end of a windy, cloudy day, David met Frank on the road at the edge of Parramatta. The grazier smiled happily, and David was equally pleased to see him again. They greeted each other warmly, and David put his blanket and other belongings behind the seat as he stepped into the cart and sat down.

The cart moved briskly down the road, the horse trotting, and Frank reminisced about his experiences. He said he had been among the convicts on the initial vessels sent to establish a colony in Australia, known as the First Fleet, arriving in the summer of 1788. The first years had been difficult, crop failures and the late arrival of supply ships resulting in famine, as well as shortages of clothing and other essentials.

With Sydney gradually becoming established, Frank had been one of those sent to build a settlement at Parramatta, then known as Rose Hill. Through unremitting labor, he had earned a land grant by the time he had served his sentence, and he had chosen the land that was now his station on the Nepean River. Married by then, he had settled down to farming and raising sheep, his flock rapidly increasing from scores to hundreds.

The sheep, a strain of Merinos brought from Capetown, had been a fortunate choice of livestock. When the first large shipment of wool from the flocks in the colony had reached England, the importations of long-staple wool from the Merino flocks in Spain had just been cut off by the Napoleonic Wars. The wool brought a premium price, and Frank and others graziers gave up commercial farming and concentrated entirely on sheep.

His flocks increasing to thousands of sheep, Frank had tried to obtain more land. None in the vicinity of the Nepean River had been available, and other graziers had crossed the Blue Mountains to establish stations near the infant settlement of Bathurst. When his station had been threatened with overgrazing, Frank had set out with his family, stockmen, horses, dogs, wagons loaded with supplies, and half of his sheep. Driving the sheep slowly westward, letting them and the horses graze, it had taken him eight months to reach the land he had wanted.

"But I ended up right back here," Frank said, ending the long narrative, "so it's just as well that I kept this place and left it in charge of a manager instead of selling it."

David was unable to see the old man's face, nightfall having come an hour before, but his voice was sadly resigned. "Many men would have sent their family back and remained there," he commented.

Frank sighed. "Aye, many would have," he agreed. "Perhaps I would have myself if my wife hadn't gone a bit odd. But I thought I should sell out and bring them back, so that's what I did."

The two men fell silent as the cart moved down the track into the station and the horse found its own way in the thick darkness. As scattered raindrops fell, David reached down behind the seat for his oilskins, a long, loose coat made of thin linen soaked in whale oil. Frank rummaged under the seat for his, and the oily fabric rustled as the men unrolled the coats and donned them.

"At least this is only rain, without sleet or snow mixed with it," David remarked. "And as yet, it isn't very heavy."

"Aye, that makes it easier to bear." Frank chuckled. "But we're almost at the home paddock in any event."

A few minutes later, David smelled wood smoke, and lighted windows shone through the rain and darkness ahead. The cart passed the bulky shadows of pens, then drew up in the yard in front of a cookhouse where whale oil lamps burned inside. A barracks was adjacent to it, and a few yards away, a lamp turned low shone through a window in the house.

The cookhouse door opened and a man came out with a lantern as David jumped down from the cart and grabbed his things from behind the seat. The man held up the lantern and stepped closer. David saw that he was an Aborigine, wearing a stockman's clothes and wide hat. Frank made the introductions as he climbed heavily down from the cart. "David, this is Kunmanara, the gardener and handyman. Kunmanara, this is David Kerrick, a new stockman who'll be working here on Sundays."

A well-built man in his twenties, Kunmanara grinned amiably, his white teeth gleaming. "Are you all right, David?" he said, his accent the twangy English of a native-born white rather than an Aborigine.

"Yes, I'm fine, Kunmanara," David replied, shaking hands with the man. "Are you all right?"

"Aye, I'll do." He moved to take the horse and the cart away. "There's hot stew and tea in the cookhouse, Mr. Williamson."

"That'll go down good," Frank replied. "Come on, David, let's go warm up and get a bite of tucker."

When Kunmanara led the horse away, Frank told David about the man and explained his accent as they went toward the cookhouse. While in the outback, the grazier had found the Aborigine as a small, orphaned boy, his parents having been killed by a wild boar. Frank had taken him in, putting him in the barracks once he was old enough to look after himself, and Kunmanara had been with the grazier ever since.

The cookhouse had a homey, cheerful atmosphere. A fire blazed in the fireplace at one end, with food bins, a cabinet, and a washstand beside it. Oil lamps burned brightly on a long, heavy table where two men sat over pannikins of tea. They stood up and Frank introduced them.

A small, wiry man with graying hair and a disabled leg was the cook and storekeeper, James Roberts. Smiling affably, he said to call him Jimbob. The other man, tall and angular, was in his forties. Cordial but more businesslike than Jimbob, Daniel Corbett was the head stockman.

After exchanging greetings with the men, David took a seat at the table as Frank and Daniel sat down, and Jimbob went to the fireplace. The grazier told David that there were four other employees who were jackaroos, trainee stockmen. They were out tending the sheep, he explained, and David would meet them the next day.

Spry and energetic despite his disabled leg, Jimbob bustled about at the fireplace, clattering dishes and pannikins. Soon, David and Frank had tin plates brimming with mutton stew, pannikins of tea, and a plate stacked with pieces of damper, stockman's bread made with flour, salt, and water. The rich, hearty stew, full of large chunks of meat and vegetables, and the broth thickened with pearl barley, was the most delicious food that David had eaten in a very long time.

Jimbob sat down at the table, and Kunmanara entered the room. As the men talked, David learned from their remarks that Jimbob and Daniel had been in the outback with Frank. Like Kunmanara, years of close association and shared experiences in the distant region had created a close bond between the two men and the grazier.

After the meal, Frank went to his house and David to the barracks with the other men. His bed, a wooden cot with its hard boards covered by layers of cured sheepskin, was as soft and comfortable as the best feather mattress, but it seemed only a short time before the other men were stirring again in the darkness before dawn. David went to the cookhouse with the others, and Frank joined them for a breakfast of fresh damper and thick slices of smoke-cured bacon.

At the first light of dawn on the cold, rainy morning, David went with Daniel to saddle horses. The home paddock was the area around the house and other buildings, which included a shearing shed and its adjacent holding pens. At one side of the buildings was a large garden, and there was also a chicken yard as well as a few head of cattle and pigs in other pens. The head stockman told David that the grazing area was divided into the north paddock, bordering on the Parramatta road, and the south paddock where he and David were headed.

As they rode south over the hills dotted with trees among the grass and brush, Daniel told David that the jackaroos remained with the two flocks of sheep, periodically going to the home paddock for food and other supplies. Shortly after, a flock of some fifteen hundred sheep came into view. The two youths with the sheep were loading a pack horse and taking down a fold made of poles and rope where the animals were penned at night, preparing to move the flock to another part of the paddock.

Reining up beside the youths, Daniel introduced them to David. A tall, fair boy, Silas Doak was about sixteen, and the other one, heavy-set and with an unruly shock of dark brown hair, Ruel Blake looked about fifteen. The head stockman told them that he and David would move the sheep, and they could go to the home paddock to get more supplies. The youths grinned happily, racing for their horses.

The two men completed the preparations to move the flock. The head stockman explained that sheep would graze grass down to the roots and destroy a pasture if kept in one place too long. He pointed out tufts of grass, showing David how to tell when the animals should be moved. Then, calling in the four dogs with the flock, Daniel demonstrated how to control them from a distance with hand signals.

With the fold rolled into a bundle of poles and ropes, Daniel tied a rope from it to the pack on the horse for the animal to drag it. He mounted his horse, taking the halter rope on the pack horse, and told David to drive the sheep ahead. David whistled to the dogs and motioned them to go around the flock to start the sheep moving, which resulted in total confusion.

The sheep, having spread out to graze, were scattered over a wide area. The dogs misunderstood David's intentions and dashed through the center of the flock, frightening the sheep and spreading them even farther apart as clusters of animals ran to and fro. Daniel, offering neither help nor advice, sat on his horse and waited.

It took David an hour of growing frustration to find out that his signals to the dogs were confusing them. Concentrating on that, he guided one dog at a time to gather the sheep which by then were spread far apart and madly milling about. When he finally had them together and moving in one direction, Daniel dryly reminded him that the flock was to be taken eastward, not to the home paddock where they were headed.

At midday, David finally had the flock flowing slowly over the rolling terrain to the east. But they were bunched instead of in the required wide column when being moved. The dogs still occasionally misunderstood his intentions, making clusters of a dozen sheep break away when they charged straight at the flock. Sending the dogs after the strays and trying again, David at last had the flock formed into a column.

During the late afternoon, the sheep reached the new grazing area. As he and Daniel were unloading the youths' belongings from the pack horse and putting up the fold, David commented wryly on his difficulties with the sheep. "No, that was nothing," the head stockman disagreed firmly. "Mr. Williamson said you would learn fast, and he was right. It usually takes a new stockman as many days as it took you hours to learn how to handle a flock. When Silas and Ruel get here, we'll go back to the home paddock. Mr. Williamson wants you to help him with some sick sheep."

The two youths arrived a few minutes later, and David and Daniel rode back across the hills. At the home paddock, David unsaddled his horse and put it in a pen with the other horses, then joined Frank at a holding pen where a score of thin, sickly sheep were standing about listlessly. The grazier opened a wooden box of medicines and primitive medical instruments, and David helped him doctor the sheep.

Most of them had infections around the stubs remaining from their tails. Frank explained that when the tail was cut off a lamb, the skin around the anus was removed so no wool would grow, a process known as mulsing. When it was improperly done, wool grew and collected clots of dung called dags, drawing blowflies. Even in winter, blowflies laid eggs in the dags that hatched into worms and caused the infections.

Trimming away the dags and opening the pockets of infection was nauseating, but David grimly accepted the fact that it was part of working with sheep. When he and the grazier finished, they went to a pen that was isolated from the others with quicklime spread around it. It contained a dozen sheep with patches of raw skin showing through their thin, ragged wool.

As they crossed the quicklime and went into the pen, Frank cautioned David to touch the sheep only with his hands. "They have what's called scab," he explained, "and it can be passed on to other sheep very easily. If you brush your clothes against one of these sheep and then against another one, that's enough to pass it on."

"Very well. What do you use to cure it?"

"A hammer between the eyes is the best cure," Frank replied, taking an earthenware pot from the box of medicines. "But I've been trying this. It's sulfur and alum mixed into a paste with whale oil."

"Has it been curing the disease?"

The grazier cheerfully shook his head. "Not yet, but it might need more time. We'll do this, then call it a day. As I mentioned before, you can use a horse to return to Parramatta, and Kunmanara will ride along with you to bring the horse back. But first we'll see what Jimbob has fixed for dinner." He opened the earthenware pot, laughing heartily. "There's nothing like doctoring sick sheep to work up an appetite."

David laughed wryly, moving toward the sheep with Frank. David was certain that any other grazier would have destroyed the sheep rather than risk spreading the disease to the flocks, confirming a general conclusion he had drawn about Frank and his station. There were too many employees for the some three thousand sheep at the station, and at the same time, the place was large enough for thousands more. It evidently made a profit, but that was secondary to Frank. In his autumn years, Frank was keeping his friends from the outback around him and working with his sheep however he wished, simply enjoying the time remaining to him.

The next day, Francis Greenway came to the construction site during the morning, exuberantly happy. In a recent shipload of convicts, there had been two building contractors, partners who had been convicted of fraud. The two men had been assigned as overseers at construction projects in Sydney, and had proven to be capable as construction supervisors.

The governor was pleased, and Greenway was even more gratified, because he was no longer involved in the details of construction. It was also good news for David. The construction of the barracks was on schedule and starting to draw ahead, and his chances of receiving a pardon appeared favorable. However, it had appeared at least possible that he might receive a pardon contingent upon his working as a construction supervisor.

During the afternoon on Wednesday, a clergyman came to the construction site with a young woman. As much a girl as a woman, she was about sixteen and apparently a convict or a servant, wearing a plain dungaree dress and a castoff coat. But she was meticulous. The coat had been carefully mended, and her hair arranged tidily under her mobcap.

The clergyman, a small, mild man with an air of patient concern, introduced himself as Terence Carlson. He asked David if they might speak privately, then told David that the young woman was Auberta Mowbray, and she was a convict.

"However," he added, "she lives with a family in the village and works as a maid. She doesn't stay in the Female Factory. I understand that a man named Enos Hinton works here. He forcibly interfered with Mistress Mowbray, and now she is in a delicate condition."

David frowned, understanding that Hinton had raped the young woman and she was pregnant. "That sounds like Hinton. Well, if you want to charge him with an offense, you need to talk to the commandant, not me, Vicar."

The man blinked owlishly, then shook his head. "No, I would like for him to do the honorable thing and marry her."

"Marry her?" David exclaimed. "You don't know

Hinton, Vicar. To start with, I'd wager my right arm
that he's never done an honorable thing in his life.
And there can't be a woman on earth who is so utterly
worthless as to deserve to be married to him."

"I understand he's a disreputable sort," the clergyman agreed. "However, when the family Mistress
Mowbray is staying with finds out her condition, they
will order her out of their home. Then she will have to
go to the Female Factory, and she is completely unlike
the women there. In addition, this is what Mistress
Mowbray wants."

"Are you quite sure about that?" David asked her.
"I've never met a man more detestable than he is,
Mistress Mowbray."

"I don't need to be told about him, Mr. Kerrick,"
she replied quietly. "Notwithstanding how he is, this
is what I want."

Although she was very young, as well as distraught
over her predicament, her face and eyes reflected a
spirited, determined personality. Studying her, David
reflected that she would make a good man an excellent
wife. Then he dismissed the thought, accepting her
decision. He called to a laborer, telling him to get
Hinton from the saw pit.

A few minutes later, Hinton came around the
building, covered with sawdust. As soon as he saw the
woman and clergyman, guilt was plain on his coarse
features, his icy eyes reflecting apprehension, but he
tried to bluster his way out of it. Vicar Carlson began
talking to him in a soft, reasonable voice, and Hinton
interrupted him, "I've never bloody seen her before in
my life! And what flaming concern of yours is it?"

"You control your tongue, Hinton!" David snapped
angrily. "That's a man of God you're talking to, not
some swine like yourself!"

Hinton turned and glared, then looked away as
David stared him down. Recovering his composure to
an extent after Hinton's outburst, the clergyman
began talking quietly again, encouraging him to ac-

cept his responsibilities and marry the woman. Hinton shook his head, stubbornly insisting that he had never seen her before. Auberta chimed in, her voice trembling with distress, and described the time and place where he had assaulted her.

Workers found reasons to pass nearby, exchanging winks and grins as they overheard the conversation, and they told others. Within a few minutes, workers all over the site were laughing and talking about it, enjoying Hinton's chagrin. He continued arguing with Vicar Carlson and the woman.

"All right, that's enough," David said, interrupting the conversation. "Hinton, everyone here knows you're lying through your teeth. You can either decide now to marry her, or you'll stay in a cell at the guardhouse on half rations until you do decide to do it."

The unblemished side of Hinton's face flushed with rage, his pale blue eyes bulging and his thick features trembling. "You can't bloody do that to me!" he bellowed. "You can't put me in a cell on half rations for not marrying her!"

"No, I can't," David agreed. "It'll be for malingering."

"Malingering?" Hinton roared. "I've been working my bloody arse off in that flaming saw pit, and you can't say that I've been malingering!"

"Yes, I can!" David snapped. "I'm the one who judges the work here, and the commandant will accept whatever I say. So you'll go into a cell for malingering, and I'll decide you've had enough when you decide to marry this woman. Now do you want the church or the guardhouse, Hinton?"

The man was speechless with fury for a moment, then he shrugged helplessly. "Aye, I'll marry her, then," he muttered grimly.

"What sort of arrangements do you want to make, Vicar?" David asked, turning to Terence Carlson. "Do you want to post the banns on Sunday?"

The clergyman hesitated, the problem having been settled quickly, then nodded happily. "Yes, the banns will have to be posted on two consecutive Sundays, then the wedding can be performed."

"Very well," David replied. "Go on back to work, Hinton."

The man slouched away, grinding his teeth in frustrated rage. The clergyman and Auberta expressed deep gratitude for David's help, thanking him over and over, then left. As he returned to work, David had strong doubts about the outcome. The decision was up to Auberta, but he believed she would be far better off in the Female Factory than married to Hinton.

Instead of passing, the incident remained very much alive at the construction site, the workers gleefully amused over what had happened to Hinton. They taunted him about it, occasionally bringing him out of the saw pit with his fists cocked and his thick features twisted in rage, ready to fight. During the remainder of the day, as well as through the rest of the week, David had to intervene to prevent a fight.

On Saturday evening, David was waiting at the edge of the village when Frank came down the road in his cart. Sunday was another long, busy day with David spending part of the morning at the smithy shed with Kunmanara, learning how to shoe horses. After that, he went out into a paddock and moved sheep to fresh pasture, then he worked until well after dark with Frank, again helping the grazier doctor sick sheep.

At muster the next morning, both Hinton and Crowley were absent. When he finished calling the roll and dismissed the craftsmen and their helpers, David talked with the laborers and asked if they knew where the two men were. They shook their heads and shrugged, none of them having seen either Hinton or Crowley since Saturday.

After he assigned tasks to the men, David went to the convict compound office. Captain Barrett was there, poring over a report. He stroked his chin musingly as David told him about the two men who were missing, then handed over the report he had been reading. It had been made up the previous day when a farmer from the Windsor settlement had come to the office to report that two horses and an assortment of foodstuffs had been stolen from his farm, the theft having occurred on Saturday night.

"The conclusion is inescapable," the captain commented as David handed the report back. "We have two more bushrangers at large."

"The theft of two horses and food on the night they disappeared can't be mere coincidence," David agreed. "I'm not surprised, though, because Hinton and Crowley are both troublemakers."

"Well, hopefully they'll be captured soon. I'll send a couple of men to replace them and report this to Sydney. If you hear anything more from your workers about Hinton and Crowley, let me know."

David replied that he would, then left. As he went back toward the construction site, he met Vicar Carlson, who was on his way to the office. The clergyman had been to the site to talk with Hinton about the wedding, and he listened with increasing dismay as David told him about the most probable explanation for Hinton's absence.

"Dear, dear," he sighed despondently. "This is most distressing, Mr. Kerrick. Whatever will Mistress Mowbray do now?"

"Frankly, I think she'll be better off, Vicar. You saw what kind of man Hinton is, and he would have made her life miserable."

"Perhaps she might have reformed him," the clergyman suggested, shrugging. "One never knows, does one? But now she'll be cast out of where she lives, and she'll have an illegitimate child. And she'll go to the Female Factory." He sighed again. "Well, good day, Mr. Kerrick."

David replied, then went on to the construction

site. As he began working, he thought about the two replacement laborers who would be assigned, wondering if they would be good workers or as much trouble as the ones whom they replaced. Other things claimed his attention, but in addition, he felt a twinge of pity for Auberta Mowbray that tugged at him and made the cold, late winter day seem even gloomier.

He was kept indirectly reminded of the woman as the workers around him discussed the two absent men. When the conversation about Hinton and Crowley began to die down by the next day, the replacement laborers arrived. Apparently good workers, David assigned them to tasks, and each time he glimpsed one of them, it created fleeting thoughts of Auberta Mowbray.

Later in the week, while David was checking the plumb lines for the stone entrance steps in front of the building, Vicar Carlson stepped up behind him. "Good day, Mr. Kerrick," the clergyman greeted him cheerfully. "I dropped by for a moment to bring very good news."

"Good day, Vicar," Kerrick replied. "What good news is that?"

"It concerns Mistress Mowbray. Do you happen to know of a Mr. James Underwood, who is a businessman in Sydney?"

Kerrick nodded, having heard of the owner of a shipyard in Sydney. "Yes, I know of him, Vicar."

"Well, I'm acquainted with Mr. Underwood and his wife, and I happened to see them yesterday. I explained the . . . ah, Mistress Mowbray's predicament, and they agreed to hire her as a maid."

"That's very good news, Vicar."

"I knew you'd be happy to hear about it, so I came by to tell you. Well, I must be on my way. Good day, Mr. Kerrick."

David replied and turned back to his work, relieved as well as pleased that the young woman's plight had been resolved, and through a means far better for her than by marrying Hinton.

On the second Saturday in September, spring having arrived with longer days, sunset was still a short time away when David waited for Frank. Instead of the grazier, Kunmanara came for him with a spare horse. The handyman explained that Frank had remained at the station that day because the ewes had started lambing.

Dusk was gathering when they reached the track, and dense smoke rose from behind a hill at one side. Kunmanara turned toward it, telling David that Frank was tending to one of the flocks there with Silas and Ruel, while Daniel was at the second flock with the other two jackaroos.

A few minutes later, the flock came into view, part of the sheep in a fold. The others were ewes, scattered about in clusters, with the dogs spread around them. The smoke billowed up from green limbs on fires near the ewes, some of them already with lambs, while Frank and the two youths bent over ewes lying in labor on the ground.

As the handyman and David rode up, Frank raised his voice over the roar of bleating that rose from the ewes: "Kunmanara, fetch more wood and green branches for the fires. Then ride over to the flock in the other paddock and see if they need anything there."

Kunmanara rode away as David tethered his horse with the others near the fold. Tossing his blanket and coat down among the other belongings in front of the hut beside the fold, he joined Frank. The smoky fires were intended to drive away the flies that had become worse with the warmer weather, but they were only partially effective. Drawn by the blood and afterbirth of the lambing, clouds of insects buzzed about.

The fires also provided illumination, the flames

making pools of ruddy light among the mass of sheep as the darkness increased. Frank had just finished with an ewe and was putting the newborn lamb in front of it. When the ewe began licking the small, long-legged creature, the grazier plunged his hands into a bucket of water.

Rinsing his hands and shaking the water off, he told David of the problems involved in lambing. He explained that older ewes that had given birth before rarely had difficulty with only one lamb, but some of them could experience trouble in giving birth to twins.

"Some young ewes have a hard time with one lamb," he added, "but the main problem is with young ewes that have twins in them."

David looked around at the dozens of ewes straining and bleating madly. "How do you know which ones are having trouble?" he asked.

"By the sounds they're making, and you'll soon learn to tell the difference between one that's only lambing and one with a lamb that's stuck. All right, let's get you started on some."

The grazier knelt beside one of the ewes in labor and carefully pushed a hand into the birth canal. He felt around, then withdrew his hand. "This one's laid wrong, David," he said. "Just nudge it around, then it'll come right out." Moving aside for David, he laughed. "After cutting wormy dags off sick sheep, this shouldn't bother you too much."

David laughed wryly, kneeling beside the ewe. He gingerly inserted a hand into the birth canal, feeling for the lamb. Pushing at it gently, he slowly turned it. As he withdrew his hand, the ewe began straining. A moment later, the lamb started sliding out.

"That's fine, David," Frank said in approval. "When you get the lamb out, wipe it off with a twist of grass and put it in front of the ewe to lick. Then wash your hands, because I've found that it generally prevents infections to have clean hands when helping them lamb."

After following Frank's instructions, David rinsed his hands in a bucket and followed Frank to another ewe. It was a more difficult situation, a young ewe with twins in the birth canal, and Frank explained how to separate the lambs and get them out one at a time. When that was done, the grazier watched and gave advice with two more ewes, then moved away and left David on his own.

A short time later, as the grazier had predicted, David was able to distinguish between ewes bleating in labor and those in distress. The latter seemed innumerable, another immediately claiming his attention as soon as he finished with one. Frank, Silas, and Ruel had been working for hours, but while the jackaroos were weary, the grazier seemed tireless.

He also kept an eye on the youths, suddenly calling out to one of them, "You, Silas! You didn't wash your hands before going to that ewe. If you do that again, you'll get a drink from one of these buckets. By the time you finish chundering, you'll remember to wash your hands."

"I'm sorry, Mr. Williamson," Silas replied, going to a bucket. "I'm so fagged that I don't know what I'm about. The next thing you'll be at me about is having my hand in a ewe's mouth instead of t'other end."

The grazier laughed heartily. "Never mind, lad," he said sympathetically. "Hard work will make a good man of you. When Jimbob gets here with tucker and tea, we'll have a little rest."

As the work continued, the chill of the spring night intensified. The combination of the cold and smoke from the fires gradually thinned the dense clouds of flies. The cook arrived, driving a cart up beside a fire. David washed his hands and joined the others as Jimbob dismounted and took covered buckets of damper, fried pork, and tea out of the cart.

The cook passed out the food and pannikins of tea, talking with Frank about the lambing, and Ruel offered an opinion. "If I ever get to be a boss cockie,"

he commented, "I'm going to have ewes bred at
different times of the year so they won't all lamb at
once."

"Then you won't be a boss cockie very long," Frank
replied, he and Jimbob laughing. "Part of your sheep
will be woolies that are overdue for shearing, part too
young to shear, and the rest somewhere in between.
You'll be trying to breed, lamb, and shear all at the
same time."

Ruel shrugged ruefully, and Frank and the cook
laughed again. The conversation continued a few
minutes longer, then the respite was over. Jimbob put
the empty buckets into the cart and drove off into the
night, and David and the others went to the ewes that
were bleating frantically.

Late in the night, the jackaroos lay beside a fire
while Frank and David still worked. The grazier's
energy finally gave out and he lay down, then David
unrolled his blanket near a fire. It was still dark when
he woke. A ewe bleated in distress a few yards away,
and as he attended it, Frank got up and woke the
youths.

At dawn, when Ruel and Silas turned out the
wethers and barren ewes in the fold to graze, they were
joined by hundreds of ewes that had one or two lambs
teetering along beside them. Hundreds more remained near the fires, dozens in labor at any one time.
Jimbob arrived with more food and tea, then the work
resumed when he left.

The afternoon was mild, with flies a constant torment and then diminishing once more when the
temperature dropped after nightfall. Later that night,
Kunmanara came for David, but David kept working
and delayed leaving until the last possible moment,
reaching the village as dawn was breaking.

The work on the new barracks was ahead of schedule, and Greenway had been coming to the site
periodically to monitor the progress. He visited again

in the middle of the week, highly pleased as he looked around. With the carpentry and stone work virtually completed, only moldings, windows, and finishing touches remained to be done on the building. The next day, glaziers and joiners arrived from Sydney to do the final work.

The following Saturday, Frank met David and expressed satisfaction with the lambing as they rode toward the station in the cart. The last few ewes had lambed Monday, he told David, with an adequate number having had twins. The lambs that had been born first were now old enough to be mulsed and have their tails trimmed, work that was more methodical than the frantic rush of lambing.

The conversation then turned to David's chances of receiving a pardon. Frank was confident that he would. "Governor Macquarie is far better than the ones who were boss cockies when I wore canaries," the grazier said. "He's very free with pardons and tickets-of-leave."

"That's true," David agreed, "but I won't be at ease until I have it. Once I do, I can set about getting together the funds I'll need for a sheep station. That might take years, but so be it."

"There's a way that wouldn't take years," Frank told him, "but it entails taking risks like a gambler and working like a navvy. You could graze a flock on shares, which would give you half the clip and half the lambs at the end of a year. But you'd be on your own, and just think of dealing with the lambing by yourself. Also, if something happened to the flock, you would have to repay the owner for it."

"I couldn't drive a flock to the outback by myself, Frank."

"No, but I could write a letter for you to carry to Pat, asking him to give you a flock on shares. With my recommendation, he would do it."

"It's certainly something to think about," David mused. "I would need a horse, supplies, and equipment, but I could earn enough to buy those in a relatively short time."

"No, Pat would provide your supplies for the time that you have the flock on shares. As far as a horse, weapons, and equipment are concerned, I would see you right on that."

"No, Frank, you've already been very—"

"I'll hear no argument about it," the grazier said firmly, interrupting David. "When I'm gone, my family will probably break up my station to sell as farms, or do whatever else it takes to get the most with the least trouble. In view of that, I'll do what I please with what I have, David."

The grazier's relationship with his family a sensitive issue, David returned to the main point. "Well, grazing a flock on shares is certainly worth considering," he mused, "but so are the problems."

Frank agreed emphatically, pointing out that David could end up in debt for years if he took a flock on shares and something happened to it. The conversation continued until he and David reached the home paddock, and they discussed the subject at length the next day, while working together on the lambs. But the grazier avoided making a recommendation, leaving the decision entirely up to David.

David pondered the idea the next week, knowing the time was approaching when he would have to decide. That time became defined when Greenway told him that the governor would inspect the new barracks the following Wednesday. Then, on Saturday evening, David told Frank that if he received a pardon, he would go to Wayamba Station and ask Pat to let him graze a flock on shares.

The following Wednesday, the workers had just finished sweeping out wood shavings and other debris when the governor arrived at the building with a party that included several aides and Greenway. Their footsteps echoing through the large, empty rooms, the men slowly went from one part of the barracks to another, inspecting them carefully.

When they finished and went back to the entrance, Governor Macquarie turned to David. "As I mentioned before," he said, "those sentenced for capital offenses can never leave the colony. However, I will grant you a conditional pardon that leaves you to your own devices within the colony."

"I'm very grateful, Excellency," David replied. "It wouldn't have been possible to have this building completed by now without the efforts of a number of workers who did far more than was required of them. If I may, I would like to ask you to take their sentences under review and possibly grant them a pardon or ticket-of-leave."

"Very well, I'll consider it and ask the advice of other overseers for whom they have worked. Come and see my secretary tomorrow and leave a list of their names. He will also have your pardon document."

David thanked the governor again, then Governor Macquarie and his party went down the stone steps to the official coach. As the vehicle moved down the street, it passed Frank in his cart, who had come to ask if David had received his pardon.

Chapter Five

West of Bathurst, among the tracks that wandered between the sheep stations and the village, David found one that was scored with deep wheel marks left by heavy vehicles. The ruts having been made by the drays that took supplies to Wayamba Station each year and returned with wool, the track led to the west.

During most of his life, he had been accustomed to constricted spaces in a land where disputes over a few inches in fields had led to lawsuits. Here, when the Blue Mountains fell behind, he felt like a tiny mote on the scale of the vast landscape around him. Though his horse kept up a good pace for hours, at the end of each day he seemed to have made little progress, the wilderness seeming to reach endlessly to the horizon.

The track led across vast stretches of rolling terrain covered with deep, lush grass, thickets of shrubs, and open forest. It was veined by creeks with tall, glistening eucalyptuses and matted undergrowth lining their banks. Parrots were bright splashes of color darting through the trees, their jarring shrieks blending with the loud, snapping call of the whipbird and more melodious chirping of pipits, swallows, thrushes, and bush wrens.

Emus scurried from thickets, and kangaroos bounded across the grassy valleys. High in the eucalyptus groves, koalas stared blandly at David and munched leaves. Occasionally he glimpsed a wombat, and bandicoots peered from holes. The spiny anteater, remotely resembling a hedgehog, curled into a tight ball for defense when David passed.

Flies and mosquitoes were a nuisance on days when the air was still, and snakes slithered across the track, many of them poisonous. At a creek one afternoon, David saw a wild boar. Both hammers on his double-barrel musket cocked, he waited as the boar snorted and dug at the ground in a display of temper, its long tusks gleaming. Then it finally turned and disappeared into the brush, and David rode on.

At first he failed to notice the widely-scattered Aborigines, because he was accustomed to those who loitered about the villages where they were conspicuous. Here they were part of the landscape, blending in almost perfectly. When a bright spot of yellow on a hillside caught his eye one day, he studied it and saw the small face under it.

It was the bright blond hair of an Aborigine child, which darkened into black as they grew older. Then he saw the others, a man, woman, and youth, in the broken shadows of brush beside the child. Absolutely motionless, they were in full view and yet almost invisible in the mottled play of light and shadow on their dark bodies as they watched him pass.

He saw others from time to time, always at a distance and motionless. Recalling what Frank had said about bushrangers, he watched for fresh hoofprints on the track. As the days passed, the terrain became more arid, the vegetation changing. Savannas were covered with deep spinifex grass, varying from

soft green to the color of ripe wheat. Mallee covered
hillsides below barren spines of black granite, and
desert oaks were mixed with the stands of eucalyptuses. With summer approaching, the creeks were
drying into billabongs, oxbow ponds in curves where
the channels were deeper.

It was a harsh land where predator and prey struggled for survival, but it lacked a cruel aspect because it
was utterly impersonal. Its immensity difficult to
comprehend, the land had a rugged, compelling beauty. The soft dull light of early dawn gave way to a
blinding brilliance as the sun rose, illuminating the
scenery with an almost painful clarity. After sunset,
dusk came as a deepening blue that closed in from all
sides, lighted by an afterglow from below the horizon.
As David traveled onward into this entirely new
world, his past sorrows were sealed off in a remote
part of his mind, like his watch remaining in his
pocket with its lid closed.

Late one afternoon, he crossed a hill overlooking
the Cobdogla River. Making camp beside it, he saw
that it fit the Aborigine description as a land of plenty,
because the wide belt of lush green vegetation flanking
it teemed with animals. The river also fit Frank's
description of flowing upside down as the water was
extremely muddy.

The days grew warmer west of the river, the midday
heat warning of the torrid intensity that would come
in December. The water sources were more scattered,
and David made sure to keep his canteen, a leather-
covered bottle, full. Once every two or three days, he
had to make a dry camp at sundown, sharing the
water in the canteen with his horse.

One day, as the noises from birds were fading in the
midday heat and being replaced by the throbbing
chatter of cicadas, David glimpsed a ground parrot a
few yards ahead. Frightened by something, it darted
from the brush on the right side of the track and
crossed it in a flash of green. The horse cocked its ears

and looked at the foliage, then David saw a musket barrel in the branches, pointing toward him.

Smoke puffed from the flash pan on the musket as David kicked out of the right stirrup and dived off the left side of his horse. The musket tracked him, firing, and the horse shrieked as its right foreleg folded and it went down. David clutched his musket, hitting the ground, and scrambled into the undergrowth on the left side of the track.

"You bloody bastard!" a man in the brush across the track bellowed. "You flaming get! You made me shoot the bloody horse, you scurvy swine!"

The man's voice, enraged and with a frenzied, irrational edge, rang out harshly over the horse's screams of pain. Its right foreleg was limp, blood foamed from its lips, and the animal had been shot through the shoulder and lungs. Lying behind a clump of acacia, David cocked a hammer on his musket and aimed at the back of the horse's head to end its torment.

As he fired, the horse jerked and then quieted. The man on the other side of the track thought the bullet was meant for him, and a pistol fired with a sharp crack, the ball clipping through the branches over David's head. The shot was followed by another raving outburst as the man promised David a slow, painful death because the horse had been shot.

Quietly sliding backward, David put a screen of foliage between himself and his pursuer, then reloaded the spent barrel in his musket as he moved parallel to the track. A few yards from the horse, he crept back to the edge of the undergrowth. The man's foot stirred the grass behind the brush where he hid as he craned his neck, looking for David.

Both hammers on his musket cocked, David aimed at the foot. He squeezed a trigger and fired, then ducked to one side of the gunpowder smoke to aim the other barrel. As the ball ripped into his foot, the man screamed in pain and shock, involuntarily sitting up in full view. David aimed at his chest and pulled the other trigger.

Just as the hammer fell, the man realized his mistake and threw himself to one side. He was an instant too late as David swung the musket barrels and tracked him in the sights as the weapon fired. The heavy ball slammed into the man's chest, the impact knocking him flat on his back.

David reloaded as he crossed the track. The ragged, unkempt man in the brush on the other side was near death, gasping hoarsely for breath as blood trickled from his mouth. He glared at David in feral hatred, his breath catching in his throat as he whispered an oath.

"Is there anyone you'd like to have informed that you're gone?" David asked. "I might be able to get a message to them eventually. Or is there anything else you'd like done?"

The man's lips curled in a sneer as he hissed another oath, then his eyes became wide in pain and fear as he jerked, blood gushing from his mouth. His limbs quivering convulsively, he choked for a moment, then the movements stopped and his eyes became lifeless.

Searching the body, David found an old letter from England addressed to a Henry Bolton at the convict barracks in Sydney. Another pocket contained a watch with the same name engraved inside the lid, along with a purse containing well over a hundred guineas. The man had been a bushranger, who apparently lost his horse, and had been waiting beside the track to ambush a traveler to get another one.

After burying the body, David took his bedroll and canvas bag from behind the saddle on his dead horse. Now afoot and still a long distance from Wayamba Station, he knew his situation was uncertain, if not perilous, and he could carry only so much. In the bag was a pouch of mail for Wayamba Station that he had picked up from the postal office in Sydney, along with instructions to place it in Patrick Garrity's hands.

Making up a pack with his blanket, he put the mail, a supply of food, and his ammunition in it. He tied his canteen and the bushranger's musket to the pack, then hoisted it to his back. With the pistol in his belt and his double-barrel musket under his arm, he went down the track.

It was late afternoon of the next day before he found water. His canteen was almost empty, and his feet were blistered. After drinking his fill from the billabong, he soaked his feet in the damp mud at the edge of the water. The next morning, his canteen full, he shrugged off the pain in his feet as he trudged down the track.

During the following days, his feet gradually toughened, and he was able to walk comfortably, but water was a constant problem. Two and sometimes three days passed before he came to the next small brook or billabong near the track, and he also needed more water as the days grew hotter. With his wide hat pulled down against the glare of the sun, he walked form sunrise to sunset, never allowing his canteen to become completely empty.

Being on foot made him feel less capable of coping with anything that might arise, as the wilderness seemed more forbidding and threatening. Thinking about the bushranger's irrational behavior, he remembered what Frank had said about the way the outback affected some people. Although he enjoyed the solitude, he could understand why some would react otherwise. Being totally alone in the vast spaces could be oppressive.

One morning, after the air had been unusually still, a gust of wind rustled the brush and trees. David was walking up a long, low hill, the foliage partially blocking his view, but the horizon to the south seemed hazy. He dismissed it, continuing up the hill and tugging his hat down firmly as harder gusts blew.

When he reached the top, the wind was a steady gale and felt like a blast of hot air from a furnace. It whipped up dust that obscured his vision, and a thick, dark cloud of dust swept from the south. For a moment he considered stopping until the dust storm passed, but his canteen was less than half full and he needed to find water.

The velocity of the wind increased, and the dust, blotting out the sun and turning the day into twilight, blinded David. Just when he decided he would have to stop, he realized he was off the track, dimly seeing a deep ditch in front of him as he stepped off the edge.

He tried to stop, but the edge crumbled under his feet. Falling and sliding through the brush on the steep side of the ditch, he rolled to the bottom. He huddled there in the choking dust, closing his eyes and covering his face with his sleeve so he could breathe.

Hours later, when the wind died away, David was covered with fine dust. He climbed the steep bank, hoisted his bundle on his back, and started to return to the track. He went several yards in one direction, then in another without finding it.

He was surrounded by dense growth that limited his vision to a few feet, but it was not sturdy enough for him to climb to look around. Deciding to return to the ditch and begin a methodical search for the track, he discovered he had moved about so much he was unable to find the ditch.

For the remainder of the day, he broke limbs on the brush to mark his path and crisscrossed the terrain. Still unable to find the track by nighttime, he drank sparingly from his canteen and tried to eat a piece of leftover damper. His mouth was too dry for him to eat, and he went to sleep.

The next morning, David headed west until he broke out of the brush and came to a hill. From the top of it, he saw no sign of the track. But far to the west was a mass of dark green foliage, possibly a source of water, and he set out toward it.

During the breathlessly hot afternoon, he came to a grove of trees beside a dry creek bed. His hunger was a gnawing pain, and his mouth was completely dry. He took a sip of water and continued walking. At nightfall, he drank the last of his water and fell asleep.

At dawn, David was weak with hunger, and his mouth was parched. He struggled to his feet, lifting his back pack and picking up his musket, then stumbled onward. Each laboring step seemed to take his last strength, but he found more and forced himself to keep moving.

He became delirious as time passed in a daze. There was a fleeting impression of darkness, then it was daytime again. His tongue swollen, he was unable to close his mouth. Having lost his pack and musket, he crawled up a barren slope toward a patch of shade in a rock outcropping to escape the glaring sun that was beating down on him mercilessly.

When he regained consciousness, it was late afternoon, and his mouth was damp with water bitterly tasting of minerals. He was sitting against a boulder near the top of a stony ridge, and an old, naked Aborigine woman knelt in front of him. She was pouring sips of water into his mouth from a small wooden vessel made from a section of tree limb.

He gulped the water greedily, then she moved aside. A few yards away, a young Aborigine man and an older man looked at him impassively. Both of them stood on one foot and leaned on spears, their other foot tucked behind the knee of the leg on which they were standing.

Two young women, three youths, a girl, and two small children whose hair was still blond crouched against a boulder at one side, gazing at him. His pack, muskets, and other belongings were stacked near him, the Aborigines evidently having gathered them from where he had dropped them.

The scene had an eerie quality to David, its colors tinted a deeper hue by the rich, rosy light of the setting sun. The Aborigines were absolutely silent as they gazed at him inscrutably, all but one completely motionless. The girl held a length of dried plant stem, a wisp of smoke rising from smoldering fire in its pulpy center. Occasionally she waved the stick gently to keep the ember burning.

They were entirely different from the Aborigines near the villages both in appearance and attitude. Instead of wearing castoff clothing, they had only woven grass belts that held their stone tools and weapons, and the men's spears were tipped with stone points. More than primitive, they were ancients, living as their forebears had eons ago.

David spoke to the older man, who was evidently the leader of the small group. "Do you understand English?" he asked.

It was apparent that neither he nor any of the others did when the man replied softly with a syllable that meant nothing to David. From a subtle, uncomfortable stir among them, it was also clear that his voice, while weak and hoarse to him, sounded jarringly loud to them.

The man glanced at the old woman beside David and nodded toward him. She gave him another drink, then joined the other women and children, as the man silently motioned to them. They gathered up woven grass bags and other belongings, the two young women having water vessels similar to the old woman's, and stepped between two nearby boulders.

David saw why his voice had sounded loud to them, because they communicated in gestures and soft murmurs. The two men sat down at one side while the others made camp. One of the women had a bundle of sticks, which they broke up. The girl blew on the end of the firestick, then touched it to thin slivers of wood. A moment later, a small fire burned, and the women and children moved around it, rummaging in their bags.

Darkness fell, and the people were silhouetted against the firelight. A few minutes later, the old woman came to David with a piece of something that had been roasted over the fire, and what looked like two small, wild figs. David thought that the roasted flesh was lizard or some other reptile, as he choked it down quickly. Then he ate the small bitter fruit.

The Aborigines ate and settled themselves to sleep as the fire burned down. David lay down, resting his head on his pack. The food burned in his stomach, making him nauseous, and he had a severe headache, but he was exhausted and immediately fell asleep.

The next morning, two of the youths carried his muskets and pack, and David followed the Aborigines into the brush at the foot of the hill. The men led the way, the women and children following, and David almost lost sight of them. They spread out, moving as silently as shadows, and he caught only intermittent glimpses of one or another of them.

An hour later, David's legs had become very unsteady, making him stumble occasionally. A feverish weakness gripped him, and he was ravenously hungry. An agonizing headache pounded in his skull, but most of all the effort of walking had given him a raging thirst.

Almost as though she could read his thoughts, one of the young women was suddenly in front of him. Removing leaves that reduced evaporation from the water vessel she balanced on her head, she handed it to him. David took a deep drink from it and gave it back, then the woman replaced the leaves and put the vessel back on her head, moving into the brush.

He struggled to keep up, and just when he felt that he could go no farther, the tall brush opened out. A short distance ahead, the Aborigines filed through spinifex grass toward the edge of a wide, deep ravine. A dry watercourse, it contained a raging river during heavy rains.

The Aborigines climbed down into the ravine and crossed it to the deep shade under a wide shelf of rock undercut by flood waters, and David followed them. The men, youths, and children stepped under the overhang and sat down. David collapsed weakly near them, but the women and the girl went back to where the rock was only a few feet above the floor of the ravine.

Putting aside their bags and long, polished staffs, the women and the girl used sticks and pieces of bark to dig a hole. When it was a few feet deep, the girl handed her firestick to one of the young women and climbed down into it. She threw out sandy dirt, and the others shoveled it away. As the hole became deeper, the other young woman took the girl's place.

A short time later, the hole had become so deep that the digging was very difficult. At the bottom of the hole, the young woman handed up dirt on slabs of bark to the other one, who hung headlong down into the hole with the old woman holding her feet. Occasionally they changed places, and David saw that the dirt on their slender, naked bodies was damp.

He realized that the Aborigines had some practical knowledge of geology, having located a gnamma hole. A stratum of granite or other stone that water was unable to penetrate was under the ravine. Water soaked into the ground during floods, then was held in the lower levels of the soil by the stone. When a hole was dug down to that level, water collected at the bottom of it by drainage from the surrounding soil.

After a while, the young woman at the bottom of the hole handed up the small, wooden water vessels full of water, which the girl carried around until everyone had their fill. His thirst finally quenched, David gave his canteen to the girl to fill. She was puzzled by its purpose until he poured some water into it from a wooden vessel, then she took it to the hole and brought it back full of water.

When all of the water vessels were refilled once again, the women and the girl pushed the dirt back into the hole, stamping it down and removing all traces of their work. They then opened their grass bags and took out lizards, small snakes, and handfuls of witchetty grubs. The older man beckoned David, he and the others eyeing the reptiles and the worms in anticipation as they gathered around. Not quite that ravenous, David opened his pack and took out leftover damper from several days before.

The young man finished his share of the food, exchanging a few words with the other man, then left with one of the youths. The others finished, and the man and youths lay down, while the women mended their grass bags and did other tasks as they talked softly. His hunger partially satisfied, David took a drink from his canteen and lay down. The women looked at the canteen in fascination, talking and continuing with their work.

David fell asleep, then woke during the afternoon as the Aborigines moved about. They set out again, two of the youths carrying his belongings as he tried to keep up, and he wondered where they were going. They were heading north, as they had been that morning, but David had no idea where the track to Wayamba Station was. It occurred to him that they could have decided to take him into their group, and he could end up traveling around with them indefinitely, starving and dying of thirst his only alternative.

His headache returning, David struggled to keep up with the Aborigines as the afternoon passed. At sunset, he saw the young man and the youth who had accompanied him coming down a hill to meet the other man, the youth carrying a small kangaroo they had killed. The women, having spotted the kangaroo a moment before David, gathered firewood.

Camp was made in a gully at the foot of the hill, and the women took the kangaroo. David had food in his pack that he could have cooked, but he was too tired. Ravenously hungry again, he watched the preparations to cook the kangaroo, reflecting that it would be far more palatable than raw lizards, snakes, and fat, squirming worms.

When the food was ready, the young women took part of it to the men, and the old woman brought a large piece of the meat to David. Softly murmuring, she also gave him several fungi the size of an egg that she called *witita*, and a handful of small, onion-like bulbs that were called *nyiri* in her language.

The tough, stringy kangaroo meat had a strong, gamy taste, but it was rich and filling. The taste of it was countered by the fungi and bulbs, which had an unusual, but very agreeable, flavor. When the meal was finished, the Aborigines settled down for the night.

The possibility of wandering forever in the outback preying on his mind, David again tried to communicate. "I need to go to Wayamba Station," he said to the older man, pointing westward and hoping that was the right direction. "Wayamba Station. I must go there."

Again there was an uncomfortable stir, the Aborigines finding his voice too loud, but he was successful. "Wayamba," the man said softly, pointing northwest. He said something else, then repeated the name.

Greatly relieved, David smiled and nodded happily. The man smiled in response. The others commented quietly among themselves, pleased by the exchange and understanding. They went to sleep, and David, sighing in satisfaction, settled himself comfortably.

Shortly after dawn the next morning, they headed northward again at a steady pace. His full strength starting to return, David kept up with the Aborigines during the morning hours, then he began tiring. At midday, he was trudging grimly through tall brush behind the group when the foliage opened and he saw all of them waiting for him. As he walked toward them, he saw that they were standing on the track.

"Wayamba," the older man said, pointing down the track to the west.

Kerrick opened his pack and gave his hatchet to the older man, and his knife to the young man. Then he handed his canteen to the old woman. They smiled in delight, examining the things and murmuring excitedly. The older man said something, apparently expressing thanks, and led the Aborigines back into the tall brush. David hoisted his pack and picked up his weapons, then walked down the track.

During late afternoon, he reached a small brook. Unsure of how far he still had to go, he measured out a small portion of his remaining food and cooked it. After eating, he bathed, washed his clothes, and shaved in the last light of the setting sun. The next morning, carrying his billy full of water, he continued his journey.

Two days later, David saw dust from a flock of sheep several miles south. He turned off the track, crossing the rolling terrain toward the flock. Near sunset, he climbed a last hill toward a fold, hut, and horses at the top of the rise.

Alerted by his dogs, the stockman was wary of bushrangers. He called out from a clump of brush near the fold, telling David to identify himself. David did and said he was en route to see Patrick Garrity. A tall, bearded man stepped out of the brush and shook hands with David as he introduced himself as Tom Mason, an employee at Wayamba Station.

Cheerful and friendly, Tom was delighted to have a visitor with news of the outside world. As he and David talked, he mixed a pan of damper, put on peas and rice to cook, and cut generous pieces from a quarter of mutton hanging beside the shelter, putting them on the spit. He had a spare horse and suggested that David ride it to the home paddock, an offer that was promptly accepted with thanks.

After the large, satisfying meal, they smoked their pipes and drank more tea. They talked for another hour, Tom apparently content when alone, but enjoying conversation with his infrequent visitors. Then he kindled the fire to burn through the night and went into his hut, and David unrolled his blanket beside the fire.

The next morning, after breakfast, David left on Tom's spare horse. Riding to the immense sheep station, the miles and hours passed, then he saw dust in the distance to the north and south from flocks of sheep.

The home paddock of Wayamba Station came into view from the top of a low hill, and Kerrick reined up. It was an island of civilization in a vast expanse of wilderness, an isolated, self-contained community. At the center was a creek lined with towering river gums and quandongs with their vividly green foliage, along with whitewoods and ironwoods that resembled willows. A rambling bungalow with tall water tanks behind it was in the deep shade of the trees, with an expanse of gardens up the creek from it and a row of small houses for married stockmen down the creek. Farther down the creek was a cluster of huts where Aborigines lived.

The shearing shed was set out into a level, open expanse from the houses, and it was huge, with acres of holding pens adjacent to it. On the opposite side of the shed from the pens were storage warehouses, barns, a barracks, cookhouse, and other buildings. David gazed at it for several minutes, hoping he would someday have the same, then rode on down the track.

At the holding pens, he met the head stockman, Fred Johnson, a wiry man in his forties. He greeted David amiably, then told him that Pat was out in the paddocks. "He should be back tomorrow," Fred added. "Put the horse in the pen over there, and somebody can take it back to Tom in a few days. There's ample room in the barracks, and the cook has tucker ready at sunrise, midday, and sunset."

David thanked him, leading the horse away. As he went to the horse pen, he met a couple of stockmen who introduced themselves, immediately interested upon seeing a stranger. After he put the horse in the pen and carried his belongings to the barracks, word quickly spread that a visitor had arrived at the station, and other men came in to meet him.

At sunset, David went to the cookhouse. Inside, the long trestle tables had been built to accommodate twenty or more at shearing time. The half-dozen stockmen who worked at the home paddock were there, as well as the storekeeper and cook, both of them older men who had once been stockmen. The food was plentiful and appetizing, fresh pork roast with potatoes and vegetables from the garden, and damper and tea.

The men questioned David about events in Sydney and beyond, as Tom Mason had. Also like Tom, they had a detached attitude toward David's information, and he saw that they were only mildly curious and gleaning topics for conversation rather than truly interested.

Wayamba Station was their world, their only real interest. David recalled what Frank had said about those who could live at peace with themselves and others in the outback, and he realized that the grazier had been absolutely correct. The men were adjusted to their isolation as a part of life, and they were also a special breed, with some ineffable quality that made them fit in with the remote region.

After the meal, David and the men went out to the benches on the cookhouse veranda. The cook brought out a lantern to light pipes, and Fred joined them. The conversation continued for another hour, as insects swooped out of the darkness and circled around the lantern.

At the fires around the Aborigine huts down the creek, didgeridoos began droning softly, building up to a steady throbbing of rising and falling notes. They were accompanied by a rustling clatter of rhythm sticks tapping in cadence, then a moment later by chanting, men's and women's voices harmonizing. The sounds melded into a velvet, hypnotic whole.

"That's the first corroboree they've had down there for some time," Fred said to David. "I wonder what it's about."

"Maybe somebody's died," a man suggested gloomily. "They have a corroboree every time somebody dies at the station."

"Well, nobody's died that I know about," Fred replied, "and that's not the only reason they have a corroboree. They have them when a baby is born, and for any number of other reasons." He yawned, standing up. "Well, it's time I found my blanket. I'll see you men tomorrow."

As he left, the other men moved off the veranda, and David went with them. In the barracks, as at Frank's station, the cots were covered with layers of sheepskin, and David fell asleep, listening to the corroboree.

The next day, David looked around the home paddock and its buildings, observing how the huge enterprise operated. While crossing the wide yard between the shearing shed and the houses, David met Mayrah Garrity who carried a basket to the gardens to collect vegetables.

Slender and in her early twenties, she wore a stockman's hat with a blouse and skirt made of dungaree, but her bearing made her more striking than any society matron decked out in costly finery and jewelry. In her own domain, she was proud and regal in spite of the deep scar on her forehead.

She talked with David for a few minutes in her broken, heavily-accented English. "Frank Williamson all right?" she asked.

"He was well when I last saw him," David replied, "and he asked me to convey his best wishes to you and your children."

"Good, good. Barracks and tucker good enough?"

"They're excellent, and I'm very grateful for the hospitality."

She smiled and nodded briskly, moving away. "G'day."

David answered, lifting his hat, then continued looking around the home paddock. While he was at the cattle and oxen pen, a rider approached from the south and a stockman working near the pen said it was Pat. David returned to the barracks to get the mail pouch out of his pack, then he went to the horse pen where Pat was unsaddling his horse and talking with Fred.

David met few men as large as himself, but he and Pat were the same height and within a few pounds of each other. In his thirties, with a thick, neatly-trimmed beard that partially obscured granite features that matched the level gaze of his blue eyes, he was covered in dust and held a coiled stockman's whip as if it were a part of him. He was a reserved man who could quickly become brusque, but as he and David looked at each other, there was instant mutual respect.

Shaking hands, they exchanged greetings amiably, and David briefly explained his purpose for being there. "Frank Williamson said I would like it here," he continued, "and he was absolutely right. He suggested that I come and talk with you."

"I'm glad you took his advice," Pat replied. "Is he all right?"

"He's bearing the weight of his years well, but as you know, they're more than a few. You have a letter from him in the pouch."

Pat opened it and looked through the mail, handing Fred several letters. "Those are for men at the home paddock," he said. "There's also mail here for men out in the paddocks, and whoever takes supplies to them the next time can deliver the letters." He closed the pouch, turning back to David. "Come to my house about sunset for dinner."

"Very well, and thank you for the invitation.

There's one other thing. Frank told me that you have a commission as a justice of the peace, and I killed a bushranger on my way here. I found identification and other personal belongings on him that I should turn over to you."

"Aye, I'll have to make a report on it to the chief justice in Sydney. Bring the things with you when you come to the house."

David exchanged a nod with Pat and went toward the barracks, more than pleased by his first meeting with the man. While their backgrounds were different, they had much in common through having similar goals and attitudes. Whether he was ever able to establish a sheep station, David knew he had found a friend in the outback.

Shortly before sunset, he went to the station owner's house, taking the bushranger's letter, watch, and purse. Pat met him at the door and led him into a spacious, comfortable parlor, the homemade furniture sized to fit large men. Pat poured pannikins of rum, and David handed over the bushranger's things.

Pat opened the purse and looked in it, then returned it to David. "Put that back in your pocket, David."

"It doesn't belong to me, Pat."

"It doesn't belong to me, either," Pat replied, going to a shelf and taking down a box of papers. "Nor does it belong to the clerk in the chief justice's office who'll pocket it if I send it to Sydney."

Pocketing the purse, David sat down and drank the rum. Pat sorted through the papers in the box, explaining that the chief justice's office sent him names and descriptions of convicts who escaped, in the event they came to the outback.

"Aye, here he is," Pat said, looking at a paper. "Henry Bolton, who disappeared from Sydney two years ago. Well, I'll send a report on him with the stockman who takes my yearly order for supplies to Sydney." He put the watch and letter in the box with the papers, then set it aside and drank while he asked David about his journey.

After David had related the details, including his experiences with the Aborigines, Pat told him how they had known the name of the station. "It's named for a landmark hill south of here that the Aborigines call Wayamba," he explained. "In our language, that means broken hill or something like that. But they would probably have known your destination even if you hadn't thought to mention the name of the station."

"How could they have known, Pat? After all, I could have been a bushranger or someone simply wandering about."

Pat hesitated, then shrugged. "You'll find that the Aborigines sometimes know things that reason says they couldn't know," he replied. "They have none of the weapons, tools, and such that go with our way of life, so we regard them as simple. In that respect they are, but they're complicated in ways that we're simple, ways that don't even occur to us."

He started to say more, but at that moment Mayrah entered the room and announced that dinner was ready. The men finished their rum and followed her down the hall to a spacious dining room, where the two Garrity children were waiting at the large, home-made table.

Colin, the eldest child, was a handsome, alert boy of about ten. He had his father's fair complexion and blue eyes, his features revealing his Aborigine bloodline. The girl, Sheila, was a year or two younger and just the opposite. Her features were Anglo-Saxon, but her skin was almost as dark as her mother's, and her hair was in the process of changing from bright blond to black.

The meal was the same ample, tasty food as at the cookhouse, and Mayrah passed around dishes as the men talked. The station owner said that he paid the head stockman's wife, who had a good education, to teach basic subjects to the children at the station. Turning to his son and daughter, he asked them about their progress with their classes.

It was evident that the children's personalities were as different as their appearance. The boy was serenely good-natured like his mother, while Sheila had her father's scant tolerance before becoming ill-tempered. Colin expressed satisfaction with school, Sheila boredom.

"You must give it your full attention, Sheila," Pat told her firmly. "If you don't, what are you going to do when you're grown?"

"What do you want me to do when I'm grown?" she retorted quickly.

Pat was momentarily at a loss for words, then he frowned. "I want you to have less sauce on your tongue, so start now," he replied curtly. "You pay attention to your schooling, and I want to hear no more about it."

From their attitudes, clashes between Pat and his daughter were anything but unusual. As the man talked about his children, David saw that he intended for them to be raised in his own culture and not their mother's, Mayrah apparently wanting the same. That was evident a moment later when Sheila started to say something to her mother in the Aborigine language. Mayrah tried to shush her, but Pat heard the girl.

"I've told you to speak English all of the time, Sheila!" he snapped. "To your ma as well, because she understands English."

"I know that," the girl shot back. "But I can't understand half of what the bloody hell she says when she answers me in English."

The reaction to Sheila's retort was a study in personalities. Colin placidly ate, Pat's face flushed with anger, and Mayrah expressed annoyance with her daughter. "No sauce, Sheila!" she ordered brusquely.

Stabbing a finger at the girl, Pat heatedly told her

again to speak only English. Sheila frowned resentfully as she nodded, then the disagreement was quickly forgotten, as before. The meal continued, and Pat talked about other things, but David felt sympathy for the woman whose task it was to teach the small, belligerent girl.

Later, the men returned to the parlor. As they lit their pipes, the station owner commented that he intended to leave the next day to take supplies to stockmen in his north paddocks. "I'd be glad of your company if you'd like to come along," he added.

"Yes, I'd be more than pleased to go with you, Pat."

"Very well, we'll leave at dawn. Concerning your taking a flock to graze on shares, I'm perfectly willing to agree to it. We'll work out all of the details while we're out in the paddocks."

"I certainly appreciate that, and I'll do my best to make sure that we both make a profit from the arrangement."

"I'll be surprised if we don't, David. With Frank's recommendation, of course, I'd agree to it. But now that I've met you, you don't need the recommendation." He paused, then shrugged. "There's also another reason why I would agree to it. I was just starting to tell you about it when we went in to eat."

"What reason is that?"

Pat puffed on his pipe, seeming to change the subject. "Were you down at the huts yesterday, or around any of the Aborigines?"

"No," David replied slowly, thinking. "I saw them, of course, but it was from some distance away. Why do you ask?"

"Well, anyone can tell by talking to you that you're not an ordinary stockman," Pat mused. "But I should think it would take a keen eye indeed to see it from a distance. In any event, they had a corroboree last night, and Mayrah told me it was because they think there's going to be another big sheep station hereabouts." He laughed, puffing on his pipe again. "So if that's what the Aborigines think, I don't believe I should stand in the way of it. Would you like more rum, David?"

David was dumbfounded, silent for a moment, then he nodded. "Yes, after that, I could use another drink of rum, Pat."

Chapter Six

Cresting a hill, David and Pat reined up, the pack horses behind them stopping. A flock grazed in a valley below, and across the valley, a stockman sat beside his horse and watched the sheep. "That's John Bowen," Pat said. "His area is the north part of Bulloo Paddock, which will graze about three thousand sheep."

Recalling what Pat had said about the names and locations of the paddocks, David knew they were at about the mid-point of the station, near the north boundary. They had worked their way across from the northwest corner of the station, replenishing the stockmen's supplies. So far, that had taken two days while riding at a steady pace, and David reflected that his estimate of the acreage of the station kept increasing.

As they crossed the top of the hill and started down its side, the stockman's dogs alerted him. Trained not to bark, which could panic the sheep, they moved about restlessly as they looked toward David and Pat.

The stockman stood up and shaded his eyes against the sun as he looked across the wide valley, then he waved and jumped on his horse.

A small, thin man in his early twenties, John Bowen beamed with pleasure at having visitors as he rode up, exchanging greetings. "Will you be able to stop for the night, Mr. Garrity?"

"No, there's plenty of daylight left, and we have miles to cover," Pat replied. "Where's your fold and hut?"

The stockman replied, pointing to the north, and Pat reached for the halter rope on the pack horse that David led. The two men rode away with the pack horses, and David remained to watch the flock. A short time later, the supplies at the stockman's hut replenished, the two men returned.

David and Pat rode on to the east across the rolling, brushy terrain, the flocks miles apart in the paddocks. Hours later, they came to a valley that reeked with the putrid stench of decay. Pat frowned darkly as he and David searched and finally found the source of the odor, the mangled remains of some ten or twelve sheep in a ditch. Near the ditch, the carcasses of two dingoes hung from a tree limb.

The flock, a few miles away, was larger than the last one and was tended by a stockman and a jackaroo. The stockman knew he was in trouble over the dead sheep and tried to explain, but Pat cut him off.

"If you'd kept your eyes open when you had the sheep in that valley," the bearded man said gruffly, "that many wouldn't have been killed. Also, there are more than two dingoes around here. Your jackaroo could watch the flock while you're tracking the rest of them down."

"Aye, I'll do that, Mr. Garrity," the stockman replied contritely. "The value of the sheep can be docked from my wages."

"I don't want the money, I want my sheep kept alive. The next time the head stockman or I bring supplies, I want you to have a lot more than two dingoes hanging in trees around here. Have your jackaroo lead the way to your fold and hut, and I'll measure out your supplies."

The stockman apologized again, then beckoned his helper. As they followed the youth away from the flock, Pat explained to David that stockmen in the more remote areas of the paddocks had to be especially watchful for dingoes, because the animals were less frightened of humans. "They aren't as bad as they used to be," he added, "after having had a taste of what firearms will do. That won't be the case when you set out into land that's never been grazed, so dingoes will be a very serious problem for you."

At the fold and hut, Pat measured out the flour, salt, rice, tobacco, and other supplies for the stockman and jackaroo. He and David then rode eastward, with only one more stockman's supplies remaining to be delivered. The stockman farther on to the east of that one would be the first on the next circuit that either Pat or Fred made, one of them visiting every stockman at least once every two months to deliver supplies and make certain that all was well.

Near sunset, they stopped at a billabong and made camp. The amount of supplies to be delivered looked large to David for one stockman, which he mentioned to Pat while they were eating. The station owner explained that the stockman, Adolarious Bodenham, had an Aborigine woman who had borne him several children.

Continuing in an amused tone, Pat said that Bodenham was a recluse who wanted nothing to do with anyone except the woman and children, and had shown up at Wayamba Station the previous year, after years of roaming the wilderness. He was evidently from a very good family in England, a life he had abandoned for the one he had found in the outback.

"That's sketching pads," Pat went on, pointing to a bundle wrapped in oilskin. "He's an artist, and it costs me a few guineas to support him and his mob, but between them they graze more sheep than any other stockman." He laughed, drinking his tea. "Adolarious is an odd one, but you find all sorts among stockmen."

"That's true," David agreed, laughing. "Kunmanara is a good workman for Frank. Do you have any Aborigines as stockmen?"

Pat shook his head, explaining that Kunmanara was an exception because most Aborigines were unable to understand the concept of individual ownership. "If one of them had a flock, he would give the others all the sheep they wanted and see nothing wrong in it. Also, they might leave at any time on a walkabout, and nothing will stop them when they decide to go on one."

"What is a walkabout, Pat?"

"It's a sort of wanderlust that can strike them suddenly. Mayrah told me that it's much more than that, but I'm never able to grasp half of her meaning when she talks about Aborigines. I think it's because we don't have words in English for what she wants to say. In any event, the Aborigines at my station hunt down dingoes and do chores, but nothing else."

"Well, I'd be dead if it weren't for some Aborigines. If I ever have a station and some want to come there, they'll be welcome."

Pleased by David's attitude, Pat smiled and nodded. They talked awhile longer, smoking their pipes and drinking tea, then they unrolled their blankets beside the fire.

At dawn the next morning, they had a quick breakfast, then broke camp and rode on to the east. Some two hours later, smoke from a cooking fire rose among the hills ahead, the fold coming into view a few minutes later. Instead of a hut, there was an encampment beside the fold. Washing hung on a line near two large shelters made of bark, and an Aborigine woman and several small children moved about the fire.

When they saw Pat, the woman beamed in pleasure, and the children squealed in delight. As the supplies were being unloaded, Pat took out a tin of sweets and handed it to the woman. The children whooped joyfully and bounced around as the woman gave each of them a piece of candy. When the supplies were stacked beside the fire, she pointed to where the flock was grazing, over the next hill.

The huge flock was spread out across a valley. The dogs and several more children, ranging up to early teens, were scattered around the sheep. The children greeted Pat, then directed him to a clump of brush near a horse that was tethered and grazing. Pat and David rode over to the brush, reining up their horses a few yards from it.

"Are you there, Adolarious?" Pat called.

"Yes, I am here, Mr. Garrity," a man answered from the brush. His accent that of an Oxford don, his tone was one of patient resignation over the intrusion upon his solitude with the woman and children.

"I see you're teaching the children English now," Pat said. "I hope you're also teaching them sums as well as reading and writing."

"I'm doing all you suggested, Mr. Garrity," Adolarious replied. "However, I must say that I still retain the same strong reservations about cluttering the minds of unspoiled, natural creatures."

"That isn't what they are, Adolarious. They won't know how to forage like Aborigines when they're grown, so they'll have to work, and schooling will be a great aid to them. I brought more drawing materials for you but I trust that you're not drawing any more live dingoes."

"No, I'm using dead ones for models. But they aren't the same."

"Indeed they aren't, and the sheep would agree most heartily if they could talk. Well, I'll be on my way. G'day, Adolarious."

"Farewell, Mr. Garrity."

Riding away, Pat led the way at a steady canter. During the early afternoon, he and David came to a deep stand of boxwood, the ground bare of other growth between the trees. Immediately to the north was a low, barren, rocky mountain of stone and shale. Several miles long, it was oriented almost due east and west.

They rode up the mountain, and from the crest, the land to the north was like an Eden. Rolling terrain covered with lush, deep spinifex, saltbrush, and mallee stretched to the horizon. Excellent graze for sheep, it was dotted with open forest and thickets that marked waterholes.

"I call this Barren Mountain," Pat said, "and it's my northern boundary. I've always been concerned that another grazier would come in here and encroach to the south. I can fight for my land if need be, but I'd rather have a friend on this land."

"It certainly looks like good land," David mused.

"Aye, from here it does. Wayamba keeps me busy, and I've never been farther north than Barren Mountain, but I've heard talk about it. At a distance to the north, there's a creek that the Aborigines call Tibooburra. Far beyond that is a line of sharp hills that look like spires. Between here and those hills is as much land as you could ever want."

"If I can get a foothold on it," David added.

Pat agreed, then talked about specifics of an arrangement. "The money in that purse the bushranger had looked like about a hundred guineas," he said. "For that much, I'll sell you horses, dogs, all the equipment you'll need, and a thousand sheep. That'll give you the lambs and wool, and you can also take a flock on shares."

"How large a flock, Pat?"

"As large as you want to take. It would entail work that would grind most men into the ground, but you can take four thousand, if you wish. Then you'll have your own flock within two years at the most."

"Or debt for many years to come, if I lose them to

dingoes, in a flood, a grass fire, or any number of other things."

Pat stroked his beard, smiling. "If you don't want to take risks, then you don't want to be a grazier, David." He chuckled.

David laughed, agreeing. Pondering for a moment, he realized he was unable to make an informed decision as too much depended upon chance. Then he decided that any risk might as well be a large one. "I'll buy a thousand and take four thousand more on shares, Pat," he said.

Pat smiled, putting out his hand. David shook hands with his friend, sealing the bargain between them, then they turned their horses and rode back off the mountain toward Wayamba Station.

A week later, David drove five thousand sheep northward on the station. His two pack horses were loaded with supplies and equipment, the second one also dragging poles for a temporary fold. Cracking his stockman's whip, he kept the sheep moving at a walk as five dogs patrolled each flank of the long column to head off those that tried to turn aside.

At sunset each day, he put the sheep in the temporary fold, a rope stretched between the poles. He knew the rope contained the sheep only because they thought it did, accustomed to being in a fold at night. If anything frightened them, the sheep would trample the rope and scatter for miles in the darkness, some of them going too far for him to find.

It was part of the risk he had accepted, and one of the disadvantages of having such a large flock to manage alone. He slept no more than two or three hours a night, waking and going to look when any of the sheep stirred. As he moved the flock at a steady pace, he began dozing in his saddle for periods of a few minutes, becoming ever more weary.

The day that Barren Mountain came into view, his beard was thick and he was covered with dust as well as so tired that he was numb. Later that morning, he woke from a nap in his saddle to see another flock a mile away to the west, and the stockman hastily turned his sheep. David whistled to his dogs, summoning them to the left side of his flock.

If the flocks were too close, the sheep would flow together like quicksilver. Of more importance to David than the trouble of separating two flocks was that he might not get his original sheep back. Along with wethers for food and several rams, he had chosen only ewes in their prime, many of which should give birth to twins.

As the dogs raced to the left side of the flock, the sheep veered eastward. David exchanged a wave with the other stockman as the two flocks moved safely apart. A few minutes later, he signaled the dogs and turned the sheep back toward Barren Mountain.

The flock moved at a good pace across the mountain, then slowed in the lush graze on the other side, cropping mouthfuls of grass, saltbrush twigs, and mallee seed pods. David cracked his whip, keeping the flock at a walk. When he arrived at a billabong during late afternoon, he put up the fold while the sheep drank and grazed.

The next morning, with the dogs scattered around the grazing sheep, he began building a permanent fold. He felled trees, then split the logs with wedges and a mallet. As the rail fence took shape, he transplated clumps of acacia to the fence so that over the years the brush would interweave with the rails and make a thick wall of brush and wood.

Knowing the scent of the flock would eventually draw dingoes, he began patrolling around the flock during late afternoons, when the wild dogs started their evening hunt. The first time he saw one, the tawny yellow animal charged boldly out of the brush toward the sheep, and he shot it. He glimpsed several dingoes slinking away from the flock through the undergrowth, and that night he heard their dismal howling nearby.

The next afternoon, he carried both his double-barrel musket and his spare one, which he had loaded with bird shot. Some of the dogs began bristling, and he rode around the flock toward them. As two dingoes raced into the open toward the flock, he killed one and wounded the other. Then he lifted the second musket, aiming at other wild dogs fleeing through the brush. The pellets ripped through the foliage and stung several of them, their yelps blending with those of the dingo wounded by the bullet.

That ended the threat during the afternoons as the dingoes had been frightened away by the gunfire. David occasionally glimpsed them lurking in the brush, but no more attacked the sheep. There was still danger at night, however, when the wild dogs could make the sheep break out of the temporary fold if they attacked, and he hurried to finish the permanent fold.

When it was completed, and for the first time since leaving the home paddock at Wayamba Station, he had time to bathe, shave, and wash his clothes. He could also sleep soundly at night, but found that he no longer needed to. Sleeping lightly and rising at any sound to check on the sheep had become a familiar routine, no longer making him weary the next day.

After the fold was constructed, his days were still filled with activity. He occasionally killed and dressed a wether to provide food for himself and his dogs. He fleshed the skins and cured them with the inner bark from peppermint trees, a process Frank had told him about. Using some skins to make a comfortable bed, he cut and sewed others into a warm, thick coat for the coming winter.

As a first step in establishing his station, David intended to divide the land into paddocks, with a permanent fold in the center of each one. Following that plan, he moved the flock eastward for several miles, then began building a second fold. He had trouble with dingoes again, driving the wild dogs away by killing and wounding several of them.

When he moved the flock once more, driving the sheep to the northwest, the weather had become cold and rainy. Counting the notches he had made on a hardwood stick to keep track of the date, David saw that March had arrived. The weather was miserable, his anxiety over the sheep was a constant burden, and his daily labor from dawn until dark was unrelenting. But he was supremely happy, attending the flock that was the seed stock for flocks of his own, and exploring the vast land where they would graze.

June and winter came by the time he worked his way north to Tibuboburra Creek, a wide, swift stream flanked by thick forest. At a curve in the creek, he found a tall hill that gave a panoramic view of the surrounding terrain. Below the top of the hill was a sheltered plateau, a perfect location for a house. It was a place of surpassing beauty with the hill dominating miles of rolling landscape, and David knew he had found where he would eventually build the home paddock for his station.

During midwinter, Kerrick reached the line of hills that Pat had told him about. Like Barren Mountain, they made a natural boundary for a sheep station of immense size. The first time he glimpsed the hills, he had to agree with Pat that they did resemble church spires, and he decided to call them Steeple Hills. Drainage from the slopes made the graze to the south of them exceptionally lush, but the land was slashed by ravines that warned of flash floods. Finding a wide, grassy knoll that rose above the low-lying land, David built a fold out of danger from floodwaters.

On a raw, damp morning two weeks after the fold had been completed, the wind rose and light showers that had been falling for the past few days turned into steady rain. David began driving the sheep back to the fold early as the ditches started to fill with water.

When he reached the hill where the fold was located, the rain was a downpour and gullies overflowed with foaming, roaring freshets that were flooding the ravines.

On the exposed slopes of the hill, the wind was a howling gale, lashing the driving rain in all directions. By the time David had the sheep in the fold, his bark hut had been flattened and his campfire extinguished, but he had far more urgent concerns than his comfort. The surrounding land was starting to flood as runoff from Steeple Hills reached it, and animals were fleeing to higher ground.

In addition to a vast variety of other animals, dingoes came up the hill. Snakes did as well, most of them harmless, but they included a few adders, copperheads, and deadly taipans. Carrying a heavy stick to kill poisonous snakes, David patrolled the fold with his musket, an oilskin over the locks to keep the gunpowder in the flash pans dry. The dogs drove away most of the dingoes, and he shot those that fought the dogs.

To keep his gunpowder dry while reloading in the heavy rain, David crouched beside the fold and sheltered his powder flask inside his sheepskin coat. He had just finished recharging both barrels of the musket when he heard the dogs snarling and fighting on the other side of the fold, and the dogs nearby raced around to join them. David followed them, expecting dingoes.

Coming around the fold, David was confronted by a large wild boar the dogs had at bay beside the rail and brush fence. The dogs darting and snapping at it, the animal squealed in rage as it lunged and slashed with its long, gleaming tusks. Then it turned to David and charged, and the dogs swarmed around it and clung to it with their teeth.

Aiming at the boar's back to avoid hitting one of the dogs, David pulled both triggers. One barrel misfired, the bullet from the other one ripping into the center of the animal's back and breaking its spine. Its hindquarters collapsing, the boar dug at the muddy ground with its forefeet and tried to get to David amidst the bedlam of its shrill, enraged squealing and the snarling of the dogs as they tugged it back.

The uproar battering his ears, David knelt beside the fold and poured gunpowder into the flash pan on the barrel that had misfired. He walked up to the boar and put the musket to its head, its jaws snapping and slavering in its fury. The musket fired, killing the animal. David called the dogs to him and looked them over to make certain none had been injured, then he reloaded his musket and resumed patrolling around the fold.

During the afternoon, the wind abated and the rain tapered off to sprinkles. The hill was surrounded by a sea of floodwater, the tops of trees and other high spots in the terrain jutting above it. Kangaroos, wallabies, wombats, bandicoots, and other animals peacefully shared space in their mutual peril, and no more came to the hill.

Under the remains of the hut, David found enough dry wood to start a fire. He roasted pieces of mutton on the spit, then fed the dogs and ate as darkness fell. The sheep were hungry and thirsty, bleating and moving about restlessly in the fold. They kept it up through the long hours of the damp, frigidly cold night as David sat beside the fire, animal eyes gleaming around the edge of the firelight.

At dawn, the flood had subsided to scattered ponds at low spots in the marshy ground, and the snakes and animals were gone. David turned the sheep out of the fold and trailed them with his horses. In the wet bottomland around the hill, the animals waded about in the mud, gulping down water from the pools and greedily cropping the foliage.

The ground became drier during the day, the ponds shrunk, and by the following morning, the only evidence of the flood was brush and driftwood hanging in

trees. A few days later, David drove the flock back to
the south, toward Tibooburra Creek.

The last days of August and early spring had arrived
by the time the flock was back across the creek. The
lambing began late one night, when David was awakened by a ewe bleating in distress. After hastily
kindling a fire beside the fold, he pulled the ewe to the
light and fumbled inside it to straighten out the tangle
of small limbs and bodies. Before he finished assisting
the ewe in lambing, other ewes were clamoring in
pain.

Through the remainder of the night, he brought one
ewe after another to the light of the fire to help it lamb.
In the meantime, scores of others were giving birth
without difficulty. When dawn came and he turned
out the flock to graze, many of the ewes had lambs
stumbling beside them, and others lay down to give
birth.

The lambing continued all day with numerous ewes
in labor all the time and several of them having
difficulty. Driving the flock to the fold that evening
was slow and tedious, ewes lambing along the way. At
nightfall, David hastily cooked for himself and the
dogs, in between helping the ewes. Then he was on his
feet through the night, assisting them.

After the second night without sleep, time passed in
a blur of fatigue. His body aching, somehow David
found the strength to continue, stumbling about and
responding automatically to the bleating of a ewe in
distress. The nights and the days running together, he
occasionally woke from a few moments of sleep while
kneeling beside a ewe to assist it or kindling a fire to
cook, then he went on with what he knew he had to
do.

Amid the crushing toil, the dingoes came, drawn by
the scent of blood and afterbirth. Lean and ravenous
at the end of winter, they were bold. An outburst of
snarling by the dogs and panic-stricken bleating on the

other side of the flock one afternoon gave David a
burst of renewed energy. He picked up his muskets,
leaped on his horse, and rode around the sheep.

The dogs fought some of the dingoes, while others
dragged away four struggling lambs. The ewes clam-
ored and vainly tried to save their offspring. Intent on
their attack, the wild dogs failed to notice David until
he began firing. He killed two, then as they fled, he
cocked his other musket and sprayed them with
pellets, bringing down two more and wounding the
others.

The lambs were injured beyond recovery, and
David had to kill them. He carried the carcasses to a
bare spot on the ground, where he piled up wood and
burned the small forms to keep the dingoes from
feeding on them. Returning to his work, he assisted
the ewes as he moved the flock slowly toward the fold.
When the sheep were safe for the night, he arduously
gathered wood and built fires around the fold, worried
that a large pack of dingoes might have moved into
the area.

There was a large pack that attacked that night in
force. In a daze of fatigue, David moved among the
ewes then heard the dogs growling in warning at one
side of the fold. Carrying his weapons, he ran to the
fence just in time to see a wave of thirty or more wild
dogs race into the light of the fires beside the fold.

Firing his musket loaded with bird shot, David
killed two and wounded the others. The remainder
swarmed into the firelight, and the dogs attacked some
of the dingoes and the rest leaped for the fold. David
shot one with his pistol and two more with his musket
as they scrambled up the side of the fold, then he used
the double-barrel musket as a club to sweep dingoes
off the rail fence.

The heavy barrels broke bones, and the wild dogs
yelped in agony and flailed as they fell. When they
stopped trying to invade the fold, David vaulted the
fence and joined the dogs. As the wild dogs finally

broke away and retreated into the darkness, the dogs turned on injured dingoes beside the fold, and David followed them, swinging his musket.

When it was all over, a dozen dead dingoes lay on the ground. All of the dogs had been bitten, but none was seriously injured. Through the night, while attending to the ewes, David occasionally saw eyes gleaming in the dark beyond the firelight. Each time, he fired a musket at the eyes, and a howl of pain rang out as the bullet hit the dingo.

At dawn, along with spots of blood where some of the dingoes had been wounded, five more dead dingoes were scattered about. The day passed without attacks, but David glimpsed the wild dogs lurking nearby and looking for an opportunity to drag away a lamb. That night, he fell asleep in the fold for some two hours before being awakened by bleating as the lambing finally tapered off.

The last of the ewes gave birth the next day, and for the first time, David surveyed the sheep as a whole and had a full grasp of the over-all results from the past few days. The vast majority of ewes had lambed without difficulty, about half of them having given birth to twins. The flock had become massive, well over seven thousand lambs among the sheep.

When the flock was in the fold that evening, he cooked the first full meal for himself in days, then slept until dawn without being awakened. The following day, dingoes shadowed the flock, and he watched the brush and waited for the right shot. Then, taking careful aim at a tawny form through the brush, he fired and wounded the dingo.

As it yelped and fled, he left the dogs around the flock and followed the trail made by spots of blood. Presently, he came to a barren, rocky hill. At the foot of it, he found a hole with dingo hair around it and a smear of blood where the wounded animal had gone inside.

On the slope above the main entrance, Kerrick

found four more holes. A very large den with inter-connecting tunnels was where the pack lived. He stacked rocks beside the holes on the slope and collected a large pile of dry wood and brush at the foot of the hill, then returned to the flock.

At dawn the next morning, when the dingoes would be in the den after their nightly hunt, David rode to the hill. He pushed the wood and brush against the main entrance and set it on fire, then hurried up the slope and tumbled the stacks of rocks over the four holes. As he rode away, yelping and scuffling came from underground as smoke streamed from around the rocks covering the holes on the hill, and the stones stirred as the smothering dingoes vainly tried to force their way out.

The danger from dingoes eliminated, Kerrick began mulsing, docking tails, and castrating the rams among the lambs. It was backbreaking labor as he bent over lambs from dawn until dark, working carefully to avoid permantently injuring them. The weather remained cool, with relatively few flies to infect the open wounds on the lambs. When he finally finished, he knew that unless some calamity occurred, he would have a large flock of his own from his sheep and his share of the lambs.

Several days later, Kerrick was ready to start driving the flock back toward the fold during the late afternoon when the dogs looked toward the south. Their behavior indicated that someone was approaching, and he rode around to the south side of the flock. Then he saw the tall, heavy-set Patrick Garrity a few hundred yards away, leading a pack horse.

Surprised and intensely pleased, David rode toward him, waving. Pat waved back, a beaming smile on his bearded face. They greeted each other warmly, and Pat explained why he had come. "I thought you'd be running short on supplies, and I wouldn't want you to have to live on mutton."

"Mutton is about all I have left," David replied, laughing. "I certainly appreciate the supplies, Pat. How did you find me?"

"It took some searching, because you've laid yourself out quite a lot of land, so I followed the trail your sheep made in grazing from one place to another. Those are very good folds you've been building, David."

They talked as they rode toward the flock, and Pat reined up in astonishment as the flock came into full view. "Good Lord, David!" he exclaimed. "You must not have lost a single sheep, and it looks like most of the ewes had twins."

David nodded in satisfaction. "About half of them, I'd say, and the lambs are strong and healthy as well. I've had good fortune."

"You've also worked bloody hard. I'll go to the fold so I can take a look as they go in and get a better idea of how many there are."

Pat circled the flock, leading the pack horse. David summoned the dogs and sent them around the sides of the flock, crowding the sheep closer together, then cracked his whip to start them moving.

Dust boiled up as the sheep flowed toward the fold. Pat sat on his horse near the gate, looking at the sheep as they approached and went inside, then he dismounted and helped David close the gate. As they unsaddled their horses, he told David that he unquestionably had his first flock.

"And a large one," he added, "some six thousand or more. That'll be a hard flock to handle, David."

"If I can handle five, I can handle six," David replied, smiling.

Pat laughed and nodded in agreement as he and David carried the supplies to the hut. With the flour, salt, tea, rice, tobacco, there were delicacies that included treacle, pots of jam and pickles, and cheese. "I also brought some seed," Pat said, pointing to several bags. "I thought you might like to plant a garden, so I brought seed for potatoes, onions, cabbage, and such."

"Yes, I've cleared some land for a garden at the creek where I intend to make my home paddock," David said. "I know little about gardening, but the soil appears to be fertile. I certainly appreciate your bringing the seed as well as all these supplies, Pat."

Pat shrugged off David's gratitude, building up the fire as David made preparations to cook. During their conversation, David commented that he would need to order supplies himself, because he would be grazing his own flock next year. "You'll have the money to pay for them," Pat told him. "The price of wool varies from year to year, but you should get at least three hundred guineas for your share of the wool clip."

"That's far more than I'll need for supplies."

"Aye, but you'll have to start hiring stockmen soon, and your percentum of profits will be less then. No stockman will attend a flock the way you have this one, and you'll also have the expense of wages and rations for the stockmen. Even so, you should still have decent profits."

"I hope I will, Pat. How do you pay for your supplies?"

"Through a bank account in Sydney. When I send my order, I'll order your supplies and send a message to the bank to set up an account and pay for them out of your share of the wool clip. I'll need to give them the name of a station, so do you intend to call your place Kerrick Station?"

"No, I'll call it Tibooburra Station, Pat."

Filling the billys with water to make tea, Pat said that it was a good name for a sheep station. David glanced out at the surrounding terrain in the afterglow of sunset. Before, it had been land, but now it seemed subtly different, with a name. Although it was only a beginning, his sheep station was a reality, and he was blissfully happy.

He had found the new life for himself that he had envisioned, a life of grueling labor and hardship, but also one of complete contentment on his own sheep station in the solitude of the outback. Months had passed since he had last looked at his former wife's picture and tormented himself with the bitter sorrow of his love for her.

That was now in the past, as distant from him as the outside world. With nothing and no one within hundreds of miles to resurrect that agony of grief within him, he knew that it would remain in the past while his flocks expanded and he built on what he had begun.

Part II

Part II

Chapter Seven

"Everyone knows that Australia is destined to be a great land," Mary Reibey commented humorously. "After all, most of the population here has been especially chosen for Australia by the best judges in England."

Alexandra Hammond laughed, but the subject was a sensitive one, because Mary was an emancipist. As she replied, Alexandra chose her words carefully. "Your presence here is a great boon, Mrs. Reibey. You've contributed immeasurably to progress and to the welfare of people in the colony."

The woman scoffed, retorting that what she had done had been for her children and herself, but her eyes were sparkling with humor, and Alexandra knew she was being gently teased. She was fully aware of the woman's generous contributions to various charities, and she also knew that Mary Reibey was easily able to afford those contributions.

Transported to Australia at the age of thirteen for

thievery, Mary had married a free immigrant merchant. When he had died in 1811, leaving her with seven children and a struggling firm, she had begun expanding the business. Now she owned farms in the outlying districts and buildings in the center of Sydney, along with warehouses and coastal trading brigs.

The other guests in the large, well-furnished parlor of the Hammond home were also emancipists who had achieved financial success, in addition to being clients of Alexandra's father, Nevil Hammond, an attorney. While he had other clients who were free immigrants, the two groups never mixed socially. Alexandra viewed that as tiresome, having friends among both groups which she had to be careful to keep separated.

A maid served drinks before dinner as Nevil and his wife, Augusta, chatted with guests. In addition to his law practice, Nevil had investments in property, shipping, and other interests that were managed by Alexandra's brother, Creighton, who was talking with guests in another part of the room with his attractive wife, Martha. Tall and dapper in his neat suit, he was thirty-two, thirteen years older than Alexandra.

Alexandra smiled wistfully, replying to a question from Mary Reibey about how she liked Australia. "Far be it from me to belittle the colony," she said, "but I still miss London. My younger brother, Robert, is attending school there, and I do envy him."

"Indeed?" Mary mused. "I thought you might be settled in here happily now. For some time, gossip has had it that you're keeping company with that lawyer who works with your father at times."

"John Fitzroy? No, that's making far too much of it, Mrs. Reibey. I have a number of friends in the town, including Mr. Fitzroy."

"He's probably the one spreading the gossip," Mary suggested with a smile, "and trying to keep others away from you." Her smile fading, she arched an eyebrow. "Although he works with your father, I hear that he'll have nothing to do with anyone but the bunyip aristocracy. I daresay that's true, because he isn't here this evening."

"I'm informed that he's working on an urgent matter," Alexandra replied, telling the truth, even though she knew that what John had told her was untrue. As long as she had known him, John had been a snob.

Changing the subject, Mary asked about Alexandra's maternal grandmother, Christine Waverly, who lived with the family. "She's very well for her age," Alexandra told Mary. "She is over seventy, of course, and she chose to remain in her room this evening. She might have become too tired."

Mary agreed emphatically, then the conversation moved on to other subjects. Andrew and Henrietta Thompson, wealthy landowners, were talking nearby with Henry Kable and his wife, Jane, who controlled a large proportion of the sealing and whaling industry in Australian waters. One of them made a remark that drew Mary's attention, and she began talking with them.

Alexandra walked away, moving toward the maid. Some of the guests were still without drinks, and the maid was making too much of a bustle as she pushed the serving cart about. Although she was inept, her job was secure because servants were difficult to find and to keep in Australia. Alexandra began helping her and the maid smiled gratefully. As they moved among the guests, most of the conversation was about the new governor, Sir Thomas Brisbane, who had arrived a short time before.

Not unexpectedly, the guests were dissatisfied with the change, because Brisbane was stricter with convicts than his predecessor. The concensus was the opposite among free immigrants, who had regarded Governor Macquarie as much too lenient toward convicts. Alexandra was inclined to agree with free immigrants on the issue, because it seemed to her that

Governor Macquarie had been entirely too lax in at least one instance.

Her cousin in Leeds, Wesley Hammond, had been murdered by a man named Kerrick, who had been transported to Australia for the crime. She knew nothing about it except the bare facts, and the one time she had met Wesley, he had seemed a handsome, coltish scapegrace with no worthwhile interests. But he had been murdered, and Governor Macquarie had granted Kerrick a pardon, which had enraged her family.

The maid was capable of keeping glasses refilled, and when all of the guests had drinks, Alexandra resumed circulating among them. Overhearing an interesting remark made by a man named Samuel Terry, she moved toward him. Known as the Rothschild of Botany Bay, Terry had once been an illiterate Manchester laborer, transported for theft. Upon being granted a ticket-of-leave, he had become a pub keeper and moneylender. Now he owned tens of thousands of acres in farms with scores of convicts working them, and he was a principal shareholder in the Bank of New South Wales.

He was talking with Simon Lord and his wife, Alma, the owners of factories in which candles, soap, glass, and other commodities were manufactured. They were discussing the outback, which more than interested Alexandra. Ever since she had first heard of the enormous reaches of unknown, unexplored land to the west, it had fascinated her.

They were talking about people who lived there, which surprised Alexandra. "I understood that very few have even ventured into the outback," she commented, "and that it hasn't even been explored."

"That's true," Terry replied. "Only a handful of people have seen it, and you'll find no maps of it. But a sheep station called Wayamba Station was established there some years ago, and recently an account was set up at the bank for another one. It's called Tibooburra Station."

The names seemed evocative of the remote, mysterious region to Alexandra, and she asked why colonial officials knew nothing about it if people lived there. "This is a penal colony," Terry pointed out, "and the officials have no curiosity about it. The area that's presently settled is enough for the colony, and officials in London take a dim view of any effort that produces no immediate worthwhile result."

Alexandra pursued the subject, wanting to know more than the sketchy and seemingly fanciful tales she had heard about the outback, but Terry had told her all he knew. Also, as he had said about the colonial officials, he had no curiosity about it. After a while, she moved away and conversed with William Redfern. Although he was an emancipist, he was one of the very few who was more than welcome among free immigrants.

As a young naval surgeon, he had been convicted of supporting the mutiny of 1797 among sailors in the fleet based at the Thames estuary. He was by far the most skilled physician in the colony, consulted by emancipists, free immigrants, and colonial officials alike, and he was the family doctor to the Macarthurs, the wealthiest and most elite of the free immigrants. However, he devoted as much effort to diseases, infected lash cuts, and bastard births among convicts as he did to his paying clientele.

At the Sydney Hospital, he had a clinic for convicts and the poor. For a time, Alexandra had helped him there during afternoons with the women and children patients until her father had found out and exploded in rage. While they were talking, the doctor made a humorous reference to the incident. "Having been invited to dine here this evening," he remarked, "it appears that I'm back in your father's good graces."

"Or perhaps his gout is troubling him again,"

Alexandra suggested. "It could be that he expects to consult you soon."

Dr. Redfern laughed heartily, agreeing. They talked for a few minutes, then a gong sounded in the dining room. The guests moved toward it, the doctor offering Alexandra his arm and escorting her. As they went through the hall, Alexandra's father gave her a piercing glance, evidently irritated at her for something she had done or failed to do.

The house, among the largest and most well-furnished in Sydney, reflected Augusta Hammond's efficient supervision and skill as a hostess. In the dining room, the crystal, china, and silver gleamed on the snowy Irish linen in the light of tall, heavy candelabras spaced down the long table. Alexandra assisted her mother in helping the guests find their place cards, then went to her own chair. After the toasts to the king and the governor, the housekeeper and a maid served from dishes other maids carried in from the kitchen and placed on the sideboard.

Seated between the Thompsons and James Underwood and his wife, Arlene, Alexandra chatted with them during the meal. A delicious turtle soup was followed by the fish course, smoked haddock steamed to a tender, flaky consistency in butter sauce. The main course was juicy, spicy beef Madras with curried rice, served with a mellow, full-bodied Capetown wine.

Henrietta Thompson was an amateur horticulturist, as was Alexandra. They discussed their problems with their flower gardens in the different climate and soil of Australia, and their plans on what they were going to plant when spring turned into summer. While they were talking, Henrietta mentioned in passing that she had heard that John Macarthur had recently planted vineyards on his estate, Camden Park.

It verged on being a touchy subject, because Alexandra was friends with the Macarthurs and particularly with their daughter, Elizabeth. However, the only way an emancipist would set foot on Camden Park was as an employee. Alexandra knew nothing about the vineyards, but they intrigued her, and she resolved to go and see them at the very first opportunity.

Later, when the Thompsons were conversing with guests on the other side of them, Alexandra talked with the Underwoods. Among other enterprises, the couple owned the only shipyard in Sydney. It had recently been expanded, and James Underwood gave much of the credit for that to Hiram Baxter, an emancipist whom he had hired when the man had received a pardon.

"In addition to being an expert shipwright," James said, "Hiram is a very capable supervisor. Shortly after I hired him, I made him a foreman and placed him in charge of the construction of a vessel."

"But Mr. Baxter has been of no benefit to our household," Arlene added wryly. "In fact, quite the contrary. Early last spring, we hired a most excellent maid, a young woman named Auberta Mowbray. But we had her for only a matter of days before she married Mr. Baxter."

"Staffing a household here is a problem," Alexandra observed. "Servants are difficult to hire and to keep, even at the best wages."

"Well, I can't make comparisons," Arlene replied, laughing, "because I certainly didn't have servants in England. However, I've had my share of trouble in keeping them here. In the case of Auberta, though, my loss was her gain, because she and Mr. Baxter are very happy. They have a baby, a beautiful, healthy girl."

Alexandra made an appropriate comment, then the conversation moved on to other things as the housekeeper and maid served dessert. It was chocolate charlotte russe, with a sweet, fragrant malvasia wine. After dinner, the men went to the library for brandy and cigars, and the women returned to the parlor. As the group divided, Alexandra's father again glanced at her sharply, obviously still irritated with her. She was unsure of why, but positive that she would find out in due course.

She learned shortly after the guests left and her father went to his room. Her mother stopped her on the stairs, saying that Alexandra's father was annoyed because she had helped the maid serve drinks before dinner, which he considered a menial task, and her mother agreed. "You are the daughter of the house, Alexandra, not a servant," Augusta said. "You must learn the difference between when you have friends in, and when the family entertains."

Considering it a very fine and tiresome distinction, Alexandra agreed with her mother and apologized to avoid further discussion. She went to her room, and after getting ready for bed, she went to the large, well-filled book shelves at one side of her room.

Only a few days before, she had received a copy of Walter Scott's *The Heart of Midlothian*, and had been looking forward to reading it. She took it with her as she went to bed, sitting up against the pillows, and she pulled the candlestick on the nightstand closer as she opened the book.

Always waiting until her father left before going downstairs, Alexandra rose leisurely the next morning. After washing, she looked in her wardrobe and selected a bright green muslin dress with pale green lace on the bodice, cuffs, and collar. Then she sat down at the dressing table to brush her hair and pin it up with combs. Then she left her room and went downstairs to the family parlor.

Immaculately neat and matronly attractive in her early fifties, Augusta was at the desk in the parlor, going over the household accounts. Augusta's mother, Christine Waverly, was seated in a comfortable chair and wrapped in a thick shawl. Frail and bent with age, she was peering through her thick spectacles and slowly crocheting with her thin, gnarled hands.

The older woman's reply to Alexandra's greeting

was warmly affectionate, a loving smile on her wrinkled face, but Augusta's response was more restrained. "In the Bible, there is only one Resurrection," she remarked dryly, "but a similar miracle occurs in this household daily when you finally manage to leave your room, Alexandra."

"It prevents my having a disagreement with Father and sending him off to work in a sour mood, doesn't it?" Alexandra pointed out, sitting down. "Even though a bad frame of mind might be advantageous to him if he is foreclosing a mortgage and casting some poor family into the street."

"Your father merely protects the interests of his clients," Augusta told her daughter firmly. "And it wouldn't be amiss for you to bear in mind that the work he does supports you, Alexandra."

"I'd be more than pleased to do that myself, Mother."

"Alexandra," Augusta sighed patiently, "you know that your father will never allow you to work. Let's don't go into that again." She picked up a bell from the desk and rang it. As a maid entered, Augusta asked her to bring a tray of tea and scones. The maid left, and Augusta resumed reviewing the accounts. "At breakfast this morning," she said casually, "your father remarked that you might enjoy seeing the governor's formal review of the regiment tomorrow. Mr. Fitzroy is going, and he could escort you."

Resentful over her father's continuing efforts to push her into a relationship with the lawyer, Alexandra made no reply. She had gone out with John occasionally to avoid a conflict with her father, but her tolerance was near an end. As the silence lengthened, Alexandra's grandmother tried to ease the discordant atmosphere. "The summer horse races at Parramatta will begin soon, my dear," she said in her soft, husky voice. "And the yacht races as well. All of your young friends will be at them, and you'll enjoy them."

Alexandra agreed with her grandmother, although her enjoyment of the races was limited. Both emancipists and free immigrants attended them, which made the event a tightrope of ignoring no one while not offending anyone. Also, the races were often marred by drunken convicts brawling over wagers, and by soldiers brutally beating and arresting the convicts.

The maid brought in the tray and put it on a side table. Augusta poured the tea and put the scones on plates, handing them and the cups to her mother and Alexandra, then took hers to the desk. Stirring her tea, she brought up a subject Alexandra had discussed with her several days before. There was a shortage of teachers at the orphanage, and Alexandra wanted to spend her afternoons teaching there.

"I haven't asked your father about it yet," she continued, "because he hasn't been in an agreeable humor. Such things as placing yourself among the household staff last evening keep him poorly disposed toward you. Now he's uncertain as to whether you may go to the regimental review with Mr. Fitzroy."

Alexandra finished a scone and drank her tea, her temper rising. "Then I shall resolve his uncertainty. I've gone about from time to time with John because Father wished me to do so, and at dinner this evening I'll tell him that I'll have nothing more to do with the man."

"You will not speak to your father with a defiant attitude," Augusta said firmly. "I will not allow it."

Alexandra set her chin, fixing her mother with a level stare. "I shall tell Father precisely what I said and I shall also advise him that I will choose my own friends instead of complying with his choices."

"My dear," Christine cut in placatingly, "if your father has been encouraging your interest in a suitable man, it's only because he is concerned about your future welfare and wants you to be happy."

"No, Grandmama," Alexandra disagreed gently.

"Father is attempting to secure a law partner through me instead of through his business offices. And if he was concerned about my happiness, he would have left me with relatives in England, as I wished. There was so much more to do there."

"You are mistaken," Augusta told her daughter. "Your father does consider Mr. Fitzroy suitable for you, but he's said that it's unlikely they will ever be full law partners. Also, your father refused to let you stay in England because he wants to keep his family together."

"Indeed?" Alexandra laughed, her anger fading. "Then he'll be delighted to hear that I've no intention of marrying John and leaving the household. In fact, the way matters are proceeding, he has the likely prospect of a spinster daughter to bedevil him in his old age."

Both impatient and amused, Augusta sighed as she smiled wryly. "The men of this world will never allow you to be a spinster, Alexandra, because you're far too beautiful. But I shall tell your father that you don't find Mr. Fitzroy's company congenial anymore, not you."

"Very well," Alexandra replied. "It'll save me a lecture on my faults. He'll still be angry, so I suppose you'll have to wait for a few more days before speaking to him about my teaching at the orphanage."

"A few weeks would be better," Augusta commented dryly. "And that's assuming that you don't make him angry in the meantime, which is a rather large assumption. What do you intend to do today?"

Alexandra finished her tea, standing up. "At dinner last evening, Henrietta Thompson said that the Macarthurs have planted a vineyard. I'm going to Camden Park to see it and to visit Elizabeth."

"Camden Park?" her mother mused, frowning in concern. "That's too far for you to ride without an escort, Alexandra."

"It's a fair distance, but riding there is like being on

the streets of the town, because there's a public road all the way. I've been to Parramatta and to Camden Park before without an escort, Mother."

"That's true, but that makes it no less imprudent. Why don't you go to your brother's office and see if he has time to escort you?"

"If Creighton had nothing better than that to do," Alexandra replied patiently, "he would be with his family. My friendship with the Macarthurs is one of the few things I've done that pleases Father, so I'm sure that he would offer no objection to my going to Camden Park alone."

"Well, I'm not so sure," Augusta said, "but go ahead, if you must. Do be careful, and return well before dinner."

Alexandra replied that she would, kissed her mother and grandmother, then left the parlor. In the hall, she saw a maid going toward the stairs and stopped her. "Amy," she said, "please go to the stables and tell the groom to saddle my gelding."

The maid curtsied and turned down the hall toward the back door as Alexandra went upstairs to her room. While putting on her hat, riding cape, and gloves, she thought again about her mother's concern over her going alone, then dismissed it, certain nothing untoward would happen.

Opening a cabinet to take out her riding crop, she looked at her pistol on the shelf beside the crop. Creighton had given it to her as a present on her last birthday, infuriating her father. He considered familiarity with firearms inappropriate for a woman, but her brother had long since taught her how to shoot both pistols and muskets.

She thought about taking the pistol with her, in the event anything threatening occurred. Then she laughed at herself, reflecting that she was allowing her mother's overcaution to make her own imagination run wild. She closed the cabinet and tucked the riding crop under her arm as she left the room.

Chapter Eight

At thick, stone towering gateposts that formed a high arch, Alexandra turned her horse off the road, riding through the gate and up the wide, tree-lined avenue into Camden Park. It was a magnificent estate, a luxurious English country home in the antipodes. The Georgian mansion was huge, with large sprawling wings on each side, and was made of brick with lower courses, wide entrance steps, and a trim of native granite.

At the house, Alexandra tethered her horse, then went up the steps and tapped the knocker on the wide double doors. A maid opened the door, bobbing in a curtsy as she greeted Alexandra. She said that none of the family was home, having left the house early in the day.

"I see," Alexandra mused, disappointed. "Do you happen to know where Mistress Elizabeth went and when she is expected to return?"

"No, mo'm. She and her father left together on horseback, and I know only that the cook isn't expecting them to be here for tiffin. Would you like to come in to wait or to have refreshments, Mistress Alexandra?"

"No, thank you. Please give my regards to Mistress Elizabeth and tell her that I'll call again. Good day."

The maid replied and curtsied, closing the door as Alexandra went back down the steps to her horse. She circled the house to look at the vineyard. Behind the house were large, formal flower gardens, with paths winding through the flower beds, and farther back from the gardens were crop fields, orchards, and cow pastures.

Farther back were sheep pens, a barracks, cookhouse, shearing shed, and other buildings. In a pasture at one side of the pens, a few score of thoroughbred Merino breeding stock grazed. Flocks were scattered over the rolling terrain that lay beyond the pens and pasture, the estate consisting of some sixty thousand acres.

Seeing the vineyard near the orchards, Alexandra rode down the fenced edge of the crop fields and orchards to it. As she dismounted and went in the gate, a gardener was hoeing weeds at the other end of the large vineyard. The aged and wiry Hodgkins and Alexandra had become friends during her visits. He walked toward her, waving and smiling.

"G'day, Mistress Alexandra," he replied to her greeting. "When we planted these vines, I knew you'd soon be here to see them."

"Indeed, because I heard of them only last evening, Mr. Hodgkins. Mr. Macarthur intends to make wine, then?"

The gardener nodded, pointing toward a corner of the fence. "Just over there, Mr. Macarthur intends to put up a building with a grape press and fermenting tuns, and the ageing cellar will be under the building. We should have enough grapes this year to make a few dozen gallons."

"That's very interesting. How are the vines fertilized and mulched?"

Hodgkins explained how the vines were cultivated, leading Alexandra through the vineyard and showing her around. When he finished, they were at the edge of the vineyard adjoining the orchards. They turned back, walking through the rows of vines toward the gate and her horse.

"Improvements are constantly being made here," she commented. "From year to year, there are always new kinds of produce."

"Aye, that's true," Hodgkins agreed. "During the years that Mr. Macarthur was in England, attending to affairs there, the mistress made many improvements. Most of the fruit trees were planted then."

Alexandra went out the gate to her horse, and the gardener followed her. "You've been here a very long time, haven't you, Mr. Hodgkins?" she asked.

"Aye, I have, Mistress Alexandra. When I came here, there was about a thousand acres. Now it's sixty thousand, and still growing. Mr. Macarthur and Mistress Elizabeth are looking at some land today with a view toward buying it when it becomes available."

Starting to mount her horse, Alexandra turned back. "I wanted to see Mistress Elizabeth today, but the maid at the house didn't know where she had gone. Do you know where the land is located, Mr. Hodgkins?"

"Aye, it's a sheep station just south of the road between Parramatta and Bathurst, and east of the Nepean River. A shopkeeper in Sydney named Williamson approached Mr. Macarthur about it. He said that his father owns it, and it'll be for sale when he dies, which is expected to be soon."

"That's a distance of some miles from here, isn't it? Considering the time it'll take them to get there and back, talk with the owner, and look at the land, they'll probably be gone all day."

"No, I don't think so, Mistress Alexandra. The shopkeeper said that no one is to talk with the owner, because he doesn't want the station to be sold or broken up. Mr. Macarthur and Mistress Elizabeth took the most direct route, so they should be back early afternoon."

"What route did they take?"

"They went to the track on the east side of the river, then north on it to the station. That's much shorter than going by way of Parramatta."

Glancing up at the sun, Alexandra saw that it was several hours before she had to start for home. She knew nothing about a track on the east side of the river, never having been in that area, but the directions sounded easy to follow. She decided to ride up the track and meet Elizabeth and her father while they were riding back.

Gripping her saddle, she hopped up lightly as she told Hodgkins what she intended to do. The gardener frowned worriedly and shook his head. "You don't have an escort," he pointed out, "and that track beside the river is well out of the way, Mistress Alexandra. It might be better for you to wait until Mistress Elizabeth and her father get here."

"If I do, I'll have to leave for home shortly after she arrives, Mr. Hodgkins. But if I meet her on the track, we'll have time to talk while we ride, and it's been some time since I've seen her."

"Well, I suppose you know best," Hodgkins said doubtfully. "But you be very careful, Mistress Alexandra. G'day to you."

Alexandra replied and waved, turning her horse. She rode around the corner of the fence, then past the pens and pasture where the Merinos were grazing. The rolling, grassy hills of the estate opened out ahead of her, and she turned her horse to the northwest, toward the Nepean River.

For the first few miles, she saw flocks of sheep off to the sides with stockmen nearby. Occasionally she glimpsed buildings in the distance on adjacent properties. Then the grasslands changed to brushy, open forest, with no sign of anyone in any direction.

The river came into view, lined with tall, thick trees. Approaching the trees, Alexandra slowed her horse, then saw the track. It was more a path than a track, but on it were fresh hoof prints leading to the north, apparently made by Elizabeth Macarthur and her father.

Encouraged by the hoofprints, Alexandra turned her horse up the track at a canter. When the track suddenly curved into the forest, she leaned over the saddle and reined back, a branch almost knocking off her wide hat. The horse slowed to a trot, and the huge, ghostly gray gum trees surrounded Alexandra in the twilight under the dense canopy of foliage.

Colorful parrots screeched, and bellbirds made their chiming call. But in a more profound way not touched by the noise of the birds, the forest seemed eerily quiet to Alexandra. While she was accustomed to riding about without an escort, this was the first time she had a sense of being completely alone.

She recalled what Hodgkins had said about the track, not having fully considered it before. As he had said, she was far from the roads between Sydney and the villages. She thought about stories she had heard of bushrangers who prowled the remote paths of the hinterlands, attacking isolated farms and solitary travelers.

Just as she was on the point of turning back, the track curved out of the forest. With bright sunlight beaming down and wide, open verges on each side of the track, Alexandra dismissed her fears. As she continued up the track, the hoofprints sustained her hope that Elizabeth and her father would come into view around the next curve, then the following one.

The track turned into the forest again, but it was more open, less dark and threatening than before. Alexandra leaned over the saddle, maintaining a

canter. The track curved deeper into the forest, but
was blocked by a fallen tree. She slowed the horse to a
trot and tugged a rein, guiding it around the right side
of the thick mass of limbs.

As the horse passed the obstruction, Alexandra
turned as she glimpsed a movement on the left from
the corner of her eye. The most terrifying man she had
ever seen sprang at her from behind the fallen tree,
and two others charged out of brush a few yards away.
Ragged and bearded, the man had thick, ugly features
that were covered on one side by a crimson birthmark.

Leaping out of concealment, he snatched at the
horse's reins, frightening it and making it shy away. At
the same instant, Alexandra instinctively whipped her
riding crop down and hit the man across the head.
The blow with the heavy crop knocked the man's hat
off, staggering him as his fingers closed on the reins
behind the bit.

The startled horse neighed in fright and tried to rear
up, pawing at the man with its forefeet. As a heavy
hoof thudded against his leg, the man's grip on the
reins loosened. For a split second, Alexandra was only
a hairbreadth away from escaping as the other two
men were still too far away to seize the horse. She
hammered at the man's arm with the riding crop.

He clung to the reins, his cruel, pale blue eyes
glaring at Alexandra and his ugly, birthmarked face a
mask of rage. Catching her arm with his free hand as
she beat at him with the crop, he jerked her off the
horse. She plummeted from the saddle, sprawling on
her face.

"What the bloody hell's holding you up, Crowley?"
the man roared. "And you, Snively! Get your arses
over here and hold this horse!"

The two men dashed forward, taking the horse's
reins. Dizzy from the bruising fall, Alexandra started
to lift herself to her hands and knees when the man
snatched up the riding crop from the ground and

slashed it across her back. Searing pain coursed through her, and she cried out involuntarily as she collapsed again.

"Give it to her good, Hinton!" one of the men shouted gleefully, the other one laughing raucously. "Make her squall, Hinton!"

Hinton stood over her, beating her viciously with the riding crop. Fiery agony spread across her back, and she bit her lip to keep from screaming as the other two men howled with cruel laughter and cheered Hinton on. Then he finally stopped and stepped back, throwing down the crop.

"That's just a taste of what you'll get if you give me any more trouble, you slut!" he snarled. "Your kind has ripped the skin from our backs with the lash for long enough, and now it's our turn to even the bloody score a bit. What do you say about that, men?"

The other two shouted their agreement, laughing in fiendish delight. Hinton moved toward the horse, and he and the other men discussed it with satisfaction. Alexandra was stunned, her mind reeling in shock. Events had moved too rapidly for her. Her life had been normal one moment, then in the next she had been brutalized by a savage bushranger.

In her turmoil of terror, mixed with pain and outrage from the beating, her eyes filled with tears. Then she summoned her will and struggled to keep from crying. Refusing to surrender to the men in spirit, she also knew that her only chance lay in maintaining her composure. If she could, she might be able to talk the bushrangers into ransoming her.

A desperate battle warred inside her, fear and anguish threatening to overwhelm her attempt at self-control. Somehow, she managed to stop herself from weeping, but she was unable to overcome the terrified shaking of her hands and legs as she stood up and straightened her clothes. To hide the nervous tremor, she stiffened her legs and tucked her hands under her riding cape. But the men's crude manner and slovenly appearance made it doubly difficult for her to maintain any composure at all.

All three of them were ragged and filthy. Crowley was a large, muscular man with a long, greasy tangle of hair and beard, his sardonic face scarred from many fights. Snively was much smaller and a young man, appearing less hardened, but he eagerly aped the other two. Hinton, with his thick, coarse features disfigured by the birthmark covering the left side of his face, was by far the worst of the three. His icy, pale blue eyes inhumanly cruel, he looked like the very personification of evil.

Hinton turned away from the horse, picking up Alexandra's reticule from the ground. He looked in it, then flung it away in disgust. "No bloody money!" he snarled. "How is it that you ride a horse like that and wear such fancy garb, but you've got no bloody money?"

Steeling herself, Alexandra tried to keep her voice steady as she replied, "I rarely carry money with me, unless I intend to make a purchase. However, I can get money for you."

"How will you do that?" he sneered skeptically.

"From my father. He will pay you a ransom."

Crowley reacted with quick interest, his eyes gleaming with greed. "How much will he pay?" he demanded.

"I've no idea of how much changes hands in this sort of instance, but he will pay any reasonable amount. If you act in good faith, I should think you might expect as much as a hundred sovereigns."

"A hundred sovereigns!" Crowley exclaimed gleefully, Snively echoing him in delight. "By God, that's as many times as much as we'd get from robbing farms. What do you say, Hinton?"

"What do I say?" Hinton jibed sarcastically, mocking Crowley. "What do I say?" He stepped closer to the man, raising his voice to a roar. "I say you're a swining fool! If you two were by yourselves, you'd be dancing on a gibbet before you could steal a bag of corn!"

"But what's wrong?" Crowley asked. "Her family must be rich."

"You're right there," Hinton agreed grimly. "And they raised a conniving doxie who'll lead you to your doom. If you went to collect a ransom, you'd find soldiers and hot lead waiting instead of gold."

Alexandra spoke up quickly, "That danger could be avoided by using an intermediary. For a shilling, any boy would carry a message and get the money for you, and my father would make no attempt to—"

"You close your bloody mouth!" Hinton interrupted in a hoarse bellow, lifting a fist and advancing toward her. "You don't fool me with your sly talk! If I hear any more of it, I'll break your head!"

Her moment of hope fading into despair, Alexandra fell silent. Taking the horse's reins, Hinton told Snively to hide in the brush and watch for other travelers on the track, then he motioned Alexandra deeper into the trees, toward the river. She turned and walked through the forest, fighting once again for self-control as her eyes filled with tears of anguish.

The two men talked as they followed her, Hinton leading the horse. Crowley complained that the track was too isolated, that there would be very few travelers on it to waylay. Hinton retorted that it was safe, even if it yielded little. The trees became thicker, and Alexandra picked a path through them. Each time she slowed or hesitated, Hinton growled and shoved her impatiently.

When they neared the river, Alexandra saw a clearing in the trees where five horses were hobbled and grazing in the glade, saddles and bags piled under a tree at the far side. Hinton gripped Alexandra's arm and stopped her, handing the gelding's reins to Crowley. He laughed in understanding as he led the horse into the clearing, and Hinton pushed Alexandra toward the brush at one side.

As she realized his intentions, her terror swelled into panic, and she struggled frantically to pull away from him. His fist slammed into her temple with brutal force, and pain exploded in her head. Everything suddenly spinned around her, and she collapsed in a semiconscious daze. Numbly, she felt him lift her dress and petticoats, then jerk at her underwear, tearing it open.

Through the murky haze of the stupor gripping her, she felt intense revulsion as he pressed down on her, fumbling with her. Then there was a wrenching stab of pain. It became piercing agony as he moved rapidly, panting and grunting on top of her. The welts on her back from the riding crop stung from his heavy weight pressing her against the ground, his sweaty stench choked her, and her head throbbed where his fist had struck her.

By the time he finished, the excruciating pain had brought her back to full consciousness. He climbed to his feet, fastening his clothes, then took her arm and jerked her to her feet. A wave of nausea swept over her, a sour taste of bile rising in her mouth as her stomach heaved in a sudden urge to vomit. She swallowed and fought the retching impulses as Hinton shoved her out of the brush and toward the clearing.

Crowley sat among the saddles and baggage, waiting impatiently, and he jumped up as Alexandra and Hinton appeared in the clearing. "It's time for my turn at her," he said, a leering grin on his face.

"No, you leave her alone for now," Hinton replied.

Crowley was surprised at first, then flushed in rage. "What do you bloody mean?" he demanded. "We share and share alike!"

Hinton pushed Alexandra aside, approaching the other man threateningly. "I mean that I'm the one who says when we share and how we share alike!" he bellowed. "I said for you to leave her alone for now, and that's what you're going to bloody do!"

Crowley shouted a furious reply, and Hinton roared

at him again as the men faced each other only inches apart, their fists clenched. Alexandra's nausea had passed and she no longer had to fight to keep from weeping, because she was beyond tears. Gripped by wretched, dry-eyed misery because of her humiliation and outrage, she stood and waited numbly for whatever happened as the men fought like two dogs over a bitch in heat.

Her anguish was lightened a degree by relief when Crowley backed down, ending the confrontation. Hinton motioned her toward the saddles and baggage, and as she went to them and found a place to sit, the men sat down nearby in hostile silence. Alexandra gazed at the ground without seeing it in a bitter torment of physical and emotional pain.

Late that afternoon, Snively raced into the clearing, beckoning excitedly and saying that two riders were approaching from the north. Hinton snatched up a rope and hastily tied Alexandra's hands and feet. Then he and the other men checked their pistols, muskets, and knives as they disappeared into the trees, running toward the road.

They returned a short time later, disgruntled, and Crowley angry as well. He had wanted to attack the travelers, but Hinton had refused because the riders had been armed. As they argued, describing a man and woman riding down the track to the south, Alexandra realized that the Macarthurs had just passed on their way home.

She silently sighed with deep remorse. If fate had been kinder, at this moment she would be riding with them and happily chatting with Elizabeth. Or, she candidly acknowledged to herself, if she had used better judgment, she would be waiting at Camden Park for Elizabeth to arrive.

The bushrangers prepared to leave, Crowley and Snively sorting out the baggage as Hinton untied Alexandra. Then he went to the gelding and unfastened the girth. He tossed her sidesaddle to the ground, then turned to her. "There's no one to wait on you hand and foot now," he snarled, "so you'll have to stir your lazy arse and shift for yourself for a change." He pointed to a horse. "Put that saddle on that horse, and be quick about it."

All five of the horses were young animals, but in poor condition from mistreatment, and the thin, abused mare he indicated was the worst of them. Alexandra carried her saddle to the horse, as the men discussed what they would do that night. They were going to raid several farms and then flee to a hideout, somewhere west of the Blue Mountains.

After saddling her horse, Alexandra mounted it. When the men were ready, Hinton tied her hands behind her back, grimly warning her against trying to escape or making any noise, then they set out. Snively went a hundred yards ahead to watch for travelers, Hinton led Alexandra's horse, and Crowley followed with the two pack horses.

Through the rest of the afternoon, they moved up the track at a walk, the men ready to duck into the trees at any moment to avoid detection. At dusk, Hinton called Snively back and told him to join Crowley, then increased the pace to a canter. At nightfall, Hinton slowed to a walk again on dark stretches where the track wound through the forest.

Since the men couldn't see what she was doing in the dark, Alexandra left a trail that a search party could follow. She knew that the gardener at Camden Park would send her rescuers to the track where they would find her reticule that had been left on the ground. With her hands tied behind her back, she tugged at the edge of a torn place on the waist of her dress. Every two or three miles, she ripped off a small piece of the bright muslin and dropped it on the track.

Almost two hours after sunset, they were near the road between Parramatta and Bathurst. Hinton turned into the trees where he dismounted and dragged Alexandra down from her saddle. He tied her to a tree while the other men tethered her horse and the pack horses. Then the bushrangers rode out of the trees and up the road toward Parramatta. Alexandra tugged at the ropes to free herself, then gave up, realizing it was futile.

Alone in the darkness, with the night sounds of the forest around her, she thought about her family's consternation. By now, her mother and grandmother would be frantic with anxiety, while her father and brother would be riding through the night to Camden Park. There they would learn enough to confirm their fears, but nothing could be done until the next day.

Writhing inwardly with remorse, Alexandra knew that her life had been shattered. Even if the ropes holding her had been less expertly tied so she could escape and make her way back to her family that night, nothing would ever be the same. Tongues would wag about what had happened to her while she had been a captive, casting a shadow of disgrace over her.

For that reason, if she was rescued or managed to escape during the coming days, she knew her father would probably send her back to England. That had been what she had wanted most of all, but not at the cost of having her life in a shambles. The injustice of the situation filled her with helpless rage, and most galling of all, she remained very aware that she could have avoided the disaster if she had used better judgment.

The moon climbed higher as the hours passed, its thin light shining through the foliage. Several yards away, she saw a bark hut with a ring of stones in front of it for a fire. The high mound of ashes in the ring indicated that someone had camped there numerous times. But the hut seemed old, making it unlikely that a rescuer would suddenly appear.

The breeze in the river valley became damp and cold, adding to her discomfort. Then, late in the night, Alexandra heard hoofbeats coming down the road from the direction of Parramatta. The pounding of the hoofs were those of more than three horses, and hope swelled within her as she listened, wondering if the bushrangers were being pursued. But as they drew closer, she heard the three men laughing and whooping.

Barely visible in the dim light, the bushrangers rode into the trees with three additional horses, the stolen animals heavily burdened with plunder. The men were flush with triumph as well as drunk, smelling strongly of rum as they dismounted from their panting horses. Roaring with cruel laughter, they discussed the terror they had created at the farms.

"The best one was that second farm," Crowley gloated, "where we tied the men in the front room so they'd have to watch while we got their doxies. The more the doxies squalled, the madder the men got."

"That's right," Snively agreed exultantly. "I thought that old geezer with the gimpy leg was going to have a seizure. He got so angry that his eyes were about to pop right out of his head. But the women at the last farm were the most comely of all."

"We also got more booty at that last farm," Hinton added. "Come on, let's get part of it onto those other two horses. Soldiers will be on our trail by daybreak, and we need to get to the hideout."

The bushrangers unloaded part of the stolen goods and transferred it to the tethered pack horses. When they were almost done, Alexandra began feeling uneasy. Hinton was completely ignoring her, and she wondered if he intended to kill her. Regardless of what had happened and its consequences, nothing could quench her driving will to live.

Then he came up to her, the stench of rum mixed with the foul, sweaty reek of his body. He untied her and shoved her toward her horse. After she climbed into the saddle, he tied her hands behind her back again, then took the halter rope on the horse to lead it as he mounted his horse.

The other two men led the pack horses and followed as Hinton rode out of the trees. Alexandra tore another small piece from the waist of her dress. When the horses turned onto the Parramatta road, she dropped the fabric. Several minutes later, the horses' hoofs thumped hollowly against the wooden bridge over the Nepean River.

After crossing the bridge, she dropped another piece of cloth, then stopped tearing at the material. She knew that if one of the men noticed the hole in her dress and guessed what she had been doing, she would suffer a very painful death. She also had to concentrate on keeping her balance on the saddle, as Hinton increased the pace to a fast canter.

An hour later, in the foothills, Hinton's gelding was the only horse that could maintain the canter. As he turned back occasionally to slash Alexandra's horse with a rope, he cursed and shouted at the men to whip their horses and keep up. The horses panted and labored as they trotted, but when the road reached the mountains, the animals slowed to a walk regardless of how cruelly they were beaten.

While ascending and descending the steep slopes, Alexandra had even more difficulty balancing herself with her hands tied behind her back. Hinton shouted at the men, telling them it was still several more miles before they would turn off the road to their hideout. Alexandra prepared to tear another piece from her dress to drop at the turnoff, knowing it would be the most important one of all.

Then the first light of dawn touched the mountain peaks to the east. As the light spread across the sky, Alexandra's heart sank. It would be suicidal to drop the cloth with Snively and Crowley riding behind her. Dawn brightened into full daylight as the horses moved down the road in the western slopes of the mountains.

The men's coarse, drunken exuberance had changed into hangovers. All three of them were haggard and miserable as well as apprehensive traveling in daylight. They lashed the horses, but the animals were almost completely exhausted. They trotted heavily for a few paces when they were whipped savagely, then slowed to a walk once again.

The road was deserted, and there were no houses in the rugged, thickly-forested mountains, dashing Alexandra's hopes that she and the bushrangers would be noticed. At a valley choked with brush and trees, Hinton turned off the road. After picking a path through the dense growth for some two hundred yards, he stopped and dismounted.

Snively and Crowley tethered their horses while Hinton tied the reins on the gelding and Alexandra's horse to a tree. "I hope you try to get away," he muttered grimly, glaring at her. "That'll be reason enough for me to flay you with a whip, the same way that your kind has done to us. So if you think you can get away, then you go ahead and try."

He turned away, and he and the other men returned to the road. They slowly worked their way back to the horses, straightening up trampled brush and smoothing out all signs of hoofprints. When they reached the horses, they were more relaxed, confident that they were now safe from retribution for their foray east of the mountains. Hinton took a jug of rum from a bag on one of the pack horses and drank from it, then passed it to the men. After they drank and replaced the jug in the bag, they mounted up again.

The horses moved slowly up the valley through the tangle of brush and trees, and Alexandra leaned low over the saddle to avoid the branches. Through the tops of the trees, she glimpsed a sheer stone cliff that rose above the forested slopes at the head of the canyon. Near the upper end, a brook trickled between boulders that had tumbled down from the cliff, and the valley walls closed together into a steep, wooded incline.

Hinton dismounted and pulled Alexandra off her

horse, untying her hands. After growling another vicious warning of what he would do if she tried to escape, he shoved her toward the slope. As she began climbing it, holding onto branches to pull herself up, she found a wide path of skidding hoofmarks.

The men and horses labored up the rise behind her as Alexandra followed the path. After climbing a hundred yards, she reached a plateau at the foot of the cliff. The path led through dense trees and brush at the edge of the level expanse, ending at a grassy field about an acre in size behind the screen of foliage. It was the bushrangers' hideout, with a spring at one side of the field and a large cave in the base of the cliff.

Alexandra's remorse was more bitter than ever when she saw the hideout. Even from a short distance down the valley, the plateau and cave were completely concealed by trees and brush. The place was very secure and would be extremely difficult to find by those searching for her.

She took the saddle off her horse and hobbled it to graze, then sat down in front of the cave. After tending the horses, the men looked through the plunder from the farms. Along with rum and a large supply of foodstuffs, it included clothing, tools, housewares, and weapons. Hinton also had some money and bits of cheap jewelry.

Counting the few guineas and looking at the jewelry, he was disgruntled, having expected more money and valuables. "If we'd had time to stick some feet into fireplaces," he mused grimly, "we'd have got more that they had hidden away where we couldn't find it."

"That's more than we had before," Crowley pointed out. "We can also sell the guns and other things which will bring good money."

Hinton nodded, shrugging off his disappointment. "Aye, we'll get some money from that. In any event, I've been thinking about a plan that will fetch us plenty of money, enough to last for a long time."

Crowley asked what the plan involved, but Hinton refused to discuss it until he had given it more thought. The two men then began talking about going within the next few days to villages on the Hunter River where they could sell the plunder to shopkeepers who asked no questions.

Hinton turned to Snively who was starting to build a fire in front of the cave. "Fool!" he barked. "Soldiers will be looking for us, and they might see the smoke from a fire during the daytime."

"I'm hungry," Snively complained. "Do we have to wait until tonight before we have anything to eat?"

"No!" Hinton snarled impatiently. "We got plenty of cheese and ship biscuit from one of the farms. Find it, and we'll have some."

Snively rummaged in the foodstuffs, taking out a large cheese and a cask of ship biscuit. He cut a slice from the cheese and grabbed a handful of the biscuit, as the other two men did the same. When Snively started to sit down and eat, Hinton told him to climb up to the lookout on the cliff and watch the road for any sign of activity.

Pocketing his food, Snively went to a crude ladder at one side of the cave and climbed to a rock shelf some thirty feet up the cliff. Having no appetite, but with a gnawing emptiness in the pit of her stomach, Alexandra took a share of the cheese and biscuit, then sat down at one side of the cave to eat.

Finished eating, Alexandra returned to the plunder and took a blanket from it, then lay down where she had been sitting. Hinton glanced at her, then turned back and talked with Crowley.

Although she was almost exhausted, Alexandra's anxiety kept her awake. Shortly after, Hinton and Crowley unrolled blankets, then began snoring moments later. Hinton had failed to tie her, Alexandra reflected, and if he made a practice of forgetting to, sooner or later she would have a chance to escape. Thinking about that, she fell asleep.

Chapter Nine

The late-afternoon shadows were stretching across the grassy field in front of the cave when Alexandra was awakened by Snively shouting to Hinton. In the instant between sleep and being fully awake, with memories of this horrible experience rushing in on her, she felt as though she was having a terrible nightmare and would wake up in her bed at home. Then her heart sank as she woke completely, the nightmare all too real.

"Hinton!" Snively shouted again in fright. "The road is full of soldiers! There are scores of them up and down the road!"

Throwing their blankets aside, Hinton and Crowley leaped up and ran out of the cave to the ladder. As they climbed it, Alexandra sat up and listened to the men. Hinton snarled at Snively, accusing him of sleeping instead of keeping watch. Contritely admitting to having fallen asleep, Snively quickly added that it had been for only a short time.

He broke off, howling with pain as Hinton reached the top of the ladder and cuffed him. Then Crowley exclaimed in fear, telling Hinton to look at the road. "Snively is right," he said, "there are scores of them. They're looking at the sides of the road for hoofprints. They've figured out that we left the road somewhere, and they're looking for a trail."

Hinton agreed apprehensively. Alexandra was more regretful than ever that she had been unable to drop another piece of cloth at the turnoff. The bushrangers were puzzled as well as worried, discussing the forays they had made east of the mountains before without creating such a strong reaction, but Alexandra knew the reason. Her family had demanded action from the governor and had received it.

Hinton and Crowley discussed the possibility that the soldiers would find the hideout. Because of the thick foliage in the valley, they were unable to see how far off the sides of the road the soldiers were searching for tracks. Crowley reminded Hinton that if the soldiers spread out over two hundred yards from the road, they would find a trail of hoofprints leading straight to the hideout.

"They haven't found the trail yet," Hinton pointed out. "If they had, they'd be following it and there wouldn't be any of them on the road. And if they found it at this very minute, there's not enough daylight left for them to follow the trail to the hideout."

"Not tonight," Crowley replied, "but they can tomorrow."

"Aye, that's possible," Hinton agreed. "We can't stay here."

The conversation continued as the three men came down the ladder. Crowley wanted to leave immediately, but Hinton overruled him, saying that it was sunset and they would be unable to get far before dark.

As they came into the cave, Crowley suddenly stopped and jabbed a finger at Alexandra. "She's the

reason so many soldiers are searching!" he snarled.
"Her family is rich, and the governor has turned out
the whole Sydney garrison because they've figured out
that we have her!"

A stab of raw fear raced through Alexandra as the
three men glared at her. But Hinton was jealous of his
authority, making him quick to disagree with Crowley. "No, the governor is just trying to get rid of all
bushrangers," he speculated. "It's happened before."

"That's not it this time," Crowley insisted. "She's
the reason."

"How do you know?" Hinton demanded. "You're
not on the governor's bloody privy council. In any
event, what's done is done."

"That's easy to say," Crowley grumbled. "When we
go, we should leave her here with her throat slit, and
leave our trouble behind."

Hinton frowned, shaking his head. "Whether she's
alive or dead will make no difference as far as trouble
is concerned. We'll take her with us." He grinned
lewdly. "By keeping her, we'll have a cook as well as
entertainment to liven up the nights."

"Entertainment?" Crowley echoed angrily. "Entertainment for bloody who? For you, that's who! When
do I get my share?"

"When I bloody say, that's when!" Hinton retorted.
"Any time you get tired of how I run things, you can
bloody leave, Crowley!"

Crowley fell silent, turning away. With dusk settling, Hinton gruffly ordered Alexandra to build a fire
and cook, and she wondered how to begin. While she
could capably manage a household, her experience in
cooking was limited to having occasionally prepared
desserts for the family and light refreshments when
she had hosted friends.

When he had started to make a fire earlier in the
day, Snively had left a flint, steel, and tinder beside the
stones. Using logic, Alexandra managed to kindle a
fire, then looked through the foodstuffs. At a social

gathering, a friend had told her about damper and
how it was made. She took out the ingredients for it,
then cut slices from a side of salt pork to fry, and put
peas, rice, and tea in pans to boil on the fire.

To her, the results of her first attempt to cook a meal
seemed indifferent at best. But the men were apparently satisfied, wolfing down the food without comment. After eating, Snively unrolled his blanket near
the fire and Hinton and Crowley talked beside the fire.
Alexandra returned to her blanket at the side of the
cave.

Listening to the men, Alexandra wondered with
shrinking dread if Hinton would rape her again before
going to sleep. Then she breathed a sigh of relief as he
and Crowley finished their conversation and lay down
on their blankets. As an afterthought, Hinton got back
up and came to Alexandra with a rope to tie her hands
and feet, then he returned to his blanket and was
snoring moments later. Alexandra gradually went to
sleep.

The men built up the fire in the darkness before
dawn, awakening her, and Hinton untied her. After
making breakfast, Alexandra saddled her horse. The
men gulped the leftovers and tea, saddling horses and
loading pack horses, and Alexandra ate a piece of
damper as she put the dishes in a bag to go on a pack
horse. As dawn broke, they filed away from the cave.

When they reached the valley, Hinton turned up the
mountain to the west. It was much steeper than the
slope below the hideout, with no path through the
foliage. Hinton pushed through the thick growth,
leading the gelding. Alexandra dodged flailing limbs
as she followed him with her horse. Behind her,
Snively and Crowley cursed as they struggled up the
mountain.

Passing through a defile in the crest of the mountain, they crossed it and went down the other side. At
the foot of the mountain was another narrow valley, a
creek flowing through it. Hinton pushed Alexandra

onto her horse, then he and the other men mounted. He led the way up the center of the stream, leaving no trail for the soldiers to follow.

Several miles up the creek, they came to a waterfall that blocked the way. They dismounted again, and Hinton led the way up the mountain on the west side of the stream. After another long, difficult climb, they reached the top. The foothills were ahead, and Bathurst was a cluster of buildings at a distance to the southwest. Farms and sheep stations were scattered over the foothills and the plain west of the village.

At midday, they were on the lower slopes of the mountain, approaching the foothills. Snively and Crowley complained about the hard pace, and Hinton responded with a sarcastic, profane tirade, calling them weaklings. The two men muttered resentfully and then fell silent, trudging down the mountain behind Alexandra. As they entered the foothills, she and the men mounted their horses again. Avoiding the farms and sheep stations, Hinton led the way west across the forested slopes.

Late that afternoon, the terrain had leveled off into rolling hills covered with open forest and brushy clearings, the farms and sheep stations well to the south and behind them. Hinton reined up beside a brook at the foot of a hill, announcing they would camp there. As he dismounted, he told Alexandra not to build a fire and to hand out cold food.

Alexandra looked through the foodstuffs, finding the cheese and ship biscuit. The long, hard trek during the day had been taxing for her, but the men were wearier, lying beside the saddles and baggage as they talked listlessly. Alexandra passed out the food, then sat down with her share.

Sunset faded into twilight as she ate, reflecting that her rescue by soldiers was now unlikely, and it would soon be impossible for her to escape. If she tried to flee on a horse after the men were asleep, the stirring of the animals as she mounted one was certain to awaken the bushrangers. But Bathurst would soon be too far away for her to reach on foot.

Either she had to escape within a day or two, or endure captivity until they were near another village, which could be weeks. Thinking about her chances of succeeding if she fled that night on foot, she knew she could travel in the dark through the hills, but the men would be mounted and able to travel much faster. If they spread out and began pursuing her at daybreak, knowing that she would be headed toward Bathurst, they would probably catch her.

Pondering her escape, she absently looked up the brook beside the campsite. During the heavy rains, the narrow stream evidently turned into a wide, raging torrent, because piles of brush and driftwood were caught between large trees on both sides of it. Her gaze fixed on a pile of debris, and Alexandra suddenly knew how to escape without getting caught.

As darkness fell, the men settled down for the night, and Alexandra lay down. Her thoughts again turned to the dread possibility that Hinton might rape her, but he merely brought a rope and tied her hands and feet. He was tired and careless, leaving the knot at her wrists loose enough for her to easily untie.

Listening to the men's breathing, Alexandra waited for them to fall sound asleep. Hinton began snoring, then a few minutes later, Crowley puffed and wheezed in deep sleep. Snively was silent, but the younger bushranger had slept quietly the night before.

As she started to untie the rope at her wrists, Snively got up from his blanket. Clamping a grubby hand over her mouth, he lay down beside her. "Be quiet," he whispered hoarsely. "If you'll let me do what I want, I'll help you get away."

As he began fumbling at her breasts with his free hand, Alexandra twisted away from him. "Get away from me!" she shouted angrily. "Get away from me and leave me alone!"

Snively frantically tried to shush her and get his

hand over her mouth again, but the other two men awoke. Hinton leaped to his feet with a roar of rage. He pulled the younger man to his feet and pummeled him. Snively yelped in pain.

"Leave him alone, Hinton!" Crowley shouted irately. "He was only claiming what's his by rights!"

"I'll give him his bloody rights!" Hinton snarled, throwing Snively to the ground, and kicking him. "There's your bloody rights, you little swine! And there! And there!"

He kicked Snively several more times, as the man howled in protest then scrambled toward his blanket. "Now let that teach you a lesson," Hinton growled. "The next time you go against what I say, I'll make you wish the soldiers had caught you. And you, you conniving slut," he continued, kicking viciously at her, "you stop displaying yourself and causing trouble, or I'll throttle you!"

His toe thudded solidly against Alexandra's side as she squirmed and turned away, trying to protect herself, then Hinton went back to his blanket.

"We should have killed her at the hideout," Crowley grumbled. "That woman is more trouble than ten women are worth. We're all sharing the trouble, but we're bloody well not sharing the benefit from having her here."

"You will when the time comes!" Hinton snapped, lying down. "I told you that you and Snively can do anything you like to her when I say you can. Until then, you'll both leave her alone."

Crowley muttered under his breath, then fell silent. Her side aching where Hinton had kicked her, Alexandra had another long wait, listening for the men to go back to sleep. After several minutes, Hinton resumed snoring, and Crowley was making his usual sleeping sounds. Finally, Snively breathed with a quiet, steady rhythm. Alexandra plucked at the knot on the rope around her wrists. After freeing her hands, she pulled up her feet and untied the rope at her ankles.

Gripped with tension, Alexandra silently got to her feet and crouched low as she crept toward the brook. After wading across it, with no outcry being raised behind her, she ran up the bank of the stream. A hundred yards from the campsite, a large mass of driftwood and brush that had collected between three trees was a darker shadow in the night.

Alexandra ran around to the other side of the debris, dropped to her hands and knees, and began pushing her way into it. As sharp tips of limbs scratched her and snagged her clothes, she ignored them, crawling into the tangle. Hearing rustling sounds, she realized that small animals and possibly snakes were in the brush, something she had failed to consider. She overcame her qualms and crawled into it.

At the center of the debris, she came to a section of the tree trunk with a narrow space under it. She pushed into the opening, then settled herself to wait. When the men discovered that she was gone, they would search in the direction of Bathurst. Eventually they would give up and leave, afraid of being captured, and she was where she could see what they did. Once they were gone, she would set out for the village.

Nothing was further from her mind than sleep, and Alexandra was wide awake just before dawn, when Hinton discovered that she was gone. He roared a stream of profanity, calling to Crowley and Snively. The two men replied, then there was a babble of voices as the bushrangers talked in consternation. They were too far away for Alexandra to understand what they said, but a few minutes later, she heard them saddling horses.

As dawn broke, the screen of dead brush was less dense than it had appeared from a distance, and Alexandra felt exposed. She could clearly see the bushrangers as they took the hobbles off the other horses and tethered the animals to trees to keep them from straying. Then the men mounted their horses and rode up beside the brook, toward her hiding place and in the direction of Bathurst.

Then icy apprehension seized her as she noticed that she had left a wide, glaringly obvious hole in the brush while forcing her way into it. Not daring to move, she waited breathlessly as the men rode toward her. They passed, not even glancing at the pile of limbs and brush.

Alexandra turned and peered through the dead foliage. The men fanned out, Crowley angling off to the left and Snively to the right as Hinton rode straight toward Bathurst. When they disappeared, Alexandra crawled back to the edge of the brush and pulled it together over the hole, then returned to the tree trunk and hid under it again.

Time passed very slowly and the sun gradually rose higher. Weary from the sleepless night, she was also hungry, but most of all she was thirsty. The sound of the brook a few yards away and its fresh, damp scent in the air tortured her, causing her to lick her parched mouth and lips.

The day grew warmer, and movement in the dead, matted grass and leaves a few feet from Alexandra drew her attention. Then she stiffened in fear, her eyes riveted to a snake. Knowing nothing about Australian snakes, she was unsure if it was poisonous, but it was large, well over four feet long. Its shiny body slithered under the tree trunk a few feet from where she lay, then disappeared. As she relaxed, she heard hoofbeats approaching in the distance.

The bushrangers were together again, the three horses moving at a fast canter. Alexandra flattened herself, watching through the brush. The hoofbeats grew louder, then the men came into view. Alexandra's anxiety became almost unbearable as they drew closer, then they passed her and rode on to the camp.

Dismounting, the men went to the other horses and led them to the baggage, then began loading the pack horses. Working rapidly and silently, they finished quickly. Hinton put Alexandra's sidesaddle on the horse she had ridden and led it as he rode away from the campsite, turning to the west. The other two men followed him, leading the pack horses.

Watching the bushrangers disappear over the hill, Alexandra felt weak with relief and joyously happy. After the torment she had endured, she could scarcely believe that she had managed to get away from the men. Her first impulse was to crawl out of the brush and run toward Bathurst, but she restrained herself and pondered what to do.

While she was uncertain of the distance to the village, she was sure it would take her several hours to get there. She wanted to reach it during daylight hours, but most of all, she had to be positive that the bushrangers were completely away from the area. After thinking it over, she decided to wait until midday. The men would be far away by then, and she should be able to reach Bathurst before nightfall.

As a breeze stirred, broken clouds moved across the sky, threatening rain. When an hour or more had passed since the bushrangers had left, Alexandra crawled out of her hiding place. Peering warily around, she saw no movement other than the trees swaying in the breeze and the birds flitting about. She started to go to the brook for a drink, but her thirst was gone, lost in her compelling urge to reach the safety of Bathurst.

Hurrying toward the village through the tall grass and stands of brush, Alexandra was aware of her unkempt appearance—her dirty face, her messy hair and her torn and smudged clothing. In the back of her mind, an anguished voice told her that how she looked meant less than nothing, now that her life had been shattered. She ignored it, determined to confront with courage the gossip, snubs, and whatever else awaited her.

The breeze turned into a gusty wind, and the clouds became thicker, covering the sky, as thunder rumbled in the distance. Rain appearing imminent, Alexandra glanced up at the sky and walked faster. Then, as she came to a thicket of brush, Hinton suddenly rode out from behind it, a triumphant grin on his coarse, disfigured face and his pale blue eyes gleaming. Alexandra froze, paralyzed with terror and dismay.

A long moment passed in silence as they faced each other, the wind stirring his dirty blond hair and beard. Then he laughed sardonically. "You stupid bitch," he sneered. "Did you think you could get away from me? Between here and Bathurst are several sheep stations, and I went to a number of stockmen who were tending flocks. I told them that my wife had run away, and asked them if they had seen a woman. None had, so I knew that you were hiding here somewhere, waiting until we left."

Listening numbly, Alexandra knew that the torment she had suffered had been nothing compared to what she would endure now. His cruel smile faded and his voice became savage. "Soldiers might question some of the stockmen I talked to," he growled, "and figure out who I am. So I'll have to take my men and get well away from here, but you're going to pay for the trouble you've caused." Taking a rope off his saddle, he motioned toward the campsite at the brook. "Get on back there."

As she turned, her torture began. Hinton rode behind her, slashing her with the rope and leaving a line of burning agony across her back. Involuntarily crying out in pain, Alexandra ran as the bushranger followed her and whipped her with the rope.

The day had become dark and stormy. The thunder moved closer, and thick, black clouds swirled in the wind that lashed the trees and brush. Alexandra gasped for breath and ran as hard as she could, trying to evade the stinging rope and the horse's hoofs pounding behind her. Hinton jeered at her to run faster as he snapped the rope across her shoulders and back.

Reaching the brook, Alexandra splashed through it and started up the hill on the other side, but Hinton reined his horse around in front of her and stopped. "Now take off your clothes!" he snarled, dismounting and tethering the horse. "And be bloody quick about it!"

His demand made her hesitate, her shrinking reluctance to undress in front of him—the ultimate humiliation—more compelling than her fear. The man's coarse face twisted in brutal delight as he saw· her distress, and he leaped at her, beating her furiously with the rope. "Get your clothes off, you worthless bitch!" he bellowed. "Your kind is good at giving commands, and now you'll learn to obey them. Take off those clothes!"

Stumbling backward and trying to dodge the rope, Alexandra began hastily undressing. Hinton laughed in cruel glee as he stopped whipping her and watched, occasionally snapping the rope to make her flinch. The storm drew closer, and lightning crackled a few hundred yards away, followed by a shattering blast of thunder. The trees thrashed in the howling wind as the first few large, scattered raindrops fell.

Trembling in fear, Alexandra took off the last of her clothes. She looked away, but she could still feel his burning gaze devouring her as she stood completely exposed to his lust, the wind whipping her hair and the large, heavy raindrops splattering her naked body. In her agony of mortification, she almost felt relieved when he finally unfastened his clothes, and pulled her to the ground with him.

Alexandra bit her lips to smother her cry of pain as he took her with a savage thrust, maliciously torturing her in every possible way. Then, as he brutally continued to ravage her with his animal grunts of satisfaction, the full fury of the storm struck. The scattered raindrops turned into a heavy downpour, and the wind increased to a gale that shredded leaves and limbs from the swaying trees. Blinding bolts of lightning cut through the gloomy twilight, and battering claps of thunder resounded on all sides.

The lightning and thunder passed, fading into the distance under the shrieking wind and the drumming roar of the rain. Hinton at last rolled away from her, then stood up and fastened his clothes. Alexandra weakly climbed to her feet and put on her sopping clothes with trembling hands as the rain beat on her. When she finished dressing, she went up the hill, hiding her pain and agony behind a stoic facade. She followed the hoofprints made when the bushrangers had ridden away earlier in the day, and Hinton led his horse as he followed her.

Having only gone as far as the other side of the hill, Crowley and Snively waited under a tree, the horses nearby. Crowley moved out from under the tree, laughing sardonically and nodding in approval as Alexandra and Hinton approached. "It looks like you've been teaching her a lesson for trying to get away, Hinton," he commented. "We'll finish the lesson, and she'll never do that again."

"No, both of you leave her alone for now," Hinton ordered, stepping in front of Alexandra. "I told you that you can have her when I say you can, and until then I want her left alone."

Crowley exploded in rage. "Damn you to hell, you scurvy swine!" he roared. "I've waited bloody long enough for her!"

Hinton replied with another stream of profanity, the two men on the point of coming to blows as they pushed at each other. Alexandra moved back to keep from being shoved about, too relieved by Hinton's keeping the others away from her to wonder about his reasons. Snively ignored the furious argument, his eyes riveted to Alexandra in raging lust.

"We're all in danger because of her!" Crowley

shouted. "You talked to those stockmen, and they'll tell the soldiers about you. If I'm to have that danger, then by God I'm going to have her as well!"

"Aye, we are in danger!" Hinton roared. "And the longer we bloody stand here, the more danger we're in!" He shoved Alexandra, motioning her toward her horse, and told Snively to get the pack horses ready to go. Then he turned back to the other bushranger. "We're leaving, Crowley, and you can either come with us or go your own way."

Snively went toward the pack horses as Crowley and Hinton glared at each other in furious silence. Then Crowley turned away, grinding his teeth in rage. Alexandra climbed onto her horse, and a few minutes later, they set out through the rain, Hinton leading her horse as Snively and Crowley followed with the pack horses.

An hour later, Hinton reined up at a narrow track that had been made by draft animals, heavy drays, and horses. Leading straight to the west, away from Bathurst, the track offered a much easier path than the open countryside, and Hinton turned onto it.

The rain tapered off then stopped, and the sun shone through the clouds as it set. At a stream beside the track, they stopped to camp for the night. Hinton and Crowley were still hostile toward each other, neither of them speaking as they unsaddled their horses and unloaded the pack horses. Snively was also silent, not wanting to give either of them a reason to vent their anger on him.

Her hair and clothes completely soaked, Alexandra shivered with cold. As she unsaddled her horse, Hinton growled at her, ordering her to get out the cold rations. She took out the cheese and ship biscuit from the baggage.

Hinton impatiently snatched his food as she took it to him, and Crowley glared at her in smoldering resentment when she gave him his share. Snively stared at her in heated lust as he took his, but the three men stayed silent. Alexandra ate, then took her blanket from behind her saddle. When she lay down, Hinton tied her hands and feet tightly.

The rope biting into her wrists and ankles, Alexandra shivered as she lay on the wet ground with the damp blanket around her. Although she was very weary after her lack of sleep the previous night, her turmoil from the events of the day and her discomfort kept her awake. She thought about Hinton's refusal to let Crowley and Snively have her, hoping that he would remain adamantly opposed to it.

Thinking about his reasons, she decided that Hinton was using her to demonstrate his authority over the other two men. And when he had made the point to his satisfaction, he would turn her over to them. With that threatening thought in mind, her body aching with fatigue, she fell into a restless, uncomfortable slumber.

The next day, watching the men's actions, Alexandra became positive that she was right about why Hinton had kept the others away from her. With the attitude of one who has acted entirely within his rights, he remained stonily silent toward Crowley, waiting for the other man to speak first. When they stopped at a pond to water the horses, Crowley spoke to Hinton who gradually emerged from his silence.

Near sunset, they stopped for the night where the track crossed a creek. As they dismounted, Hinton told Alexandra to build a fire and cook, then seized her shoulder and pulled her close. "And if that fire smokes," he snarled, "I'll push your face into it."

Releasing her, he turned away and unsaddled his horse. Alexandra gathered twigs and sticks that had dried in the sunshine during the day. After building a hot, smokeless fire, she fried strips of salt pork and cooked peas and rice. She dished up the food, and when they had all eaten, she took the dishes to the creek to wash them. Hinton and Crowley sat beside the fire and talked, their dispute completely forgotten.

As she knelt beside the creek, stacking the dishes to carry them back to the fire, Alexandra heard a soft footstep behind her. Before she could turn, Snively had his arms around her and fondled her breasts as he tried to kiss her. She twisted away from him in revulsion. Neither of them spoke a word, wanting to keep Hinton from noticing their tussle and reacting in a rage which would be directed at both of them.

Snively darted a fearful glance toward Hinton, then looked back at Alexandra with an exultant, lustful grin as he moved away. Her hands shaking in anger and disgust, Alexandra took the dishes to the fire. Then grabbing her blanket, she lay down, listening to the conversation between Hinton and Crowley.

Hinton had previously mentioned that he was considering a scheme to get money, and he was telling Crowley the specifics of the plan. He intended to steal a flock of sheep and take it to the Hunter River, then sell the animals a few at a time to farmers and graziers in the area. Crowley was doubtful about the plan, pointing out a serious shortcoming.

"You always talk about the danger of being caught," Crowley said, "so we could never get away with it. Sheep can't be driven more than ten or fifteen miles a day, and soldiers would be after us within a day or two after we took the flock. They would catch up with us easily."

"Aye, that's the main obstacle that I saw," Hinton replied. "I looked at it from all sides, and I couldn't think of any way around it. But when I found that track that we've been traveling on since yesterday, I figured out a way that we could avoid that problem."

"What do you mean?"

"All of the sheep stations around Bathurst are close together, and we couldn't take a flock from any of them without drawing attention. But I've heard of a big sheep station in the outback that has flocks spread far and wide. This must be the track to that station, because we're already well beyond any of those around Bathurst. We could take a flock from it, and the others at the station probably wouldn't know for weeks or perhaps even months. By then, we could have the sheep sold."

"How far away is this station you're talking about?"

Hinton shrugged and shook his head. "All I know is that it's a long distance away. That's better, though, because the hue and cry for us here will die down while we're gone. And it'll be worth our while. Sheep will sell fast at two or three shillings each, so a thousand or more sheep will bring in enough money to last us for a long time."

His interest in the idea growing, Crowley became enthusiastic after Hinton mentioned the amount of money involved. The two men discussed the plan, as Alexandra listened in dismay.

She had thought that they would hide out for a time and then go to Hunter River where she might have a chance of escaping and reaching a village. Now they would be going into the distant wilderness of the outback, and she would remain the bushrangers' captive indefinitely.

Chapter Ten

During the following days, the uncomfortably cold night that Alexandra had spent on the wet ground became a fond memory. The farther west she and the bushrangers went on the track, the more torridly hot the weather became. Early summer was pleasant in Sydney, but here the sun glared down from a cloudless sky through the long, suffocating hours of each day.

Adding to her discomfort, her riding cape was in rags and her hat had been lost somewhere along the way. One night, she looked in the bags containing clothes that the bushrangers had stolen from the farms. She picked out a man's hat and coat to protect her from the sun, turning up the cuffs on the coat as she put it on. It was risky because of Hinton's unpredictable temper, but he said nothing when he saw her wearing the coat and hat.

He tied her hands and feet with increasing carelessness for several nights, then stopped altogether, and he showed no inclination to rape her again. It had become evident that his lust was aroused only by an urge to punish and dominate, and as long as she resisted defying him and did nothing to anger him, he ignored her.

At night, when Hinton talked with Crowley or had his attention on other things, Snively tried to catch her by herself to fondle her. She tried to avoid such situations, which would enrage Hinton if he saw them. The incidents were a reminder that her life would become unendurable when Hinton turned her over to the other men, because she would be repeatedly raped every night. At the mercy of Hinton's whim, she felt utterly helpless.

While cooking one night, she looked at a small knife among the utensils as a weapon rather than as an implement. There were pistols among the loot from the farms, but concealing one of them in her clothes would be impossible. The knife, however, was small enough for her to slide into the hem of her dress, where it would be completely hidden.

When she was certain that the men were paying no attention to her, Alexandra made an opening in the hem of her dress and slipped the knife into it. The next night and on following nights, she took it out and honed it on a stone until it was razor-sharp. While she had no idea of what she might do with it, she felt less helpless, the weight of the knife in her hem deeply comforting to her.

Along with the heat of the outback, it was plagued with flies. At ponds and streams, they were joined by clouds of mosquitoes. The men cursed and flailed their arms in vain, while Alexandra found that she could keep the insects away by carrying a leafy twig and fanning herself with it.

Despite the circumstances, Alexandra experienced moments when she enjoyed the journey. The outback was intimidating, a harsh land with perils on every side, but it had a rugged, compelling beauty. Venturing where so few had been appealed to her sense of novelty and adventure. Its enormous spaces staggered her imagination, and it was so entirely different from any place she had ever seen that she found it endlessly fascinating.

The bushrangers, however, had an intense aversion to it. The boundless reaches and isolation of the immense land were oppressive to the men, making them nervous and irritable. With a mixture of contempt and amusement, Alexandra watched them act like small children who whistled to bolster their courage while passing a cemetery. The men talked loudly among themselves during the day, and after sunset, they built a fire and sat near it to keep the vast, dark cavern of night in the outback at bay.

The men remained constantly fearful of being seen, and near the top of a hill one day, Hinton suddenly wheeled his horse around. "Get off the track!" he shouted to Snively and Crowley. "Move, you bloody fools! Get off the track and hide in the brush!"

Just before Hinton jerked the rope on her horse's bridle and turned it, Alexandra saw dust rising from the track on the other side of the hill. Then she concentrated on balancing herself on the saddle to keep from falling as her horse spun around with Hinton leading it off the track as he continued shouting at the men to hurry.

The horses cantered, plowing through the thick growth. Some fifty yards from the track, Hinton rode around a thick, tall clump of brush and stopped behind it. The other men, following closely with the pack horses, reined up.

"What's wrong, Hinton?" Crowley asked.

"Someone's coming down the track toward us," Hinton replied, then he turned to Alexandra. "If you make a sound, it'll be the last thing you ever do," he warned her grimly. "Do you understand?"

She nodded, watching the track through the screen of brush in front as she heard heavy wheels rumbling, and saw a thick cloud of dust. A moment later, seven huge drays drawn by oxen passed over the top of the hill where Hinton had turned off the track. They were loaded with large, canvas-covered bales of wool, and four armed riders led them.

"That wool is worth a fortune," Hinton commented sourly. "Why should some rich swine have all the gold it'll bring? That would be more than enough to last us for the rest of our lives."

"Well, we can't get that," Crowley replied, "but we can get some of his sheep that the wool came from. That'll satisfy me."

Hinton laughed sardonically, agreeing. When the drays disappeared around a curve, he turned his horse and rode back to the track. Alexandra's mount and the others followed. Then the horses settled back into the routine of traveling up the track at a fast walk.

Finally, they camped beside a pond. When she went for water, Alexandra took a wine bottle that was full of water as well as a bucket. The distance between sources of water becoming farther, she had concluded that the time might come when they would be unable to find water. She had mentioned it to Hinton, who had merely laughed sarcastically, and she had begun keeping the wine bottle full of fresh water.

At the pond, Alexandra emptied the water from the previous day out of the bottle and refilled it, then dipped up water into the bucket. Hiding the bottle under her coat, she returned it to where she kept it in a pack of foodstuffs. She then set about preparing the usual meal of salt pork, peas, rice, damper and tea which she knew the men wanted. But Alexandra knew that as a steady diet, the food would eventually cause scurvy. Among the foodstuffs was an earthenware pot of pickled cabbage which prevented the disease, but the men disliked its vinegar taste. The one time she had put it on their plates, Hinton had thrown it at her. More than willing to let them get scurvy, Alexandra filled their plates with what she had cooked, then added a helping of the pickled cabbage to her own plate.

After the meal, the bushrangers built a roaring fire as they always did, since the vast, surrounding darkness made them uncomfortable. Their conversation was the usual topic, their dislike for the outback. Crowley had suggested several times that they turn back, and he became more insistent about it as Hinton refused once again. Their exchanges verged on an argument, then they built up the fire once again before they unrolled their blankets beside it.

The following day, while they were riding up the track, Hinton shouted at Crowley and pointed to a kangaroo in the brush some two hundred feet away. "You see that kangaroo over there, Crowley?" he called. "See if you can hit it."

Crowley lifted his musket and fired at the animal. He missed, and the kangaroo bounded away. Hinton jeered as he cocked his musket and looked around. A few minutes later, he saw another kangaroo and fired at it. It tumbled over, thrashing on the ground in its death throes.

"That was closer than the one I shot at!" Crowley shouted angrily.

"No more than a few feet," Hinton replied, laughing and reloading his musket. "Let's see if you can do any better on the next one."

A short time later, they saw another kangaroo, and Crowley fired at it. The bullet wounded the animal, and the men howled with laughter as it bled heavily and struggled frantically to flee, falling down every few feet. Then, when Snively joined in, the bushrangers took turns shooting at the animals and wagering pence on being able to hit them.

Alexandra was revolted, knowing why Hinton had started the shooting. None of the men were intelligent, but Hinton was sly and had thought of a way to distract Crowley from the journey. But it was savagely brutal, at the expense of pain and death for unwary animals that had stopped to gaze curiously at the travelers.

However, it worked as a way of diverting Crowley's attention from the journey, and the wantonly cruel sport continued during the following days, filling the hours of traveling for the men. When sitting beside the fire at night, they argued over the settlement of the wagers they had made that day, and not over whether they should turn back toward Sydney.

Alexandra saw far more animals than the men who spotted only those that were in the open. But in addition to having discovered that she had more physical endurance than the men, she had long since found out that her eyesight and hearing were keener than theirs. However, they saw enough to leave a trail of dead and wounded animals behind.

While she was washing dishes at the edge of a billabong one night, Snively once again sneaked up on Alexandra. This time he managed to get within a few feet of her before she detected him, then he rushed her. As he threw his arms around her, squeezing her breasts and trying to kiss her, she knocked over the tin plates and pannikins in her furious effort to twist out of his grasp.

Hinton, hearing the clatter, stood up beside the fire. "What the bloody hell is going on over there?" he growled, peering toward the billabong. Seeing them in the moonlight, he charged away from the fire. "Snively, I warned you about that, you little swine!" he roared.

"She told me that I could!" Snively yelped, dodging to get away from Hinton. "She said that I could if I wanted to!"

"I don't give a bloody damn what she said!" Hinton bellowed, chasing him. "I'm the one who gives the orders here, not her!"

Catching the smaller man's sleeve, Hinton spun him around and hit him in the face. Blood burst from Snively's nose and mouth as he stumbled back and sprawled on the ground. Following him, Hinton kicked him again and again as he scrambled about frantically on the ground and tried to get away, his face covered with blood. Finally, after kicking Snively around to the other side of the fire, Hinton turned back.

"So you told him that he could, did you?" Hinton snarled, stamping toward Alexandra. "I warned you about causing trouble, you slut!"

Knowing that it would be useless to protest and contradict Snively, Alexandra steeled herself, trembling in fear. She ducked as Hinton's fist lashed out, but it still struck the side of her head hard enough to daze her. Catching her hair as she fell, Hinton dragged her to her blanket, then threw her down on it. He dropped on top of her, pushing up her clothes and unfastening his, and then pushed into her with a vicious thrust.

When Hinton fastened his pants and went back to the fire, Crowley's lust was aroused and they argued fiercely over her again. Numb with pain and her mind still reeling from the blow on her head, Alexandra lay, listening as they raged at each other, Crowley demanding to have her and Hinton refusing. The argument ended in hostile silence, and Alexandra pulled her blanket closer and waited for sleep as an escape from her misery.

The atmosphere of discord remained the next morning, and Snively's face was swollen. Later in the day, the hostility between Hinton and Crowley faded, and they shot at kangaroos again. Snively joined in later, the aftermath of the night before passing, and Alexandra earnestly hoped that he would leave her alone.

Two days later, a situation that she had foreseen occurred. Throughout the day, she and the bushrangers rode up the track without passing a billabong or a stream. Hinton cursed irately and increased the pace to a canter, but the track continued winding through the arid, sun-baked terrain without a sign of water.

When dusk gathered, the men's disquiet in the vast, isolated land came to the fore. They stopped, making a dry camp beside the track, and kindled their usual large, blazing fire. Alexandra asked Hinton if he and the others wanted cold rations, then had to jump back as he slapped at her viciously, cursing and snarling that they were too thirsty to eat.

As the men sat morosely beside the fire, Alexandra quietly took her water bottle out of the foodstuffs, along with cheese and ship biscuit. Intensely regretting that she was unable to give the horses at least a sip, she went to her blanket. After the bushrangers were asleep, she ate and drank, then fell asleep. The next morning, she concealed the bottle under her coat and returned it to its place in the baggage.

There was still no sign of water as the morning passed, the sun rising higher into the cloudless sky and the breathlessly still air becoming torridly hot. Instead of shooting at kangaroos, the men were glumly silent in their raging thirst. Alexandra's satisfaction over their suffering was offset by her pity for the horses with dried foam crusting on their lips as they plodded wearily along.

Early that afternoon, she saw bright green foliage through the shimmering heat waves. A short time later, the horses lifted their heads and flared their nostrils as they smelled the water, and they broke into a canter. The bushrangers exchanged perplexed comments and looked ahead, seeing nothing that was different. Finally, when they were near the billabong at the side of the track, Snively and then the other men saw it.

When they reached it, the men ran to the water and drank, but Alexandra restrained the horses from drinking too rapidly and foundering. The nine large animals were frantically thirsty, and she had to struggle with them. Gripping the reins and halter ropes, she dragged the horses back after they had gulped down a few mouthfuls. Then, their frenzy of thirst passing, she got them under control and made them drink slowly.

Alexandra drank when the horses finished, then she opened a bag of supplies to get out the cheese and ship biscuit. As they wolfed down the food, Hinton opened another pack that contained jugs of rum stolen from the farms. Selecting a jug that was less than half full, he emptied out the remainder of the rum on the ground.

Turning to Alexandra, he handed her the jug. "Here, fill this and keep it full from the waterholes along the way," he ordered gruffly. "That's what you should have been doing all the while, you stupid cow."

Silently taking the jug, Alexandra carried it to the billabong. As she knelt at the edge of the water, the angle of the sun on its surface made it almost like a mirror. For the second time since the bushrangers had captured her, she was aware of her appearance.

She was barely recognizable with her face sooty from campfires and her hair a tangle under the dusty brim of a man's hat. Under the grimy, shapeless man's coat, her dress was in dirty tatters. Dipping the jug into the water, she desperately yearned to be free of the bushrangers. And with equal intensity, she longed to avenge what they had done to her.

A few days later, there was a lavish abundance of water when they camped beside a wide, muddy river. West of the river, however, the terrain was even more arid than before, with long stretches between sources of water. Crowley finally became bored with the bloodthirsty sport of shooting kangaroos, and again brought up the subject of turning back. He gradually became more insistent, arguing with Hinton about it.

When they were debating the subject beside the fire one night, Hinton became angry. "Have done with your bloody whining, Crowley!" he snapped. "It can't be all that much farther to the sheep station."

"You've been saying that for weeks," Crowley retorted. "Having a go at that woman now and again would make this bloody place easier to bear. When am I going to get my turn with her?"

Lying only a few feet away, Alexandra looked at the men and listened to the conversation more closely as Hinton made his usual reply. "Like I've told you," he growled, "it'll be when I say you can."

"Aye, that's right," Crowley agreed. "You give the orders and no one's questioning that. I'm just asking you when it'll be."

Apprehension gripped Alexandra, because of the man's wheedling tone instead of his usually demanding one. Having learned much about Hinton and his childish, overbearing self-importance, she knew that Crowley had taken an approach that might be successful.

Hinton frowned, stroking his greasy, blond beard as he pondered, then shrugged. "It'll be when we have the sheep," he replied. "Then she'll be yours and you can do whatever you bloody like to her."

It was too far in the future to satisfy Crowley, who nodded glumly and reached for his blanket to unroll it beside the fire. Her heart sinking in dismay, Alexandra turned and looked up at the stars, the time now more or less defined when an even worse nightmare would begin for her.

Along with her dread, she deeply resented being treated as chattel, completely dependent upon the whims of another. For the first time in her life, she was eager to kill, but that offered no solution. Her only weapon was the knife in the hem of her dress, and even if she attacked the men while they slept, she knew she would be unable to kill all of them.

During the following days, with growing apprehension, she noticed a gradual change in the foliage. Even to her inexperienced eye, it appeared to be better pasturage than the terrain they had crossed. The men failed to observe it, making no comment about it, but the barren stretches became more and more infrequent. Then, shortly after they set out one morning, fear gripped her as she saw a cloud of dust several miles to the southwest. It was being raised by a flock of sheep.

Hours passed, but none of the men noticed the dust as Alexandra watched it anxiously from the corners of her eyes. At midday, it was straight to the south and much closer, seeming painfully obvious to her. Snively finally saw it. "Look there!" he called out excitedly, pointing. "Look at that dust. Do you suppose a flock of sheep is stirring it up?"

The other two men peered to the south, then exclaimed in satisfaction. "That's what it is, Snively," Hinton replied happily. "Tie the pack horses to this brush here, and we'll go take a look."

Snively hastily tethered the pack horses at the side of the track, then mounted. They set out to the south across the rolling hills at a fast canter. Dust boiled up, and Alexandra hoped the stockman would notice it, but Hinton foresaw that possibility. After they had covered over half the distance to the flock, he slowed the pace to a trot, raising little dust.

When Hinton led the way into the concealment of trees on top of a hill, the flock was in a wide valley a mile away. The sheep had just been driven from another grazing area to the valley, the dust they had raised dissipating. They milled about in clusters and cropped the foliage as a stockman and several dogs watched over them.

Alexandra noticed a second stockman, or possibly a youth who was an apprentice, and three horses on the far side of the valley. He was beside a copse, building a hut at the edge of the trees. Dust in the distance caught her eye, and she looked at it more closely. It was from another flock that was several miles away.

As the bushrangers were discussing how they would deal with the stockman, their attitudes grimly nonchalant, Alexandra interrupted them and pointed out what she had seen. The men gazed across the valley.

Crowley shook his head skeptically and said that he saw nothing. "I don't see any of that either," Hinton agreed. "How about you, Snively?"

The younger man was silent for a moment, peering closely, then he nodded. "She's right," he announced. "There's two or three horses over by those trees, and I believe a man is over there. And there's dust from sheep over in that direction. She's got some eyes in her head."

"And a bloody big mouth," Crowley added, noting Hinton's sudden wary attitude. "Hinton, if there is another stockman, we can deal with two as easily as one. And another flock doesn't make any difference."

"It bloody does make a difference," Hinton replied emphatically. "If there's another flock only a few miles away, how far do you think we'd get with this one before we had men chasing us?"

"Bloody hell!" Crowley snarled. "I didn't come all this way to listen to reasons why we can't do what we came here for!"

"And I didn't come all this way to be shot down by a mob of bloody stockmen!" Hinton retorted, reining his horse around. "We'll find another flock that's safer to take, and that's the end of it!"

Crowley was speechless with rage, his scarred, bearded face pale and his eyes glaring. He turned to Alexandra, and she braced herself to duck, thinking for a moment that he was going to lash out at her. Then he jerked on his reins, wheeling his horse around to follow Hinton.

The two bushrangers were furiously silent until they were back at the track. Snively retrieved the pack horses, then Hinton and Crowley argued fiercely again. This time it was about the direction in which they should go. Hinton intended to leave the track and ride northwest to find another flock, but Crowley wanted to stay on the track and continue west.

"This bloody place is bad enough when we're following a track!" Crowley barked. "But at least we know that we're going where others have been. If we get off the track, we could bloody well get lost out here."

"Lost?" Hinton sneered. "Are we sniveling brats, or are we men? We can find our way about without getting lost!"

"How do you know? I've never been more than a few miles from a road or a track, and neither have you! In any event, why leave the track? We found one flock while following it, and we can find another!"

"And be seen with it, you fool! We saw the dust from a flock while we were on the track, so stockmen can see the dust from a flock that we drive on the track! We're going to have to get off it!"

The men raged and cursed at each other for a time, then the dispute ended as the other one had. Hinton angrily shouted that they were going northwest, and he was through arguing about it. Then he turned his horse off the track, leading Alexandra's horse. The other two men followed, but Crowley was furious.

Crossing the rugged terrain was far more arduous than traveling on the track, and the pace was much slower. Alexandra dodged flailing limbs as the horses pushed through thick brush and stands of trees, laboring over the rolling hills. Late that day, Hinton reined beside a small stream in a valley to camp for the night.

The argument between Crowley and Hinton resumed, the two men ranting and raving at each other. Along with his rabid anger, there was a taut edge of quaking fear in Crowley's voice as he insisted that they could become lost in the far reaches of the outback. Snively was prudently silent, but his attitude reflected complete agreement with Crowley.

Snively gathered wood for a fire, and Hinton roared at him that the smoke might be seen. Hearing that, Alexandra stopped measuring out the peas and rice and took out the cheese and ship biscuit. She cut slices of cheese and gathered up handfuls of the biscuit, then passed them out to the men.

Alexandra ate then pulled her blanket over her. The lack of a fire made the men's disquiet in their surroundings more acute, Hinton and Crowley sitting near each other despite their hostility. Looking up at the stars, Alexandra smiled as she heard them stirring uneasily, then she went to sleep.

The next day, she saw that there was ample reason to doubt Hinton's ability as a leader in the wilderness, because he had a very poor sense of direction. After skirting around steep hills and other obstacles in the line of travel, he often veered far off a northwesterly direction. They passed two flocks during the day, one so near that Alexandra could smell the sheep, but the bushrangers failed to detect them.

When they made camp that evening, Crowley heatedly insisted that they have a fire. "I'm not going to go through another dark night in this bloody weird place," he snarled. "And there's no reason not to have a fire, because it'll be seen by nothing but bloody wild animals!"

Obviously wanting a fire himself, Hinton relented. With a fire blazing, Alexandra prepared the usual hot meal, adding a generous portion of pickled cabbage on her plate. As the men were eating, she noticed with satisfaction that Crowley and Hinton had crusty brown spots on the back of their hands, the first sign of scurvy.

The following day, Hinton found a flock, a cloud of dust billowing up as it moved from one grazing area to another. He led the way in a wide circle, getting in front of the flock to look at it as it passed. Concealed in a thick stand of brush, Alexandra and the bushrangers watched as the sheep came into view a few hundred yards away.

Alexandra's attention was drawn by the people with the flock, a stockman, an Aborigine woman, and their offspring. The dozen or more children ranged from a baby the woman carried and the toddlers on her horse to youths who were driving the sheep. The man was most unusual of all, looking completely out of place in the outback.

Instead of stockman's garb, he wore a broadcloth frock coat, a high collar and cravat, and a top hat with a flared crown. Moreover, he was the only one doing nothing to help move the family and sheep. Small children helped the youths drive the sheep, while even the toddlers on the woman's horse clutched halter ropes and led five pack horses laden with supplies and equipment. The man worked over a sketchbook on his saddle horn, completely oblivious to the activity around him.

Crowley was eager to steal the sheep, commenting gleefully about the large flock. Alexandra knew what the fate of the family would be, and she had to restrain herself from voicing her horror. Then she relaxed as Hinton said that some of the youths were old enough to use firearms or might escape with word of what had happened. Another violent argument began, the two men screaming at each other for hours once again.

For the next two days, as they headed northwest, the men found no more flocks, and Crowley insisted that they had gone too far from the track to find any. It appeared to Alexandra that he was correct, because she saw no evidence of sheep herself. But on the morning of the third day, they came to a wide swath of tramped ground and foliage where a very large flock had been driven northward a few weeks before.

For once, Hinton and Crowley conversed instead of shouting at each other. Crowley expressed reservations about following the trail and going any farther from the track, wanting to turn back before they became lost. Hinton acknowledged that they were many miles from the track, but insisted that the trail made by the flock appeared very promising. The two men finally agreed to find the sheep and to examine the situation, and to turn back toward the track if some reason prevented their stealing them.

The trail the sheep had made led straight through a deep belt of boxwood. On the other side of the forest, the flock had been driven up and across a bare, rocky mountain that stretched east and west. As she rode across the crest of it with the bushrangers, Alexandra scanned the terrain ahead and saw where the flock was located. Miles away to the north, she saw a very faint smudge of dust on the horizon.

It took the bushrangers four days of tediously tracking the flock to find out what Alexandra had learned in a moment on the mountaintop. The trail first led northwest to several hundred acres of savanna, with a hut and a huge, well-built fold of logs and brush in the center of it. The sheep had grazed there for a time, and after searching for a day, the men found the trail where they had been driven to a similar pasture to the east. From there, the flock had been driven northwest again.

During the afternoon of the fourth day, Hinton led the way across a dry creek bed and up a forested slope on the other side of it. In the trees at the top of the hill, he reined and lifted a hand for the others to stop. A valley some three miles long and almost a mile wide lay ahead where the flock grazed. Crowley and Snively moved up beside Hinton, and the three men looked at the flock, discussing it.

Alexandra leaned from side to side, peering through the trees. At the top of a hill on the opposite side of the valley was another of the large, secure folds, with a hut in the shade of trees near it, and a pond surrounded by tall trees at one side of the hill. Below the fold was a wide swath of bare ground where the sheep had trampled down the grass and brush when they had been taken to pasture and returned at night.

The sheep were loosely bunched at a distance up the valley, and some ten dogs were scattered around them. Three horses grazed on a rise overlooking the flock, two of them hobbled and the other one with a saddle. A man sat on the ground near the horses, and Alexandra's anxiety increased as she craned her neck and scanned the entire valley. Although the flock was a very large one, it appeared that only a single stockman tended it.

The bushrangers had come to the same conclusion, and Crowley commented in a grimly gleeful tone, "This is the one we've been looking for, Hinton. It's a long way from other flocks, the biggest one that we've seen, and there's just one stockman."

"I can't see but one from here," Hinton agreed cautiously. "Let's go closer on foot and get a better look."

When the horses were tethered, Alexandra followed the bushrangers as they went down the hill, angling up the valley toward the sheep. As the trees thinned out, Hinton led the way through the thickest brush on the slope, working closer to the flock, then stopped several hundred yards from it.

At the lower elevation, all of the valley's shallow hollows and contours were in clear view, and Alexandra saw that there was indeed only one stockman with the flock. The bushrangers discussed that in ruthless satisfaction, then talked about how to steal the sheep.

"We'll make camp at that dry creek on the other side of the hill," Hinton said, "then wait until just before dawn. It'll be easier to deal with him then, and less chance that one of us will get shot. The sheep will also be in the fold and easier for us to handle."

While the men talked, Alexandra watched the dogs. When she and the bushrangers had come down the slope, the dogs had been sitting and lying down as they watched the sheep. Now the nearest dogs were pacing restlessly, glancing over the sheep and looking toward the brush where she and the men were hidden. She hoped they would bark in warning, but they merely continued moving and looking.

The stockman stood up, tucking a double-barrel musket under his arm. He took the hobbles off the two spare horses, then led them by their halter ropes to the saddled horse and mounted it. He rode around to the side of the flock toward the head of the valley, then uncoiled a long whip and snapped it, the loud report ringing out like a gunshot.

A surge of motion passed through the flock, each sheep turning away from the crack of the whip and trotting a few paces. The sheep now headed toward the pond and fold, and moved down the valley at a slow walk, grazing along the way. The dogs raced back and forth at the sides of the flock, heading off sheep that tried to break away.

"That stockman looks familiar," Hinton mused, combing his fingers through his ragged, blond beard. "He looks a lot like that bloody foreman who tried to make me marry that woman I knocked up."

"The foreman?" Crowley replied, shaking his head. "What would that bastard be doing here, Hinton? That stockman is a hefty size right enough, but he couldn't be that foreman. I wish he was, though, so we could spend about a week at doing him in an inch at a time."

Hinton laughed grimly, then shrugged. "Whoever he is, he's seen his last sunrise. Let's get back to that dry creek bed and make camp."

The man also seemed vaguely familiar to Alexandra, but he was too far away for her to see his features. She followed the bushrangers as they began moving quietly back up the hill, and glanced over her shoulder at the stockman, trying to think where she might have seen him before. Then she dismissed it, thinking about the situation confronting her.

If the men's plans materialized, Hinton would turn her over to Crowley and Snively the next day. Her only hope of escaping that fate lay in doing what the most basic considerations of humanity demanded of her. She had to find a way to help the stockman, or at the very least warn him that the bushrangers were nearby and intended to kill him.

David Kerrick already knew that someone was nearby. As always when they detected strangers, his dogs had been uneasy. Someone had been across the valley from the flock, but the behavior of the dogs now indicated that the intruders had left the valley.

As he followed the flock toward the pond, David speculated that the dogs had detected some Aborigines. They wandered through the area from time to time and often wanted some mutton which he always gave them. Sometimes they loitered in the vicinity for a day or two before revealing themselves, and what had happened that day had occurred before.

Other than Aborigines, the possibilities were few. Although he was grazing his own flock now, he was sure that Pat Garrity would visit to bring some supplies and see how he was faring as a gesture of friendship. However, he had left Wayamba Station only a few weeks before, so it was much too soon for Pat to visit, and if it had been him, the station owner would have simply ridden down into the valley.

The sun was low when the sheep reached the pond, swarming around it and drinking thirstily. The dogs joined them, and as David rode through the sheep and into the water to let his horses drink, he weighed the single remaining possibility of who the strangers could be—bushrangers, intending to kill him and steal his sheep.

It was unlikely since his station was hundreds of miles from where bushrangers usually prowled, but he recalled an incident that Pat had told him about. Many years before, bushrangers had attacked Pat and Mayrah, intending to murder them and steal their sheep. Pat had been shot through the leg and Mayrah had been left with the deep scar across her forehead.

After the animals drank, David signaled the dogs.

Racing around the flock, the dogs moved the sheep away from the pond. David cracked his whip, riding around the flock, and the dogs took their positions on the flanks as the sheep moved up the hill to the fold. Following them, David continued musing about the strangers' identities.

In all probability, he reflected, the dogs had detected Aborigines, but a warning voice in the back of his mind kept him from dismissing the more ominous possibility.

Chapter Eleven

"What happened to all of it?" Hinton roared, slapping at Alexandra. "There was a whole cheese and a full cask of ship biscuit!"

Alexandra dodged the slap, moving back from him. "They were simply used up," she protested. "They could last only so long."

"No, you wasted them, that's what happened!" he bellowed. "You're a bloody useless slut! Bloody useless!"

"It's just as well that they're gone," Crowley grumbled, "because I'm sick of cheese and biscuit. Hinton, there's no reason why we can't have a fire and cooked rations. That stockman won't see the smoke."

Hinton hesitated, looking around at the edge of the trees beside the dry creek bed as dusk settled. Then he shrugged and nodded. "Go ahead, then," he growled. "I don't want a big fire, though. And keep the horses tethered instead of hobbling them. They want water, and they might wander over into that valley where that stockman will see them."

The men tethered the horses as Alexandra gathered firewood, then took out the water jug and bags of food. A few minutes later, with a fire blazing at the edge of the sandy creek bed, the men sat around it and talked as she prepared the meal. Very little of the salt pork remaining, she had only a few thin slices of it frying in a pan.

"She's been wasting the pork as well," Hinton growled, eyeing the pan. "But tomorrow we'll have all of the mutton we can eat."

Crowley commented in agreement, then suddenly reached out and pinched Alexandra's thigh with brutal force. "Mutton won't be the only thing that I'll have tomorrow," he added, grinning lewdly.

The bushrangers howled with laughter, and Alexandra bit her lip to keep from crying out in pain as she moved away from Crowley.

"Mutton won't be the only thing I'll have either," Snively remarked happily.

"You'll wait your bloody turn!" Crowley snarled. "You'll get what's left when I'm finished with her, and that won't be much."

"It'll be enough for me," Snively replied, leering at Alexandra. "As long as she's still alive and kicking, I'll be satisfied."

The men laughed raucously again, and Alexandra's thigh throbbed painfully and her stomach churned with fear and revulsion. As she finished cooking and served the food, the men spoke of their plan to kill the stockman and drive the sheep eastward. Alexandra stepped away from the fire with her plate, then put it down untouched, in too much of a turmoil to eat.

Listening to the bushrangers, she was acutely aware that she had no plan of her own. Once she aligned herself with the stockman against Hinton and the other men, she was certain she would be doomed unless the men were killed. But the stockman was only one man against three murderous criminals, and at an extreme disadvantage. She needed to help the man fight the bushrangers, but she knew of nothing that she could do.

It occurred to her that even if the bushrangers were killed, she could be exchanging three cruel tormentors for one who would be no better. From what she had heard, at least some stockmen were dissolute, shameless men. She thought about the man, wondering if she had really seen him before, or if he had only reminded her of someone whom she had met. Then she dismissed it, as the bushrangers were still very much the immediate problem.

When they finished eating, she went to get the dishes. As she stacked the plates and pannikins, Crowley reached to pinch her again, and she dodged away. The bushrangers howled with laughter. "Come tomorrow, you'll have to move faster than that to get away from me," he sneered, smiling grimly. Then he turned to Hinton. "She'll have to be left here while we're dealing with the stockman."

"Aye, that's right," Hinton agreed. "But to make sure that she can't cause us any trouble, I'll truss her up like the swine she is."

Alexandra moved away from the fire again. Using a sparing amount of water from the jug, she washed the dishes and listened to the conversation. Replying to a question from Snively, Hinton said that they would go to the stockman's hut on foot since the horses would make too much noise. Then he added that they would stay awake all night to avoid any chance of oversleeping, so that they would arrive at the hut just before dawn.

After washing the dishes, Alexandra covered herself with her blanket, then suddenly thought of the muskets and pistols among the things the bushrangers had stolen. After the men left, she reflected, she could free herself with the knife in her hem, take some of the weapons, and follow them. When they were near the hut, she could begin shooting, hopefully killing at least one of them while alerting the stockman with the gunfire.

Her hopes starting to soar, she firmly controlled her optimism, separating wishful thinking from what she realistically might be able to do. Then it seemed a possibility, but no more than that.

She had seen the weapons only once, when the bushrangers had sorted out their plunder at their hideout, and she was unable to recall if there had been gunpowder flasks and bullet pouches among the loot. Logically, the men had taken them as well, but if there were none in the baggage, the weapons would be useless. Or if there were, Hinton might remember the weapons and take them with him as an extra precaution.

Despite the uncertainties, she was still eagerly hopeful. At least there was the possibility that she might be effective, a promise that tomorrow would bring her freedom from the bushrangers instead of worse torture. She turned and looked at them, the scene like a somber, tortured Hogarthian spectacle.

The flames highlighted the planes of Crowley's scarred, bearded face and cast the hollows into shadows, making it look even crueler. Snively's eyes and teeth shone in a fixed, malevolent grin as he and the other two discussed their evil, murderous scheme. Hinton was fiendish, his birthmark looking like blood in the firelight. Spittle gleamed on his thick lips, his icy blue eyes were merciless and his ugly face was framed by his greasy, blond hair and beard. Filled with loathing for the three men, Alexandra turned away from them.

The conversation between the bushrangers gradually became fitful, then died away. One of them occasionally tossed wood on the fire, which flared for a few minutes and then burned down. Alexandra lay and looked up at the slow movement of the moon and stars as the hours passed, fervently hoping that her plan against the bushrangers would work.

Late in the night, Hinton suddenly snarled an oath and cuffed Snively roughly. "I said to stay awake!" he barked angrily. "If me and Crowley can stay awake, then you can too!"

Snively yelped in pain and surprise, falling over from his sitting position and sprawling, then he climbed to his feet. "I wasn't really asleep," he said defensively. "I just closed my eyes for a minute."

"You were asleep! Now stay awake!"

Snively sighed, tossing wood on the fire as he sat down again. The fire blazed once more as the men sat around it in silence, then it began to die. Alexandra was too tense to sleep, but she closed her eyes and tried to rest for what the next day would bring. She listened to the insects chirping, the mournful call of night birds, and the other chorus of sounds of the outback at night, waiting for time to pass.

At last, Hinton muttered to the others, throwing wood on the fire. The bushrangers stood up, stretching and yawning, and checked their weapons. Hinton picked up lengths of rope from the baggage and bent over Alexandra. He took her arm and jerked her over onto her stomach, then twisted both of her arms behind her back.

"You're not going to get loose from this," he growled, wrapping a rope tightly around her wrists and tying it. He kicked her feet together, then tied her ankles, pulling on the rope and making it bite into her as he knotted it. "There, that'll hold you until we get back."

"And I'll take it off when we get back," Crowley added, chuckling in anticipation as he stooped over Alexandra.

"Leave that until later," Hinton said irritably. "We've got more important things to do now. Get a light over here and make sure there's no sharp rocks or anything she can use to cut that rope."

Crowley went to the fire for a burning stick, then returned to Alexandra and searched the area around her. Satisfied, he returned to the fire and flung the stick onto it. She waited breathlessly to see if Hinton or the other men would think of the weapons in the baggage, then relaxed with a sigh of relief as they went into the trees and started up the hill.

After forcing herself to wait until she was certain they were gone, she gathered up the skirt of her dress with her fingers and slipped the knife out of the hem. Wedging the knife between her feet, she sawed at the rope binding her hands, and gasped in pain as the rope bit deeper into her wrists. The rope finally went slack, slipping off her wrists.

She cut the rope around her ankles and quickly went to the baggage. Finding the long, heavy pack containing the weapons, she dragged it to the fire and opened it. She pushed the muskets and pistols aside and smiled happily when she found a dozen shot pouches and powder flasks. Then her heart sank as she looked at the weapons more closely. The flints were gone from the hammers.

Without flints to ignite the gunpowder in the flash pans, the weapons were as useless as they would be without ammunition. Emptying the pack, Alexandra searched in vain for at least one flint, then sat back with a despondent sigh. It appeared that at some point, Hinton had thrown away the flints in the event she managed to get and load one of the firearms without being seen. With her only weapon now a small knife, her plan was impossible, and she thought again about what to do.

She looked at the baggage, then at the horses tethered nearby. For the first time since the bushrangers had captured her, she had ready access to ample supplies and the horses, a perfect chance to escape. Hours would pass before they returned, giving her time to leave, and she could strand them by taking all of the horses.

Nothing had ever been so tempting to her because she would be free of the men at last. But she would be entirely alone in a perilous, unfamiliar wilderness, and fleeing also smacked of cowardice to her. A man had been marked for death, and to flee and leave him to his fate without even trying to warn him was craven.

Of equal importance, a fiery yearning for revenge against the bushrangers seethed inside her. Stranding them in the wilderness was not enough. She detested them with a searing intensity more demanding than any emotion she had ever known, and she wanted them dead.

Pondering the situation again, she was unable to think of any way to balance the odds between the bushrangers and the stockman. But Hinton and the other two men thought she was securely tied, which gave her the advantage of surprise. Further, she knew that her only opportunity to help herself had arrived and time was running out. She had to do something—anything.

Finally, she decided to follow the bushrangers and look for any circumstances she could exploit, and then to shout and alert the stockman if nothing better offered itself. While that seemed very little, at least it was something. She moved toward the trees.

When she reached the other side of the hill, the moon had set, but the sky was clear and the stars bright in the hour before dawn. As she went down into the valley, the trees thinned and she could see a few yards ahead. Then the forest fell behind her, and she walked rapidly through the tall grass, the clumps of brush thicker shadows in the dim light.

Straining her eyes, she could barely make out the hill where the fold and stockman's hut were located almost four hundred yards away. The bare swath below the fold where the sheep had trampled down the foliage was a light blur, flanked by tall brush and grass. Alexandra started across the valley, watching and listening for the bushrangers, but they were apparently well ahead of her. As she ran from one stand of brush to the next, the first light of dawn touched the horizon.

Alexandra ran the last hundred yards, angling toward the brush on the right side of the bare stretch below the fold. Reaching it, she peered up the slope and made out the forms of the bushrangers creeping toward the hut. She hesitated for a moment, then drew in a deep breath, cupped her hands around her mouth, and screamed at the top of her voice.

As her scream shattered the stillness, the dogs began snarling beside the fold at the top of the hill. Then pandemonium erupted in the fold, the sheep frightened by the dogs and surging about as they bleated. His voice ringing out over the bedlam, Hinton roared in fury, "I'll kill you for that, you conniving slut! Come on, men!"

The bushrangers raced on up the slope, and Alexandra watched the hut for movement. Seeing none, she gasped in dismay as the men ran inside it. The stockman had failed to react, and his dogs were unable to help him, because for some reason they were apparently tethered beside the fold. Alexandra waited for the shots that would end the man's life.

But there were no shots. A moment later, as dawn spreaded across the sky, the bushrangers came back outside. Baffled and enraged, they looked around in the thin light as the uproar at the fold continued. Hinton lifted his musket, venting his fury at Alexandra. "You sly bloody cow!" he roared. "I'll teach you to set yourself against me!"

As he shouldered the musket, Alexandra started to jump into the brush. Then, halfway up the slope in the foliage on the left of the bare ground, she saw a bright flame in the lingering light. The flare of gunpowder igniting in a flash pan was followed by a tongue of flame from a musket barrel as the sharp report rang out over the noise from the fold. Snively, who was standing completely in the open, staggered back and fell.

The other two men scrambled for cover, running into the dense growth down the slope from the hut.

Alexandra leaped into the brush beside her, realizing that the stockman had known all along that the bushrangers were near, and had been waiting for them. But the issue was far from settled. The stockman was one man against two wily, vicious criminals. She crept through the foliage up the hill to get Snively's weapons.

The men traded shots on the other side of the open swath as Alexandra worked her way up the hill. The stockman was well-armed, firing three times in quick succession as the bushrangers tried to rush him. Crowley bellowed an oath in pain, apparently grazed by a bullet, then he and Hinton became more cautious. The acrid haze of gunpowder smoke wafted across the bare ground to Alexandra as she passed the men.

The sun was rising as she stepped out of the brush near the top of the hill, and the sheep still bleated in a tumult that muffled the gunshots down the slope. Snively moved feebly, and Alexandra took her knife out of her coat pocket as she crossed the bare expanse below the fold to where he lay a few yards from the hut.

Then she saw that he was no longer a threat. Shot through the lungs, he was near death, his shirt soaked with blood and his face blanched. His eyes followed her as she picked up his musket, then he weakly lifted a hand and put it on the pistol in his belt as she started to take it. "Help me," he whispered. "Please help me."

"There's nothing I can do," she replied coldly, pushing his hand aside and taking the pistol. "And nothing I wish to do, because the world will be a better place without you." She took his shot pouch and gunpowder flask, putting them in her coat pocket as she stood up. "You chose the way you would die when you chose the way you lived, Snively."

Moving away from him, she listened to the shots and watched the gunpowder smoke rising from the foliage. One of the men was straight down the hill from her, while the other one was off to the right and farther down, trying to work his way around the stockman to catch the man in a crossfire. Carrying the long, cumbersome musket and the heavy pistol, Alexandra went down the slope toward the nearest bushranger.

Creeping quietly through the brush, Alexandra looked at the weapons and saw spots of rust on them. They had been neglected, and the touchholes—the openings through which fire traveled from the flash pan into the breeches to ignite the charges—could be plugged with gunpowder soot and rust which would make the weapons misfire. With no time to check them, she stopped long enough to pour extra measures of gunpowder into the flash pans in case the touchholes were partially clogged.

The dense growth was a mixture of bright light and thick shadows in the early sunlight, as Alexandra descended the hill. When a shot rang out some thirty feet away, she craned her neck to look ahead as she eased from one wiry bush to the next. Then she glimpsed the bushranger. It was Crowley, lying on his stomach behind a clump of matted growth and hastily reloading his musket as he peered down the slope.

The long, heavy musket was awkward for her to handle in the close confines of the foliage, and Alexandra put it down as she knelt behind a bush. She pulled the hammer back on the pistol and held it with both hands, resting the thick barrel on a limb in the bush. Peering down the barrel at Crowley's back, she drew in a deep breath and steeled herself against jerking when the hammer fell, then slowly squeezed the trigger.

The hammer slapped forward, the flint in its jaws knocking the flash pan lid open and spilling a shower of sparks onto the gunpowder. Hearing the loud, metallic snap of the lock, Crowley propped himself on one elbow and looked over his shoulder. His callous, bearded face reflected astonishment and terror as a fountain of fire and smoke boiled up from the overcharge in the flash pan on the pistol, and he rolled to one side.

Her teeth clenched, Alexandra ignored the fire as it singed her eyebrows and covered her face with soot. She squinted through the smoke and swung the pistol, tracking Crowley with it. An instant later, smoke belched from the pistol as it fired with a loud report. A large hole appeared in his shirt above his belt, the heavy ball ripping into his stomach. His face twisted in agony and shock for an instant, then in rage as he lurched up from the ground and swung his musket toward Alexandra.

As Crowley stood up, Alexandra prepared to jump back into the thicket brush, then a shot rang out down the hill. The musket ball tore through Crowley's neck, and his throat was suddenly a mass of raw flesh, blood spurting. His eyes and mouth opening wide, he dropped his musket and collapsed. He uttered choked, gagging sounds as his limbs jerked convulsively, stirring the foliage, and his life ebbed.

At a distance to the right and down the hill, Hinton fired at the stockman who fired back. Her eyes stinging from the gunpowder soot and her hands trembling with tension, Alexandra blew down the pistol barrel and on the flash pan to dispose of any hot sparks. She reloaded the weapon, setting the ball and powder charge with the ramrod under the barrel, then poured gunpowder into the flash pan and closed the lid. While Hinton and the stockman occasionally exchanged fire, Alexandra picked up the musket and crawled down the slope toward the bushranger.

When she was about forty yards from Hinton, he apparently became concerned because the other bushrangers had stopped shooting. "Crowley!" he shouted. "Where are you? Are you all right?"

"He can't answer you, Hinton!" Alexandra called, laughing in satisfaction. "He's burning in the fires of perdition! When you join him presently, you and he will be in suitable company again!"

Hinton roared a stream of profanity, then the foliage thrashed as he crouched low and ran down the hill. Alexandra raced after him, determined to keep him from getting a horse and escaping. The wiry limbs clawed at her and caught the musket barrel as she dashed through the brush, but Hinton ran with a slow, clumsy pace, and she gained on him.

At the foot of the hill, the bushes were smaller and thinning, and Alexandra glimpsed the bushranger. She stopped and dropped the musket, then cocked the pistol. As he zigzagged between clumps of foliage, she held the weapon at arm's length and took aim, waiting for a clear shot. When he ran across an opening, she squeezed the trigger and tracked him as the hammer fell and the flash pan flared.

The ball clipped twigs behind Hinton and forced him into a burst of speed. Pushing the pistol under her belt, Alexandra picked up the musket and dashed from one thicket to another while crossing the valley, reaching the other side without Hinton's stopping to fire at her. Certain that he would, she veered to the left as he went straight up the slope on the other side of the valley.

Over the noise she made as she ran, Alexandra clearly heard Hinton's awkward, pounding footsteps and his heavy crashing through the growth. Some fifty yards to his left, she gradually pulled abreast of him. He stopped, evidently intending to wait and shoot at her. She slowed to a fast walk and moved quietly up the slope. When he resumed running a few minutes later, Alexandra had reached the trees near the top of the hill.

Entering the forest, she crossed the hill and went down the other side. At the dry creek bed, she moved stealthily through the edge of the trees toward the camp. Just as she saw the horses, she heard Hinton sliding and stumbling as he hurried down the slope.

Alexandra eased forward from tree to tree until the camp was in full view, then she stood behind a large eucalyptus and peered around it, cocking the musket.

Hinton slid to a stop beside the saddles and baggage, looking back and holding his musket ready to fire as he panted breathlessly from running. After a moment, seeing no pursuit, he relaxed. Lowering the musket, he watched the forested slope as his breathing gradually became even. Finally, he loosened the pistol in his belt as he put down the musket, then he picked up a saddle and turned toward the horses. Alexandra stepped from behind the tree, aiming her musket at him.

Hinton recoiled in shock as he dropped the saddle. Moving toward his musket, he stopped as her finger tightened on the trigger. The unblemished side of his face was pasty white, his pale blue eyes gleaming with fear as he licked his thick lips. "I didn't do anything that really hurt you," he muttered defensively. "It wasn't anything that somebody else wouldn't do sooner or later. Let me take one horse, and I'll leave you all my money and everything else."

"No. You destroyed my life, and now I'm going to take yours."

Beads of sweat shining on his ugly face, he licked his lips again. Then he waited for her to pull the trigger, ready to try to avoid the bullet in the fraction of a second between the flare of the flash pan and when the weapon fired. Alexandra braced herself to swing the heavy musket and keep it pointed at him as it fired, then she tugged on the trigger.

As the hammer fell, fire and smoke shot up from the overcharge in the flash pan. Hinton threw himself to one side, falling to the ground and rolling. Her eyes stinging from the fire and smoke, Alexandra ignored the pain and tracked the man with the musket, keeping it aimed at him. Then the smoke dissipated, and the weapon misfired.

Hinton scrambled to his feet, jerking the pistol from under his belt and training it on Alexandra. As he seized control of the situation, his fear was instantly replaced by his usual overbearing, swaggering attitude, and he laughed in gleeful triumph. "So you're going to take my life are you?" he sneered. "You'd best think again, you stupid bitch!"

A movement at one side catching her eye, Alexandra glanced and then looked. The stockman had just stepped quietly through the trees, out of Hinton's line of vision, and was aiming a double-barrel musket at the bushranger.

As she looked back at Hinton, he smiled sourly. "You conniving slut!" he jeered. "Trying to make me look the other way so you can run into the trees, aren't you? Well, I'm not that stupid, and you'll never get rid of me. I can get rid of you, but you'll never be rid of me."

He started to say more, then broke off in shock as both hammers on the musket fell with a loud snap. As he started to turn his head to look, the weapon fired with a shattering roar, a cloud of smoke boiling from the barrels. Hinton's hat flicked off, the hair on the left side of his head stirred, and the right side of his skull exploded into a spray of bloody tissue, bone, and hair. The impact of the bullets pitched him sideways, his pistol firing harmlessly into the ground as he fell.

The stockman stepped through the gunpowder smoke, and Alexandra immediately recognized him from when they had met in Parramatta. The shock of recognition, combined with the overwhelming relief she now felt, rendered her momentarily speechless. The stockman, too, seemed very withdrawn, gazing at her in somber silence. Alexandra was the first to recover herself.

"My name is Alexandra Hammond," she told him, "and I'm most grateful for your timely assistance. You helped me once before when my situation was far less dire. It was in Parramatta, and you replaced a wheel that had come off my buggy. But perhaps you don't recall the incident."

Still reserved, it appeared that he had to exert an almost physical effort to draw his gaze away from her. Then he nodded, turning to the baggage. "Yes, I remember it well," he replied quietly.

Puzzled by his aloof attitude, it suddenly occurred to Alexandra that her grimy, disheveled appearance might have led him to believe that she was the bushrangers' woman and had turned against them for some reason. "In the event you think I wanted to be with those men, let me assure you that you're entirely mistaken. They abducted me near Sydney—"

"How could I think such a thing?" he interrupted impatiently, frowning at her. "It's obvious that you were abducted." He turned back to the baggage and began sorting through it. "I can see that you're anything but a trollop, Mistress Hammond, as could anyone with eyes in his head."

"Then I'm on beam's ends in trying to understand the reason for your manner," she retorted. "Could you at least be so kind as to tell me your name? Even though our conversation is strangely halting, considering the circumstances, I would like to know to whom I am speaking."

He glanced at her again, then picked up two pack-saddles and carried them toward the horses. "I'm David Kerrick."

In the aftermath of the rapid flow of events during the past hour, it took Alexandra a second to recall why the name was so familiar. Then she gazed at him in shock, realizing that he was a convicted murderer and her family's deadly enemy, the man who had killed her cousin.

An hour later, at the hut below the fold, Alexandra was still trying to come to terms with what had happened. She looked down the hill, watching David Kerrick. After stacking the baggage beside the hut, he had used three horses to take the bodies to the foot of the slope, where he buried them.

When he finished and came back up the hill with the horses, Alexandra experienced a growing discomfort that overcame all her other feelings. It was something entirely new to her, a reaction to David Kerrick simply as a man and unrelated to him personally. Analyzing it, she realized that the brutal mistreatment by the bushrangers had created a lingering effect of distrust within her toward men in general.

He stopped at a tree near the hut, where he had tethered the other horses. As he untied them, her gaze met his in mutual wariness, a silent acknowledgment of the abyss of hostility between them. Gathering up the halter ropes, he started to turn away, then looked back at her. "That mutton hanging beside the hut is fresh," he told her. "Make free use of it or anything else here that you might need."

Her sense of courtesy demanding a response, Alexandra managed a cold nod.

David led the horses to the fold where he untied his dogs. Then he opened the gate, and the sheep poured out and down the slope. As the dogs raced beside the sheep and kept them in a wide column, David followed the flock, riding a horse and leading the others.

When he was gone, Alexandra sat beside the smoldering ashes of the fire in front of the hut. She idly tossed twigs on the coals, a confused muddle of thoughts tugging at her mind. Most of all, she remained dazed by the twist of fate that had freed her from the bushrangers only to leave her with David Kerrick.

For weeks, her every waking moment had been dominated by her urgent need to escape from the bushrangers. Now that she was free of them, she remained trapped in another way, this time by hundreds of miles of deserted wilderness that separated her from her family. Even trying to find the stockmen to the south would be perilous. She could get lost or die of thirst and starvation. And of all people on earth, no one was near except her cousin's murderer.

Wisps of smoke rose from the twigs as she threw them onto the coals, then the wood burst into flames. Alexandra looked at the fire, her innate refusal to be defeated asserting itself. While she was far from her family, the bushrangers were dead and she no longer had to live in constant terror of being brutally raped. Somehow, she would eventually make her way back to her family and try to rebuild her life.

Alexandra stood up, thinking about her immediate needs and forcing aside other matters for the moment. She was hungry and weary, but her ragged, grimy state was her first concern, having galled her for weeks. At the foot of the hill, the pond fed a brook, a place where at last she could bathe in privacy. She searched the baggage for a dress and other things among the clothes the bushrangers had stolen.

Looking back, David saw that Alexandra was moving about the hut. Although she had resurrected the array of tormenting emotions that he had thought he had left behind, he felt sympathy for her. He knew how she must have suffered as a captive of the bushrangers, and he was relieved that she was busying herself instead of merely sitting dejectedly, as before.

He wanted to help her and to comfort her, and at the same time, he had a driving urge to run away from her. The agonizing memories of betrayal that she had brought back to him were a somber warning of the penalty he had once paid for being drawn to beauty and charm. Cracking his whip, he kept the sheep moving at a fast walk up the valley until it curved, wanting to leave the hut and the beautiful woman behind.

Near the head of the valley, the sheep cropped the foliage. He hobbled the horses and sat under a tree, watching the animals. The valley looked the same as before, yet at this moment it was entirely different.

During the previous days, it had been a scene in the new life he had made for himself. Now his past had reached out and caught up with him, his old life and all of its turmoil intruding upon the new.

The bushrangers had been little more than an annoyance, merely a physical threat. Disposing of them had been hazardous but straightforward. However, they had brought with them one who was completely innocent of any wrongdoing, but who was a far greater danger. She created an attack from within him, one he was unable to fight.

In a sense, it was also an assault in which he conspired, savaging himself. Although his love for his former wife was poisoned with a sense of betrayal, turning it into a caustic, devouring force that was agonizing, he resisted giving it up. Instead, he had put it aside and occupied his mind with other thoughts, but that love still remained too much a part of his very being for him to exorcise it from his life.

For the first time, in almost two years, he took out his watch and opened it, looking at the miniature. From when they had first met, his love for his wife had been his sole purpose in life. Everything else had been subordinate, including his work which had merely been a source of money to buy presents that would bring a smile to her lovely face. His lack of moderation had laid the ground for disaster, blinding him to her faults, and leaving him with no refuge when that infirm foundation of his life had collapsed.

The hours passed, as Kerrick sat gazing at the portrait. When late afternoon arrived, he had mixed feelings as he moved the flock back down the valley. He was reluctant to return to the hut, wanting to avoid Alexandra, but he was concerned about her after her ordeal and wondered what she was doing. At the same time, which created a far more severe conflict within him, he also looked forward to seeing her.

The hut came into view. Smoke rose from the fire and as he drew closer to the hill, David saw that

Alexandra had on a dark dress instead of the ragged clothes she had worn, and she was cooking. The flock reached the pond, the thirsty sheep and dogs wading into it to drink. David rode into the water to let the horses drink, then he signaled the dogs and drove the flock up the hill.

As he followed the sheep to the fold, he passed several yards from the hut. Alexandra ignored him, not even glancing up as she knelt beside the fire and stirred a pot. Upon reflection, it was nothing more than the attitude that David had expected her to have toward him, a convicted murderer who had killed her relative.

He tried to regard her with similar reserve, but it was impossible. She was bewitching, her face having a delicate, classical beauty, yet revealing the proud, determined spirit that the bushrangers had been unable to break. It was framed by long, thick brown hair that caught highlights in the setting sun. Wearing a shapeless dungaree dress and heavy shoes, she was still incomparably lovely, just as she had been in the costly clothes she had worn the first time he had seen her.

After securing the sheep, David tethered the horses for the night and went to the hut with the dogs following him. Having eaten nothing since the previous evening, he was famished, and the food that Alexandra was preparing smelled far more appetizing than when he cooked. She continued to ignore him as he put his musket down beside the hut and walked to the fire. A strained, hostile silence hung between them.

Glancing around, David saw that she had been hard at work during the day. The baggage and cooking utensils around the fire and hut were in meticulously neat order, and a large pile of firewood was stacked tidily at one side. "There's no need for you to do any work here," he told her. "It certainly isn't expected of you."

"I don't like to be idle," she replied coldly, still not looking at him as she turned the mutton on the spit. "While I'm here, I'll do my share of the work. Dinner will be ready soon."

In the hut, David gathered up his shaving gear and went to the pond. Later he returned to the hut, put his things away, and sat down beside the fire.

There was a tense, awkward quiet between them again, a wall of silent distrust. Alexandra took one of the mutton roasts off the spit and cut it up, feeding the dogs, then dished up the food for David and herself. She concentrated on what she was doing, trying to control the uneasiness she now had over being near any man, and her aversion to David in particular. Taking her plate and tea, she sat on the other side of the fire.

As he ate, David found that the food not only smelled more appetizing than what he cooked, but it tasted much better, and Alexandra had supplemented his supplies with those in the baggage. The roast was tender and juicy, and the excess fat that sometimes gave mutton a strong flavor had been trimmed off. The peas and beans were seasoned with bits of fried pork, and the pickled cabbage was a delicious accompaniment.

"The food is very tasty," he commented.

Alexandra shrugged, glancing across the fire at him, then looking away. "It will suffice for a meal," she replied indifferently.

With the firelight shining on her lovely face, she was a vision of beauty, and David had to keep himself from staring at her. After a moment, he spoke again, "I know you want to return to your family as soon as possible. Wayamba Station is south of here, and it's owned by Patrick Garrity. He can help you get back to Sydney, but I can't leave my flock and take you to Wayamba. However, I'm sure that Pat will visit, and you can go back with him."

The remarks indicated concern which surprised

Alexandra. David's reserve had led her to expect nothing of that nature, and after the weeks of the bushrangers' callous brutality, being treated with kindness by a man almost seemed strange to her. "I realize that you can't leave your sheep," she told him. "When do you expect Mr. Garrity to visit?"

"It'll probably be late summer, after the worst danger of grass fires is past. When you leave, you can take those horses and the bushrangers' belongings because they're yours as far as I'm concerned. They're worth more than enough to hire an escort to take you to Sydney."

"My father will pay for my transportation costs. The chestnut gelding is my horse, but the other horses and the rest of the things are yours by right of forfeiture. You killed the bushrangers, not I."

"I had a great deal of help, which I appreciated."

Alexandra dismissed the subject with a shrug, and both of them fell silent again. After they ate, she washed the dishes in a water bucket, and David got his blanket and brought it to the fire. Sitting down, and puffing on his pipe, he looked across the fire at Alexandra. "You can sleep in the hut, if you wish," he suggested.

Alexandra nodded her thanks, stacking the dishes beside the fire. She went to the baggage for her blanket and took it into the hut. Surrounded by Kerrick's belongings, she experienced a twinge of the disquiet that she now felt when near a man. She shrugged off the feeling, wondering if it would continue to haunt her after she returned to Sydney. That seemed irrelevant, however, because she knew no man of her choice would show an interest in her after her captivity.

Looking out the doorway at David, she thought about his attitude toward her. His kindness toward her had seemed to be motivated by something more than an innate sense of courtesy. Although he had murdered her cousin, she had to admit that he was anything but a common criminal. No man could be more different from the bushrangers.

As he smoked his pipe, he took a hardwood stick and a knife from his coat pocket. His back to Alexandra, she was unable to see what he was doing, but he appeared to whittle on the stick for a moment before putting it and the knife away again. Then he took out a watch and opened the lid. At first she thought he was looking at the time, but he continued gazing at the watch as the minutes passed. He was still sitting beside the fire and staring at the watch when Alexandra fell asleep.

She woke before dawn when David stirred the ashes of the fire and stoked it. He went to check on the sheep and horses, and the dogs followed him into the thick darkness away from the fire. Alexandra rolled up her blanket and left the hut. Picking up the utensils, she prepared breakfast, making porridge and tea. Hearing David's footsteps, she put the pan and billy on a rock beside the fire.

After sitting down, David ate. "This is very good," he commented, "and I appreciate your preparing it. But you're under no obligation to see to anything other than your own needs."

"I realize that," she replied. "But I am being accommodated, and as I told you last evening, I'll do my share of the work while I'm here." She put leftover pieces of mutton and damper in a cloth, then tied up the corners. "This is for your tiffin."

David reached to take it, but instead of handing it to him, she placed the cloth on a rock between them. Then she moved away, going to the other side of the fire. Having noticed that she avoided being near him, David had concluded that it was simply a measure of her antagonism toward him.

Taking the cloth containing the food, he went to the horses. After saddling and mounting one, he led the others and opened the gate in the fold. The sheep

poured out and down the slope as David followed
them. When he passed the hut, Alexandra turned
from the fire and glanced at him. He touched his hat,
and she nodded in response.

While the sheep and horses grazed, David felt more
content than the previous day. Instead of an oppressive sense of invasion by an outsider who had only
reminded him of an old sorrow, he had a feeling of
companionship in the valley. Despite the hostility
between them, Alexandra was a fascinating woman.
Rapturously beautiful, she was also the most coura-
geous human being he had ever met, having withstood
the bushrangers' cruelty and abuse.

His feelings were shadowed by a warning voice in
the back of his mind that recalled the turmoil he had
endured because of another woman. But he knew the
situation with Alexandra was temporary and would
last only a few months at the very most. He would
never see her again after she left with Pat and returned
to her home in Sydney.

There were other compelling reasons why his past
experience was a false basis for drawing conclusions
about Alexandra. While eating the food she had
wrapped in a cloth for him, he thought about her
insistence on doing her share of the work. She did
what she considered right, whether or not she wanted
to. His former wife had lacked such principles, living
more for the moment and whatever enjoyment it
might bring.

Long before, he had logically reasoned that it was
unfair to judge all women by his former wife. However, the depth of agony he had suffered had made it
impossible to accept that emotionally, and further-
more, he had not wanted to. Clinging to the bitter,
tarnished fragments of his love, he had wanted nothing to do with women. But as the afternoon passed
and he thought about Alexandra, that was changing.

Chapter Twelve

Late that day, as he drove the sheep down the valley, David knew Alexandra would be at the hut, but he had an irrational, demanding need to reassure himself of it. When only one shoulder of a hill was between him and the slope where the hut stood, he rode away from the flock and out into the valley, looking toward the hut. Alexandra was watching for him, shading her eyes with a hand and gazing up. Seeing him, she turned to the fire as he rode back to the flock.

Over dinner that evening, their conversation was less constrained, the reserve between them fading. In reply to his compliment on the food, she said that her experience in cooking had been limited until very recently. As she began explaining, evidently having to refer to cooking for the bushrangers, she broke off and fell silent. Understanding her reluctance to talk about the men, David quickly changed the subject and asked her how long the mutton hanging near the hut would remain fresh.

"For another two more days or so," she replied. "After that, it will be too strong to eat."

"Very well, I'll bring in the flock earlier the day after tomorrow and butcher a wether. I have plenty to spare."

"Indeed you do because that's the largest flock I've ever seen. Do the sheep belong to you?"

David nodded, explaining how he had acquired them. "It's a risk for a single stockman to graze this many," he continued, "but I did it last year without serious losses. If I can do the same this year, I'll hire some employees to help me with them next year."

"I'm sure you will succeed, and I wish you the best of fortune, of course. Is this Tibooburra Station?"

"Yes, it is," David answered, surprised. "How did you know?"

"I heard about it in conversation with Mr. Samuel Terry, one of the principal shareholders in the Bank of New South Wales. He mentioned that an account had been set up for a new sheep station in the outback and mentioned it by name. Were you a stockman or a farmer in England?"

"No, I'm an engineer by training."

It was Alexandra's turn to be surprised, but only to a degree. David was obviously well-educated as well as different in many other ways from the average farmer or stockman. He was a cosmopolitan man and an interesting conversationalist, and with a strong, compelling personality, he seemed more accustomed to exercising authority over others than to working alone.

While Alexandra washed the dishes, she mentioned having seen a flock similar in size to David's at the station to the south. The stockman was accompanied by an Aborigine woman and numerous children. David told her that the stockman was Adolarious Bodenham, and described Bodenham's family and the man's eccentricities in such amusing terms that Alexandra smiled, almost laughing.

It was the first light, cheerful moment she had experienced since the day the bushrangers had captured her, and she was still amused when she went to bed. Lying on her blanket in the hut, she looked out the doorway at David. Like the previous night, he sat beside the fire and looked at his watch, and he was still staring at it when she fell asleep.

The following day, after David left with the flock, Alexandra thought about their conversation of the night before as she went about her tasks. She reflected that it had been exceptionally fortunate for her that the bushrangers had chosen David and his flock as the target for their evil scheme. At least some men who were capable of killing the bushrangers would not have had the gentle nature David had shown toward her.

She also realized that she had been fortunate that her captivity had ended in the distant reaches of the outback. The combination of snubs, salacious curiosity, and well-meant, but intrusive, solicitude that she would have met with in Sydney would have been unbearable immediately after her ordeal with the bushrangers. Here, she had simple work to occupy her hands and solitude to help her adjust to what had happened as well as to prepare for what she would face when she returned home.

At dinner that evening, Alexandra and David conversed even more than they had the night before. Through an unspoken understanding, they talked only about safe, neutral subjects, and Alexandra enjoyed it. It was evocative of conversations with her friends in Sydney, which seemed so very long ago. After cleaning up, instead of going to bed, she sat down again.

David smoked his pipe as he told her about the grazier near Parramatta who had helped him and taught him how to care for sheep. "Frank Williamson also helped Pat," he added. "Frank hired Pat when he was a boy, and Frank was the original owner of Wayamba Station. He sold out to Pat and moved back to the Nepean River. But it wasn't called Wayamba then and was much smaller, with only a fraction of the sheep that Pat grazes."

"I think I've heard of Mr. Williamson," Alexandra mused, then she recalled the conversation at Camden Park with the old gardener who had mentioned Williamson. "Yes, now I remember. Mr. Williamson has a son who is a shopkeeper in Sydney, and he approached Mr. John Macarthur with an offer to sell his father's property. I'm sad to say that it seems your friend was in poor health and was not expected to recover."

David frowned somberly, shaking his head. "I'm very sorry to hear that, and Pat will be as well. But Frank came here on the First Fleet. If he has passed away, he had very good innings."

"Why did you choose to be a grazier? As an engineer, you could have done very well for yourself in Sydney."

"Yes, I probably could have. But in Sydney, I would have always been a former convict and an engineer. Here I'm simply a grazier."

The answer came close to a subject that puzzled Alexandra, a fact that was at complete odds with what was obvious about David. While he was entirely unlike an ordinary criminal, he was a convicted murderer. Knowing that she would have to ask him about it sooner or later, she broached the subject. "Why did you kill Wesley Hammond, my cousin?"

The question violated their tacit agreement to discuss only uncontroversial subjects, but David had been expecting it. Her cousin's death was the foundation for the antagonism between them, and with their mutual reserve fading, it had to be brought into the open. As he replied, he watched for Alexandra's reaction. "Because I returned home unexpectedly one day and found him in bed with my wife."

Her beautiful face revealed nothing, but in her

large, blue eyes, he saw at least understanding, if not agreement, with what he had done. She nodded as she stood up and entered the hut to go to bed. The conversation was over for the night, and David was more than satisfied with how it had ended, not wanting her to think ill of him.

Putting aside his pipe, David took out his knife and calendar stick to make a notch in it. He put them away and fed the fire for the night. Then, having no urge at all to look at the portrait of his former wife, he slept.

The next morning, while he was eating breakfast, Alexandra reminded him that they needed fresh mutton. "I'll have everything ready to butcher a wether as soon as you put the flock into the fold," she added.

"Very well, I'll bring the sheep back an hour or two early. When I've seen to the wether, I'll kindle a fire at the bottom of the hill and burn the rest of that other carcass to keep dingoes from getting it."

"No, I'll have time to do that today. The canvas that protects the mutton from flies is quite grubby, so I'll also wash it."

The conversation created a domestic atmosphere between them that David found extremely pleasing. She put leftover mutton and damper in a cloth for his midday meal, still placing it on a stone instead of handing it to him. But when he took the flock down the slope, she smiled at him as he rode past. It transformed her lovely face, making her so radiantly beautiful that the sunrise seemed dim by comparison.

Then he firmly reminded himself that a woman like Alexandra Hammond would never make her life with a stockman, or even a grazier. With an energetic, practical nature, she would turn her hand to the most common labor if she thought she should, but her birthright placed her in the wealthy, privileged class. Misfortune in her life had made their paths cross, but eventually her path would lead her in an entirely different direction than his.

While driving the flock, he noticed that the mulga

and grass were thinning. Within a very few days, he would have to move the sheep northward to another paddock. It was risky as the flock would be vulnerable to attacks by dingoes when separated from the permanent folds, as well as laborious. But with Alexandra attending to the time-consuming tasks of making camp and cooking, it would be much easier for him than before.

As the sheep grazed, David kept himself from thinking about the months in the future when Alexandra would be gone. In his impatience to see her and talk with her again, the hours passed very slowly. To fill the time, he moved the sheep twice to better forage. Then, about noon, he steered the flock back down the valley, letting the sheep graze along the way.

His first glimpse of her brought him pleasure, and even from a distance, she was poignantly beautiful, waving back as he waved to her. While the animals drank at the pond, she went to the fold. David drove the flock up the hill, and Alexandra waited beside the gate, then closed it behind the sheep and helped him attend to the horses.

"Everything is ready," she told him. "I chose a place down there in the trees away from the hut, and dug a hole to bury the offal. The knives, rope, and canvas are there."

David nodded, taking the saddle off his horse and putting it aside. "Very well, I'll fetch a hammer and pick out a wether."

"Don't knock it on the head in front of all the others, David!" she exclaimed. "There's no point in terrifying the poor creatures, and the hammer is with the knives."

It had never created visible distress among the sheep, but David nodded in agreement, amused by the contrast between the practical and tender sides of her nature. He selected a wether from the fold and led it down the hill as Alexandra walked ahead. At the place she had prepared, he removed his coat and rolled up his sleeves, then she turned away as he took the hammer and dispatched the wether with a single, swift blow.

A rope around its rear feet, he hoisted the animal up to a low limb. Alexandra rolled up her sleeves and tied a piece of canvas around herself to protect her dress, then helped him skin and clean the sheep. Her chin set at a determined angle and her lips in a pale, thin line, she appeared to be fighting her squeamishness, and David told her that he could attend to it by himself, as he was accustomed to doing.

"No," she replied firmly. "This is as much my task as yours, and two can finish it far more quickly than one."

They worked side by side, and a moment later, David found out that at least a large measure of her disquiet had nothing to do with the goriness of the work. As he was tugging the skin off a foreleg, his hand slipped and brushed against hers. She jerked her hand away as though she had been burned, retreating from him.

"It isn't you," she explained, flushing in confusion. "After being with those savage men, I find it vexing to be near any man, and—" She broke off, shrugging helplessly. "I know that it's strange and unreasonable, but I'm unable to rid myself of it. I didn't mean to offend you."

Realizing that was the reason she never handed him anything and kept a distance between them, David shook his head. "I'm not offended, Alexandra. Now that I know about it, I'll be careful not to distress you. You see, I've had feelings myself that aren't entirely unlike yours."

"What do you mean?"

He turned back to the sheep, pulling at the skin. "After my wife betrayed me, I was inclined to distrust any woman. That is even stranger and more unreasonable than your feelings, Alexandra."

As she moved back toward the sheep, Kerrick edged

to one side of it. They finished the work in silence. Alexandra wrapped canvas around the carcass to protect it from flies as David buried the entrails. She took the canvas from around her dress and wrapped the knives in it, then picked up David's coat and went toward the hut. With the carcass over one shoulder, he gathered up the skin in his free hand and followed her.

Alexandra left his coat beside the fire and went down the hill. After hanging the carcass, David put the skin on top of the hut to dry and went inside to get his razor, soap, and mirror. When he arrived at the pond, Alexandra was washing the canvas and knives.

She glanced at him as he knelt at the edge of the water to rinse the blood off his hands and arms. "In some respects, what happened to us is similar," she observed. "We both suffered through the iniquity of others, and we both met with circumstances that destroyed our lives."

"What happened to us is also dissimilar," he countered. "You are completely innocent of any wrongdoing, but my trouble was mostly of my own making. I didn't have to kill your cousin."

"Yes, that's true. It was poor judgment to allow your anger to rule your actions. But those bushrangers were able to abduct me only because I used poor judgment in being without an escort."

"Perhaps, but a woman should be able to go wherever she wishes by herself. And if those who live only to prey on others are ever dealt with as they should be, women will be able to do that. In any event, circumstances did destroy my life, as you say. But that happened only because I permitted it, and you must avoid doing the same thing."

"How can I avoid it? It is done."

"No. nothing in life is final except death. Even after I was transported to Australia, I could have overcome my bitterness and put the past behind me. But I didn't, because I didn't want to. You must dismiss what happened and go on with your life as before."

Alexandra sighed impatiently as she wrung water from the canvas, her manner indicating that he had missed some vital point. She silently picked up the knives and canvas and returned to the hut. As he took off his shirt to wash and shave, David thought about the conversation, but he was unable to find any further meaning in what she had said.

The sun was low when he went back up the slope, where Alexandra was cooking. Her attitude not inviting conversation, he put his things in the hut and began checking the equipment to see that it was in good condition for when he moved the flock northward. After looking at the packsaddles among the baggage, he carefully inspected the rope he used to make a temporary fold.

When dinner was ready, he put the coils of rope away and went to the fire. Alexandra talked with him as they ate but only about commonplace, impersonal subjects. Avoiding the more meaningful previous communication about themselves, she apparently regarded him as unable to understand her feelings.

During a pause in the conversation, he broached the subject they had discussed at the pond. Even if it annoyed her, he considered it important to warn her against his mistake. He told her that she had to take control of her life and put what had happened behind her. "It's simply a matter of determination," he continued, "and I know you have that—"

"No, it is not," she interrupted curtly. "David, my life as I knew it is destroyed. To be painfully blunt and bold about it, as far as my marriage prospects are concerned, I am damaged goods."

"Nonsense!" he replied emphatically, then thought again. "Well, perhaps to those with the narrowest minds, and the spineless sort who rely upon others to make decisions for them. Why would you care what they think? You were a victim of criminals, with no control over the situation, and that is all any sensible man will think of what happened to you."

Studying him, Alexandra wondered if he was merely trying to cheer her, then she saw that he was as completely sincere as he was wrong. She had seen the effects of a blemished reputation and the crushing weight of public opinion that few men would challenge. David was one of those rare men with the inner strength to follow his own convictions, and she reflected that his former wife had been very stupid to betray him.

"No, you're wrong," she said, stacking the dishes. "Also, in more general terms, what has gone before shapes the present, and trying to dismiss the past is futile. But let's not talk about this."

"Very well. I've set up the paddocks here so a flock of two or three thousand sheep can be grazed on them indefinitely, but the size of the one I have now must be moved. I'll have to do it soon."

Alexandra was pleased as this place held unpleasant associations for her. "When do you intend to move it?"

"Within the next two or three days. We'll go north, to my home paddock. I planted a garden there during the spring and I want to see how the vegetables are growing."

"I daresay that you'll find weeds doing well," she remarked, amused. "One doesn't plant a garden and then leave it."

David laughed, saying that keeping the sheep in good graze was more important than the garden. They discussed moving the flock, and Alexandra asked how he kept the sheep together at night. He described the procedure for making a temporary fold, then explained its shortcomings and the risks involved in moving the flock between paddocks.

Their conversation lasted longer than usual, and the fire waned. David put wood on it, then took out his knife and the hardwood stick that Alexandra had noticed before. The stick had rows of notches on it, and as he added another, Alexandra realized its purpose.

"That's how you keep account of the date, isn't it?" she commented. "I've quite forgotten the date myself."

"It's very easy to do when away from towns," David replied. "One day is much like another in the outback, but it's necessary for a stockman to keep track of the date, because sheep must be taken in at the right time for shearing." He glanced over the rows of notches, counting, then put the stick away. "Today is the fourteenth of November."

Gazing into the fire, Alexandra recalled that the fateful day she had ridden to Camden Park had been the eighth of September. It had seemed about two months to her since the bushrangers had abducted her, but she had been unsure of the precise length of time. Some fact in connection with the date hovered at the back of her mind momentarily, then she listened to David as he spoke again of moving the flock. Then, the hour growing late, she went to bed.

Sitting beside the fire, David pulled out his watch and opened the lid. After staring at it for a moment, he closed the lid and then hurled the watch far into the night. Sitting up in surprise, Alexandra started to call out and ask why he had thrown away his watch, then she changed her mind.

It was apparently connected with his past, which he thought he could dismiss, but Alexandra knew he was wrong. A cut on a child's finger remained as a scar, however faint, when that child became an adult.

The following day, after David left with the sheep, Alexandra thought about her family as she performed her tasks. She longed for a way to send them a message so they would at least know she was still alive. In particular, she was concerned about her grandmother and the effects of constant anxiety on her as the weeks had turned into months.

While musing about those months, a related fact occurred to her, one that had barely brushed her thoughts the night before. Until this moment, the date had meant nothing to her as she had spent every waking moment occupied with trying to evade the bushrangers' brutality. But the exact date of events during the past few weeks was abruptly crucial. It seemed as if over a month had passed since her last menses.

Walking blindly toward the fire, Alexandra tried to force aside her chilling, somber dread so she could think clearly. Starting with the previous day, she began recalling specific events and counting the days between them. When she reached twenty-eight days, she could still recall things that had happened over the course of a week or so since her last menses.

Mounting horror gripped Alexandra as she frantically counted the days again, searching for a mistake. She was less than certain about the time between some events that had occurred three and four weeks before, but the possible error was only two or three days at the very most. The conclusion was just as inescapable as it was disastrous. Her menses a week or more overdue, she was pregnant by Hinton.

Now the ordeal she had anticipated upon returning to her family would be infinitely worse than the pity, snubs, or knowing smiles. Her disgrace would have a visible result—a bastard child who would always bear the additional stigma of having been fathered through rape by a hunted criminal.

She was suddenly beyond sorrow, her future promising only unending grief. Hinton's final words had been prophetic, because she was still unable to rid herself of him, even though he was dead. During her torment as a captive, she had never surrendered to despair, but this final, crushing blow was too much, plunging her into hopeless anguish. Collapsing beside the fire, she burst into bitter tears.

When her tears were exhausted, she continued

sobbing dryly in abject misery, her life now worse than meaningless. She lay numbly beside the fire, the hours passing in a blur that was an eternity to her in one way and an instant in another. Then it was late afternoon, and she heard the distant murmur of the sheep bleating as they moved toward the pond.

Reacting to a sense of responsibility and necessity, Alexandra climbed shakily to her feet, her grief an immense burden. Her eyes burning and swollen from crying, she proceeded mechanically about the routine of preparing their meal.

A moment later, hoofbeats pounded up the slope at a headlong run. The horse slid to a stop and David leaped off and dashed to her. "What's wrong, Alexandra?" he exclaimed worriedly. "What happened?"

Unwilling to talk, Alexandra silently shook her head as she cut pieces from the mutton. David looked all around anxiously, then ran a few paces past the hut and looked down the other side of the hill. He turned back. "Alexandra, I can see nothing that's amiss. Please tell me what's wrong."

Shaking her head again, Alexandra motioned him away, then carried the mutton to the fire. David looked around once more and hesitated for a moment in perplexity, then reluctantly went to his horse. "I must see to the flock, but I'll be back as quickly as I can."

He mounted the horse and rode back down the slope as Alexandra put the mutton on the spit. She fanned the fire, then mixed a pan of damper and put on the rice and peas to cook, numbly proceeding about the tasks without thinking.

A short time later, after the sheep passed with the dogs racing beside them, David reined in. The spare horses behind him stopped as he looked at Alexandra for a moment, then rode up the hill. A few minutes later, he hurried back to the fire. "Alexandra, you must tell me what's wrong," he insisted. "Please tell me, and I'll do anything I can to help."

Grimly resigned to the fact that she would have to explain sooner or later, Alexandra started to speak, but her voice broke. As a flood of tears began again, she buried her face in her hands. "I'm with child," she wailed, her shoulders shaking with sobs. "I'm with that vile swine's child."

David started to say something, then shrugged helplessly as he sat beside the fire. Alexandra wiped her eyes and picked up a fork with a trembling hand. She turned the mutton on the spit, then stirred the food and moved the damper off the coals. Then she fed the dogs and filled a plate for David.

Having lost his appetite, he carried the plate aside and emptied the food on the ground for the dogs. He sat down, filled his pipe and smoked. The hours passed as they sat in silence.

Late in the night, he brought Alexandra's blanket out of the hut and put it around her shoulders. Physically and emotionally exhausted, she slept fitfully for a few hours, waking each time he built up the fire. She woke again near dawn, when he stirred.

After taking his tiffin, David went toward the fold. As the first gray light of dawn spread across the sky, he returned with her gelding sidesaddled. He tethered the horse beside the hut, entered it and came out with the man's coat and hat she had worn.

"Come with me, Alexandra," he told her, then he lifted his hand as she started to refuse. "No, you mustn't be alone today. The flock needs to go to pasture, but I can't leave unless you come with me."

As she nodded in resignation, he returned to the fold. Alexandra put on the coat and hat, then checked the saddle on her horse. The girth somewhat tighter than she liked, she adjusted it and then mounted. Prancing about, frisky from its days of rest and good graze, the horse quickly came under control as Alexandra exercised her deft, practiced skill.

When he passed with the flock and spare horses, Alexandra followed David, holding her horse to a walk. At the foot of the hill, he whistled and motioned to the dogs, sending them around the flock to turn it up one side of the valley. Alexandra rode toward the other side, letting the gelding canter to expend its excess of energy.

The wind against her face gave her the feeling of fleeing from her crushing burden of anguish, and she relaxed the pressure on the reins. The young, powerful horse lunged into a full run, its hoofs pounding. It was a complete escape from grief for Alexandra, the headlong pace among the brush and other obstacles requiring her full concentration and all the skill she had learned as a girl while riding cross country in England.

While the sheep moved slowly up one side of the valley, she rode back and forth on the other side, leaping over ditches and brush. Then, when the sheep began grazing and the hobbled horses were browsing on a slope, she rode up the valley to them. She dismounted, and David helped her unsaddle and hobble the gelding. "I've seen some very good riders," he commented in admiration, "but you're the best I've ever seen."

Alexandra nodded to be polite, knowing that her riding skill was now largely irrelevant, because she would never again be invited to join a hunting club. Seeking the shade of a nearby tree, she sat down, writhing inwardly in abject misery, and David sat in silence beside her.

The hours passed, but David made no attempt to speak. At midday, he put a water bottle and the cloth containing leftovers between them. "Try to eat something, Alexandra," he urged, untying the cloth. "Please, just try."

She took a small piece of the damper, which stimulated a gnawing emptiness in her stomach as she ate. Then she took a piece of the mutton.

"Perhaps this isn't a good time to talk about your situation," he said as he ate, "but I don't think there'll ever be a good time. Considering how you feel, though, I don't think you'll want to go back to Sydney now."

Tears rose to Alexandra's eyes as she realized that he had gone to the very heart of the matter, pointing out a conclusion that she had avoided even thinking about, because it was too painful. But it was true, completely inescapable. In addition to what she would endure herself, she would inflict humiliation upon her family, even if she returned to England.

Holding back her tears, Alexandra wiped her eyes. "No, I can't go home now," she whispered brokenly.

"Then it follows that you'll have to stay here. In time, though, much of your sadness will pass. It's natural for you to miss your family, and that can't be helped. But as for the rest of it, you can put it behind you in time and make a good life for yourself, Alexandra."

Wiping her eyes again, Alexandra made no reply. As before, she knew he was wrong in believing that the past could be buried. Somehow he had blinded himself to the fact that joys and regrets were the harvest of previous actions and decisions. As for making a life for herself here, she was unable even to think about it. She could only grieve because any semblance of her former life was now lost to her.

Chapter Thirteen

Alexandra peered into the shadows under a bush, searching for the animal that David had pointed out, then she saw it. Frightened by the sheep, dogs, and horses, it had curled into a ball of yellow and brown bristles. "It looks a bit like a hedgehog," she mused, "but only a bit. What is it?"

"An anteater," David answered. "Those bristles do make it resemble a hedgehog, but they're a kind of fur, not quills. It's a very strange creature in many ways. Instead of giving birth to young, they lay eggs and carry them about in pouches on their stomach."

As he talked, they rode past the bush. During the past few days of moving the flock northward, David had constantly pointed out things to her. Alexandra knew he was trying to take her mind off her sorrow, and, to a degree, he had been successful. While she had seen a few kangaroos and other unusual animals near Sydney, the outback teemed with bizarre creatures.

While the sheep browsed on tender shoots and seed pods growing in a wide stand of mallee, David called Alexandra's attention to a large mound of leaves, twigs, and dirt off to one side. Atop the mound, a speckled bird somewhat smaller than a hen was digging furiously with its long, powerful legs.

"That bird is large enough to be a predator," Alexandra observed. "Is that some small animal's den, and the bird is trying to dig it out?"

"No, the bird is a mallee fowl, and it eats only these seeds you see here. That mound is its nest, with its eggs under the debris."

"Its nest?" Alexandra echoed in astonishment.

"Yes, apparently it uses a combination of heat from the sun and from decaying vegetation to hatch its eggs. The egg is about the size of a goose egg, and the bird knows how to keep the temperature in the mound constant. On hot days, it covers the mound with more dirt to protect the eggs from the sun. On cooler ones, it scratches away the dirt."

"I suppose that when the eggs are ready to hatch, then, the bird digs them up in order to keep the chicks from smothering."

"No, the chicks dig their way out of the mound. When they do, they have full feathers and are entirely capable of caring for themselves. As far as I've been able to tell, they never see the parent bird. They must know how to survive and how to go about that complicated means of hatching completely by instinct. That's very interesting, isn't it?"

Alexandra sighed despondently, glancing away. "Yes, but equally disheartening to me in my present situation. It suggests that the child I have might well become a criminal, come what may, and I know that already."

"No, it will be a human being with free will to choose between right and wrong, not an animal. Also, children can be trained, Alexandra. A sapling will grow tall and straight if it's supported properly."

"We aren't prisoners of the past, but we are its result, reaching back to our birth. People choose between crossroads, but the junctions they come to are a result of previous choices. And properly supporting a maple sapling will never turn it into a tall, straight oak."

The basic point was one on which they could never agree, and David made no further comment. Alexandra also fell silent, reflecting that she was venting moodiness by taking an argumentative attitude instead of discussing the issue. During the past days, her sorrow had been joined by helpless rage, a frustrated, smoldering resentment at her situation. Her temper flared occasionally, but David never became angry in return.

He began talking about the garden at the home paddock, naming off the various vegetables he had planted. "I'm looking forward to seeing what you think about it when we get there," he added.

"As I mentioned, most of my experience is with flowers, but I enjoy working with plants, and I'll be pleased to see what I can do with the garden. We'll be there within a few days now, won't we?"

"Yes, within three or four," he answered, glancing up at the sun. "There's a billabong a short distance ahead, with a spring on a small hill just above it, and we can camp there tonight. You made camp when we stopped yesterday, so I'll ride ahead and do it today."

Alexandra reached back to a ring on her saddle, untying the halter ropes on the pack horses she was leading, then leaned over and handed them to him. David turned and disappeared into the thick growth, circling the flock. Uncoiling the spare stock whip he had given her, Alexandra watched the sheep.

For the first time in her life, she could take part in all the activities around her, which she enjoyed intensely. David had showed her how to control the dogs and sheep, and she knew that his purpose had been to distract her from her grief. But he was also willing to share any of the work and let her do what she wished, a novel and rewarding experience for her.

In addition, in subtle ways that never required a response or exerted any kind of pressure on her, he had expressed increasingly deep feelings for her. But that involved the future, and her calamity was too recent for her to think of what might lie ahead, or to do anything other than endure her sorrow and moments of seething, helpless fury. David was a pleasant, interesting companion with characteristics that she liked and admired, and she refused to search her feelings further than that.

As she followed the flock out of the mallee, the billabong was on the other side of an open, grassy field where the horses were hobbled and grazing. Among the scattered trees on a low rise overlooking the water, David had stacked the packs under a tree and was gathering firewood. The sheep smelled the water, and their woolly backs bobbed as they trotted toward it.

The sheep and dogs waded into the water as Alexandra's horse pushed among them. After setting up camp, David came through the trees as the sheep drank their fill and began moving back into the field to graze. He watched over the sheep and put up the temporary fold at the foot of the hill as Alexandra unsaddled and hobbled her horse, then put it with the others to graze.

She went to the camp and grabbed the water buckets, then carried them to the spring. It was a small pool of deliciously cold water in a natural stone basin, shaded by trees and granite boulders. While filling the buckets and drinking, she noticed carvings on the boulders that appeared to be highly stylized representations of people, birds, and other animals. The lines in the granite were blurred from age, evidently made by Aborigines centuries before.

Alexandra carried the water to the camp, then kindled a fire and began preparing dinner. When the sun started to set, David drove the sheep into the temporary fold. A few minutes later, he came up to the camp with the dogs. Alexandra mentioned the carvings at the spring, and he told her about others he had seen.

Then he broke off and fell silent as a dingo howled in the distance, a hauntingly dismal sound. Another dingo somewhere in the mallee replied. Just as its call was fading away, a third one near it wailed mournfully.

The dogs bristled and bared their teeth, and Kerrick frowned as he listened to the howls. "Those dingoes sound fairly close," he mused. "Once they've learned what firearms will do, they're usually more cautious about getting this near a flock unless they're very hungry."

"Have you ever shot any dingoes here?" Alexandra asked.

"Yes, but that was sometime ago," he said, listening to yet another howl from a different direction. "These could have recently moved into this area, and it sounds like a fairly large pack. We could have trouble with them, so I'll sleep beside the fold tonight."

Dropping the subject, he talked again about Aborigine carvings. Dingoes continued howling occasionally as Alexandra finished cooking, and the dogs looked out into the darkness, growling. She fed the dogs, then served David and herself.

As they ate, Alexandra brought up a comment he had made the previous evening. Their conversation had touched on the bushrangers, and David had implied that he had known them in the past. Remembering the conversation between Hinton and Crowley about a foreman in Parramatta, she asked if he had been the one the bushrangers had mentioned.

David nodded, telling her that he had been in charge of a building project where the two men had been laborers. "They caused trouble far more than they worked," he added, "so they weren't missed when they fled."

"Did they flee because they were about to be sent to confinement at Norfolk Island, or something of that nature?"

"No, that would have probably happened eventually, but it wasn't an immediate prospect. I was forcing Hinton to marry a woman named Auberta Mowbray, but I believe that only set the time when he and Crowley left. I think they had been planning all along to leave."

"Yes, Hinton mentioned a woman. She was with child by him, wasn't she?"

His expression reflecting regret that he had mentioned that aspect of the situation, David nodded.

Burning hatred for the dead man swelled within Alexandra, joined by her helpless rage at her fate. Struggling to control her feelings and to think of other things, she wondered what had happened to the woman. She asked David, and he replied that a clergyman had secured her a position as a maid in an affluent Sydney household. He pondered for a moment, then remembered the people's name. "It was a family named Underwood."

Alexandra nodded, recalling a discussion with the Underwoods about the same maid who had married a shipwright named Hiram Baxter. As they finished eating, the dingoes still howled intermittently in the distance and David picked up his blanket and two muskets, then went down to the fold with the dogs.

After cleaning up, Alexandra went into the hut and listening to the wails of the dingoes and other sounds of the night, she fell asleep. Hours later, she was awakened when the dogs began snarling furiously at the foot of the hill. It changed into the scuffling and yelping of a savage fight, and the sheep were bleating in terror. A musket shot rang out, then another as Alexandra leaped up and ran out of the hut.

Looking down at the fold, she could see nothing in the darkness but shadowy movements. The pandemonium grew louder, a pitched battle raging between the dogs and dingoes, and David fired again. The gunshot was almost lost in the uproar from the sheep, then she heard a more ominous sound. In a sudden, drumming thunder of pounding hoofs, the sheep charged out of the temporary fold and bolted.

Thick dust billowed up to the camp as the sheep raced away to the east, their hoofbeats gradually fading. The struggle between the dogs and dingoes continued, and David shouted in rage as he beat at the wild dogs with his musket. Alexandra ran down the hill and past the horses tethered at the edge of the trees. The fight ended as the dingoes scattered into the darkness. David called the dogs to him and examined them.

"Are you or any of the dogs injured, David?" Alexandra called.

He spoke to the dogs, checking them, then answered, "No, I'm all right. The dogs have a few bites, but they gave far more than they got."

Alexandra followed the sound of his voice, then found him, he and the dogs barely visible forms through the swirling dust and darkness. "Is there anything I can do to help?"

"No," he replied despondently. "It could be that there's nothing at all anyone can do now, Alexandra. I'll saddle a horse and follow the sheep, and see if I can find them when daylight comes."

"Perhaps they won't have gone far," she suggested hopefully.

"Perhaps, but that isn't likely. The way they bolted, they'll undoubtedly run for miles. I'll be back when I've had a look around."

He went toward the horses with the dogs. Alexandra returned to the camp, where she stoked the fire and filled a billy with water, hearing the hoofbeats as David rode away. She drank her tea as she waited for daybreak.

At dawn, she went down the slope, looking at the scene of desolation. Seven dead dingoes and a sheep that had its throat torn out lay on the ground. The poles and rope from the temporary fold were scattered, and the wide path the flock had made in the foliage was dotted with dead sheep that had been trampled by the others.

After gathering the rope and poles, Alexandra led the horses to the camp. She saddled hers and loaded the packs onto the others, getting everything in readiness to leave in case David wanted to immediately set out after the flock when he returned.

An hour later, she glimpsed David in the distance, driving sheep toward the camp. When she saw him clearly, her heart sank. The sheep numbered no more than fifty. She placed the billy of water on the hot coals, then made tea for David.

He entered the camp, his strong, handsome face set in somber lines. Drinking the tea, he talked in a quiet, grimly resigned voice, relating what he had found. The sheep had remained largely in a flock while fleeing eastward for several miles. Then, at a rocky bluff that rose abruptly from the surrounding terrain, the flock had divided. Part had gone north and the rest to the southeast, all of them still running.

"Because of that," he summed up, "I'll lose almost half of my flock. When they get over their fright and stop running, they'll begin clustering, because they don't like to be alone. But they'll be scattered out over two widely-separated places."

"You can't gather one part of them, then the other?"

"No, it'll take several days to collect one part of them. By then, the others will have scattered too far to find."

"Or they'll be dead of thirst," Alexandra mused.

"Yes, those that don't happen upon water will, because they can't spot it from a distance, like someone on horseback. Well, I should have hired a stockman this year, but what's done is done."

"Did the sheep split up fairly evenly at that bluff?"

"No, judging from the path they made, more than half of them went to the north," David said. He drank the last of the tea, then visibly dismissed his remorse as he stood up. "Those are the ones I'll go after. If I can find most of them, and if I have a fairly good lambing next spring, I'll have another large flock within a year or two."

"That's a year or two lost," Alexandra pointed out.

"It is, but as Pat said, those who don't want to take risks shouldn't try to be graziers. Will you be all right if I leave you with those sheep down there and the spare horses? The dingoes won't be back, and I'll return within a few days."

Alexandra stood up, shaking her head. "No, I don't want to stay here. I'll go after those sheep that went to the southeast, David."

"That's out of the question, Alexandra," he replied firmly. "You know full well that you can't go wandering about out here by yourself."

"I won't be wandering about, I'll be gathering sheep. And I won't be by myself, because I'll have some of the dogs with me."

David brushed her comments aside, repeating that she would be alone. He reminded her of his experience, when he had become lost on his trek to Wayamba Station and had almost perished. She pointed out that he had been on foot and without ample supplies of food and water at the time, while she would be mounted and would have everything she needed.

As they debated, David insisted that she might become lost. "No, I will not," she shot back. "You said that the home paddock is due north of here, on Tibooburra Creek, and the sheep are to the southeast. I'll simply gather as many sheep as I can find, drive them north to the creek, and then go upstream until I reach the home paddock."

Silenced by her full, logical grasp of directions and

the essential features of the region, David hesitated for a moment, then tried to dissuade her again. "Alexandra, those sheep aren't worth the risk."

"It's a minor risk, and they're worth it to me," she told him, turning to the horses. "Shall I take half of the pack horses?"

"No, more than one would be a burden to you, and it would be better for me to keep the rest. But this is extremely ill-advised, Alexandra."

The discussion ended as far as she was concerned, Alexandra took the packs off the horses. David sighed, reluctantly helping her. Looking through the packs, they took out the equipment she would need, along with cooking utensils and foodstuffs to last her for several days. Alexandra chose a musket and a pistol, and David divided the fresh mutton, wrapping it in canvas, then they bundled the equipment and loaded it onto a pack horse.

With the pistol under her belt, Alexandra mounted, balancing the musket across the horn of her saddle. David handed her the halter rope on her pack horse, then walked ahead as she rode down the slope. Summoning the dogs, he picked out half of them to go with her.

When she was ready to leave, David tried once more to discourage her from going. "Perhaps you and I could go and gather the sheep that went to the north," he suggested. "With us working together, it shouldn't take long, then we could see about the others."

"No, you know that it would take both of us almost as long as it'll take you by yourself, David. This is the logical solution."

"It's also a dangerous one. Be very careful, Alexandra."

"And you. I'll see you at the home paddock in a few days."

He nodded and tried to smile as he touched his hat. Alexandra turned her gelding away, and the pack horse followed. The dogs hesitated, looking at David until he motioned them after Alexandra. They raced to catch up, then trotted beside her horse as she rode away to the east.

A few hours later, after passing the rocky bluff, she found a dozen sheep huddled in a ditch, off to one side of the trampled path that the main group of sheep had made. After driving them out of the ditch, Alexandra tethered her pack horse and searched the ditches and thickets on each side.

The intelligent, experienced dogs perceived what she was doing and began searching. Sheep bleated on all sides as the dogs found them in pairs, threes, and fours. Alexandra found more, driving them toward the others, and the cluster grew. When she began driving them ahead of her, leading her pack horse again, there were over fifty of the animals.

The number also grew as she drove the sheep slowly, looking for water. The sheep bleated with thirst, a sound that was audible for hundreds of yards in all directions. Other small groups and isolated sheep were drawn to it by their instinct to flock together, and the dogs continued to find a few. Near sunset, as Alexandra drove them toward bright green foliage that indicated water, she had almost seventy-five sheep.

In the midst of the green foliage was a mudhole covered by an inch or two of tepid, stagnant water. It satisfied the animals, but Alexandra drank a sparing amount from her water bottle. After stringing a rope between saplings for a temporary fold and putting the sheep into it, she cooked a quick meal for herself and the dogs, then fell asleep beside the fire.

Rising before dawn, she was ready to leave when it was light enough to see. She moved along the trampled path through the brush, and the flock grew rapidly. Only a few isolated sheep wandered about, the animals having found each other and gathered in clusters of a dozen or more. Alexandra searched on each side, while the dogs went far out on the flanks, racing about and driving in groups of sheep.

At sunset, when she stopped at a small pond for the night, there were over four hundred sheep in the flock. After the sheep, dogs, and horses drank, the pond was liquid, scummy mud, with no indication that the water would clear for hours. Alexandra had to drink the small amount remaining in her bottle, but she also had to use a full coil of rope to make a temporary fold for the larger number of sheep.

As she kindled a fire and prepared to cook, she saw that she would have to butcher a wether the next day. The mutton was very strong, and also mostly bone and gristle. She made damper and cooked some peas and rice for herself, and roasted the mutton for the dogs. They were still hungry after gulping it down, sniffing about for more and growling at each other over the stringy tendons and bones.

From the first few minutes after she set out the next morning, the flock grew by leaps and bounds. The path the sheep had made became diffuse and disappeared, but Alexandra knew she was following the main group because of the number of wethers and ewes she found. They had gathered in even larger clusters, groups of a dozen up to a score joining the flock.

Coming through the brush and out of ditches on each side, the sheep were crazed with thirst, bleating piteously. Some were weak and unable to bleat, their tongues swollen in their open mouths as they staggered through the brush to join the flock. With some of the sheep in reasonably good condition and others barely able to stay on their feet, the flock became increasingly difficult to control and moved at a very slow pace.

By midafternoon, the flock was too large for Alexandra to count the number of sheep accurately, but she was certain there were more than seven hundred.

They were almost impossible to control but the dogs worked furiously to turn back the sheep that tried to wander away, while they moved at an increasingly slower pace. Crossing a low rise, Alexandra saw a patch of deep green and turned the flock toward it.

When the sheep smelled the water, Alexandra had to ride around in front of the flock to slow them and prevent weaker ones from being trampled. The animals spread apart, hurrying frantically toward the water. It was a spring-fed stream that sank into the parched soil a short distance from its source, with room for only a few score of sheep. Alexandra rode among them, driving the first ones out of the water so others could drink.

The dogs lapped up quick sips as they charged into the sheep, helping her move them and keeping a crush from developing. Part of the flock began moving away and cropping the lush grass around the water, and the congestion of animals gradually diminished and the weaker ones found room to drink. When the last sheep moved away, Alexandra drank at the head of the stream.

After hobbling her horses, she made camp. Then she realized that she was procrastinating over the extremely disagreeable task of butchering a sheep. Steeling herself against her squeamishness, she prepared for the task.

At a distance from the stream, she found a tree with a convenient limb for hanging the carcass to skin and clean it. She dug a hole to bury the offal, then gathered rope, knives, and canvas. The heaviest implement she had was a hatchet, and she placed it under the tree with the other things.

The dogs watched the preparations, evidently surmising that a feast of fresh, roasted mutton would shortly be forthcoming, and followed her as she walked among the sheep. Looking them over, she reflected that it would be shameful to kill one that had been tortured by thirst. At the same time, she was

reluctant to select an identifiable wether among the
first ones she had found, having grown to know them
in a way.

The lack of distinguishing marks also seemed an
unfair criterion for being doomed, but Alexandra
chose one that was like many others, unsure of when it
had joined the flock. She drove it away from the rest of
the sheep, and the dogs eagerly helped her. At the tree,
they gathered around to watch, panting happily in the
afternoon heat and wagging their tails.

Standing in front of the sheep, she picked up the
hatchet. The dogs stopped panting, becoming intent,
their eyes following the gleaming steel. Raising the
hatchet high, Alexandra lifted to her toes and gathered her strength. Then the wether looked up at her.
She froze, gazing down as it somberly surveyed her,
then she slowly lowered the hatchet.

The dogs stirred impatiently, scratching at fleas.
Alexandra moved around to the wether's shoulder,
out of its line of vision, and held its neck as she lifted
the hatchet again. The dogs became quiet, their eyes
raptly fixed on the hatchet once more. Alexandra
composed herself, looking at the spot David always
struck on the wethers he killed.

Then she thought about the bulging muscles in his
brawny arm, the crushing force he put behind a heavy
hammer to kill a wether with a single blow. She had a
sudden vision of the wether thrashing about on the
ground, merely wounded and its last moments passing
in mortal terror and agony as she hacked frantically,
trying to finish it off. She lowered the hatchet once
again and turned away from the wether, going toward
the camp.

The dogs hesitated, looking between her and the
wether, then ran to catch up with her. As they trotted
beside her, a couple of them growled and bared their
teeth. At the camp, she dropped the hatchet and
picked up her pistol, then returned to the tree.

Standing at the wether's shoulder with the pistol cocked, Alexandra took a firm grip on the skin at the back of the animal's head. With the barrel against the top of its head, she closed her eyes and turned her face away, pulling the trigger. The sheep jerked when the pan flared, as did Alexandra. Then the pistol fired and the woolly skin was pulled from her grasp as the wether dropped to the ground, killed instantly.

Hoisting the animal up to the limb by a rope around its rear feet was a struggle of a different nature, Alexandra heaving her weight against the rope. The dogs circled and watched, offering encouragement in the form of eagerly happy whines. The sheep finally dangling off the ground, Alexandra tied a piece of canvas over her dress and set to work.

The next obstacle was getting it to the camp, and Alexandra staggered from side to side under the heavy weight of the limp, canvas-covered carcass on her back. It was finally hanging from a tree at the camp, and none of the other sheep had seen one of their number killed. She wearily put up a temporary fold and drove the flock into it, then kindled a fire.

With no appetite, but hunger gnawing in her stomach, she put a large cut and a small piece of mutton on the spit. The dogs eyed the roasting meat and whined in anticipation as Alexandra prepared the rest of the meal. As soon as the large cut of mutton had cooked, she took it off the spit and fed the dogs.

Comfortably gorged, the dogs lay around the fire as Alexandra dished up her food. When she tried to dismiss her qualms and eat a morsel of the mutton, her stomach rebelled. Controlling the urge to retch, she spat it into the fire, then threw the rest of the mutton to the dogs. They gulped it down, and Alexandra ate the damper and rice and peas.

Having slept poorly the previous two nights, she was sagging with fatigue after another long, hard day. But when she lay down, the howling of dingoes in all directions kept her from sleeping soundly. They woke her several times, and when it happened again an hour before dawn, she stoked the fire and made tea.

The next day, driving the sheep on to the east, she found what had drawn the dingoes. Sheep that had died of thirst were scattered in the brush, the carcasses mangled where the wild dogs had fed on them during the night. A few dingoes still slinked about, and the birds rose and the carrion-eating lizards scuttled away from the dead sheep as the flock passed them.

The dead sheep were evidence that Alexandra was following the path the sheep had taken, but she began wondering if she would find any more alive. With dingoes about, that seemed even more doubtful. Crossing a rise, she scanned the surrounding terrain in the bright sunlight. The vast wilderness stretched to the horizon in all directions, and she saw foliage that indicated water in the distance ahead of the flock.

All morning Alexandra followed the flock at a slow walk, not even finding any more dead sheep. At noon, the water was straight ahead, in a valley over a low hill. The flock went over it, and when she reached the top of the elevation, Alexandra suddenly reined up, gazing down into the valley in amazement and delight.

The grassy valley below was dotted with sheep in bunches of two score or more. Estimating their number, Alexandra speculated that there were almost twice as many in the valley as those she had gathered. At the end of the valley was a large billabong, shaded by dense trees. The sheep had found ample water and graze, then remained there.

Scanning the sheep again, Alexandra saw no carcasses on the ground among them. The dead ones she had passed since daybreak had kept the dingoes satisfied, and the wild dogs had killed none in the valley. Smiling happily, Alexandra drove the flock down the slope.

When she took the dogs and circled the valley to

gather the sheep, she saw that they were the very best of those that had broken away to the southeast. In their prime, the young, strong animals had continued eastward when the others had become exhausted and fallen behind. She sent the dogs into the thickets on the surrounding slopes, finding a few more, then drove all of the sheep to the center of the valley.

At one side of the valley was a granite cliff over a hundred feet high, its base dipping back to form an immense, lofty cave. As Alexandra unloaded the pack horse in it, she noticed Aborigine carvings and paintings from past centuries on the high ceiling. With the horses hobbled and grazing, she watched the sheep as they browsed. There were far too many for her to count, but she was certain that they totaled nearly two thousand.

Late in the day, the trail of scent left by the sheep she had driven to the valley drew dingoes that had been feeding on the dead sheep. Alerted by the growling of the dogs, Alexandra went around the flock and waited until the wild dogs were within close range. She shot one with her pistol, then dropped it and took aim with her musket as the dingoes raced away, bringing down another one.

The danger from the dingoes eliminated, she made a temporary fold in scattered trees near the cave, using all the rope she had. After taking the sheep to the billabong to drink, she drove them to the fold, which was barely large enough to contain them. As dusk settled, she kindled a fire at the front of the cave, the stone floor stained by fires of long ago.

Along with mutton for the dogs, Alexandra put a small piece for herself on the spit, roasting it until it was very well done. She tasted it gingerly, then found that she could eat it with her other food. Aching with fatigue, she still slept only lightly, any unusual noise or a stir among the sheep waking her.

Near dawn, as she made tea, Alexandra decided to stay in the valley that day. She was unsure of the distance to Tibooburra Creek, and of finding water along the way, but she did know that some of the sheep remained weak from their days without water. At daybreak, she drove the flock out into the valley and hobbled the horses again.

As the animals grazed, she thought about how bizarre her situation was compared to a few months before. In her wildest flights of imagination, she never would have dreamed that she would be tending a flock of sheep in the outback. But it was deeply gratifying, because she finally had the freedom and independence for which she had always longed.

Looking around the cave, she concluded that the Aborigines must have erected a scaffolding to carve and paint on the lofty ceiling. No trace of it remained, and the generations of ancient artisans who had made the enigmatic figures and symbols had been dead for centuries. The sole evidence that they had ever lived was markings on stone in a cave in a remote place in the immense wilderness of the outback. Only the immutable, eternal landscape endured, the people fleeting shadows against it.

Pondering that, she saw her own life on the same scale. In that context, her upheaval over her abduction, as well as the entire course of her life, was as transient as the glint of a dust mote in a sunbeam. She came to terms with what had happened to her, an inner tranquility replacing her frustrated rage, and then she no longer hated the life that was growing within her womb.

At the first light of dawn the next morning, she drove the sheep north. Seeing a small spot of bright foliage a few hours later, she left the flock and rode to it. Among the trees was only a patch of mud, its surface dried into a maze of cracks. That afternoon, she saw bright greenery to the northwest and rode to it, finding another waterhole that had dried up in the summer heat.

At sunset, only the duns and browns of the parched

land and sun-baked foliage extended to the northern horizon. In a wide, sandy valley, Alexandra used a straggling stand of small trees to make a fold, stretching the rope between them. The thirsty sheep bleated plaintively in protest as they moved reluctantly into the fold ahead of Alexandra and the dogs.

The other animals craved water, the dogs whining and the horses too thirsty to do more than nibble at the brown, dusty grass that grew sparsely near the trees. Alexandra tried to ignore her demanding need for water, as she gathered wood. After kindling a fire, she took out her water bottle and tin plate.

The dogs gathered around eagerly, lapping up the water as she filled the plate twice. She went to the horses and gave each of them a brimming plate of water, then the bottle was empty. Too thirsty to eat or to sleep, she roasted a single piece of mutton for the dogs and then sat beside the fire, waiting for dawn.

The next morning, the sheep were easier to keep moving at a fast walk than the previous day, because they were too thirsty to eat and made no attempt to graze. Later that morning, she saw foliage that indicated water during some seasons, but she made no attempt to investigate it, harboring her strength and that of her horses.

Nothing but the dry, rolling hills covered with seared foliage stretched ahead and Alexandra wondered if the animals could last through another night without water. Her own thirst was an unrelenting torment, her mouth parched and her lips cracked. But her determination provided reserves of energy, while the animals would end their torture by giving up and lying down to die.

When the heat reached its full, torrid intensity during the afternoon, the sheep slowed. The older and weaker ones gradually drifted to the rear of the flock, and Alexandra had to crack her whip every few minutes to keep them walking. The dogs were also becoming exhausted, their tongues hanging out as they panted breathlessly. The horses were in the same condition as they plodded with slow, dragging steps.

Alexandra knew that she might lose all of the sheep if she wasted her energy in struggling blindly to save each of them, but she was reluctant to give up a single one. Cracking her whip over those that straggled, she drove them back into the flock. Every time an old ewe or wether tottered feebly out of the column ahead of her, she shouted hoarsely to one of the dogs and motioned it to turn the sheep back.

Concentrating on the flock, she looked ahead less often. When she did and saw a smudge of a different color in the distance, she suppressed her exuberant surge of hope, fearing the crushing backlash of disappointment if she was mistaken. Fighting the urge to gaze ahead, she watched the sheep for what seemed an eternity, cracking her whip and keeping them together. Then she looked up again, seeing a broad band of shimmering emerald foliage that stretched from the eastern to the western horizon.

She was unable to rejoice, because the last miles were a struggle to keep the sheep moving, dozens of them faltering in the burning heat. Many of them dropped in their tracks, then lurched weakly back to their feet when Alexandra cracked her whip over them. The weary dogs moved listlessly back and forth as she stormed at them in her cracked, husky voice, sending them to turn back sheep that reeled out of the flock ahead.

Going over the last low rise before the creek, the sheep smelled the water, which brought another crisis. A ripple of movement passed through the flock, those that could breaking into a trot or run. Weaker ones stumbled and fell in the crush, in immediate danger of being trampled. Alexandra called to the dogs and sent them to the front of the flock as she rode up through it, cracking her whip to clear a path.

The sheep spread apart as they dodged the dogs in front of them and the loud cracking of the whip. The flock disintegrated into a disorganized mass a hundred feet wide, with a ragged group of sheep running and trotting across the valley toward the creek. The weaker, slower ones fell far behind, some still tottering down the last rise.

Urging her horses into a canter, Alexandra rode ahead of the sheep. The creek was wide and shallow, lined with trees that were flanked by acres of lush spinifex and mulga. Splashing into the water, the horses slid to a stop and dipped their muzzles, drinking frantically.

Alexandra tugged on the reins, trying to get the horses out of the water before they drank too much. Finally lashing them to make them stop drinking, she rode back out of the water and tethered the pack horse to a tree. By then, the first of the sheep had reached the creek. She rode back into it, cracking her whip to drive the sheep to the other side before they could drink too much.

The sheep gulped down water, dodging the whip and floundering across the creek. On the other side, the edge taken from their thirst, they began greedily cropping the grass and mulga. Riding up and down the creek, Alexandra drove more sheep across as they reached it. The dogs lapped up water, helping her chase the sheep to the other side.

With her lips and mouth parched, the cool, fresh water splashing as high as her saddle was an excruciating torture. But she denied herself, knowing the sheep would be violently ill and could die if they were bloated from the water. If she paused to drink, a sheep might drink too much, and she was determined to save every one of them.

After a while only those having difficulty reaching the creek were left. Taking the dogs with her, Alexandra rode back to them. Some stumbled and fell every few, feeble steps, while others dragged their hindquarters, only the scent of the water keeping them from giving up. The loud, cracking whip and the dogs frightened them into making a final effort, and Alexandra drove them slowly toward the creek.

The water revived them, and the last of the sheep crossed the creek ahead of Alexandra and the dogs. She followed them, motioning the dogs around the flock and moving it farther from the creek. Then, leaving the dogs with the sheep, she tethered her horse, and took off her dusty coat and hat, dropping them on the grassy bank. She waded into the creek and sat down, the water soaking through her clothes up to her chest as she dipped up handfuls and drank. She splashed it on her face, then held her breath and lay back, letting the deliciously cool water cover her.

Four days later, when she detected a faint odor of wood smoke in the breeze blowing down the creek, Alexandra turned her horse and rode to one side of the flock. Away from the dust and smell of the sheep, the aroma of wood smoke was distinct.

She gazed a few hundred yards up the creek, at a curve in the stream. A tall hill rose well above the surrounding terrain and just below its crest was a sheltered plateau where a large hut stood, a wisp of smoke rising from the smoldering campfire. It was the home paddock, and Alexandra was suddenly jubilant, a sense of joyous anticipation gripping her.

The intensity of her feelings surprised her, and she realized that she was looking forward to David's pleasure upon seeing the sheep. More than that, she eagerly awaited his smile when he saw her. Although she had not been lonely, she had missed him.

A short time later, the home paddock came into full view. The garden, some five acres surrounded by a rail fence, was on the near side of the hill, with a water wheel in the creek to irrigate it during dry periods. On the other side of the hill was a permanent fold, somewhat larger than those in the other paddocks, made of thick timbers and brush.

The flock grazed south of the hill, and on a rise overlooking the sheep, David leaped onto his horse and rode toward her. As his horse raced across the rolling terrain, he disappeared and then came into view again. When he drew closer, his tanned, handsome features were wreathed in a glowing, boyish grin of delight, and he looked only at her, not even noticing the sheep as he passed them. Then he reined in beside her, his horse panting heavily from the run.

For a long moment, neither of them said anything, a tingling, magnetic silence between them. Her discomfort when near him was gone, replaced by a completely opposite reaction. His fresh, male scent was pleasant, and the thought of his muscular arms holding her gave her a warm, melting feeling. His blue eyes gleamed with radiant joy, reflecting his intense love for her. Newly conscious of her own feelings for him, Alexandra's answering smile rose from the very depths of her being. In their mutual elation at being together after days of separation in the immense wilderness, words were pitifully inadequate, and at the same time, unnecessary.

Finally, he took off his hat and pushed his hair back, sighing happily. "I can see that you're all right, Alexandra."

"Yes, are you?"

"I am now, but I was becoming more and more worried. If another day or two had passed, I would have left the sheep to do what they would and come searching for you." Turning to look for the first time at the sheep she was driving, he gazed in astonishment. "Good Lord, Alexandra! There are well over two thousand sheep here!"

"I'm sure I failed to find quite a few. And unfortunately, some died of thirst before I could collect them."

"You still did far, far better than many stockmen would have. The total loss to the flock is no more than a few hundred, which is a miracle. Considering the difficulty I had, I can only imagine the trouble you experienced in gathering these sheep and driving them here."

"Difficulty?" Alexandra echoed in pretended surprise. "Trouble? No, I merely collected them and drove them north to the creek, then here. Nothing could have been simpler or easier, David."

He fell silent in perplexity, and with more than a hint of skepticism. Unable to contain her amusement, Alexandra laughed, then he laughed merrily with her. They began driving the sheep toward the others as Alexandra related what had actually happened during the past few days.

When all of the sheep were together, David left the dogs to watch them and rode to the hill with Alexandra, pointing out where he intended to have the complex of station buildings. They stopped at the garden, which he had planted with cabbage, cucumbers, potatoes, onions, and other vegetables. Weeds had sprung up, the soil richly fertile and damp from irrigation by the water wheel at the creek, but the crops had flourished.

"This garden is in much better condition than I expected, David," Alexandra told him. "It only needs mulching and weeding, which I'll attend to within the next few days. The cabbage and cucumbers are more than large enough to eat, and I'm sure they're delicious."

"They undoubtedly are," David said. "I've been waiting for you to get here before I have any." He pointed up the hill. "I plan to build the station house just back from where that hut is."

They rode up the slope to the hut, stopping beside it. The level plateau where it stood was over an acre in area, protected from the prevailing winds by the crest of the hill behind it. Alexandra glanced around, then turned to survey the surrounding terrain.

She gasped, captivated by the striking scenic beauty of the view from the hill. In the afternoon sunlight, with a few luminously fleecy clouds casting shadows over the countryside, it was a panorama of rolling grasslands and open forest stretching for a distance that staggered the imagination. In comparison with the immense landscape, the previous scenes of her life had been small and confining, dwarfed into insignificance.

"How magnificent, David," she sighed in awe. "I haven't seen nearly this much of the outback all at one time before. In the entire world, there can be few views that are even remotely as lovely as this."

"I feel the same about it as you, but not everyone would. Many prefer to have busy streets on all sides of them."

Alexandra laughed as she dismounted and unsaddled her horse. "I did at one time, and the busier the better, but now I've grown to love the outback. That's a large, stout hut you made, David."

"It'll do for now," he said, unloading her pack horse. "But one day there'll be a house here that will match the view. I'll get on back to the flock and put these horses with the others."

"Very well, they can use the rest and graze. My gelding has become a bit thin, as I have myself."

"Every woman on earth can only wish she looked like you," he told her firmly, leading the horses. Then he mounted his horse. "Similarly, I can only wish I could find the words to tell you how happy I am that you're here. I'll see you a bit after sundown, Alexandra."

With a wide, beaming grin on his face, he turned and led the horses away. She smiled and flushed in pleasure. When he was gone, she gazed at the landscape again for a moment, then went into the hut, and searched through the baggage, taking out clean clothes.

At the creek, Alexandra found a washstand David had made from split timbers, his razor, mirror, and earthenware pot of soap on it. Nearby, freshly-laundered clothes hung over a rope between two trees. Alexandra bathed and washed her hair, then dressed in the clean clothes and washed those she had been wearing, hanging them over the rope.

She returned to the hut for a bucket and went to the garden, where she gathered the vegetables. After washing them in the creek, she took the bucket to the hut and began cooking.

Near sunset, David drove the flock to the creek to drink, then to the paddock. A few minutes later, the dogs followed David as he came up to the hut after washing and shaving, his tanned face ruddy from the cold water. He smiled at Alexandra as he sat down beside the fire, commenting that the food smelled very appetizing.

Her appetite also keen from smelling the food cooking, she fed the dogs, then filled plates and handed one to David. As he ate, he emphatically remarked that the food was delicious. Alexandra thought the same, even the commonplace mutton and damper tasting better when accompanied by the tart, tangy cabbage in vinegar, the crisp cucumbers, and the fried potatoes and onions mixed with crisp, savory bits of pork.

Alexandra refilled David's plate and put another small amount of cabbage and cucumbers on hers. When he finished his second helping, he shook his head reluctantly as she offered him more. "It's so tasty that I wish I could, but I can't eat another bite," he told her. "Royalty never had a better meal, though. And," he added with a smile, "any king would envy the companionship I have at dinner."

Alexandra smiled as she picked up the dishes. "The produce from the garden will be substantial, far more than we'll need. Some thought must be given to storing it for winter."

David agreed, taking out his pipe and tobacco. Alexandra said that a cellar would be best for storage because of its constant temperature, and he replied that he would begin digging one at the side of the hill within the next few days.

While David smoked his pipe, he spoke again about his plans for the station, saying that he intended to have amenities that would make life there pleasant. Then he suddenly put down his pipe and reached over, taking her hand.

"But all this will mean nothing to me unless you share it with me, Alexandra," he said earnestly. "Since I've known you, I've found more meaning in life than I ever knew existed, because I've learned what love truly is. Please tell me that you'll marry me."

Although she had anticipated it, his manner forewarning her, somehow hearing him say the words had the impact of surprise. But they were also the words she yearned to hear more than she had ever wanted anything. Joyful happiness soaring within her, she smiled at him, nodding. "Yes, I will, David," she replied.

He took her in his arms and kissed her ardently. A warm glow suffused her as his lips moved over her face. "Pat is a justice of the peace," he murmured against her lips. "When he comes, he can perform the ceremony for us."

Alexandra nodded, pulling back from him and standing. "Very well, David. In the meantime, we have no neighbors to spy on us and gossip. From now on, we'll share the hut."

He stood up, pulling her into his arms again, and kissed her as he carried her into the hut. When he put her down on their blankets, for an instant she experienced a fleeting hint of the outrage she had felt at the times when Hinton had seized her. But this was different and it passed, lost in the mounting sensations that his tender, gentle hands created.

The night air cool against her bare skin, and the feel of his muscular body beside hers stirred a demanding need to be closer, a burning ache for more intimate contact. His lips evoked a growing urgency that turned into an exquisitely torturous yearning inside her. As she pulled at him, he moved over her, his weight gently on her.

She felt a momentary pang of fulfillment which faded into a numb grasping for a still greater pleasure. It drew closer and then retreated tantalizingly, time standing still as it ebbed and flowed, approaching nearer each time. Then she clung to him and met his surging passion with her own in a throbbing wrenching peak of ecstasy.

The aftermath was utter quiescence, the most complete contentment she had ever known. It was enriched by his arms around her, his lips moving over her face. Then he lay back, holding her close. "You've made me the happiest man alive, Alexandra," he said.

"And I'm the happiest of women, David." She sighed, placing a hand on her stomach. "The only thing that could make my happiness more complete would be for this baby to be yours."

"But it will be," he assured her. "You'll be my wife when it's born, and it'll have my name. Who will know anything more than that?"

Alexandra said nothing at the moment, pulling the blankets over them. Turning her head, she looked at the smoldering fire and the vast landscape beyond, its features indistinct in the soft moonlight. A few minutes later, David breathed with the slow, regular rhythm of sleep, and then she whispered, "Fate will know."

Chapter Fourteen

At the fire in front of the hut, Pat doffed his hat and bowed as David introduced him to Alexandra. "This is indeed a pleasure, Mistress Hammond," he said. "David told me what happened to you, and you have my deepest sympathy. Now that the ones responsible for your misfortune have met a just end, I trust that you're happy and comfortable here."

"I'm very pleased to meet you, Mr. Garrity," she replied. "Yes, what began as an ordeal has ended very happily. I wouldn't give up my place here with David for any situation a woman could have."

"Then I'm pleased for you and for David. As I told him, I need witnesses to perform a marriage ceremony, but that's easily arranged. When I return to my station, I'll make preparations to bring my family and others here within a few days. I'll also send a rider to Sydney with word of your whereabouts so your family will know you're safe and well."

"That's very obliging of you, Mr. Garrity. I hope

that it won't interfere in any way with activities at your station."

Pat shook his head, assuring her that it would not. They continued talking, and David glowed with pride in Alexandra. Radiantly beautiful, her spirited, independent nature gave her a compelling personality. While she was now five months pregnant, her loose, dungaree dress concealed the slight thickening of her body. For the first time since David had known him, the burly, self-confident Pat was a trifle abashed as he talked with Alexandra, exerting himself to be correct.

"Dinner will be ready presently," she said, ending the conversation. "In the meantime, I'm sure you would like some refreshment after your long journey." She poured pannikins of rum, handing them to Pat and David, and turned to the pans around the fire as they moved away.

The two men picked up the supplies the station owner had brought, carrying them into the hut, then sat down. Pat drank his rum and shook his head in amazement, looking at Alexandra. "David, I've met people who've had good fortune," he commented quietly, "but none that would begin to compare with yours."

"I can hardly believe my good fortune myself, Pat, particularly the fact that she's agreed to marry me."

"No," Pat disagreed. "You could search the world over and not find another like her, but you're a rare sort yourself, David. You say she collected part of your sheep when they bolted? One might think that a woman from her station in life could never do anything like that, but she has a very steady look in her eyes."

"She can do anything she sets her mind to, Pat. In that instance, she did much better than many stockmen would have."

"Aye, she certainly did. You're taking unnecessary risks in grazing such a large flock by yourself, David. You should hire some help."

David agreed, but primarily because he wanted to stay close to the home paddock as Alexandra's pregnancy advanced. "Do you have any good, steady jackaroos you can spare, Pat?"

"I can do better than that. If you like, I'll send Adolarious Bodenham and his mob up here to work for you."

The offer surprised David, as Bodenham was an extremely valuable employee. Pat explained that the number of flocks on his station had increased while Adolarious had been there, and nearby stockmen occasionally visited him, which he disliked intensely. He was dissatisfied, considering the station too congested with people, and was threatening to leave.

"I've told them to stay away from him," Pat added, "but it does no good. When a stockman runs short of tobacco, salt, or something, he'll go to the nearest stockman to get some. There's no changing that."

"If that's his complaint," David mused, "then Adolarious would be happy for the rest of his life in my northwest paddock. It's isolated, and the graze is so sparse that I'll never have more than one flock there."

"Adolarious would be glad to hear about that, and his oldest boys could work here at your home paddock. You'd have to pay them jackaroos wages, but you have more than ample funds in your bank account."

"More indeed, because I found a heavy purse on Hinton. Also, you saw that plunder in the hut that the bushrangers had with them." David swished the remaining rum around in his pannikin, then drank it. "Even this rum is from their loot, and I don't like gain of that sort."

"I can understand that, but it's yours by rights, David. It can never be returned to the rightful owners, and you deserve much more for putting those three in the ground, where they belong. If you have any extra pistols and muskets, I'd be more than glad to trade sheep for them. Some of my stockmen's are so old and rusty that they're worthless."

David smiled wryly as he led his friend into the hut and opened the pack containing the weapons, and Pat exclaimed in surprise, "You could arm a company of soldiers with what you have there, David! Show me how many you can let me have, and I'll make you a fair deal for them."

After selecting several muskets and pistols for his own needs, David motioned to the remainder. With a wide, happy smile on his bearded face, Pat looked at the weapons as he and David carried them outside. They bundled the firearms in canvas, ready to put on Pat's pack horse the next morning, then Alexandra called them to dinner.

Though it was late summer, with March only a few days away, the garden still produced vegetables. So to accompany the mutton and damper, Alexandra had prepared fresh peas, carrots, and potatoes, along with a salad of lettuce and cucumbers. The food expertly cooked and seasoned, Pat complimented Alexandra on it, then commented on how well the garden had done.

"Alexandra is due credit for that," David told him. "Through her knowledge of gardening and hard work, we have enough vegetables stored in a cellar to last a number of people through the winter, as well as several bushels of dried beans and peas put by."

"If you have the Bodenhams here, the vegetables won't go to waste," Pat commented wryly. "I've almost sprained pack horses' backs taking rations to that mob, because they like their tucker."

David and Alexandra laughed, then the subject turned to the weather. During many late summers, when the foliage was parched, lightning in dry thunderstorms ignited raging grass fires that raced with the speed of the wind for miles, consuming everything in their path. This year there had been only minor grass fires, and Pat speculated hopefully that the situation would continue until the autumn rains came.

After the meal, Pat went to the pile where his saddle, bedroll, and supplies were stacked, and brought a large leather pouch back to the fire. He took foolscap, an ink bottle, and a pen out of the pouch, and suggested that Alexandra might like to write a letter to her family.

Thanking him gratefully, Alexandra took the writing materials as the men talked and smoked. Pat raised the subject of the weapons, commenting that he had been thinking of what would be a fair trade. "If you're going to hire Adolarious and his mob," he said, "I'll send him with three thousand sheep and enough supplies to last until you get your supplies next spring, and I'll make sure that most of the sheep are young ewes in lamb."

"That sounds like a fair deal to me, Pat."

"Well, I'm not through yet, David. Weapons are scarce and valuable out here, and sheep are cheap. I'll also give you six cows in calf and a dozen pigs. You have more than enough horses now, so that will provide you with a good start on all the stock you'll need."

"I think you're giving me too much, Pat."

"No, you know yourself that a good musket costs up to forty guineas, and I have ample cattle and pigs. When I come back for your wedding, I'll bring wagons and men to make a track into here. Next spring, you'll have upwards of twelve thousand sheep, if all goes well, and it would be senseless to drive them to my station for shearing."

"That's true, and the drays could deliver my supplies for the next year. But I'll need a shearing shed, a barracks for the shearers, and a storage building for the supplies."

"Aye, you will. When I talk to Adolarious, I'll tell him that you want his two oldest boys to work here. They can help you gather timber and get started on the buildings, and while I'm here with my men for the wedding, we should be able to more or less finish them."

"That'll be a big help, and I appreciate it, Pat."

The older man shrugged off the thanks, bringing up details of what they had discussed. They decided upon the best route for the track into Tibooburra Station, one that would require the least labor, and would pass a number of water holes while following a reasonably straight line. David then described his northwest paddock and the easiest way of reaching it with a flock so Pat could pass the information on to Adolarious.

While he talked with his friend, David occasionally glanced at Alexandra as she sat beside the fire and wrote her letter. With the glow of the flames highlighting her lovely face, she was so strikingly beautiful that looking at her made his ardent love for her swell to a bittersweet ache. He knew that the letter was a difficult one for her to write, because she had set herself against her family by agreeing to marry him and her father would be enraged when he learned of it.

When they had discussed the subject, she had said that it was regrettable but unavoidable. He knew that it was far more important to her than her quick dismissal suggested, because her loyalties ran deep. However, he had found that she possessed the strength of character to endure what she could not change and to go on cheerfully with her life.

In addition, he knew that her loyalties had been transferred to him, because she loved him. That continued to be a source of wonder to him, a new keystone that supported everything meaningful to him. He had felt content on his land with his sheep, but in comparison, it had been a dull, gray existence that she had turned into a richly colorful life of joy. In the outback, he had found the life he had wanted, and she had made it complete.

Pat left the next morning, promising to send Adolarious and the sheep within a few days, and to return himself as soon as he and his men could make a track into the station. David drove his flock to pasture, taking an ax with him. During the previous spring, when he had planted the garden, he had also cut rings around scores of trees. In a grove near the grazing sheep, he began felling and trimming limbs from the dead, seasoned trees.

During the following days, the thickets at the home paddock became littered with logs, and David watched for some indication that Adolarious had arrived. A week after Pat had left, a faint haze of dust was on the horizon when David drove his flock to pasture that morning. As the sun rose higher, the dust slowly inched to the north, indicating that a flock of sheep were being driven to the northwest paddock.

Late in the morning, David put down his ax as the dogs at one side of the flock moved about restlessly, indicating that strangers were near. Mounting his horse, he rode around the sheep to the dogs. Adolarious rode out of the thick brush nearby, accompanied by two youths of about fourteen and fifteen riding bareback on a second horse.

The tall, middle-aged man wore his usual frock coat, high collar and cravat, and a top hat, all considerably the worse for wear. As he lifted his hat and greeted David in his rich Oxford accent, the pained expression on his face revealed his urgent desire to keep the conversation brief and to return to his privacy with his family.

Adolarious motioned the youths off the horse and pointed to the eldest. "That is Cornelius, and his brother is Eustace, Mr. Kerrick," he said. "You will find both of them to be excellent workers."

"There's plenty for them to do, and they'll be treated well," David replied. "If you keep your sheep headed the way they are now, you'll find the northwest paddock just south of a line of sharp hills I call Steeple Hills. There's a permanent fold in the center of the paddock."

"Very well, Mr. Kerrick. When do you plan to shear?"

"The shearers and drays will come here after they finish at Wayamba Station, which will be about the third week in September. The spring lambs should be weaned and grazing by then."

"Yes, they should. I'll see you then, Mr. Kerrick."

Adolarious lifted his hat again as he rode back into the brush, leading the spare horse. David turned to the youths who were surveying him with meekly amiable grins. Both of them were large and muscular for their age, with dusky skin and Aborigine features. They were clad in loose, heavy canvas trousers and shirts, their belongings rolled in tattered blankets slung over their backs.

The oldest boy pointed to himself and then to his brother, speaking in a mixture of Oxford English and stockman's slang, with an Aborigine accent, "I'm Corley and he's Eulie. That's easier to say, ain't it?"

"Yes, it is," David agreed, laughing. "Go take the hobbles off two of the horses over there, and I'll get you settled. You can use any horse except the chestnut which belongs to the mistress."

When the youths were mounted, David told them to move the sheep a short distance. Corley and Eulie signaled the dogs, skillfully moving the flock to where David had pointed. Satisfied that either of them could be left in charge of the sheep, David took them to the garden where Alexandra was working to introduce them to her.

She greeted them warmly and chatted with them for a few minutes, the boys bashfully stuttering replies. David then showed them around, telling them what they would be doing. When he finished, he sent Corley to watch over the sheep, and had Eulie help him stack the logs he had felled and trimmed. Using teams of horses, they dragged the logs to the opposite side of the hill from the garden.

By that evening, David saw that Adolarious had

understated his sons' abilities as workers. Skilled in the wide variety of tasks that stockmen had to do, the youths were eager to please, laboring with concentrated, unflagging energy. The next morning, they were up before David, chopping firewood and carrying water from the creek.

A few days later, when he had a large number of logs near the fold, David planned the dimensions of the buildings and their locations. The number of sheep he would have within the next two or three years justified only a small shearing shed, and he would need no more than a modest-sized building for storing supplies during that time. But eventually he could end up with a jumble of small buildings instead of a well-organized complex of large ones if he built only for his present needs.

When he discussed it with Alexandra, she had no doubts about what he should do. "Build to last, David," she told him. "The time will come when we'll be grazing tens of thousands of sheep, and everything on Tibooburra Station should be built to last through the years."

With her opinion as the determining factor, David and Eulie cleared brush and other growth from the large, level expanse at the side of the hill near the fold. After he decided each building's site in the complex, David paced off a large shearing shed, barracks, and warehouse as Eulie followed him and drove stakes into the ground. They then rolled large stones into place and fitted them together into low, thick walls with smaller rocks, making impregnably solid foundations for the buildings.

When the foundations were completed, the arduous labor of squaring logs into massive sleeper beams began. Late in the day, Corley and Eulie helped David slide the beams up inclines of stones and into place on the foundations with levers.

After the work on the buildings was begun, David started spending part of his time on other things.

Using the rough slabs he had split off the logs, he and Eulie made shelves for the cellar and pens for the cattle and pigs that Pat would bring. When the youths saw that containers were needed to store the vegetables neatly in the cellar, they wove grass baskets during the evenings, a skill they had learned from their mother.

David was working on the buildings again early one afternoon when Alexandra called to him from the hut. She came down the hill to join him, pointing to the south. Stepping onto a pile of logs, David saw Pat approaching across the paddock and exchanged a wave with him.

Pat reined up and dismounted, taking off his hat as he bowed and greeted Alexandra. He shook hands with David, then gazed in wonder at the work that had been accomplished. "David, when you set your mind to do something, you proceed quickly, don't you?" he commented with a laugh. "I didn't expect to see anywhere near this much done."

"Eulie and Corley have been a big help, Pat. Alexandra and I discussed it, and we decided upon large buildings that will suit both present and future needs, rather than small ones that would only suffice for now."

"Aye, I can see that, and they'll be fine buildings. It's easy to tell that you're an engineer, with knowledge of all sorts of levers and such. Some of those sleepers must weigh a ton, and I wouldn't want to try to move them without a half-dozen or more strong men helping me."

"I used inclines and levers to raise them onto the foundations, but I didn't attempt to get any of the uprights into place. That's going to take a block and tackle, with several men hauling on it."

"Well, I brought both," Pat said, "as well as whipsaws for cutting logs into boards and everything else we'll need. The wagons are five or six miles away and should get here an hour or two before sunset. Would you like to have the wedding tomorrow?"

Both men turned to Alexandra as the decision was hers. "Yes, let's have it tomorrow morning," she replied. "I'll get busy and start preparing food for everyone this evening, and I'll—"

"No, no," Pat interrupted, smiling and shaking his head. "The men cook for themselves, and Mayrah cooks for my family. It would be too hard on you to cook for the whole mob, and I won't let you. We brought along the wherewithal for a good feed after the wedding, and the men will prepare it. You're to enjoy the occasion, not work like a navvy."

"That's very kind and thoughtful of you," Alexandra told him, "but I insist that you and your family have your meals with David and me. Dinner will be ready when you arrive."

"Aye, very well," Pat replied, liking the arrangement. "Mayrah has been looking forward to meeting you, and that'll give her plenty of time to visit with you. I'd best get back to the wagons now."

He bowed to Alexandra again, then mounted and rode away. David resumed working around the foundations of the buildings, and Alexandra left to get an early start on the evening meal. When he finished the work he had started, Kerrick went to the washstand beside the creek to shave and get ready to receive the visitors.

They came into view later in the afternoon, two jackaroos in front to chop down brush and saplings. Pat and three other men rode behind the youths, followed by two wagons drawn by horses. At the rear, a third jackaroo herded the cattle and pigs. As they moved toward the hill, they left behind a trampled path that wound across the rolling terrain like a ribbon. It was a visible means of contact that reached across the wilderness, Tibooburra Station no longer isolated from the outside world.

David and Alexandra greeted the visitors at the foot
of the hill, the stockmen and jackaroos bowing awkwardly and mumbling as they were introduced to her.
She and Mayrah Garrity liked each other immediately, warmly exchanging pleasantries, then Mayrah introduced her children. Colin was shyly courteous, and
liking Alexandra as much as her mother did, Sheila's
habitual reserve melted into a wide smile.

The stockmen parked the wagons near the fold and
put the cattle and pigs into the pens awaiting them.
The Garrity family went to the hut with David and
Alexandra. Alexandra put the finishing touches on the
meal, as Mayrah and the children helped her, and the
men sat, talking over pannikins of rum. Once again,
Pat commented on how fortunate David had been to
meet Alexandra.

"It was like finding a mountain of gold," David
agreed, "except that she's more precious than any
amount of gold. She's happy here, but I know that
she's looking forward to hearing from her family."

"It might not be long before she does," Pat said.
"The rider I sent to Sydney was mounted on a good
horse. If nothing untoward occurs, he should get there
within four or five weeks. I told him to wait for a reply
from the Hammonds, and if all goes well, he should be
back here by late autumn."

He explained that the rider was also carrying a
report about the three bushrangers to deliver to the
chief justice.

As dusk fell, they ate, and during dinner Alexandra
and Mayrah discussed the dingoes. The Aborigine
woman said that they were something more than
simply a threat to sheep. In her broken English, she
explained that dingoes had an important role in the
outback.

"What they eat," she said, "it goes away. Something
not good or not wanted, it is no more if dingoes eat.
They make bad things not bad."

"Aye, they're scavengers," Pat interposed, laughing.

"If a dead 'roo or something is lying about and smelling the place up, they'll eat it. Everyone knows that, Mayrah. For my part, though, I'd rather do away with dingoes altogether and leave dead animals to the parrots."

Mayrah made no reply, but judging from her resigned smile at her husband, it seemed to David that Pat's interpretation of what she had said had been entirely wrong. It had been too literal, but at the same time, David was unsure himself of precisely what she had meant.

He exchanged a glance with Alexandra, who appeared to share his feelings.

At the end of the meal, the men lit their pipes. Near the wagons at the foot of the hill, the stockmen and jackaroos sat around a blazing fire after their meal, their voices and laughter carrying faintly up to the hut. Then as the fire burned low, the men and youths unrolled their blankets and lay down around it. Colin became sleepy and went to his bed in one of the wagons while Sheila remained beside the fire and listened as her mother and Alexandra conversed.

Pat yawned occasionally, and David also felt weary. However, the quiet conversation between the two women at the fire showed no sign of lagging; the daughter of a well-placed English family and the one of a Stone Age people had formed a warm friendship. Finally, Pat stood up and announced that it was time for bed, and they moved off into the night, walking down the slope toward the wagons.

At first light the next morning, the fire near the wagons blazed in the fading darkness. The stockmen dressed the extra pig Pat had brought and put it on a spit over the fire, then prepared large pans of vegetables to simmer slowly on the edge of the coals.

Late in the morning, everyone at the wagons came up to the hut. They took their places, Pat standing in front of David and Alexandra, Mayrah and her children behind them, and the others in a line at the rear.

Pat took off his hat, and the other men removed theirs. Then he opened his Book of Common Prayer and began reading the marriage service.

While it was a very simple ceremony, to David it was infinitely more meaningful because there were no embellishments to obscure the significance of the event of a man and woman being united in their love. The setting was more appropriate than the most lavish wedding with the immense vault of the Australian sky instead of a cathedral ceiling, and the organ music replaced by the whisper of the late-summer breeze. Most of all, it was the fulfillment of the need for his life to be complete.

When the ceremony ended, Alexandra and David turned to each other for the traditional kiss. Their lips had often met in passion, but that light touch of her mouth to his was more exhilarating than ever before because she was now his wife.

The silence among the small gathering broke up into conversation and laughter as the men shook hands with David and then shuffled awkwardly into line to claim their kiss from the bride. The formalities completed, the people trooped down the hill to the wagons where the stockmen had set up a make-shift trestle table near the fire. They took the pans of vegetables off the coals and placed them on the table.

The pig was done to a turn, and an appetizing scent wafted from it as Mayrah and Alexandra carved it. David took a plate with a rich, juicy slice of the fresh pork on it, then piled the plate high with vegetables. The food was less tasty than what Alexandra prepared, but his exuberant mood made it just as delicious as anything he had ever eaten.

When he finished eating, Pat took a jug of rum out of one of the wagons and placed it on the table with the pannikins. As the stockmen moved quickly toward the table, he warned them not to imbibe too freely, because work on the buildings would begin soon. David and Pat poured the rum, then moved aside as they talked.

Pat suddenly broke off in the middle of a comment and frowned suspiciously at Sheila. A few feet away, the girl was a picture of well-fed contentment, sucking her teeth and smothering belches. With one hand on her hip, she had a pannikin in the other and was sipping from it. "Sheila!" Pat snapped. "What do you have in that pannikin?"

"The same as you have in yours!" the girl retorted. "And it fits my hand as well as that one does yours!"

"You get a civil tongue in your head!" Pat said angrily. "I'll not have saucy remarks from you, and put down that rum!"

Mayrah walked up to the girl, frowning darkly, and took the pannikin. "No sauce!" she ordered. "And no rum!"

Glowering resentfully, Sheila turned away. The stockmen and jackaroos also turned from Pat, their faces crimson as they struggled to contain their laughter. Alexandra was both disapproving and amused, which matched David's feelings as he exchanged a glance with her.

Pat sighed heavily, drinking from his pannikin. "That girl will be the death of me," he grumbled. "The way she keeps my bile churned up, I'm certain to have a seizure one of these days. But I wouldn't trade her for every head of sheep on the face of the earth." He changed the subject, talking in a quieter voice, "David, Mayrah brought up something to me before we went to sleep last night . . ."

"Yes?" Kerrick prompted him.

"Well," Pat continued uneasily, "I'd never have guessed it myself, but Mayrah said that Alexandra is fairly along with child."

"Yes, that's true. Alexandra intended to tell Mayrah about it at some point, but she didn't say anything to me about having mentioned it. And like you say, it isn't obvious, so how did Mayrah know?"

"David, if you ever figure out how Aborigines know some things, then we'll both have learned something if you'll explain it to me. I've asked Mayrah, but I never get an answer that makes any sense to me. The reason I brought this up is because Mayrah wants to be here when Alexandra's time comes. Is that agreeable to you?"

"Absolutely," David answered emphatically. "I'll be very grateful indeed if she is here, Pat."

"Then I'll tell Mayrah, and she can tell Alexandra when they talk about it. Mayrah has ways of figuring out within a few days of when a baby is due, so she'll be here in plenty of time to attend to everything. She'll probably bring Sheila and some other women with her."

"Very well, and I appreciate it very much, Pat."

Pat dismissed the uncomfortable subject with a nod and discussed how to proceed with the work on the buildings. David felt vastly relieved. From time to time, he had thought about the dangers of childbirth that Alexandra would face within a few months. Now that an experienced woman would be with her, those dangers would be much less perilous.

When the visitors left, the area at the base of the hill had taken on the appearance of a home paddock. Off to one side of the fold stood the large shearing shed, barracks, and warehouse, needing only steps and other details to be completely finished. In addition, there were stacks of sawed boards and beams for future construction.

While he was gratified by the buildings, they made David even more aware of the shabbiness of the hut. With the nights becoming cool, Corley and Eulie slept in the barracks where they had a fireplace, while Alexandra still had to cook over an open fire. Construction of a house was still in the future, because they had discussed it and decided upon a large, stone house which would require materials from Sydney.

When he suggested that she move into one of the buildings for the present, she declined. "I prefer it here on the hill," she explained. "It has a view that touches my heart each time I look out over the countryside, and a fresh, pleasant atmosphere. The hut has its drawbacks, of course, but I'd rather remain here, David."

"Perhaps I'd better build a small house for now."

"Build to last, David," she reminded him. "We intend to have a stone mansion, not merely a house. The hut will suffice for now."

He pursued the subject no further, but it remained a source of dissatisfaction to him. Every time he saw Alexandra shivering beside the fire in the crisp early-morning air, it galled him. On each occasion when he rode back toward the hill, the contrast between the hut and the large buildings near the fold was painfully evident.

Another problem of less importance to him was the condition of the paddock, which was becoming grazed down. Although there were thousands of acres of grasslands in the vicinity, the exceptionally large flock had been pastured there for weeks at the end of the dry season when no new grass would sprout. However, the jackaroos were too inexperienced to take the flock to another paddock, risking encounters with dingoes while en route, and David was reluctant to leave Alexandra until the baby was born.

While exercising her horse, Alexandra noticed the lack of good graze and raised the issue with David. She suggested that he and one of the jackaroos move the flock to another paddock, leaving the other one to take the cattle to graze and the pigs to forage in the forest. When he refused, she pointed out that she was perfectly healthy, having rarely even experienced morning nausea during her pregnancy. He continued to refuse, knowing that he would endure constant anxiety about her if he left.

This time it was Alexandra who was dissatisfied,

saying nothing more on the subject. David was acutely aware that she was a strong, healthy woman, that Mayrah Garrity would be with her when the baby was born, and that the sheep needed better graze to insure healthy lambs and a good wool clip. However, Alexandra was his very life, and he wanted to be with her.

The first autumn rain came during the dark, early hours one morning, after a cool, clear day. Although the clouds moved in suddenly, the wind and the steady patter of raindrops on the hut awakened David. He dressed and pulled on his oilskins, then went out and built up the fire to keep the rain from extinguishing it.

When he went back into the hut, rain was dripping through the roof onto the blankets, and Alexandra was feeling for her oilskins in the dark. David helped her find them and spread the oilskins over the blankets, then he put his own on top of them. He undressed and went back to bed, but the blankets were damp and Alexandra shivered as she nestled against him for warmth.

At dawn, breakfast was miserable. Alexandra crouched beside the smoking fire in the rain to prepare porridge and tea, then she and David huddled together inside the dripping hut to eat. It was a familiar experience for him, because huts always leaked, and being cold and wet was a part of rainy weather, but he knew that Alexandra needed to be comfortable.

That morning, David and Eulie worked on the hut. Even with layers of bark so thick that the frame began sagging, the steady rain found its way through the roof in a few places, but Eulie knew how to protect the fire from the rain when there was little wind. He planted thin poles around the fire with connecting sticks at the top of them to support a tilted roof of bark so the rain would run off one side.

The next day, the rain continued and the ground around the hut was a quagmire of mud. David knew he had to do something. After weighing present needs against future plans, he came up with a solution. He sent Eulie to get two horses, then they hitched the team to a load of lumber beside the buildings and dragged it up the hill.

When they took the second load of lumber to the plateau behind the hut, Alexandra came out. "Building a wooden house now is contrary to what we agreed to do, David," she told him.

"Not the house that I have in mind, because it will become the kitchen and scullery at the rear of the house we'll eventually build. The interior walls won't support the roof, so I'll be able to pull them down. A stone house must have an interior frame of wood, and this will simply be a part of that frame when it has stone over it."

Alexandra hesitated, weighing what he had said, then she smiled. "I'm very fortunate to be married to such an intelligent, ingenious man," she commented. "Hurry and get it built, David."

David laughed as he and Eulie stacked the lumber with the first load as Alexandra returned to the hut. As the jackaroo led the horses away to bring more lumber, David paced off the full dimensions of the mansion that would one day stand on the plateau. When he decided where the kitchen and scullery would be, he gathered stones for a foundation.

Only part of the foundation had been completed at the end of the day, but the prospect of having a dry, warm house made the clammy cold of the hut easier for David and Alexandra to endure. The discomfort also faded the next day when the rain stopped and the sky cleared. During the following days, the warmth of late summer returned, as the sun beamed down on the grasslands that were tinted bright green with new growth.

The nights remained crisp, with the feel of a change in season in the air as work on the house progressed. Although this section would eventually be only part of the house, its proportions were substantial, divided into four rooms. When the floor and framework for the outside walls were completed, David began work on the fireplaces in two of the rooms. Lacking lime to make mortar, he used fine clay from a deposit down the creek to cement the stones, as he had done on the fireplace in the barracks.

The fair weather continued while the clay was drying and being baked into a solid bond between the stones by roaring fires, then clouds moved in again. The rain lasted for two days, accompanied by gusty winds that stirred the bark on the hut and warned of more violent storms that would come during the following weeks. When the sky cleared once more, the sun had lost its intensity and late autumn had arrived.

David devoted most of his time to working on the house, but he occasionally went out into the paddock to inspect it. With the new growth, the graze was adequate, but not abundant. The pasture was also becoming seriously damaged in places where the sheep had eaten the grass down to the roots before fresh sprouts had developed.

It needed months of not being grazed to recover, but David dismissed it, still determined not to leave Alexandra. She worked on the house with him, drilling holes to peg boards into place and doing other light tasks. Working together on their house was one of the most enjoyable experiences of David's life, but it seemed as if winter storms would arrive before the house was finished.

Early one afternoon, as Alexandra moved about and cleaned up wood shavings on the floor, she paused and looked into the distance. "Riders are coming down the track, David."

David straightened up from trimming a board and looked. The only visitor he had been expecting was a messenger from Wayamba Station, hopefully with letters to Alexandra from her family. If all had gone well, the rider who had been sent to Sydney should be returning at any time. But instead of one rider, in the distance were five, leading three pack horses and moving down the track at a slow walk.

"Who do you think they are, David?" Alexandra asked.

"I have no idea," he replied musingly. "I know they aren't bushrangers, though, because they never travel in groups larger than two or three, and they don't move about in broad daylight where they can be seen." He turned to the edge of the plateau where Eulie was leading the horses up with another load of lumber, and shouted, "Go put a saddle on one of those horses and bring it to the hut, Eulie! Hurry!"

The jackaroo hastily unhitched the horses and ran back down the hill with them as David and Alexandra went to the hut. She asked if she should begin preparing a meal for the riders, and David shook his head firmly. "No, there's no need for that. We'll provide them with rations, which is customary, but they can cook for themselves at the barracks. At least we can accommodate visitors now."

"That's true," Alexandra agreed, looking at the riders in the distance, then she sighed wistfully. "I do hope they've brought mail."

"So do I, love. We'll know soon."

She smiled and nodded, sighing again. A moment later, Eulie rode up, leading the saddled horse. David mounted it and rode down the hill. At the foot of the slope, he turned toward the track at a canter.

On the rolling contours of the terrain, the men were lost from view most of the time. As he crossed a rise, the riders also on a high point in the track a mile away waved at him. David rode down through a swale, and a few minutes later, the men came into sight again a little more than a half mile away. As they shouted greetings, David waved back, recognizing the employees from Frank Williamson's station on the Nepean River.

As he drew closer, he saw that the men were ragged,

and their horses were weary and bony. Only two of the pack animals, carrying crates wrapped in canvas, were in good condition. Silas Doak and Ruel Blake had grown into men, while the other three appeared much the same. A wide, cheerful smile wreathed Kunmanara's dark face, and Daniel Corbett, the head stockman, was soberly reserved. Jimbob, the old cook, sat at an angle on his saddle to favor his bad leg, seemingly impervious to the passing years.

The men greeted David warmly and with the respectful attitudes of workers toward a station owner. Daniel took an oilskin package from his coat pocket and handed it over. "There was some mail for your station at the postal office in Sydney, Mr. Kerrick," he said. "There are also some letters to the mistress from her family in that. Her clothes, books, and other belongings are in the boxes on those two pack horses there."

"She'll be very glad to get them, particularly the letters. I take it that you met up with the rider from Wayamba Station, then?"

Daniel nodded and explained as they rode down the track that Jimbob had been working at the inn in Sydney where the man from Wayamba Station had stayed. In talking with the man, Jimbob had found out about David and Alexandra, then had contacted Daniel. The head stockman had met Alexandra's brother, who had given him the letters from her family and her belongings, and the two horses to transport the crates to her.

"Apparently you haven't been working for Frank Williamson for some time now," David commented. "Did he pass on, then?"

"Yes, sir. Shortly afterward, his sons sold the station."

Daniel related what he and the other men had been doing since the station had been sold. Two of the jackaroos had found good jobs at Camden Park, but the others had been unable to find employment that satisfied them. In addition, Daniel, Jimbob, and Kunmanara had longed to return to the outback, and Silas and Ruel wanted to accompany them.

"So that's why we're here," Daniel summed up. "When I heard about your station, I got in touch with the others, and we all decided to come and see if we could work for you."

"Dan, that might be the best thing that could happen for me in two or three years from now," David said. "But for now, I'm grazing only about ten thousand sheep, which doesn't justify very many employees."

"We expected that," Daniel replied quickly, "and ten thousand is many more than we thought you'd have. If you can provide rations, we'll work for wages in arrears until you can pay us."

They reined up at the hill, the men anxiously waiting to hear what David would say. "Well, we can certainly talk it over," he told them. "Right now, I'm sure you'd like a rest and a good meal. Pick out a wether from the flock to butcher, and I'll send some vegetables to the barracks."

Satisfied by his reply, the men left the two pack horses with David and headed for the barracks. David ascended the hill, separating four letters to Alexandra from the others in the oilskin package. When he reached the hut and told her who the letters were from, she eagerly took them.

As Eulie helped unload the four heavy crates from the pack horses, David told him to take a basket of vegetables to the barracks and to put the horses with the others.

Alexandra sat beside the fire and pored over her letters, and David put on water to heat for tea, then looked at the other mail. It consisted of letters from wool brokers and supply factors soliciting business, reflecting that Tibooburra Station was becoming well-known in Sydney.

When the water boiled, Kerrick prepared the tea

and waited for Alexandra to finish reading her letters. They were obviously anything but heartening as her beautiful face reflected sorrow and disappointment as she scanned the lines. Only once did she smile, and then it was wistfully, accompanied by a pensive sigh.

She folded the letters and told David as she drank her tea that two were from her grandmother and mother, who wished her well in her new life. "However," she added, "they appear to believe I've met with some terrible doom. My letter to them was very cheerful, but it seems they consider my life here a tragic fate. My brother's letter is less distressed, but he's very sad that we'll be so far apart. There is nothing from my father, nor any mention of him in the letters. We were often at odds, and it appears that he's now dismissed me entirely from his life."

"I'm very sorry to hear that. Who is the other letter from?"

"Amy Godwin, a maid in my father's household. She's discontented there and wants to come and work for us."

"That could easily be arranged. She could come with the drays that bring supplies and the shearers, and I think it would be good for you to have another woman here with you, Alexandra."

Depressed by her family's letters, Alexandra agreed absently and sipped her tea, looking into the fire. Then shrugging off her mood, she asked about the five men. David told her who they were and why they had come to the station.

Eager to take her mind off the letters, Alexandra listened intently, interested in the men's offer. "The flock could be moved to better pasture immediately," she pointed out when David finished. "Also, it could be divided into two flocks that could be kept in paddocks indefinitely, which would eliminate the danger of losing sheep from moving them about."

"That's true," David agreed. "There would be advantages to hiring the men, and we could probably

provide rations for them. But we would have eight
employees and ten thousand sheep, which isn't very
sensible."

"If we're ever to have more sheep, those ewes must
have better graze so they'll give birth to strong lambs.
I'm sure we can provide the rations. We have abundant vegetables, as well as fresh beef and pork on the
hoof. We'll urgently need stockmen within a few
years, and in the meantime, there's plenty of work to
be done here at the home paddock."

David liked the men and wanted to hire them, but
he was inclined toward caution in expanding. Alexandra was more in favor of taking advantage of opportunities that promised future benefits, even if
temporary imbalances occurred that jeopardized
profits for a time. As they talked and the chill of the
autumn evening settled in, she swayed him to her
point of view.

"Well, we'll try it, then," David mused, throwing
wood onto the fire. "I'll have more help with the
house, so it should be finished soon."

"More importantly, the sheep will have better
graze. They're our livelihood and should be our first
concern."

"No, you're my first concern, Alexandra," he said
firmly. "I'll go down to the barracks and tell the men
what they'll be doing."

As he moved away from the fire, Alexandra began
preparing dinner. He glanced back at her, seeing that
her lovely face was melancholy again, and knew she
was thinking about the letters once more. It troubled
him deeply, his love making her pain his, but he knew
there was nothing he could do. Sighing heavily, he
went down the hill.

At dawn the next morning, some three thousand of
the sheep moved away toward the paddock to the
southeast with Silas and Corley driving them. Ruel
and Eulie followed the rest of the flock moving it

toward the southwest paddock. As the sheep left,
Daniel and Jimbob worked the house. Kunmanara
took the horses, cattle, and the few wethers remaining
at the home paddock to graze, along with the pigs to
forage in the patches of forest for roots and plants.
Later, when he returned, he helped work on the house.

The work proceeded rapidly because both Daniel
and Jimbob had experience as carpenters. During the
evenings, the two men assembled shutters and doors
by the light of the fire in the barracks. At their fire,
David and Alexandra split blocks of wood into shingles for the roof and whittled out pegs to fasten the
boards.

More than skill, Kunmanara had a talent for working with wood, and in the barracks at night, he used
limbs with curved forks to make the arms and legs of
chairs and settles. After constructing the frames and
scraping the wood down to a smooth finish with
sandstone, he upholstered the furniture with layers of
sheepskin.

While the house neared completion, the furniture
for it was stored in the supply warehouse. At dawn on
a cold, windy May morning, dark clouds harbingered
an early-winter storm that promised to be severe. The
wind blew gustier as the morning passed and David
and the men pegged down the last shingles on the roof
and put the shutters on the windows. Then they
brought the supplies from the hut to the house and
carried up the furniture from the warehouse.

Late in the day, David and Alexandra had moved
into the warm, snug house. The storm struck while
they were having dinner, rain pounding on the shingles and howling wind making the flames in the
fireplace leap higher. After dinner, David removed the
canvas from the crates that Alexandra's brother had
sent and opened them for her. She examined her
belongings reminiscently then she put them away.

Sitting beside the fire and smoking his pipe, David
watched her as she moved about the room. Although

she was heavily pregnant, her steps were still light. She took out snowy muslin undergarments and dresses in costly, colorful fabrics, filling chests and a clothes press that Kunmanara had made of hardwood. Next were books by the dozen, rapidly taking up the space on the shelves.

As she almost dropped a book from a stack and then caught it, David sat up in his chair when she made the sudden move. "Are you certain you don't want my help?" he asked.

"No, thank you," she replied, carrying the books to a shelf. "I've looked forward to doing this, and I prefer to do it myself. What I don't finish tonight, I'll do tomorrow."

David built up the fire to make more light for her, then sat back again and smoked as he watched her. The shelves were filled with books when she finished taking them out of a crate, and she commented that they would make the evenings more enjoyable. David agreed, the lack of reading material the only disadvantage he had found in the outback. When she was through for the night, with one crate still full, the books, pictures, and china ornaments she had placed about had banished the stark, spartan atmosphere of the house, turning it into a home.

The next morning, as David went to the barracks, he thought about how the work still to be done at the home paddock seemed endless. A cow calving in the wind and rain the night before emphasized that fact and determined the next project as the cow huddled in a corner of the pen, trying to protect the calf from the cold, driving rain. After raising a bark shelter for the cow and her offspring, David and the men prepared to build barns for the horses and cattle, and a shed for the pigs. As before, David paced off the dimensions of structures that would be large enough for the foreseeable future.

Two days later, when the shed for the pigs had been completed and work on the barns well begun, the

storm ended. Late autumn returned for a time before
the full onset of winter, the sky hazy and the feeble
sun barely dispelling the nighttime chill by afternoon.
The construction of the barns proceeded rapidly
during the cold, dry weather, and the one for the cows
was finished just in time for a second cow to calve in
it.

When a third calf was born, Jimbob pointed out the
benefits if one of them was used for veal. Without a
calf, the cow would provide milk and butter, and the
rennet from the calf was an essential ingredient for
cheese which he knew how to make. Agreeing with the
cook, David told Jimbob to butcher a pig at the same
time. David then sent Daniel to check on the flocks,
taking with him a portion of the veal and pork,
along with fresh supplies for the stockmen and
jackaroos.

Another storm had arrived when the head stockman returned a week later, reporting that all was well
with the flocks. During Daniel's absence, David and
the other two men had finished the barns, and on the
side of the hill overlooking the paddock buildings,
they had constructed a furnace to make clay pipe. The
day after Daniel returned from the paddocks and
while working at the furnace with the men, David
noticed riders and a wagon coming down the muddy
track in the rain, and rode out to meet them.

Two stockmen were with Mayrah and Sheila, all of
them bundled in thick sheepskin coats that draped
down over their saddles. In the wagon, a dozen
Aborigines huddled with their belongings under a
canvas cover, the rain pouring off it. David exchanged
greetings with Mayrah and thanked her for coming,
then turned to Sheila, who was surveying him somberly as rain dripped off her oversize stockman's hat.
"Are you all right, Sheila?" he asked.

"Do I bloody look all right?" she responded crossly.
"I'm soaked to the skin and frozen to the bone, that's
what I bloody am."

"No sauce, Sheila!" her mother snapped. "Be polite!"

"I was answering his flaming question, wasn't I?"
the girl grumbled irately. "Where's the bloody fault in
that? And the longer we sit here in this scurvy rain and
clap our jaws, the wetter and colder we'll be."

The stockmen barely concealed their amusement,
and Mayrah seethed with disapproval. David shared
both reactions as they moved on down the track. At
the foot of the hill, the wagon turned toward the trees
lining the creek, and David led the others up to the
house. As Alexandra met Mayrah and Sheila at the
door in an exchange of joyful greetings, the girl's surly
mood evaporated. David carried their baggage to the
room Alexandra had prepared for them, then took the
stockmen down to the barracks.

By the next day, the visitors had settled in comfortably. Smoke rose from fires in front of huts the
Aborigines had built in the trees beside the creek,
while Mayrah and Sheila chatted happily with Alexandra as they helped with chores around the house.
David and his men continued working at the furnace,
the stockmen from Wayamba Station helping them.

Along with his supplies for the next year, David
intended to order the parts to make a windmill and
pump to provide running water at the house. He and
his men had dug a deep trench, which they lined with
firewood and covered with blocks of sod, leaving an
opening at each end for an air intake and an exhaust
vent. In a shed beside the furnace, racks were filled
with straight, smooth lengths of slender tree trunks
that were covered with thick layers of clay from the
deposit down the creek. In the furnace, the tree trunks
were reduced to ashes as the clay baked, producing
lengths of hard, durable pipe for the water, as well as
for drains from the house.

Even in the cold and rain on the exposed hillside,
the area around the furnace was a comfortably warm
place to work. On the windward side, a large air

scoop, made of bark fastened to a framework of poles, funneled the wind into the air intake. The draft of forced air from the gusty wind made flames shoot out of the exhaust vent for several feet with a drumming roar, the intense heat warming the ground all around the furnace.

On the fourth evening after the visitors' arrival, Alexandra moved around restlessly shortly after she and David had gone to bed. Then she touched his arm, asking him to get Mayrah. As he was hastily pulling on his clothes, Mayrah entered the room with a candlestick.

She glanced at David then went to the bed. "Please, you go to the barracks now," she said quietly.

"No, I want to stay with my wife," David objected. "If there isn't anything I can do, I won't interfere. But I want to stay."

The woman shook her head firmly, repeating what she had said. In the flickering light of the candle, Alexandra smiled entreatingly at him and asked him to leave. Reluctantly, David dressed and then left the room.

When he went into the front room, Sheila was going out the door, carrying a lantern. Pulling on his coat and hat, he went outside and through the light, steady rain and darkness, he saw the spot of light from the lantern moving down the hill toward the Aborigines' huts in the trees.

In the same inscrutable way that Mayrah had known, the Aborigines at the huts were also apparently aware that the forces of nature were approaching a climax at the house. Fires were blazing in front of the huts, and a moment later, a didgeridoo groaned in the night. Others joined it, building up to a throbbing dirge of two deep, resounding notes.

Rhythm sticks clattered in cadence with the didgeridoos, then voices harmonized as they rose in a chant. The sounds blended into a pulsing whole that seemed to come from all directions, thick smoke from the fires billowing up the hill. Sheila returned from the huts, becoming dimly visible in the light of her lantern as she passed a few yards away. Carrying a basket of herbs, she went into the house. David turned and walked down the hill toward the barracks.

The men in the barracks were out of bed and dressed, building up the fire as the cook filled billys to heat water for tea. "We heard the corroboree," Daniel explained as David entered.

The men moved benches from the table to the fireplace, and David took a seat as the others settled themselves. "What's the corroboree mean, Kunmanara?" Jimbob asked as he put the billys on the fire. "What are they saying when they sing out like that, and what's it all in aid of?"

"Don't ask me," Kunmanara replied. "I've been eating mutton and damper too long, and I know no more about it than you do."

The men laughed, then became quiet. All of them life-long bachelors, they had no advice or encouragement to offer David. When the tea was ready, Jimbob passed it around. Daniel exchanged a few comments with the stockmen from Wayamba Station, discussing the sheep there. There were other moments of desultory conversation between long silences, when the only sound was that of the corroboree.

The time he had dreaded having arrived, David sat, staring into the fire, the tea in his billy untouched and cold. As Alexandra endured the agony and peril of childbirth, he suffered in fear of losing her, of having his very purpose in life taken away from him.

Each minute seemed an eternity, but somehow they passed and joined into hours. The men dozed on the benches as the fire burned low. When the encroaching chill awakened one of the men, he put wood on the fire and fell asleep again. The fire roared for a time, then gradually settled into ashes until one of the men woke once more.

A steely silence suddenly fell during the early-morning hours as the sounds from the huts abruptly ceased. David sat up with a jerk, which woke the other men. The barracks were cold and dark, and the men commented about the quiet as one of them put wood on the coals in the fireplace. As it blazed, David put on his coat and hat to go to the house. Just then, the door opened and Sheila entered with a lantern.

"Is it over, Sheila?" one of the men from Wayamba Station asked.

"You attend to your own bloody flock and leave others be, dag worm," the girl replied acidly. The man she had addressed and others burst into laughter as she turned to David. "If you can tear yourself away from your mates, your wife would like to see you. You have a son."

"How is Alexandra?" he asked, moving toward the door.

"Well enough," Sheila replied, her tone and the expression on her small, brown face cordial for once. "My ma says she'll be all right."

The tension from the long night suddenly leaving him, David followed the girl outside, feeling weak with relief. Holding up the lantern in the rain and early-morning darkness, Sheila ran to keep up with his long strides as they climbed the hill. At the house, he hurried into the bedroom, then a twinge of his anxiety returned when he saw Alexandra.

In the candlelight her beautiful face was pale and drawn in sorrow, as well as lined with fatigue. Mayrah walked away from the bed and motioned Sheila to follow her as David moved toward it and bent over Alexandra, kissing her. "How do you feel, love?"

Ignoring the question, she turned to the baby nestled beside her. "Hinton said I would never be rid of him," she whispered bitterly, "and he told the truth. The baby has a birthmark, David."

Concerned only with her, David looked at the baby for the first time. She pulled down the edge of the soft cloth around it, showing him the birthmark on the tiny shoulder. It was the same crimson color as the birthmark that had covered the side of Hinton's face.

"That means nothing whatsoever," he assured her. "Our son will grow up to be a fine man, one who is respected and admired." Searching for a way to take her mind off the birthmark, he thought of the name. "As we discussed, shall we name him Morton, after your uncle in London?"

Alexandra sighed and nodded, then smiled wanly. "You're a good man and a good husband, David. A woman who bears another man's child would suffer recriminations from most husbands, but your only thought is to make me cheerful. I'm a fortunate woman, and I love you so much."

"I love you just as much, and I'm the one who is fortunate. And there's no reason to feel anything but cheerful good spirits. You're going to be all right, and we have a son who'll make us very proud of him."

Her smile had a hint of its usual radiance as he kissed her again, but a haunting shadow of apprehension lingered in her blue eyes.

Chapter Fifteen

Six years had passed since her wedding feast, and though she had seen Patrick Garrity from time to time since then, Alexandra now noticed streaks of gray in the burly man's hair that had not been there on that memorable occasion. As he bowed and replied to her greeting, he made an indirect reference to what she had observed. "I'm well, Mistress Kerrick," he said, "but I'm feeling the weight of the passing years a bit now."

"No one would know it," she assured him. "You seem as hale and hearty as when we first met some years ago. Please come in, and I'll have your things taken to a room. David and I are eager to hear about Mayrah and the children, and I'm sure you would like some refreshment."

The stable boy held Pat's horse, ready to take it to the barn. Pat untied his bedroll and other belongings from behind the saddle. He tucked them under his arm, and the boy led the horse down the tree-lined avenue through the landscaped grounds from the front of the house to the edge of the plateau. Alexandra and David turned on the front steps to go inside, but Pat paused looking up at the house.

Built of native stone, it was three stories high, with wings reaching back on both sides. Except for the entrance portico supported by columns, the front of the house was plain, the unadorned window openings emphasizing the massive expanse of the building. The lack of architectural detail provided an elegant simplicity, while at the same time, the straight, uncluttered lines evoked a sense of authority. The huge house towered like a great stone keep, dominating the surrounding terrain.

With lawns flanking the avenue in front, at the sides and rear of the house were flower gardens and large trees. On the mild spring day in October, the flower beds were starting to blossom and the trees were alive with birds. "I never tire of looking at this house," Pat commented as he went up the wide, stone steps with Alexandra and David. "It's well worth the ride from Wayamba Station just to see it again."

"That's a ride we wish you could make more often, Mr. Garrity," Alexandra told him. "It's been far too long since we've seen you."

"Aye, and too long for me as well," Pat agreed. "But at times graziers have too much work to be able to enjoy the fruits of their labor. I'm sure it's much the same with you, David."

David nodded, replying that he had returned only the day before after some three weeks of making the rounds of the paddocks. In the wide entry hall, they were met by the maid, Emma Bodenham, one of the eccentric stockman's many children. She took Pat's belongings and went up the staircase to put them in a guest room as the men followed Alexandra into the parlor, where a low fire burned in the marble fireplace.

The men sat in the large, comfortable armchairs. At

the liquor cabinet, Alexandra filled a glass with port for David and another with the rum that Pat always preferred, then handed the drinks to the men.

She left and went upstairs to fetch her sons to greet Pat. On the mezzanine overlooking the entry, she turned down the wide hall into the east wing and went into the first room. It was a classroom, with desks, bookshelves, and large chalk boards with stools in front of them.

Two boys worked on sums she had written on the boards that morning. Morton was a slender, blond-haired boy with pale blue eyes and well-formed features. A reserved, moody child, the six-year-old glanced up at Alexandra and turned back to his chalk board. His brother, Jonathan, a fair, cherubic boy of five, grinned at Alexandra, radiating a sunny disposition.

Putting down her knitting, Amy Godwin stood up from a chair under the window as Alexandra entered the room. Thirty years old and very stout, the former maid in Alexandra's home in Sydney had come to the station with the drays that had brought the supplies and had hauled away the wool. As a nurse, she had turned out to be perfect. Loving and endlessly patient, she viewed caring for the children as a pleasure rather than work.

Alexandra checked the sums that Jonathan had completed, pointing out errors. Reacting with his characteristic good nature, he hastily corrected the numbers. But when she did the same with Morton, he was peevishly defensive. While she loved him devotedly, the same as Jonathan, Alexandra was determined to crush his tendencies to be like his biological father, and it seemed to her that he had several.

"These are the same sort of sums that we've been working on for days," she reminded him. "Don't you understand them? If not, we'll begin over. But if you're merely not concentrating, that's another matter."

The boy shrugged sullenly in reply, turning away from her.

"Morton, I must know what the difficulty is, or I can't help you," she insisted. "Now kindly tell me why you made the errors."

"I'll change the numbers that are wrong," he mumbled sullenly.

"That isn't the point, Morton. I can't follow you through life and correct every error you make. I can only help you learn how to avoid errors. Now why did you make those mistakes?"

"I don't know!" he replied angrily.

"Don't defy me!" Alexandra snapped. "Look at me when I speak to you!" The boy turned to face her, and she pointed a warning finger at him. "I've told you before that I shan't tolerate defiance. If you form a disposition now of setting yourself against rightful authority, it will bring you to no good end when you're a man. I shall not allow you to do that."

The boy looked up at her in morose silence, and the atmosphere in the room tensed. Jonathan was always disturbed when Morton was reprimanded, while Amy had a protective attitude toward the children, invariably defending them regardless of what they did. "Madame," she began hesitantly, "it's such a lovely day outside, and they find it hard to sit here and . . ."

Her voice faded at Alexandra's searing, sidelong glance. Controlling her anxiety over her son, Alexandra knelt beside his stool and held him, the scent and feel of his small body in her arms a joy. "Defiance is a barrier to improvement, Morton," she said in a soft, imperative voice. "When I point out faults, it's because I love you and want you to avoid that which will bring you harm and pain. If you defy me, I must punish you until you stop. Please don't make me do that."

The boy nodded and murmured a reply, but his tone was defensive rather than apologetic. And while he made no overt move to pull away from her,

Alexandra could sense his withdrawing into himself. Dismissing the entire matter for the present, she stood up and pointed out the mistakes he had made. He corrected the numbers, then she led the two boys out of the room and downstairs.

Smaller than his younger brother, Morton also lacked Jonathan's exuberant energy. He walked sedately down the hall and stairs, while Alexandra had to correct Jonathan to keep him from bounding down the steps and disturbing the household. When they greeted Pat, the marked differences in their personalities were more than evident.

The boys bowed politely, as Alexandra had taught them, but Pat wanted more than that. Laughing merrily, he pulled the boys to him and hugged them affectionately. Jonathan was ready to climb onto his lap, always willing to be friendly, but Morton drew back from Pat, just as reserved as his brother was outgoing.

When she took the children back upstairs, Alexandra told Amy to let them go outside and play when they finished their sums, then she went to the kitchen to plan dinner with the cook. In her forties, Flora Blainey was married to a stockman and, having worked in several homes in Sydney as a cook, was highly skilled. Just as importantly, she and her family enjoyed life in the outback, an essential requirement in a dependable employee.

Knowing that Pat preferred somewhat plain, bulky fare, Alexandra considered and then dismissed several choices for entrees that were more flavorful than substantial. She decided upon capon Kiev with vegetables in butter sauce and potatoes au gratin. "Not too much garlic on the chicken," she told Flora. "We'll have the Camden Park riesling with dinner, and it doesn't stand up well to an abundance of spices."

"Yes, mo'm. Chicken broth would do well for the soup, then."

"It will, and thicken it with pearl millet. For the fish

course we'll have dried cod, steamed in butter to coordinate with the main course. No egg glaze on the bread, please. Our guest's teeth aren't as sound as they once were. For dessert, we'll have pommes au riz."

The cook nodded, and she and her helper began moving purposefully in the large, spotless kitchen as Alexandra left.

Returning to the parlor, Alexandra refilled the men's glasses and poured a small glass of sherry for herself, then sat down and joined the conversation.

For four years, the wool clip at Tibooburra Station had been so large that separate drays had been coming from Sydney for it, instead of those that went to Wayamba Station. Ever since then, the contacts between the stations had diminished. When the subject turned to the breeding of sheep, Pat was surprised to find that Alexandra and David had bought several purebred Merino rams from Camden Park during the past year.

David explained that Alexandra was friends with the Macarthurs, who had agreed to sell her the rams, and two stockmen had been sent to drive the sheep to the station. Within the next two or three years, he added, the cost of the rams should be offset by an increase in wool production. Pat asked to be informed of the results, then when David mentioned showing him improvements in the home paddock, he regretfully replied that he would have to leave early the next morning. David objected, trying to talk him into staying longer, but Pat insisted that he had to return to his station as soon as possible.

Alexandra added her protests to her husband's, but she had already suspected that the visit would be a short one. Sensitive to nuances of attitude in those she knew well, she had concluded that Pat had come for some specific reason that he would reveal in his own good time.

A few minutes before dinnertime, when the children were having their meal in the staff dining room off the kitchen, Alexandra went to check on them. After spending a few minutes with the boys, she left, feeling frustrated and uneasy. Morton had been eating heartily until she had gone into the room, then he had begun picking at his food.

Dinner went well, the food prepared as expertly as always, and the men ate well. Alexandra suspected that Pat might have preferred a billy of tea to the riesling, and even though she liked the wine, it was a preference she could understand. From time to time, she longed for tea from a fire-blackened billy, with its overtone of eucalyptus smoke.

After dinner, they returned to the parlor, where the men filled their pipes, and Alexandra poured brandy for David, more rum for Garrity, and a small glass of mint cordial for herself. For an hour, the conversation continued to be that of friends who have been apart for a time. Then, when Pat began talking about an official in the chief justice's office in Sydney, Alexandra knew he had arrived at the purpose of his visit.

"As a justice of the peace," Pat continued, "I've exchanged correspondence with him frequently over the years. We've become quite friendly, and he's notified me of various things that happened there. In his last letter, he said that the governor and his staff have decided to concentrate on surveying crown lands so they can be sold to raise revenues."

"Does he think that will affect us?" David asked. "This area hasn't even been officially explored, Pat. It can't be surveyed, because on the maps of the colony in Sydney, it's still a complete blank."

"Aye, for now," Pat agreed. "But some of the blanks are starting to be filled in." He took a folded sheet of paper from his pocket and handed it to David. "That's a copy of the latest map from the colonial surveyor's office, and you may keep it."

After glancing over the map, David handed it to Alexandra as he and Pat continued talking. Holding it to the light of the lamp on the table beside her chair, she studied it. While it was primarily of the east coast to the north and south of Sydney, it was more complete than any map she had ever seen. New villages were shown, and it included river systems and other features in an arc some two hundred miles inland from Sydney.

She folded the map and put it aside, listening to Pat. He speculated that within a few years, the region would be explored, then declared crown lands. "We have only grazing licenses, David," he pointed out. "That's far from property titles, so we'll be on a slippery slope."

"Perhaps, but there are rights by tenure and useage. I'm not a lawyer, but I know that such rights exist in common law."

"Well, there's a lawyer in Sydney who I've done business with a few times, and I've written to him about this. If my station is threatened, I'll try the courts first, then lead and gunpowder last. But I thought I'd best warn you and Mistress Kerrick so you can plan your own measures."

David expressed his thanks, and Alexandra added hers. Turning to other things, the discussion continued for a time. Their friendship sealed by years of shared experiences, all three of them were reluctant to end the evening. Finally, the hour growing late, David showed Pat to his room as Alexandra went to the children's rooms.

Jonathan was sound asleep, but he immediately stirred when she bent over his bed to kiss him. He drowsily put his arms around her neck and kissed her, then fell back to his pillow, asleep again almost instantly.

Her other son was awake, his breathing shallow, but he acted as if he were asleep. "I shan't give you any peace and let you rest until you give me a kiss, Morton," she said teasingly.

He turned and kissed her, but it was perfunctory, and she could sense his coldness. Ignoring his attitude, she combed her fingers through his hair, tucking the covers around him, then left his room.

In their room, David prepared for bed as Alexandra sat in front of the dressing table and brushed her hair. They briefly discussed the problem of the land survey, then Alexandra mentioned her concern about Morton. "He seems more resentful and very cold toward me of late," she mused. "I wonder if I'm being too severe with him."

"Severe?" David echoed, laughing. Standing behind her, he pushed her hair aside and kissed the back of her neck. "You're so sweet and gentle that you can't even be firm with the boys unless it's fully deserved."

Alexandra smiled at him in the mirror, then smothered a sigh and continued brushing her hair when he moved away. Long before, she had found out that he had a lack of moderation in his feelings, a characteristic that had made him suspicious of all women after his first wife had betrayed him. Instead of being loved, she was adored, with no faults as far as he could see. It was richly gratifying, but it also had its disadvantages.

The next day, after Pat left, Alexandra worked with the boys on their lessons for an hour before leaving them to go riding. She rode down the hill and out on the track to be alone for she had three things to ponder. The first was that she might be pregnant again. She and David longed for a daughter, and she weighed whether to tell him immediately. Then, not wanting to raise his hopes, she decided to wait until she was certain she was pregnant.

The other two matters—the possibility that the region would eventually be seized as crown lands, and her relationship with Morton—were far more complex, the solutions elusive. Increasingly, she had seen traits in Morton that reminded her of Enos Hinton. Just as Hinton had said, she was unable to exorcise the bushranger from her life.

Thinking about her problems, she stopped on the

track and gazed over the home paddock. The warehouses, cookhouse, barracks, shearing shed and its pens, and other structures in the complex of buildings covered acres to the west of the hill. East of it, gardens, fruit orchards, and a dozen cottages for married stockmen spread along the creek. Further down the creek was an Aborigine village. The stone mansion overlooked all of it and the surrounding countryside from the plateau on the hill.

To her, the value of the station was on a scale where money was completely irrelevant. It was a way of life, and Alexandra shrank from thoughts of losing it. The home paddock was a teeming center of activity in a vast wilderness, the focal point of over a million acres where some seventy-five thousand sheep grazed. It provided full employment for scores of people, as well as substantial income for thousands more in the path of the tons of wool that eventually reached English mills.

That train of thought suddenly gave Alexandra an idea about how to protect the property. She had considered the course Pat had chosen, which could involve years of litigation, and dismissed it. What she wanted was a means that would produce results quickly as well as conclusively, ending in a clear title to the land instead of the conditional right of occupancy that could be the result of a court settlement.

That clear title could be obtained only by a land grant, which seemed out of the question. Land near Sydney was sold in parcels that ranged up to a hundred acres, so it appeared unlikely that a request for a grant of over a million acres would be received favorably, to say the least. But as she pondered her idea, she recalled the map that Pat had brought, and a way of drawing favorable attention at the highest level occurred to her.

Her thoughts racing, she realized that even pursuing the idea was open to question, but at least it was a possibility. Deciding to investigate it, she rode back toward the house.

As she entered the house, Amy was coming down the stairs, her round, rosy face distraught. "Thank goodness you're here, madame," the nurse said. "Master Morton has been misbehaving rather badly."

Alexandra drew in a deep breath and sighed grimly as she went up the stairs, and the nurse hurried after her. "What happened, Amy?"

"I noticed that he hadn't touched his sums," the nurse explained, "so I told him that he should set to work or you would be displeased with him. Then he became very angry, and . . . Well, you'll see, madame."

The woman opened the door for Alexandra. Sitting on his stool and frowning sullenly, Morton ignored her as she entered the room. His chalk board was tipped over onto the floor, and chalk scrawls were slashed over the sets of numbers she had drawn on the board. Jonathan worked feverishly, darting apprehensive glances at her.

"Amy, take Master Jonathan out into the gardens," she said.

The nurse beckoned and the boy ran to her. Then the door closed behind them.

"Morton," Alexandra said quietly, "if you can give me a reasonable explanation for this, I won't punish you." As he silently shrugged, her patience ended: "Tell me why you did this, Morton!" she snapped.

"I was angry," he muttered, still not looking at her.

Knowing it would be useless to question him further, Alexandra tried to convince herself that it had been the act of a rebellious, willful child. She wanted to believe that, but was unable to. His anger seemed too much like the blind, unreasoning rage that she had seen in Enos Hinton, the brutal, mindless striking out at any nearby object or person.

"I must think and decide upon an appropriate

punishment," she told him. "Go and stand in the corner until I return."

He glared at her, then turned and went to a corner. Her blood ran cold as Alexandra clenched her hands into fists so tightly that her fingernails pressed into her palms, and she wanted to scream. In the instant that his gaze had met hers, she had seen Enos Hinton's feral eyes glowering out of her son's small face. Shaken to the depths of her being, she left the room.

Downstairs, she struggled to put that hate-filled glare out of her mind, and concentrated on her idea for getting a land grant and wondered if it was feasible. When she did, her difficulty with Morton fell into place with the idea, a possible solution to her problems with the boy occurring to her. She ran out of the house, looking for David.

He was at the windmill with two jackaroos helping him repair it. Going toward him, Alexandra felt the warm, comfortable sense of emotional and physical security he provided. Towering over the jackaroos, the large, powerful man she loved deeply appeared capable of anything. Alexandra knew, however, that she alone could resolve the problems with Morton, if indeed there was any solution at all.

When she took him aside and explained her idea, she was glad that she had said nothing about her uncertain pregnancy. She knew that if she had, he would have been obstinately against her traveling anywhere. He still objected, always wanting them to be together as much as possible.

"I can send for Adolarious," he told her. "Your way of going about getting a land grant is excellent, and it might well succeed. Adolarious can probably do what you need, but you don't have to go there. He should be more than glad to come here, considering the clothes and other things you've sent him over the years."

"Even so, he doesn't like to come here, and what I want done is entirely outside his duties as a stockman. But there's another reason why I want to go." She briefly explained what Morton had done, adding that she wanted to take him with her. "While we're by ourselves, away from all distractions, I may be able to reach a better understanding with him."

"Perhaps all he needs is a thrashing," David suggested, frowning.

"David, I would take a stock whip to him if I thought it would be of any avail. But defiance is only driven in deeper by a thrashing."

His frown fading, he smiled at her fondly. "Could you be seeing something of someone in the boy that isn't there?" he asked gently. "I know you've always feared that, love. But he's your son and mine, no one else's, and many boys are difficult to control."

"I'm only a mortal human being, David. If I were omnipotent, I would gaze into his nature like seeing into a crystal goblet. As it is, I can only interpret what seems to be there and act upon my beliefs."

"You're the most perfect human being God ever created," David assured her earnestly. Then he looked away, sighing and nodding. "Very well, Alexandra, I'll have some men escort you to the northwest paddock."

"David, I won't need a large escort, because I—"

"You'll have an adequate escort," he said firmly, interrupting her. "You'll also have everything else needed for your safety and comfort, because I intend to see to it myself."

Alexandra smiled, standing on tiptoe to kiss him, then returned to the house.

Jonathan would have received the news about the journey with delight, regarding it as an adventure. Morton, however, appeared to view it as the punishment for his temper tantrum, nodding glumly when she told him.

At dawn the next morning, Alexandra and Morton set out with the escort. When she had first thought of going to see Adolarious, Alexandra had anticipated being accompanied by no more than a stockman and a jackaroo, but a long procession moved away from the house. Two stockmen had four jackaroos with them, along with eight pack horses loaded with everything she might possibly need, including canvas for a tent if it rained.

There was no threat of rain, only a few fleecy clouds against the rich blue of the sky as the sun rose. Over the years, tracks had developed between the paddocks. The horses moved at a slow trot as the track wound through great sweeps of spinifex and mallee, and past groves of gaunt shaggybarks and silvery, ghostly gum trees. In places, dead trees were rotting skeletons of wood, their bare, gray limbs stretched up to the sky.

Riding beside Alexandra, Morton was silent. She knew he would eventually talk to her out of sheer loneliness, away from his brother and Amy. A couple of the jackaroos were only a few years older than the boy, but Alexandra knew he would avoid their companionship. They were boisterously playful with each other, which Morton disliked.

Alexandra made no attempt to converse with him, enjoying the journey as she waited for him to talk. Amid the constant chatter of gloriously colorful lorikeets, rosellas, and cockatoos, she watched wombats, kangaroos, and other animals race away from the horses. Around every turn in the track was another view of the land she loved, the outback.

At sunset, they camped beside a billabong, and the jackaroos kindled two fires several yards apart. Through lack of recent practice, Alexandra burned a finger slightly while cooking, but the meal was more than worth it. The most delicious cuisine prepared by the cook suffered in comparison with the simple food prepared over a fire and eaten as the after-glow of sunset faded into dusk over the immense outback.

Morton spoke to Alexandra the next day, but it was mostly grumbling. Flies hovered and he said that he wished one day to be away from insects and never to have to ride a horse again. Following up on the conversational opening, Alexandra asked him what he wanted to do in life. "Simply get away from here," he replied, batting at flies.

"Very well, you can do that," she told him. "I love it here, but that doesn't mean that you should. You could live in Sydney, if you wish."

The boy had apparently never seriously considered that he could live elsewhere, and he gazed at her thoughtfully as he weighed what she had said. Then he dropped the subject, talking desultorily about other things. At their campfire that evening, however, he brought it up again and told her about his ambitions, which were understandably vague at his age. They involved a sedentary way of life, an occupation in an urban setting.

"Perhaps a position as a functionary in the colonial government," Alexandra suggested. "Or in business, like my brother, Creighton."

"What does he do?"

Never interested in her brother before, Morton listened closely as she talked about Creighton. Since the death of their mother, he had moved into the family household with his wife and three daughters. He still managed the family business while her father concentrated on his law practice. Over the years, she had maintained an affectionate correspondence with Creighton. But she had never heard from her father, even when her mother had died.

In some of his letters, Creighton had mentioned facts about the family business. Alexandra told Morton about them, as well as what she could recall from when she had been with the family. In simple terms, she explained the principles behind investments in shipping, land, and the other business interests in which Creighton was involved.

The boy was keenly interested, and the conversation continued during the following days while they rode up the track. At noon on the day after they reached the huge northwest paddock, the permanent fold at the center of it came into view. The others dismounted to wait, and Alexandra rode ahead to the cluster of bark huts beside the fold.

Several small children peeked around the huts at Alexandra in timid curiosity, and the Aborigine woman beside the fire held a baby as well as a child almost large enough to walk. She pointed out the valley to the north where the flock was grazing, and Alexandra thanked her and turned toward it. Soon, the flock came into view. Although five of his children were employed in various positions on the station, Adolarious still had plenty of help, because four youths were with the dogs watching over the flock.

The tall, rangy man sat under a tree on a nearby slope, working over a sketchbook. As a result of the clothes she had sent him, he looked as dapper as he did out of place in the outback in his usual formal attire. Instead of hiding, as he often did when unexpected visitors appeared, he put his sketchbook aside and waited as she rode toward him.

His thin, aristocratic face, like wrinkled leather from age and the elements, broke into a smile, and he doffed his hat as she reined up. "This is indeed a pleasure, Mistress Kerrick," he said.

"As it is for me, Mr. Bodenham. I trust that I find you well."

"I am quite well, dear lady, despite my advancing years," he replied. "One need not inquire about you, for you are a veritable picture of health and happiness. Please join me in the shade."

Sitting under the tree with him, she brushed aside his thanks for the clothes and sketching materials she had sent. They discussed his children who were employed at her station, Alexandra telling him about those he had not seen for some time, then she broached the purpose of her visit. When he acknowledged that he had traveled widely in the outback before working at Wayamba Station, she took out the map Pat had given them.

"I urgently need a map of the region west of this," she told him. "Ideally, it would encompass as much of the region as possible and include the area around Tibooburra Station. As an educated man with artistic talent who has traveled the outback, it occurred to me that you might be able to prepare a map that shows what you have seen."

He made no direct reply, perplexed as he studied the map. "I'm amazed, Mistress Kerrick," he commented. "It surpasses belief that no more of Australia than this has been explored."

"Officially explored," she pointed out. "Others must have traveled about, as you did, but their findings haven't been documented. But there are indications that official explorations will be undertaken eventually."

"And the region will be designated crown lands," Adolarious added, his astute mind perceiving her purpose. "So you need the map in connection with protecting Tibooburra Station. To get a land grant, perhaps?"

"Exactly. If I can get a map of the region, I'll rename the Cobdogla River the Darling River, for the governor. That should insure at least a sympathetic review of a request for a land grant."

"Indeed it should!" Adolarious exclaimed, laughing. "What an excellent idea, dear lady. As it happens, I'm in the happy position of being able to assist you. Years ago, I drew up maps of my travels. They extended to the Lachlan and Murrumbidgee Rivers south of here, hundreds of miles to the north, and to the desert country to the west. You are more than welcome to take the maps and do whatever you wish with them."

Alexandra was delighted, having expected at best that Adolarious would draw up a map and send it to her. As they went to their horses, he called to the four youths and told them that he was going to the fold and would return soon.

On the way to the fold, Alexandra asked Adolarious about his family. In newspapers she had received with the mail, she had read about a Sir Geoffrey Bodenham who had been appointed as an undersecretary in the colonial office in London. He was from the Surrey branch of Bodenhams, a well-placed family she had heard about long ago. When she mentioned him, Adolarious reluctantly admitted that the man was his younger brother.

"I prefer that not to be widely known," he added. "More important, at present I prefer that my family in England not know where I am."

His reasons none of her affair, Alexandra quickly agreed to say nothing to anyone about the matter. At the fold, Adolarious went into one of the huts and rummaged about, then came out with three maps drawn on sketch paper. Alexandra examined them, marveling at the gigantic area they covered, as well as the detailed depiction of rivers, mountain ranges, and other features. Barren Mountain at the south boundary of the station and Steeple Hills at the north boundary were clearly shown on one of the maps. Wayamba Station was also indicated, and Adolarious had written in some names for features.

A name near the station to the south aroused her curiosity. She pointed to it, and asked, "Broken Hill? Why did you call it that, Mr. Bodenham?"

"It's a translation of Wayamba, the Aborigine name," he told her.

Knowing that the wealth of information on the maps would be received in Sydney with great pleasure and gratitude, making her chances of success more likely, Alexandra wanted to repay Adolarious in some way. When she asked if there was anything she could do for him, he replied that he would like his family in England to be notified upon his death.

"That will resolve any problems regarding inheritance of family properties that were occasioned by my departure from there," he explained. "Also, I had hoped that whatever children I had would be of a self-sufficient age by now, but my wife is a woman of extraordinary fertility. So I would like for them and my wife to be looked after."

"I'd have done that without your asking, of course, so you may set your mind at ease about them. And while I'm sure you have many years remaining, I'll promptly notify your brother when you go to your reward. Can you think of anything else I can attend to for you, Mr. Bodenham?"

"Yes, my sketches. The ones I consider my best are boxed and wrapped in canvas. I'd like for you to do whatever seems best with them."

Alexandra agreed to take charge of the sketches upon his death, then asked if there was anything further she could do for him. He could think of nothing else, the simple life he had chosen involving few affairs that would need to be settled. She continued talking with him for a while, enjoying her conversation with the interesting, eccentric man. Then, leaving him to the privacy with his wife and numerous children that he preferred, she rode back to rejoin her son and the escort.

Beside the campfire that evening, Alexandra examined the maps again with great satisfaction. She showed them to Morton and explained what she intended to do, but he was disinterested, as she had more or less expected he would be. Instead of being blunt about it, though, he courteously expressed the hope that she would succeed, which was a very promising change in attitude for him.

The conversation about Alexandra's brother resumed as they traveled back toward the home paddock, Morton remaining deeply intrigued by what Creighton did. Searching her memory for details, she elaborated on what she had told her son about the family business. At length, the boy expressed a wish to do the same himself when he became an adult.

"If you're going to do that," Alexandra told him,

"you'll have to trim your sails closer to the wind. My brother is a well-educated man, as is your father, for that matter. At your age, they were working hard at their lessons instead of sulking in front of a chalk board."

Nettled by the straightforward advice, Morton was quiet for a time, something of his former attitude returning. Alexandra also remained silent, waiting for him to speak and take the initiative for communication between them. Finally he did, although reluctantly, and asked if she would help him find out more about business activities.

"Of course," she replied. "Morton, I'll always be ready to help you achieve what you want. You do realize that I love you, don't you?"

"You say you do, but you criticize me constantly."

"Morton, you know that if you eat too much fresh fruit, you'll have a bad stomach. There are many things in life that can have a much worse effect, but instead of happening quickly like that, they stretch over a period of years. I've lived a number of years and know of these things, whereas you're very young and don't. When I correct you, it's simply to make you avoid those things, certainly not because I enjoy doing it."

The boy was silent for a time, weighing what she had said. Then, as she had many times before, Alexandra explained the importance of his concentrating on his lessons, not only for the purpose of learning them, but also to develop mental discipline. For the first time, the boy listened and seemed to understand.

Beside the campfire that evening, he raised the subject of his lessons. "I don't always know what to do with a carry-over number when I'm doing sums," he told her. "Would you show me again?"

Alexandra smoothed off a spot on the ground, picking up a stick to draw numbers in the dirt and demonstrate the procedure. Recalling errors he had made, she realized his lack of understanding on that point had been responsible for some of them. She wondered whether it had been pride, stubbornness, or something else that had kept him from telling her.

The essential point, however, was that he had told her. While she had obtained the maps she needed, she had also achieved a success of infinitely greater importance to her on the journey. She knew she would continue to have difficulties with Morton, and she would always be fearful about the origins of some of his characteristics. But at least she could now work with him, having at last broken through his cold reserve.

During the weeks that followed her return home, Alexandra discovered that she was indeed pregnant again. David was delighted when she told him, and both of them hoped for a daughter. During that time, Alexandra had to begin giving her sons different lessons. Highly intelligent, as well as older and more mature for his age, Morton had raced ahead of Jonathan in arithmetic as well as the other subjects she was teaching them. His behavior remained a problem at times, but he was obedient, if often reluctantly so, and he worked long and hard at his lessons.

Each day, when she was done with the lessons and her other responsibilities, Alexandra worked over the maps at her desk in the family parlor. On a large sheet of paper, she consolidated the maps that Adolarious had given her and the one from Pat. Converting them to approximately the same scale with a ruler, she sketched in the lines with a sharp charcoal pencil and then traced over them in ink.

After the map was completed, and the Cobdogla changed to the Darling River, Alexandra knew she had only begun on what she needed. The map would create favorable attention, but the request for a land grant had to be fully substantiated. Her request had ample justification. First of all, the station made a large contribution to the colonial economy, and secondly its land was too arid for small holdings to be self-sufficient. But there were many other reasons why the grant would be in the best interests of the colony.

Those reasons, however, had to be presented compellingly, and Alexandra labored over drafts of the request to get each sentence correct. As she worked on the request, she knew it was important to have it placed in the governor's hands, rather than have some clerk either pigeonhole it or send it to the colonial surveyor. Reasonably sure that her brother would be at least acquainted with the governor, she planned to send it to Creighton and ask him to deliver it personally to Governor Darling.

That particular part of her plans was superseded on an early-summer afternoon in December, when the tranquility of the house was broken by the thump of the knocker on the front door. Visitors were still an extreme rarity, so Alexandra curiously walked out of the family parlor into the entry as Emma went to the door. The maid opened it, and Alexandra was stunned to see her brother standing in the doorway.

Besides being untidy from his long journey, Creighton had changed through the years, his face lined and his hair streaked with gray. For the first time, Alexandra realized that he closely resembled their father. But he was still her loving brother, and an affectionate smile wreathed his face. "Creighton!" she cried ecstatically, running to him. "My dear, dear Creighton!"

Laughing in delight, he held Alexandra close and kissed her. "My lovely Alexandra," he said. "It would be worth traveling any distance just to see you. Words can't express how I've missed you."

"I've also longed to see you, Creighton," she replied. "But come, let's get you settled, then you can have a refreshing drink while we talk. I want to know all about your wife and family, as well as everything that's happened during the long, long years since I've seen you."

The stable boy led the horses away after Creighton and Alexandra, with Emma's help, had taken the baggage off the pack animal. "David is out in the paddocks," Alexandra told her brother as they went inside. "He should return within the next day or two. And as soon as you've unpacked, you can meet my sons."

Creighton nodded happily, commenting that he had been looking forward to meeting her husband and sons. They continued talking cheerfully as they went upstairs, but from subtle nuances, Alexandra knew he had bad news. Their mother and grandmother dead, it could only be about their father or their younger brother, Robert, a naval officer.

It was their father, Creighton told her when they were alone in the guest room. "He had a heart seizure," Creighton explained, taking out a letter. "He lingered on for a few days, during which he was very remorseful over how things stood between you. He wrote this to you, then passed on a few hours after finishing it."

Alexandra took the letter, a pall suddenly cast over her joy at seeing her brother. Although her father had wounded her deeply, making her resentful toward him, he had still been her father. "Very well, Creighton. After you've freshened up, join me in the garden at the side of the house."

He smiled and nodded, exchanging a kiss with her. Then she went downstairs and after telling a maid to bring refreshments when Creighton came down, Alexandra went into the garden. At one side of the path that wound through the trees and flower beds, stone benches and a table were under a large rose arbor, the shady conversation nook made fragrant by the flowers. Alexandra sat on a bench, opening the letter.

As she read the apologies and expressions of regret, Alexandra realized that her father had indeed been extremely sorrowful over the rift between them. Her resentment toward him fading, tears filled her eyes and overflowed. She clutched a handkerchief to her face and sobbed, remembering acrimonious arguments that she had done much more to create than to avoid, facing him with youthful obstinance instead of willingness to compromise.

Creighton sat down beside her, putting his arm around her. "Your tears do you credit, Alexandra," he told her. "Facing death, he wanted to be reconciled with you. But in life, he treated you very badly."

"Yes," Alexandra agreed, wiping her eyes. "But that might not have happened if I had been less willful and made him love me more."

"It's up to a parent to take the lead in coming to terms with a child. The measures used may vary from gentle to stern, but it's the responsibility of the parent. I've found that out, as you must have."

Recalling her experience with Morton, Alexandra nodded. "Even so, it grieves me that we weren't reconciled when he was alive."

"Again, that wasn't your fault. Also, he's much more at peace now, because he was a very unhappy man after our mother passed away."

The moment was reminiscent of the times in her girlhood when Creighton had soothed away her tears, and Alexandra dried her eyes. He looked more like himself, having washed up and changed into a clean suit. She asked about his family, and he replied that they were well and he now had a fourth daughter, the conversation moving on to more cheerful subjects.

When the maid brought a tray laid out with port and sherry, Alexandra told her to send the boys to the garden.

Shortly after, they appeared, Morton for once more eager than Jonathan to meet a visitor. He was still reserved, hanging back as his brother exchanged an affectionate hug with Creighton, but he was bursting with questions. Leaving her brother talking with the boys, Alexandra went to discuss dinner with Flora.

Returning to the garden, Alexandra sent her sons to play. She had to tell Morton twice to leave. He finally slouched glumly away. "Morton has ambitions to be a businessman like you," she explained to her brother.

"Yes, he said as much," Creighton replied. "He appears to have a very fine mind, so he should do well. I have some business to discuss with you, Alexandra, our father's will."

He explained to her that shortly before he had died, their father had made out a new will, specifying that his property was to be divided equally among his three children. The family business comprised the bulk of the estate, but its value was in various investments and property holdings. Money could be raised to cover Robert's share, but it would bankrupt the business if the same was done for Alexandra's share.

"You and I could become partners," Creighton suggested. "Some debt will be incurred in giving Robert his share, but that should be paid off within a year. I would draw a salary for managing the business, then we would divide the profits annually. It should be a tidy sum."

Thinking about it, Alexandra saw a way to resolve a potential problem in the years ahead. If Morton did decide upon a career in business, he would need at least a modest capital that would have to come from the resources of the station. But with a partnership in the Hammond family business, which could be turned over to him as his inheritance, he would start out as an equal to those who had been in commerce for decades.

"I'll have to discuss it with David, of course," Alexandra replied, "but it appears a very sound proposal, Creighton. Now I have a matter to discuss with you, one that concerns Tibooburra Station."

Creighton understood immediately when she explained her concern about the region being designated crown lands, then he nodded as she told him about her plan to get a land grant. "That's an excellent idea," he said. "As you say, it would be an extremely large grant, so approval is open to question. But I can assure you that the request will be placed in the governor's hands for his personal review, because he and I are on good terms."

Knowing she could ask for no more, that, in fact, she was very fortunate her brother was acquainted with the governor, Alexandra also knew the coming months would be uneasy ones. To her, Tibooburra Station was life itself. More than fear, a threat to the station created a shrinking dread within her, a menace to her very existence.

Creighton then described how Sydney had changed and gossiped about their old friends until dinnertime. The boys joined them in the dining room, and the meal was flawless, Flora having outdone herself. The beef was tender and juicy, and the dressing was robustly flavorful with spices and onions. The vegetables and other side dishes were seasoned to perfection, while the rich, fruity wine, with its overtone of the oak in which it had aged, provided the finishing touch.

After dinner, Alexandra and Creighton went to the parlor and talked until late in the night, reminiscing about the years in London.

The next morning, Creighton wanted to spend time with the boys and work with them on their lessons, and Alexandra wrote the land grant request in its final form for her brother to take with him when he left. During the afternoon, David returned from the paddocks.

Wanting the two most important men in her life to get along well, Alexandra was extremely pleased when her husband and brother liked each other immediately. The afternoon passed in lively, enjoyable conversation, followed by a delicious dinner.

That night, while preparing for bed, Alexandra told Kerrick about Creighton's proposal for a partnership in the family business. She explained the possibility of eventually turning it over to Morton as his inheritance, and David firmly agreed with her plan.

The following day, while David oversaw work at the barns, Alexandra went riding with her brother and showed him around the home paddock. When they reached the far end of the Aborigine village and turned back, Creighton commented about Alexandra's obvious satisfaction with her life at the station. "That pleases me to no end," he added. "You have reason to be content, because you live in luxury that would be envied by most of the bunyip aristocracy in Sydney. But more than content, I can see that you're extremely happy, and David is the very best of husbands."

"That's true on both accounts," Alexandra agreed. "We live well, but the outback isn't for everyone, Creighton. I'd like to keep both my sons here, but I believe Morton would be better off in what he wants to do. He would be a better businessman than stockman. What do you think?"

"I think you're right. Now that I know him better, I believe his way of going about things would be different from mine. However, he might be more successful, and I believe he has a head for business."

"Then let's discuss the partnership you proposed. David and I plan to send the boys to a boarding school in Sydney. After Morton finishes there, I'd like you to take him into the firm as an associate. When he reaches the age of majority, I'll turn over my share in the firm to him, and he will be your partner. In addition, I'd like to change the name of the firm to Hammond and Kerrick. Do you object to any of that?"

"Certainly not to changing the name of the firm," Creighton replied. "It should reflect the ownership." He hesitated and thought for a moment, then smiled wryly. "As I said, Morton's ways might be different from mine, but I should be able to cope with that. And it doesn't appear that I'll have a son in the business with me, so I'll accept those terms."

Alexandra nodded in satisfaction, and they discussed the matter further as they rode back up the creek. A short time after they reached the house, David joined them in the garden. The three of them talked about all aspects of Morton's future role in the partnership, agreeing on all the details.

The arrangement settled, Alexandra was reasonably sure that Morton's future was assured. But for her other son, his future was less secure. There was every indication that his interests would center entirely on the sheep station, but whether the station would even remain in existence rested heavily on the outcome of the request for a land grant.

The request and map were in Creighton's baggage when he rode away two days later. David left once again to take supplies to the stockmen and to check on the flocks. The house seemed very quiet after the constant activity and conversation, and Alexandra felt lonely and anxious, hoping the governor would approve the request. As she settled back into her busy routine, the loneliness soon passed.

David returned after a few days, then when the days began turning into weeks, Creighton's visit became an enjoyable memory. But the request and map remained very much on her mind, scarcely an hour of any day passing without her thinking about them.

When sufficient time had passed for Creighton to reach Sydney, her anxiety increased. Longing for a way to reach across the distance for some word about the governor's reaction, she tried to resign herself to wait for the arrival of the drays with supplies. That was months away, but she hoped for a reply to the request in the mail the drays would bring.

The reply, however, came much sooner than that. While exercising her horse on a sultry, late-summer afternoon in February, Alexandra noticed two riders with a pack horse coming down the track. Riding to meet them, she saw that one was a woman with a baby in her arms.

Stopping on a rise, the young couple looked at the home paddock in awe, the woman almost in tears of happiness and relief. The man touched his hat as Alexandra rode up to them. "G'day, mo'm," he said. "I'm Isaac Logan, and this is my wife, Mandy. I have mail for the owners here."

"Good day, I'm Alexandra Kerrick. I'll take the mail."

"I beg pardon," Logan apologized, snatching off his hat. "I should have guessed who you are, mo'm." Taking an oilskin package from his coat pocket, he leaned over and handed it to her. "I met Mr. Hammond, your brother, in Sydney, Mistress Kerrick. He said he would give me a recommendation for employment if I would bring the mail, and it's in that. He also gave me two of these horses so me and Mandy could get here."

Alexandra looked at the package, aching to open it, then forced herself to turn to the woman. "Are you and the baby well?"

"Aye, we are now, mo'm," the woman replied, smiling tearfully. "After that dreadfully long way on that tiny bit of a road, I didn't expect to see all this. It's like a wonderful, beautiful town, with that great, lovely house standing over it. It quite took my breath away."

"It took me aback as well," Logan put in. "I'd heard that Tibooburra Station was big, but I didn't think it would be like this. It's been several days since we crossed the south boundary. Can I get a job here, mo'm? I've worked with sheep and dogs ever since I was a nipper."

"Well, not everyone is content in the outback. But we can use another stockman, so we'll see how you and your family get on here. The last two houses beside the creek are empty. Take either of them, then go to the storeroom beside the shearing shed and draw rations. The storekeeper will also give you lamps and other things for your house."

The young man and woman were piteously grateful, and Alexandra controlled her impatience and smiled as they repeated their thanks again and again. At last, they rode down the track. With trembling fingers, Alexandra unwrapped the oilskin. The package contained a letter from Creighton and a much thicker one with the governor's official seal on it.

Breaking the seal, Alexandra took out a brief note and a folded parchment. The note, signed by Governor Ralph Darling, expressed thanks for the excellent map and the honor of having the large river designated with his name. After glancing over the note, Alexandra unfolded the parchment.

With large, bright official seals and the governor's signature below the writing, it was a freehold land grant to David and Alexandra Kerrick, and to their heirs and assignees in perpetuity. The grant encompassed Barren Mountain northward to Steeple Hills, then east and west from the home paddock to a total distance of four hundred furlongs, the boundaries enclosing a total area of one million sixty thousand acres.

The constant, gnawing anxiety of months suddenly lifted from her, Alexandra felt weak with relief as tears of joy welled up in her eyes. Clutching the parchment and other papers, she slowly climbed down from her saddle, her eyes blurred with tears.

She grasped a handful of soil and let it trickle between her fingers. It had always been precious, but now it was subtly different from only moments before. Now it was safe, placed beyond the grasp of any envious intruder. For vast miles in all directions, it would belong to her family down through the generations to come.

Part III

Chapter Sixteen

"I'd like to speak with you for a moment, Morton."

Looking up from the papers on his desk, Morton noted the dissatisfaction in his uncle's voice and attitude. He sat back, motioning to the chair beside his desk. "Yes, of course. What is it?"

Heavy-set and troubled with gout in his middle age, Creighton Hammond slowly crossed the office and eased himself into the chair. "I understand," he said somberly, "that you sold the firm's share in the cargo of a vessel named the *Wavertree* to Edgar Humphries."

"Yes, and it's fortunate that I did. I see from today's admiralty office postings that the *Wavertree* sank off the Cape."

"Fortunate?" Creighton echoed in disapproval. "Morton, Edgar Humphries has been a friend of mine for twenty-five years."

"I'm fully aware of that. Are you suggesting that that should have a bearing on the firm's business dealings with him?"

"Of course it should!" Creighton snapped. "Morton, how do you think something like this appears to others?"

"I don't give a bloody rap how it appears to others!" Morton shot back. "The firm doesn't own a sixty-fourth of a cargo that's on the bottom of the ocean off the Cape, and nothing else matters to me."

"But you sold it to him after the ship sank!"

"And two weeks before the sinking was posted by the admiralty office! Does he contend that I knew about it before the admiralty?"

Creighton drew in a deep breath and controlled his temper, combing his fingers through his white hair. "He contends nothing, Morton. But you know as well as I do that word of sinkings sometimes arrives by word of mouth before the admiralty office receives official notification."

"Pissmire rumors," Morton replied, dismissing it with an impatient wave. "Who listens to the ramblings of drunken sailors?"

"No, I can't leave it at that, Morton." Creighton lifted a hand as his nephew started to object hotly. "No, I'm the senior partner, and I insist that Edgar's money be refunded. I'll see to it myself."

Morton sighed irately, shrugging. "Very well, but you'll be the senior partner of a bankrupt firm if you persist in this sort of thing. Further, I sold a share of that cargo to Farrel Ibbets, but he won't get a shilling back. That was a private venture of mine, and the sale will stand."

"Farrel Ibbets?" Creighton exclaimed, suddenly amused. "That old rogue? He's swindled so many people out of money that I'm pleased to see him lose some of it. How much of a share did you sell him?"

"An eighth."

"An eighth?" Creighton gasped in astonishment. "You bought a full eighth of that cargo with your private funds? That's a very substantial investment. Did you sell it to him at the subscription rate?"

"No, I discounted it, because I needed funds on short notice."

Creighton sat back in his chair, studying his nephew with an anxious frown. "Morton, taking a loss on that share has every appearance of a panic sale. You didn't know that the ship had sunk, did you?"

"How could I have known?"

A momentary silence fell, and Creighton's brows were drawn in concern as Morton gazed back at him blandly. Then the older man slowly shook his head. "When you were an associate, Morton," he said soberly, "I often told you that principles are more valuable than money. I do hope you remember that, and I'll say no more on the matter. Have you examined the cost for that investment in the sheep station south of the Murray River?"

Morton nodded, separating a paper from others on his desk and pushing it toward his uncle. "Yes, and I think it's a very poor investment."

"Buying that land and providing money for stock and supplies would be an investment in people—four good, honest families. They'll work hard, and it should begin paying a return within a very few years."

"No, I rather expect that we would be left holding land in the wilds of the Murray River, while the people would be looking for someone else to fleece for the necessities of life. I'm adamantly against it."

"Then I'll fund it as a private venture," Creighton said in resignation, taking the paper and pushing himself to his feet.

He left, and Morton dismissed his uncle and the conversation from his mind as he brought his concentration to bear on a stack of papers. They were mortgages that were heavily in arrears, which he had bought at a deep discount from face value. Studying each one, Morton made a list on a sheet of foolscap, estimating how much profit over his purchase price he could realize after he secured full title to the properties.

Morton had bought a few of the mortgages which were on houses owned by judges, government officials, and professional people, for benefits other than direct profit. To secure those benefits, he had bought yet another mortgage, one on a house owned by the lawyer, John Fitzroy. Morton anticipated dealing with Fitzroy with pleasure.

He had sent a message to Fitzroy, asking him to meet with Morton to discuss the mortgage. It had been ignored, an example of the contempt Morton had encountered from some with high social standing yet many who had ignored him a short time before were now being very friendly toward him. Money was power, and he had merely begun to realize his objective to amass an immense fortune and dominating power.

At a polite rap on his office doorjamb, Morton looked up. As often happened, the day had faded unnoticed into dusk while he worked, and the head clerk of the firm was in the doorway. "I beg pardon, sir," he said. "Mr. Hammond went home awhile ago, and my work for the day is done. An apprentice will be here if you need anything."

"Very well. Send the apprentice with a light for my lamp."

The man left, and a boy with a candlestick entered a moment later and lit the lamp on the desk. Morton totaled up his estimated profits and made two lists, one of the names of well-placed people among the mortgages, and the other of mortgages on businesses he intended to foreclose. When he finished, he locked the papers in a desk drawer and left the office.

In the dim, quiet outer office, the boy worked by candlelight at one of the tall accounting desks. Scrambling down from his stool, he went to the clothes rack. He helped Morton on with his coat, handed him his hat and cane, then opened the door for him.

The town had settled for the evening, and the

cobblestone street in the commercial district was quiet since shops and other businesses in the half-timbered buildings were locked and shuttered. Here and there, lighted windows in living quarters on the second floors cast a dim light down on the street. While walking, Morton saw a man step out of the shadows on the other side of the street and cross toward him. He recognized the middle-aged, paunchy John Fitzroy.

"You, there," Fitzroy called haughtily. "If your name is Kerrick, I'll have a word with you."

"That is my name, but I don't conduct business on the public streets," Morton replied brusquely. "Come to my office tomorrow."

"No, I'll speak with you now," Fitzroy insisted arrogantly, reaching for Morton's arm. "It isn't my practice to patronize every—"

He broke off and stumbled back, as Morton slashed his cane at the man. "By God!" Morton snarled. "You venture to take my arm and hold me? I'll break your bloody head open, you impudent swine!"

"How dare you!" Fitzroy exclaimed in outrage. "Do you know who I am, you upstart? I'll have you know that I'm—"

"Yes, I know who you are! You're the shyster, Fitzroy, who didn't reply to my message about the mortgage I hold on you. Now you be at my office at the seventh hour tomorrow morning."

"I will not!" Fitzroy spluttered. "I'll have you know that—"

"Then take warning as to what will happen. On Sunday morning, when everyone is abroad, I'll hire ten of the scurviest, most drunken sailors I can find at the Pissmire, and I'll have them cast you, your family, and your belongings into the street for the town to see. Now if you think I won't do that, you bloody well wait until Sunday."

His sagging jowls quivering, Fitzroy shook his head.

"You wouldn't dare," he whispered, his voice trembling in fear. "I have friends, and they would take every sort of official action against you that—"

"No, they won't because they wouldn't want their own debts called to account in the same fashion. Until now, you've been dealing with bank directors who are more concerned with receiving dinner invitations than in earning profits. Now you're dealing with me, and I dine only at my lodgings. You be at my office at seven tomorrow morning."

Leaving the man standing speechless in consternation, Morton walked away. He turned the corner and went down another street to a chemist's shop. The shop closed, he climbed the steps at the side of the building and rapped on the door at the top of the stairs with his cane.

James Boland, the chemist, a bookish-looking man in his forties, was swallowing and wiping his mouth as he opened the door. "Good evening, Mr. Kerrick. I was just having a bite to eat. Would you join me?"

"No, thank you. Kindly step outside and close the door."

Nodding amiably, Boland came out onto the landing. A well-educated man and a former manufacturer in England, he had been convicted and transported to Australia for infringement of the patent rights on a steel process. He had obtained a ticket-of-leave and brought his family to Sydney, then had opened the pharmaceuticals shop.

In debt and with a large family, he was often hard pressed for money. However, foreknowledge of who was ill, recovering, and expected to die could be very useful in the business affairs of the town, which he gladly revealed to Morton on occasion. Now Boland related all the medicines he had sold since he had last seen Morton, as well as whom they were for and what illnesses they were commonly used to treat. When the man revealed all he knew, Morton gave him a coin and left.

Morton's next stop was several streets away, a public house where seamen congregated. Relatively expensive, it was patronized only by captains and other officers. The publican, Harvey Mankin, seeing Morton enter the crowded, noisy barroom, met him in a quiet corner near the door. Mankin had given Morton many extremely valuable and completely reliable bits of information, including that about the sinking of the *Wavertree*. He had overheard nothing useful since their last meeting, but he had a request. Transportation of convicts to New South Wales had ceased three years before, but many were still serving sentences. In addition, they were still being transported to Van Diemen's Land, and the publican's brother had been sent there a few months before.

Having received a letter from his brother describing the conditions there, Mankin was frantic to get him out of confinement. "If you can attend to this for me, Mr. Kerrick," he continued anxiously, "I'll never take another shilling. And I'll work harder than ever to find out things for you. But I've got to get Harold out of there before they kill him."

"Very well, I'll see what I can do."

The man wanted to continue talking, adding further entreaties. But the conversation had reached a conclusion, ending it for Morton. He detached himself and left for his lodgings.

He lived on a quiet street above Sydney Cove, in a house owned by a widow in her thirties, Clara Tavish. Her home comfortable and her children well-fed, well-clothed, and their school fees paid from the money that Morton gave her, he was the only lodger and Clara saw to all of his needs with dedicated skill and efficiency.

After she took his coat, hat, and cane, he entered the dining room. The Sydney newspaper that he had delivered to the house was on the table, along with a London *Times* that had arrived during the day. He pored over the newspapers and ate while Clara silently served the meal she had kept hot for him. When he finished the last course, she cleared the table and brought in a pipe, smoke wafting from the smoldering tobacco in it.

A few minutes later, Clara stood in the dining-room doorway. "Shall I come to your room tonight?" she asked.

Morton glanced at her absently, then shook his head as he puffed on the pipe and looked back at the newspaper. "No."

"Very well. Good night, Mr. Kerrick."

"Good night."

The house quiet around him, Morton analyzed the developments reported in the newspapers, speculating about their side effects. He had once read about a hurricane in the British West Indies, a center of sugar production, then had invested in sugar shipments out of Malaya and made a large profit. Since then, he had used newspaper reports similarly, but he was one of the few who examined news events for their indirect results. Most businessmen clung to time-worn practices, closely followed what their colleagues did, and reacted only to transparently obvious developments.

Even though he was weary from the long, busy day, he continued studying the newspapers until late, a restless, driving energy seething within him. Long before, its outlet had been anger, then it had been channeled into its present course. Begrudging the time that he spent sleeping, he knew it was essential for a clear, keen mind, and he finally blew out the lamp on the table and carried a candlestick upstairs to go to bed.

The next morning, when Morton reached his office building shortly before seven, Fitzroy was waiting. Ignoring him, Morton brushed past him to go inside. Fitzroy followed Morton, nervous and uncertain.

In his office, Morton sat down at his desk, opening his inkwell and dipping a pen into it. "I'm sure you know a number of clerks and officials at the attorney general's office," he said curtly.

"Well . . . yes," Fitzroy replied, perplexed.

Morton wrote Harold Mankin's name on a scrap of foolscap and pushed it across the desk. "There, in event your memory is as poor as your financial judgment. That man is a prisoner at Van Diemen's Land, and I want him to have a ticket-of-leave. I'll pay five guineas for it, no more."

"You intend for me to offer a bribe?" Fitzroy gasped in dismay. "I've never done anything like that in my life, Mr. Kerrick, and I can't—"

"Then offer a bloody Christmas gift!" Morton snapped irately, unlocking his desk drawer and taking out the lists he had made the night before. "Or get on your knees and beg until someone does it for you. I could care bloody less how you do it. I simply want it done today."

His splotched face quivering, Fitzroy put the paper in his waistcoat pocket. "Ah . . . Mr. Kerrick, I was under the impression that we were going to discuss the mortgage on my house," he suggested meekly.

"We are," Morton replied brusquely. "You don't have any money, so we're discussing what you'll do to pay me." He pushed a list across the desk. "I'm sure you know those people. Go to each of them and tell them that you're my legal advisor, and let them know that I hold their mortgages."

Fitzroy's eyes opened wide as he looked at the paper, speechless for a moment. "But, Mr. Kerrick," he stammered, "these people are friends of mine, and they're very important—"

"I know who they are. Just let them know that if I'm crossed, I'm a remorseless swine who knows no ends in getting what's mine. By now, you should be able to explain that very convincingly."

"But to make myself a party to this and to approach my friends in such terms is disgraceful!" Fitzroy spluttered. "It's outrageous!"

"Perhaps," Morton replied, laughing dryly. "But you'll find that you're all in the same boat. They'll quickly realize that I'll want something of them sooner or later." He pushed the other paper across the desk. "I own the mortgages on those businesses, and I want court orders seizing the buildings and their contents. Word soon spreads on something like this, so I want the court orders today, before the contents can be removed."

"Today?" Fitzroy mused doubtfully. "But filing writs to obtain court orders can take anywhere from several days up to—"

"You're very slow, aren't you?" Morton interrupted impatiently. "You have two judges on that other list. Give each of them half the names of those businesses after you've explained the situation, and you'll get the court orders immediately. Now how much do you owe green grocers, butchers, and so forth?"

Fitzroy blinked at the sudden change of subject, then pondered. "I believe my wife said it was nearly thirty guineas, Mr. Kerrick."

Morton took out his purse and opened it, counting out forty guineas on the desk. "There's extra for pocket money and household expenses. In due course, we'll determine a suitable wage. You have enough work to occupy you today, so get busy. Attend to the ticket-of-leave first."

Fitzroy looked at the money in his hand and hesitated as though he were going to protest again, then he turned and walked out with slow, heavy steps, his shoulders slumped. As soon as he left, the head clerk came in with two sheets of paper and placed them on Morton's desk. One was a list of arrivals and departures an apprentice had obtained at the port master's office that morning, the other a list of the morning postings at the admiralty office. Morton checked them, noting the arrival of vessels in which he or the firm owned shares of the cargo.

The vast majority of businessmen in the town spent

most of their time in coffeehouses, swapping rumors,
selling and buying shares in cargoes, and transacting
other affairs. Typically, his uncle would have been
there until at least noon, but Creighton came in
suddenly during midmorning. "The most terrible
news has just arrived on a cutter from New Zealand,"
he announced as he walked into Morton's office. "The
Maoris massacred a surveying party and several settlers at a place called Wairau, and the tribes are up in
arms all across North Island. It's very bad, Morton,
very bad indeed."

Knowing that his uncle was referring to more than
the deaths, Morton put down the papers and sat back
in his chair. When New Zealand had become a colony,
there had been heavy speculation in land development bonds for the new settlement area. Morton had
avoided them, anticipating events such as the one his
uncle had just told him about. However, over his
strong objections, Creighton had bought into the
bonds for the firm.

Crossing the office, Creighton sat down on the chair
beside the desk and sighed heavily as he continued.
"You were quite right in your reservations about those
New Zealand land development bonds, Morton. I
made a very serious mistake when I invested so
heavily in them for the firm."

"Yes, they'll fall sharply in price now," Morton
mused.

"Sharply?" Creighton echoed bitterly. "Very sharply indeed, Morton. When I left the coffeehouses, they
were being offered at a sixty percent discount from
face value, but there were no buyers."

The discount was extremely deep, and Morton
recalled what he had read about New Zealand. Many
of the settlers had been transported there and sold
land through a company organized by a man named
Wakefield, whose shareholders were among some of
the most wealthy, politically powerful families in
England. They would demand and get action, and in

addition, the government would not leave the hundreds of settlers in New Zealand undefended.

It was obvious to him that the businessmen were stampeding each other into a panic, either not knowing or not considering all aspects of the situation. The price of the bonds now deflated far below their actual value provided an opportunity for a very large profit. "I'll buy the bonds held by the firm," he offered, "at a sixty percent discount from face value."

"Very well," Creighton replied somberly. "I'm responsible for buying them to begin with, but I'm unable to cover any of them. Financing that sheep station on the Murray River with my private funds has almost exhausted them." He sighed despondently, pushing himself up from the chair. "I'm going home, Morton. I don't feel very well."

After his uncle left, Morton thought rapidly for a few minutes. Deciding upon a course of action, he left the office and headed for the nearest coffeehouse. Usually teeming with activity, a funereal quiet gripped the place. Men in their coats and hats sat around tables in desultory conversation as waiters shuffled about with cups.

"Are you here to gloat, Mr. Kerrick?" a man joked wryly as Morton entered. "You didn't buy any of those bloody bonds, did you?"

"No, I didn't," Morton replied, taking a seat at the table. "I hear that they're not trading very well now."

"Indeed they're not," the man agreed sourly. He took several of the bonds from his coat pocket and slapped them down on the table. "Let's you and I start them moving. There's a face value of five hundred guineas, and I'll offer them at sixty-two percent discount."

"Done," Morton replied, putting out his hand.

Dead silence fell around the table and spread as those at other tables sat up and turned to look. The man gazed in surprise, his tone having been bitterly joking, then he seized Morton's hand and shook it vigorously. The quiet was shattered by an explosion of noise, others around the table taking out bonds and shouting offers, and chairs fell over as men all about the room leaped up and ran to the table with their bonds.

When he left, Morton sent a waiter to the office for an apprentice. The boy met Morton at the next coffeehouse and took the bonds to the office, with a list of bank drafts to issue. Then apprentices ran back and forth, following him from one place to the next. Taking the lists and the bonds to be locked in the office safe, they returned with notes from the head clerk on the amount remaining in his personal funds.

Finishing that afternoon, Morton returned to the office to sign the bank drafts and to review his bank account. In his last purchases, he had overextended himself, leaving insufficient funds for normal activities while he waited for the price of the bonds to rise. He sat at his desk and pored over the cargo summaries of vessels that had arrived during the past few weeks. Then, late in the day, he went to see the commodities wholesaler who supplied all the ships' chandlers and refitters in town.

Perplexed, the man had his head clerk bring in his warehouse inventory. He leafed through it, finding the product that Morton had asked about. "I have just over four hundred hogsheads of pine tar, Mr. Kerrick," he said. "The price is an even nine guineas each, but there's very little demand for it here. Why are you interested in pine tar?"

"I'll buy the lot at six if you'll store it and handle it for me while I resell it," Morton told the man, ignoring the question.

"Well, this strikes me as more than a bit odd, Mr. Kerrick. But I'll do that at seven a hogshead if you'll remove what's left over after three months. As I said, there's not much demand here for pine tar. You probably don't know it, but most of the ships' chandlers and refitters here use kauri gum from New Zealand, which is a little cheaper."

"Let me have a piece of foolscap, and I'll write a bank draft."

As he went back to his office, having done all that he could, Morton hoped it would be enough. On his desk, he found a note from Fitzroy informing him that Harold Mankin's ticket-of-leave would go in the next mail to Van Diemen's Land. On his way to his lodgings, he stopped in and gave Harvey Mankin the news, then quickly left, in no mood to listen to the man's effusive thanks.

Rarely sleeping well, Morton slept very poorly that night. The next day, in order to conceal his financial condition, he bought a share in a cargo, leaving only a few guineas in his bank account. He was unable to sleep at all that night, but he had passed the nadir. A measure of relief came the following day, then increased during the succeeding days.

With rapid court action through Fitzroy's efforts, Morton took legal possession of the properties on which he had foreclosed mortgages. They included retail businesses with stock on hand, which other dealers were eager to buy at reduced prices. When the shipments of kauri gum from New Zealand stopped arriving, ships' chandlers and refitters discovered that the amount of pine tar available was limited. They rushed to stock up, buying all that was in the wholesaler's warehouse at twelve guineas per hogshead.

The mortgages that Morton had kept brought a change in attitude toward him in the town, the warning that Fitzroy had circulated among the debtors proving highly effective. Carriages drew up at the offices, as well-dressed men made friendly calls on Morton with vague promises of payment and concrete offers to use their influence in any way that would benefit him. Many others who had never noticed him before began going out of their way to avoid offending him, greeting him cordially on the streets.

His sister, fourteen-year-old Dierdre, was a pupil at Sydenham Academy, an expensive, exclusive girls' boarding school. When the meticulously efficient head clerk reminded Morton of her birthday, he left work for an hour to take her a set of combs and brushes. During the visit, she remarked that he was becoming an important man in the town. Even though it was said with an affectionately amused attitude that annoyed Morton, it was evidence that his reputation had become very widespread.

When the governor dispatched part of the militia to Wellington, the New Zealand land development bonds that remained in circulation began selling at discounts that diminished from fifty to thirty percent. Upon arrival of the news that warships on station at Trincomalee were speeding toward the same destination, the discount edged down to twenty percent.

Some six weeks after Morton had bought the bonds, a ship arrived from India with word that a Colonel Oliver Bethune was embarking from Bombay to New Zealand with a regiment of Bengal lancers. That day, the bonds began trading at face value. During the following days, with the price increasing into the premium range, Morton began selling off his bonds.

When the last of the bonds were liquidated, Morton had passed an important milestone, becoming a wealthy man. Others would have found a way to mark the occasion, but his lifelong reserve governed him. After following his usual routine, he left his office at the same time as always, but inwardly he seethed with joy as he went through the dark, quiet streets.

When she took his coat, hat, and cane, Clara Tavish greeted him as she always did. "Was your day a pleasant one?"

"Yes, very pleasant indeed."

The reply was a contrast to his usual noncommittal

grunt, and Clara looked at him again as she hung up his things. Gazing back at her in his tightly-contained happiness, it was almost as though he saw for the first time that she was slender and attractive, with pretty features and wide gray eyes. He also thought of a way to express his feelings.

Weeks had passed since she had been to his room, his every urge submerged into his concentration on his affairs when they were unsettled. He realized that she had become worried, wanting to hold the one who provided for her children. Studying his face, she moved closer to him and brushed her hand against his. He quickly grasped her hand, and she smiled in relief as they went up the stairs.

On her soft, yielding body, he celebrated his victory over the world at large, his achievements against those who had matched wits with him. It was a complete release for his seething exhilaration, as well as something more. His exultant joy touched her, making her respond. Only dutiful before in satisfying him, she suddenly joined him.

Sexual partners in the past, now they became lovers. Her supple body tensed as her smooth legs clenched his and her fingers dug into his back. Smothering her soft cries with her open lips against his, she met him with a fiercely demanding energy that awakened him to her, a formerly self-satisfying act becoming an entirely new world of experience for him.

Fulfilling their need had taken only minutes, but quenching their desire consumed hours as they joined again and then again. Then, late in the night, they went downstairs. She brought his belated dinner into the dining room. Her lips were bruised from their passionate kisses and they shared a new, secret knowledge of each other when their eyes met.

Thinking of his uncertain situation with her, he decided to make it more permanent. "My lodging here from month to month is unsatisfactory," he said. "Tomorrow, I'll establish a bank account for you."

"It's been satisfactory for me," she replied, smiling happily, "but I worry so much about my children and their future."

"You may put your worries to rest. Their future is secure, and I'll see to both their and your present comforts better."

Her silent, glowing gratitude, highly pleasing to him, also stirred his yearning again for that mysterious, blissful sharing he had found with her. When they went back upstairs, she started to turn toward her room. Then she smiled and went with him to his room as he took her hand.

The next day, after attending to the bank account for Clara, Morton went to his office, where the morning passed quickly as he planned strategies for the immediate future. During the afternoon, hearing his uncle talking with someone in the outer office, Morton walked to his office door. At the same time that his own financial situation had been improving by leaps and bounds, his uncle's had been declining, and the conversation indicated that Creighton was in danger of yet another financial reverse.

The visitor, wearing stockmen's clothes, was one of the men at the sheep station that Creighton had financed. The stockman was reciting a litany of woes, including illness among the families at the station and heavy losses of sheep to dingoes. Then he began talking about additional sources of revenue which Creighton had asked him to investigate.

"There's timber aplenty, Mr. Hammond," he continued, "but rafting it down the river would be very difficult and would take months. We found no coal or anything like that, but there might be some minerals." He pointed to a wooden box at his feet. "One of the men used to work in a lead mine, and he found some rocks that he thought might contain minerals. I brought some back with me in the event that you would want to have them tested."

Creighton stroked his chin, looking at the box

skeptically. "Very well. How much do you need for supplies?"

"About thirty guineas, Mr. Hammond," the man replied, taking out a list. "I have the things written down here."

"I don't need to see it," Creighton said, waving the list aside. He nodded to the head clerk, who began writing out a bank draft, then turned back to the stockman. "I hope the illness among your people isn't serious."

"No, it isn't," the man assured Creighton. "We appreciate your confidence in us, and we'll do our best to make that station pay."

Appearing less than totally confident, Creighton signed the bank draft and gave it to the man. They shook hands and the stockman left as Creighton studied the box somberly. The head clerk spoke to an apprentice, who found a knife and prised at the top of the box. Morton moved closer, watching as the boy lifted off the top and put it aside.

"Well, he told the truth," Creighton remarked dryly. "He brought me some rocks from the Murray River. What do you think of them, Morton?"

Morton examined one of the rocks, sparkling streaks of color in it, then tossed it back into the box and dusted his hands together. "I know nothing at all about minerals. But even if it is some sort of ore, transporting it to have it processed would be prohibitively expensive."

"That's true," Creighton agreed. "And as far as I know, there isn't any means in Sydney to test for minerals." He glanced around. "Well, let's put the box somewhere. With as much as I have invested in it, I don't want to throw it away, even if it is worthless. But we can't leave it here."

"It can go on the floor of the closet in my office," Morton offered. "I use only the shelves for my ledgers and files."

Creighton nodded, going into his office as Morton returned to his desk. When the apprentice brought in the box and put it in the closet, Morton thought about the chemist, James Boland, who had the experience and probably the means to test the rocks. Coal was the only mineral of value that had ever been found in Australia, and as he looked at the papers on his desk, he halfheartedly decided to take the box to Boland at some point.

When he opened the closet the next day to take a ledger off a shelf, he looked at the box and thought about it again. Then, during subsequent days, it became a familiar object that he scarcely noticed whenever he went to the closet, thinking of matters more important to him.

A week later, a visitor arrived who created an explosion of happy excitement in the outer office. Morton heard his uncle's unrestrained whoop of delight in greeting, followed by a reply in a ringing baritone that Morton knew well. It was his brother, Jonathan.

With his usual contradictory feelings toward his brother, Morton got up from his chair. He loved his brother, as well as resented him. With an amiable, winning disposition, Jonathan was easy to admire, but he was also the tall, handsome one who had never been reprimanded as a child. Drawing in a deep breath, Morton entered the outer office.

Over six feet tall and two hundred pounds, Jonathan seemed too large for the office in his stockmen's clothes, a man of the outback. Much like their father in other ways as well as size, he had bold, tanned features and a compelling personality. His blue eyes shining and his teeth gleaming in a wide smile, Jonathan brushed Morton's proffered hand aside and hugged him affectionately as they exchanged greetings.

Always somewhat overwhelmed by his brother,

Morton struggled to recover his poise. "Well, what brings you to Sydney?" he asked.

"Countless errands," Jonathan replied. "We need more Merinos from Camden Park, as well as some saddles and other odds and ends. Mother wants to have a book of etchings made from those sketches she's had ever since old man Bodenham died . . ." His voice fading, he laughed and shrugged. "Simply a host of things that someone had to come and see about."

"Well, the first thing you must do," Creighton put in firmly, "is go and greet your aunt. She'll prepare a room for you, and my daughters will see that you have ample entertainment while you're here."

Jonathan expressed his thanks for the invitation and asked about his uncle's family, and Creighton replied that they were well. Morton noticed that the apprentices were grinning and gazing at Jonathan in awe, while the head clerk smiled absently as he listened and watched. The young giant of a man always made a forcefully favorable impression on others.

Ending the conversation, Jonathan said he had to get his stockmen and jackaroos settled in an inn before he went to his uncle's home. He made his farewells, promising to spend time with Morton while he was in town, then he left. As always after Jonathan departed from anywhere, the place seemed somewhat quiet and empty.

Morton returned to his desk, experiencing his usual mixture of pleasure and dissatisfaction after having seen his brother. Then he concentrated completely on the papers on his desk, everything else fading to the remote sidelines of his thoughts.

That evening, as he walked down a quiet, dark residential street with his two pretty cousins and their escorts, Jonathan was bombarded with questions about the outback by the young men. Both of them from merchant families, they had idealized notions about the outback, regarding it as more exciting and enjoyable than life in Sydney.

"I'm sure I'd find it very pleasant," one of them remarked. "I'd like to ride about the wide, open spaces in the wind and sunshine."

"You'd get saddle sores on your bum," pointed out Dora, the youngest of the Hammond sisters. "Then you'd long for your desk and chair."

Everyone laughed, then the conversation turned to the gathering where they were going. His cousin, Leona, told Jonathan that it was entertainment the regimental band had begun providing for the townspeople a few evenings each week since the last time he had visited Sydney. It was located at the public park on Macquarie Street, and vendors sold refreshments during the performance.

"But only small beer, light punch, and that sort of thing," Leona added. "Anything stronger would draw the wrong sort, which wouldn't do at all. Dora and I often come here unescorted, as do others."

She continued talking, having made a point that Jonathan clearly understood. In addition to entertainment for the entire town, the gathering was a place for the eligible to meet. Each time he came to Sydney, his cousins introduced him to numerous attractive young women from good families, but all the young women he had ever met had seemed very vapid and shallow to him in comparison with his mother.

When they turned a corner, the music carried down Macquarie Street from the park. It was brightly lit, lanterns hanging around the bandstand, from tree limbs, and over vendors' carts. Scores of people were in the park, their laughter and voices an undertone to the music ringing out in the balmy evening, as the vendors did a lively business.

Immediately upon entering the park, Leona and Dora spotted Melissa, one of their two older, married sisters. Leading a small boy, Melissa exchanged greetings with Jonathan. "You've very smartly turned out,

I must say," she remarked. "That suit and cravat would put all of my husband's to shame. I trust that your mother and father are well?"

"Yes, thank you. How is your husband?"

"He's well," she replied. "He had to work late this evening, so I decided to take little Tommy for a stroll." She picked up the weary-looking boy and held him. "But now I'd best get him home before he falls asleep. Try to find time to visit us while you're in town, Jonathan."

He replied that he would, as Melissa walked away. The other two sisters introduced him primarily to young women. While Jonathan preferred to seek out acquaintances on his own, he knew that his cousins considered what they were doing an obligation, and he was resigned to it. As he exchanged greetings and talked with people, he observed that the social barriers of the past were becoming even more blurred, as those who were evidently children of convicts and those of free immigrants mixed in the same groups.

Moving through the crowd with his cousins, he noticed a woman at one side of the park by herself. Content to be alone, she was listening to the music. Jonathan noted that her dress and wide, matching hat had the sheen of fine muslin, a costly fabric. But muslin dresses were usually made in bright colors and decked out with frills, while hers was unadorned and in a subdued shade. He found the effect of her clothing and demeanor pleasing, giving an impression of a young woman who was very practical, and who had no need for others around her. The dress fitted her slender figure neatly, and in the edge of the light from the lanterns she seemed attractive, with dark hair.

The sharp-eyed Leona, noticing his gaze, linked her arm through Jonathan's and announced that they were going for refreshments. Turning away from the group, they went toward a vendor's cart, and stopped in front of the woman who was in their path. "Oh, good evening, Catherine," Leona said. "I almost didn't recognize you in this dim light. This is my cousin, Jonathan Kerrick. Jonathan, this is Catherine Baxter."

Exchanging greetings with her, Jonathan saw that she was far more than attractive. With the unusual, striking combination of large green eyes and gleaming, raven hair tucked up under her hat, she was bewitching, her lovely features reflecting a forceful personality. The gaze from her beautiful eyes was level and unwavering, her chin set at an assertive angle.

For an instant, Jonathan thought he saw interest in him in her eyes, but it was gone so quickly he was unsure. It was also obscured by her obvious displeasure at the intrusion. Unsmiling as she exchanged greetings with him, Catherine then turned to his cousin. "I'm in a vile mood this evening, Leona," she said. "I beg you to excuse me."

Then she was gone, walking toward the street, and Leona shrugged in wry amusement. "I barely know her," she remarked, "but I've heard that she's often abrupt. She's a teacher at the public school, so one may well pity the boys who stir her temper. And it doesn't take a wizard to fathom why she's into her twenties and not married. She's very pretty, to say the least, but her manner drives men away faster than her beauty draws them."

Watching her as she disappeared into the darkness, Jonathan considered those men fools. In the brief moment that he had spoken with her, he had seen that even in comparison with his mother, a standard that few women could approach, Catherine Baxter was anything but insipid and colorless. He was sure they would meet again. In fact, he was determined to make whatever effort it took to make that happen.

Chapter Seventeen

"You're the boss cockie, and that's your job, Mr. Jonathan," Ruel Blake said. "I don't have to tell you that."

"No, you don't," Jonathan replied. "I have other things to do, though, and you know more than I do about sheep. So it makes sense for you to pick out the rams at Camden Park."

The stocky, bearded stockman frowned in dissatisfaction as he and Jonathan stood with the other stockman and four jackaroos in front of the livery stable where their horses were. "If you're busy today, we could pick out the rams tomorrow," Ruel suggested.

"No, we said we'd be there today to pick out the rams, and that's what we should do." Jonathan pointed to the package he was carrying. "I have the letters and things from the station for my sister, and I want to go see her now. After that, there are other things I need to do today."

Corley Bodenham, the other stockman, eyed

Jonathan's neat suit, cravat, and hat. "Those other things are of a female sort, or I'll miss my guess by a mile," he speculated.

"If that's the case," a jackaroo remarked merrily, "it would be a lot better for Mr. Blake to pick out the rams. The boss cockie is liable to get mixed up and pick out ewes instead."

Ruel directed an angry glare at the youths, the laughter among them suddenly ceasing. He turned back to Jonathan and shrugged in resignation. "All right, I'll see to it. What do I do?"

"Just see the head stockman there, and he'll show you all the rams. When you've picked out a dozen, they'll be put in a separate pen until we're ready to leave. That's all there is to it."

The stockman nodded, beckoning the others and leading them into the stable to get their horses. As he walked away, Jonathan felt a twinge of guilt, knowing he had shirked a responsibility. However, it would have been after dark by the time he returned to Sydney, and he was determined that nothing would prevent his being at the public school during late afternoon when the pupils and teaching staff left for the day.

In the meantime, he crossed the center of town and turned onto King Street, which led past large, luxurious homes on a slope overlooking the bay. At the top of the hill, a high stone wall surrounded the buildings and large grounds of Sydenham Academy. In the office beside the gate, a stout, formidable woman questioned him about the purpose of his visit, then pointed out the central hall, the administration building.

Inside the wall, paths led through shady lawns to towering stone dormitories and academic buildings, a cricket ground, and other games fields. Most of the buildings were of relatively recent construction, but the ivy on the stone walls and the quiet atmosphere gave the school a venerable appearance. In the central hall, a matron showed Jonathan into the visitors' parlor and sent for his sister.

Dierdre ran in a few minutes later, breathless with anticipation, and gasped in joy as she rushed to Jonathan. He hugged and kissed her, laughing happily. With the Kerrick stature, she was tall for her age, a charmingly pretty girl who closely resembled their mother.

They sat on a couch, and Jonathan gave her the package containing presents and letters from their parents. He started to ask her about school and other usual things, but she was bursting with a subject she wanted to discuss. "Have you heard about Morton's mistress?" she asked excitedly.

Jonathan blinked in surprise, then smiled. "Well, no, I didn't know he was keeping company with anyone. Dierdre, when you use that word in just that way, it means something you don't know anything about. And don't need to. You should use it only as a title in referring to—"

"Oh, don't be absurd, Jonathan! I mean a kept woman, of course."

"Bloody hell!" Jonathan exclaimed angrily. "What are they teaching you in this . . ." His voice fading, he glanced at the door to make sure no one had heard him, then lowered his voice. "Dierdre, I apologize for swearing, but I intend to talk to the headmistress about this."

"Jonathan, Jonathan," Dierdre sighed in amused exasperation. "I'm fourteen now, not a baby. So you didn't know?"

Discussing the subject with his sister made him uncomfortable, and he tugged at his collar and shook his head. "No, none of the Hammonds mentioned it, but they might not know."

"I'm sure they do, because the woman's neighbors do. A girl here found out about it from a maid who works at a neighbor's house, then pointed her out to me one day in the public gardens. She's a widow with three children, and that's why she's Morton's mistress, of course."

"What do you mean?"

"When the girl pointed her out to me, I spoke with her. She's very pleasant, not the least bit bawdy. I saw that she's simply providing for her children as best she can. It couldn't be anything else with Morton, because he's no more romantic than a pair of smelly old boots."

Jonathan guided the discussion away from the subject, asking about her schoolwork, and Dierdre told him what she had been doing. She smiled hopefully as she pointed out that as a student in the upper forms, she could get permission to be absent for a few hours to have dinner with relatives. Jonathan assured her he would arrange for her to have dinner at the Hammond home while he was there.

When it was time for him to go, they went to the front door together. As Jonathan looked at his sister, he realized that she was growing up. In her neat school uniform, she was as tall as most women, curves replacing the gangling lines of her slender body. He was pleased, but he also missed the little girl. There remained much of a child in her, however, as she stood on the steps with her package under her arm, looking very lonely and exchanging waves with him while he went down the walk.

The public school was in a much less fashionable location, on the edge of the business district and hemmed in by commercial buildings. It was an impressive, three-story stone structure, however, designed and built years before by an architect named Francis Greenway. Shortly after Jonathan reached it, the pupils poured out the front door and scattered.

Soon after, the staff exited the school and Jonathan looked closely at each woman among them. But it was unnecessary, for Catherine Baxter stood out among the other people as if the street were empty, and she turned down it away from him. Crossing the street through the horses and vehicles, Jonathan hurried to catch up with her.

Her head high and her shoulders back, she made her way up the crowded street at a brisk pace. Coming up alongside her, Jonathan lifted his hat. "Good day, Mistress Baxter. It's very pleasant seeing you again."

Taken by surprise, her reaction was revealing, her emerald eyes reflecting delight and her quick smile radiant. She pursed her lips, controlling her smile as she walked more slowly. "Good day, Mr. Kerrick. I'm pleased to see you again."

"It isn't by chance," he told her, dispensing with customary polite fictions. "I've been waiting for you. If I may, I'd like to walk with you as far as your home so we can talk."

His straightforward expression of interest in her also took her by surprise, and a slight blush rose to her cheeks as she looked away. He waited for some response as the two of them made their way through the people on the street. Then, at a corner, she pointed to another street. "We can go that way, which is always less crowded. But only as far as the gate, because my mother doesn't like unexpected visitors."

Her reply indicated that she was at least receptive to his interest in her and Jonathan was elated that that giant hurdle had been crossed. As they turned onto the quiet street and began talking, he realized that she had indeed been upset the previous evening. Now she was amiable as well as witty and engaging, the most charming woman he had ever met.

When he asked her about her work, he found out what had been troubling her the evening before. She enjoyed teaching, she explained, but took strong exception to the headmaster's disciplinary measures. "If a boy misbehaves in my classes," she continued, "I'll bowl him out of his chair with my ruler in an instant. But to cane boys until blood runs down their legs, as he did to two lads yesterday, is savagely cruel and revolting."

"The parents don't take him to task about it?"

"They're usually so hard pressed to find the school fees that they're often in arrears, which makes them loath to object. At times, I think I would resign, but my parents made great sacrifices to pay my fees through the higher forms so I could be a teacher. I also enjoy teaching, but most of all, I would like to have my own little school in a village. However, villages usually make do with anyone who can read and write as a teacher."

Jonathan thought about the situation at the station where it was the same for the dozen or so employees' children at the home paddock. His parents had often expressed a wish to hire a qualified teacher in the unlikely event one could be found who would come and live in the outback. He started to mention it to Catherine, then decided not to for the moment. Although they were barely more than acquainted, he felt as though he might soon be searching for ways to make the outback seem attractive to her.

With that in mind, he noted with pleasure that she obviously enjoyed his company. Their lively conversation ranged from one subject to another, and they walked more and more slowly as they went up a street of modest, well-kept houses, the neat yards bordered with hedges and picket fences. Stopping at a gate in front of one of the houses, Catherine continued talking with Jonathan for a few minutes, then reached for the latch.

"This has been the most enjoyable conversation I've ever had," he told her sincerely. "I'd like to see you again tomorrow, if I may, and I'd like to meet your family whenever it would be convenient."

"I enjoyed talking with you, Jonathan, and I'd be pleased to see you again. I'll ask my mother about inviting you to . . ." She broke off, as a woman came out of the house. "Well, here's my mother now. I

presume she saw us talking and wants to meet
you."

Her tone reflected perplexity over why her mother
had come out. The woman came down the path, and
Catherine introduced her to Jonathan. Trim and
meticulously neat in her late thirties, Auberta Baxter
had a serene composure that indicated the source of
her daughter's poise. As they were introduced, she
revealed the reason she had wanted to meet Jonathan.

"I happened to look out and noticed that you're the
very image of Mr. David Kerrick," she said. "You
must be his son."

"That's correct, Mistress Baxter, and people do say
that we're much alike. It must have been a good while
ago that you knew him."

"It's been a quarter of a century, more or less, in
Parramatta. He impressed me as the very finest of
gentlemen, with a reserved manner. Your father isn't a
man one can easily forget." She turned back to the
house. "Bring Mr. Kerrick in, Catherine. He can meet
your father and brothers when they get home, and
then have dinner with the family."

Delighted by the unexpected turn of events, Jonathan smiled happily as he opened the gate and held it
for Catherine. She was anything but displeased, a
smile on her lovely face as they followed her mother
up the path. In the modestly-furnished, but spotless,
parlor, she seated him and brought in her younger
sister to introduce her. A timid girl of seven, she
quickly left to resume helping her mother in the
kitchen.

A short time later, Catherine's father and brothers
arrived home from work. Her father, Hiram Baxter,
was an affable man in his early fifties, a shipwright
who worked at a yard owned by the Underwood
family. The three sons were all much younger than
Catherine, the oldest about fifteen, and they were
apprentices at the shipyard where their father worked.
It was a closely-knit, loving family, with no squab-

bling among the children, and Hiram obviously adored his wife. The placid, hard-working man was friendly toward Jonathan, talking with him in the parlor until dinnertime. During the conversation, he mentioned that he remembered Jonathan's father from years before, when they had both been at Newcastle.

When the meal was ready, the kitchen doubling as the dining room, the long, heavy table was crowded with platters of vegetables, fresh bread, a large pork roast and homemade beer. The food was expertly prepared and heartily delicious, and the youths ate with the single-minded concentration of ravenous appetites.

As Jonathan and the Baxters talked, it became evident that the Baxters had taken an entirely different approach in raising Catherine than with their other children. Her education was far above average for artisans' children, but her brothers had received only a basic education before being apprenticed. When it was mentioned, Auberta made a comment that indicated it had been through choice.

"Mothers love all of their children the same," she remarked, "but the first-born often receives more attention."

"It seems that way," Jonathan agreed. "It always appeared to me that my mother devoted more time to my brother, Morton."

"I've heard about your brother," Hiram said. "It didn't take him long to become one of the leading businessmen here. And I've read about your sheep station in the newspapers. Your father certainly has been successful as a grazier. Does he ever talk much about Newcastle?"

"No, I know very little about his life as a young man. Whenever I've brought it up, he's always said that he put his past behind him and began a new life when he met my mother." Jonathan smiled, shrugging. "But I've heard my mother say that can't be done. According to her, each day is a brick in the house of a person's life."

"Your mother is correct," Auberta commented quietly.

Hiram laughed, shaking his head. "No, I must disagree with you and Jonathan's mother, my dear. I'm not ashamed of the fact that I came here as a convict, but I've done the same as Jonathan's father."

His wife's only reply was a silent smile, but it indicated that her opinion was unchanged. After the meal, the boys and their young sister attended to the dishes, and Jonathan and the adults went into the parlor. Not wanting to overstay his welcome, he made his farewells after an hour, thanking the Baxters gratefully for their hospitality.

Seeing him out, Catherine walked down the path in the moonlight with him. "This has been a most pleasant evening," he told her as they stopped at the gate. "It's been an evening that I'll never forget."

"It was very pleasant for me as well, Jonathan, and my mother and father certainly enjoyed it. My mother told me that you would be welcome to have dinner with us again tomorrow, if you wish."

"I'd like nothing better, but I don't want to impose."

"It won't be an imposition. I trust, though, that your cousins haven't arranged engagements that you would find more entertaining."

"Nothing can compare to how much I enjoy your company, Catherine. I could say far more, but I don't think I should yet."

With the moon shining on her beautiful face and catching glints in her gleaming black hair, she silently smiled at him and then went back up the path. Jonathan closed the gate and set out across town toward the Hammond home, his steps light with joy.

Four days later, having spent every evening with Catherine and her family, Jonathan knew with absolute certainty that he loved her and would never be content until she was his wife. It seemed favorable, because Catherine was apparently strongly drawn to him, and her parents liked him. But he speculated that they might expect him to settle in or near Sydney if he and Catherine were married. Asking her to make her life in the outback could possibly bring an unfavorable reaction from her, her parents, or both.

Time was also a problem, because he had planned to spend no more than a week or so in Sydney. The time had slipped away as he visited Dierdre every day at her school, occasionally saw Morton briefly, and attended to station affairs. When those affairs were completed, which would take another four or five days at most, his parents expected him to set out for the station with the supplies that were needed there. Even if Catherine agreed to be his wife and go with him, there was far too little time for a wedding.

After another evening at the Baxter home, Jonathan discussed plans for the next day with Catherine as they walked to the gate. The following day was Saturday, and the school closed for the weekend. Jonathan wanted hours of privacy with Catherine to talk with her, and he suggested that they go for a long drive, to Parramatta and beyond.

"I can get a buggy from the livery stable where I'm keeping the horses," he added. "It should be a pleasant outing."

"Yes, it should. Shall I prepare a lunch?"

"No, let's find a place where we can build a fire, and I'll prepare a stockman's meal. That'll be something new for you, won't it?"

"Indeed it will," she agreed, laughing. "Very well, Jonathan."

"I've obtained permission from Dierdre's school for her to have dinner at my uncle's home Sunday evening. Would you like to come to dinner then? My aunt and uncle would like to meet you, as would Dierdre."

"Yes, I will, Jonathan. I'd like to meet them as well."

Stopping at the gate, she stood invitingly close to him. As he put his arms around her and bent down to kiss her, the magnetism between them drew them into a passionate embrace. She clung to him for a moment, then pulled away and walked toward the house. With the sweet taste of her lips still on his as he went out the gate and down the street, Jonathan was euphorically happy. But he also wondered if the next day, when he asked her to spend the rest of her life at Tibooburra Station as his wife, she would consent to marry him only if they remained in Sydney.

The next morning, when he drew the buggy up in front of her home and she came down the path, his certainty that he could live nowhere but in the outback wavered. Her dress, expensive but unadorned as usual, was a pale green muslin that brought out the shimmering emerald of her eyes. With a smile on her lovely face and the sunshine highlighting the thick, raven hair arranged under her hat, she was so bewitchingly beautiful that no sacrifice seemed too great if she would be his wife.

A team of young, spirited horses hitched to the light buggy moved swiftly through the town and up the road flanking the Parramatta River. The weather was sunny, but a fresh breeze dispelled the torrid heat of early January, making the day balmy. The conversation with Catherine was as lively as usual, and Jonathan knew they were meant to be together.

Looking at the cooking utensils and bag of foodstuffs behind the seat, Catherine commented jokingly on the quantity of things for a single meal. "There might be more," he replied in the same tone. "Perhaps I've brought enough for a good while, and I intend to take you away."

Catherine laughed, then fell silent and looked out over the countryside with a reflective smile. Just as he was going to pursue the subject in more serious terms, she asked him about the station affairs he had been attending to in town. He told her about the things he had bought, along with a wagon to transport them, then the conversation moved on to other topics.

It was market day in Parramatta, farmers from the surrounding area having brought livestock, produce, and handicrafts to barter and sell. On the main street, Jonathan held the horses to a slow walk, picking a path through the congestion of vehicles and people. At the other end of the village, the last houses fell behind, and the road was deserted.

Never having been beyond Parramatta before, Catherine looked around in interest as the buggy moved down the road. With private land on both sides, Jonathan drove to the river. A few yards from the bridge, a narrow track opened on the left side of the road which Jonathan turned onto. The track led through the edge of thick trees flanking the river, and a few minutes later, coming to a grassy opening where the horses could graze, he stopped the buggy and helped Catherine out.

When the horses were unhitched and grazing, Jonathan took a blanket and the other things out of the buggy. As he searched about for stones to place around the fire, he found a circle of large stones and the rotted remains of a bark hut where someone had camped decades before. He spread the blanket beside the rocks, then gathered firewood.

Enjoying the novelty of cooking over a fire, Catherine sat on the blanket and helped Jonathan. He had bought thick slices of choice cured bacon, fresh vegetables, a bottle of Camden Park wine, fruit preserves, mustard pickle, and dark, rich treacle bread bottled by Crosse & Blackwell in London. Catherine commented that the foodstuffs were very lavish, reminding Jonathan that they had intended to have a stockman's meal.

"It won't be entirely typical," he admitted, laughing. "But stockmen don't have the company at meals that I do, either."

Catherine smiled, asking how the station was organized. Jonathan explained that it was divided into paddocks which had acquired names over the years. Some, such as Quandong and Gidgee, had the Aborigine names of plants or terrain features. In other instances, incidents had provided names. A head stockman named Daniel Corbett had been killed by a wild boar in Boar Paddock, and Bushranger Paddock was where three outlaws had been killed.

"Do very many bushrangers venture into the outback?" she asked.

"No, there was only one time when any of them were at the station. I know nothing more than that about it, because it happened years before I was born, and Mother and Dad never talk about it. What we're seeing more and more of during recent years are swagmen."

"What do they do?"

Jonathan explained that swagmen were footloose wanderers who roamed the tracks from one sheep station to another. At each one, because of the hospitality code of the outback, they were given lodgings for the night and enough rations to last them until they reached the next station. They would do odd jobs and help when grass fires and other calamities occurred, but other than that, they were always gone with the sunrise.

When the food was cooked, Catherine served it as Jonathan opened the wine. It was delicious, but to Jonathan, sitting beside the fire with Catherine in the forest glade made it the most enjoyable meal of his life. He continued talking about the station and the outback, reserving until later one fact that he had waited for days to tell her.

After they finished eating, comfortably full and relaxed from the rich, flavorful meal, he emptied the bottle into their pannikins. As they sipped the wine, Jonathan told her what he had thought about on the first day he had walked home with her from the school. He explained that there were several families at the station as a number of the stockmen were married.

"All together," he continued, "there are about a dozen children. For years, my parents have wanted to get a qualified teacher for them."

Catherine lifted her eyebrows, smiling. "Are you offering me a position as a teacher there, Jonathan?" she asked.

"No," he replied, putting his pannikin aside. He took hers and placed it with his, then put an arm around her and pulled her close. "I'm begging you to take the position of my wife there. I realize we haven't known each other very long, but I couldn't love you more if I'd known you all my life. And as much as I love you, I can't help but believe that you must feel something for me. Please say that you'll marry me, Catherine."

She looked down at her hands on her lap as he spoke, a smile that came from deep within her flowering into a blushing radiance on her beautiful face. "I love you as well, Jonathan," she whispered softly. Lifting her head, she turned to him. "And, yes, I'll marry you."

Joy exploding within him, he clasped her in his arms and kissed her, then moved his lips over her face. "What will your parents say?" he asked. "Will they object to your going so far away?"

"I trust not," she sighed. "I love them, and I want their blessing. But I will go regardless, because I love you most of all."

His happiness soaring to dizzying heights, he had to restrain himself from using the full strength of his arms as he pulled her closer and kissed her again. She used no restraint, her fingers pushing up the sides of his face and tugging his hair as they combed through it. Locking her arms tightly around his neck, she lifted herself and pushed him back onto the blanket. Then she lay across him as they kissed, her body pressing against his.

The fiery spirit that drove her moods flared into passion, and his joy ignited his raging desire. Her open mouth was damp and warm against his lips. As her hair came loose, spilling down over his face in thick, fragrant tresses, she pushed her hands inside his shirt and moved them over his chest. Unfastening her clothes and pulling them down, he caressed her soft, smooth shoulders and then the yielding firmness of her breasts.

Moments later, their clothes cast to one side, they clasped together on the blanket in a pulsing frenzy of lovemaking. Her fingers digging into his shoulders and back, she arched to meet him as her soft cries joined the chattering of the birds in the canopy of foliage. The demanding submission of her lithe, slender body enfolded him in numbing rapture, and together they exploded in spasms of ecstasy.

Passion gave way to affection and mutual gratitude as they lay in each other's arms, her heart beating against his. When she shivered in the cool, damp air off the river, he pulled the edge of the blanket over her. "No, put wood on the fire," she told him, pushing the blanket away. Then she smiled and blushed furiously in embarrassment, covering her eyes with her hand as he sat up and looked at her. "I'm shameless, but only for you, Jonathan."

Her naked body was more poignantly beautiful than the masterwork of a supremely skilled sculptor. He caressed her, then pulled her hand away from her eyes and kissed them. "You're the most wonderful, most lovely woman in the world. And I'm the most fortunate man."

She smiled at him, resting her head on her arm. "I feel the same, so we're both fortunate, Jonathan. I trust your parents will like me."

He tossed wood on the fire as he assured her they would, knowing his mother and father would be delighted with her. They discussed marriage plans, agreeing to have the wedding as soon as possible. Jonathan knew that the most simple of weddings, with the posting of the banns, would take at least three weeks. While that presented a problem, he said nothing to her about it, determined to resolve it.

Picking up the pannikins beside the blanket, he drank then handed the other one to Catherine. After drinking most of the wine, she dipped a finger in the last drops and put the pannikin aside. She touched her finger to one nipple and then to the other nipple. "Here is more wine for you, Jonathan," she whispered, pulling his hand to her body. "Now make me burn and then make it go away."

Fondling her, he buried his lips in the silky, resilent warmth of her thrusting breasts. Moments later, their rekindled desire made them impatient in their search for each other. Joining in an echo of their deep, ardent kisses, they met in a quickening ascent to rapture. Then, their passion exhausted once again, they held each other in blissful contentment.

During late afternoon, they dressed, and Jonathan helped Catherine pin up her hair, savoring the feel and scent of her glossy tresses. Dusk was falling when they reached Parramatta, and he stopped to light the headlamps on the buggy. Then they held each other and kissed as the buggy moved down the road to Sydney.

At her door, Jonathan kissed Catherine once more and left, thinking about the length of time he needed to remain in Sydney for the wedding. An obvious solution had occurred to him, but it involved his shirking another responsibility. After pondering it at length, he finally decided that he had no alternative and that his parents would understand.

When he went to church with the Hammonds the next day, the service was especially meaningful to

him, because the setting was similar to the one where
he and Catherine would exchange vows. After lunch,
he went to the inn where the stockmen and jackaroos
were staying, intending to provide himself with the
time he needed to stay in Sydney for the wedding.

In the small, cluttered room that he shared with
Corley, Ruel sat on his cot and listened in growing
dissatisfaction. Then he shook his head when Jonathan finished. "We can all wait, Mr. Jonathan," he
suggested. "Three weeks shouldn't make that much
difference."

"Yes, it will," Jonathan replied. "The saddles and
such could wait, but not those rams. It'll be March by
the time you get there, and that's none too soon for
the breeding season. But two stockmen and four
jackaroos can see to a dozen rams and the other
things."

"If the day ever came when I couldn't see to them
by myself," Ruel growled angrily, "I'd give my stock
whip to a jackaroo. But you're the boss cockie, and
your place is with those rams, not loitering about here
on some sort of bloody business or other."

Lying on his cot with his hat over his face, Corley
laughed. "That business," he commented, his voice
muffled by his hat, "wouldn't have anything to do
with Catherine Baxter, would it?"

"Yes, it does," Jonathan acknowledged. "I'm getting married."

Tossing his hat off his face, Corley sat up with a
wide grin. Ruel gazed at Jonathan in surprise, then
laughed heartily. "Well, I certainly won't try to stand
in the way of that, Mr. Jonathan!" he exclaimed.
"What do you need me to take care of besides the
rams?"

Jonathan went over the various items of business
with the stockman, and after settling all the details,
Jonathan went to the livery stable and rented a buggy.
Then he drove to the Hammond home and prepared
for the dinner that evening.

At dusk, he took the buggy to pick up Catherine at her home. During the drive to Sydenham Academy, she told him that her mother was very pleased about their engagement and had accepted that she was going to the outback. That evening, Auberta intended to tell her husband about it, expecting him to share her attitude. Jonathan and Catherine then agreed to say nothing about their engagement until after he talked to her father.

At the school, Dierdre was waiting in the gate office, wearing a pretty gown and watching the street for the buggy. Having glimpsed each other in the town at various times, Catherine and Dierdre exchanged greetings warmly and chatted amiably during the drive to the Hammonds. At the house, Jonathan followed them inside to a cheerful round of greetings. His cousin, Melissa, was there with her husband, Stephen Gilbert, a portly, bearded merchant. His other married cousin, Amanda, had declined the invitation, remaining at home with her sick child.

Dinner was a festive, lighthearted occasion, the food enjoyable and the conversation lively. Jonathan glowed with pride at the impression that Catherine made on everyone as the center of attention at the table. With a measure of sedate reserve in her smile and laughter, the enchantingly beautiful woman was charming, gracious, and quick-witted.

After the meal, everyone went into the parlor. The conversation continued smoothly for a time, then it took a controversial turn, when Leona mentioned Morton's absence to her mother. A matronly, attractive woman, Martha Hammond shrugged archly. "Morton is fully aware that he is welcome in this house at any time . . . alone."

"Are you referring to Clara Tavish, Auntie?" Dierdre piped up. "If you met her, I'm sure you'd like her, because she's quite pleasant."

A thunderstruck silence fell, with only Catherine in the dark on the subject. The others exchanged embarrassed glances and gazed at Dierdre in astonishment and dismay. A bright flush of anger spread across Martha's face, contrasting with her white hair. "Dierdre," she said in a choked voice, "kindly tell me how you know that woman's name."

Nonchalant about the furor she had created, Dierdre plucked at the sleeves of her gown. "A school friend explained the situation to me, Auntie, and pointed out Mistress Tavish in the public gardens one day. Then I approached her and we had an entertaining chat. The fact is, she's a good woman, a widow who is providing for her children as best she can."

"She might try honest work," Stephen Gilbert muttered in disapproval.

Having comprehended the subject under discussion, Catherine turned to him, her green eyes sparkling. "Spoken like a man," she said acidly. "A woman who has devoted herself to slaving for a man and children is skilled only as a char. She might be able to earn pence at best, but the bare necessities cost shillings."

"That's quite true," Melissa chimed in at her husband, her sisters emphatically agreeing. "Save your righteousness for church, Stephen."

As Stephen quieted under the women's glares, Martha lifted her hand for silence. "The issue," she announced firmly, "is what Dierdre did. My dear, I cannot but deplore it. Your school is supposed to prevent such things, and I intend to ask the headmistress why you were at liberty in the public gardens."

"She will tell you I was there for a botany class, Auntie," Dierdre replied blandly. "When I talked with Mistress Tavish, I had finished my observation notes on the plants I had been assigned, and the class was waiting for the instructor to finish her after-lunch nap under a tree."

Discomforted by the prompt explanation, as well as by the stir of amusement it created, Martha tried another approach. "Well, you didn't tell her your name, did you? That would have been disgraceful."

"And embarrassing for both of us," Dierdre added. "No indeed, Auntie. She asked, so I told her I was Lady Dierdre Augusta Juliana Hanover, the posthumous daughter of the Duke of York, the second son of King George III. I explained that my claim to the throne had been overruled in favor of my cousin, Queen Victoria, because my age would have required a regency. However, my cause was still being championed by a faction led by Lord Castlereigh, and I had been sent abroad because Prince Albert had been loath to become consort to a monarchy that might be challenged."

When she finished, the quiet was shattered by an explosion of hilarity. As he laughed heartily, Jonathan reflected that it had been characteristic of his sister. Able to mimic any accent and having unshakable aplomb, she could be very convincing. Laughing in spite of herself, Martha shook her head. "My dear, that was outrageous!" she exclaimed.

Dierdre smiled, shrugging. "If one must lie, one may as well make it as interesting and entertaining as possible, Auntie."

Catherine leaned over and kissed the girl. "You're a delight," she said, laughing. "Did the woman believe you?"

"Yes, she did," Dierdre replied gleefully. "And it did no harm when my school friend heard our conversation and addressed me by title."

Laughter erupted again and ended the pleasant evening on a cheerful note. The guests thanked their hosts in a flurry of finding coats and hats. After the farewell of hugs and kisses had been exchanged, Jonathan took Catherine and Dierdre out to the buggy and helped them in.

He left his sister at the school, then drove back through town to Catherine's home and tethered the horse at the gate. Her mother met them at the door with a candlestick, smiling at them warmly, and led them through the dark, quiet house to the kitchen. A bottle and cups had been placed ready beside the lamp on the table where Hiram sat.

The other children were in bed so he spoke quietly as he greeted Jonathan and told him to have a seat at the table. "Well, I understand that you want to take our daughter with you when you leave, Jonathan."

"That's right, Mr. Baxter. I can well appreciate how you feel, but we love each other and we want to make our lives together."

"Then you have our blessing. But if you were any other man, I'd do all I could to keep her from being taken so far away. You're a fine man, Jonathan, and she's as fortunate as you are."

Jonathan thanked him for the compliment, noticing that Mrs. Baxter's silent approval was even greater praise. Sitting at the table and holding one of Catherine's hands between hers, Auberta glowed with joy over her daughter's forthcoming marriage. Hiram poured wine into the cups, then passed them around for a toast to the engagement.

After the toast and a few minutes of conversation about wedding plans, Jonathan left with Catherine. At the gate, she moved against him restlessly as they kissed. Taking his arms from around her, she lifted his hands and placed them on her breasts. "I'm aching here for you, Jonathan," she whispered against his lips. "Make it go away."

With her moist, warm lips against his, he caressed her breasts gently and then more firmly as she murmured impatiently and nipped at his mouth. Then she sighed heavily, taking his hands away from her breasts. "Now I'm burning, Jonathan. When can we return to our place beside the river?"

"When will you resign from the school?"

"On Monday, tomorrow."

"Then we'll go to the river on Tuesday."

She kissed him with torrid intensity, pressing herself against him in a silent promise, then turned and went in the house. As he stepped to the buggy, he seethed with desire, but he knew that the hours would pass and Tuesday would eventually arrive. And he also knew that the future held a lifetime of both passion and the quieter depths of love for them.

On an early autumn day in March, Alexandra Kerrick sat at her desk in the family parlor and looked through Adolarious Bodenham's sketches. Studying one, she felt a flush rising to her face, as she always did when looking at it. In one respect, it was simply a figure study executed with consummate skill and the subtle, ineffable sensibility that imbued all the sketches with life, elevating craft to art which reached out and touched the viewer.

In another way, it gave insight into the hidden side of the seemingly mild, ascetic Adolarious's character, revealing why he had fathered so many children. The sketch, a scene of an Aborigine woman bathing, was voluptuously erotic, with delicate shading drawing the eye to the breasts, body hair, and liquid sheen of water on the thighs. The position of the hands had no particular significance, but like all of the sketches, it had purpose and meaning. The woman was washing her genitals after lovemaking, possibly having just been impregnated with one of Adolarious's numerous children.

At a quiet cough behind her, Alexandra covered the sketch with another as she turned to look at Emma in the doorway. "There are riders on the track, with a wagon and sheep, mo'm," she said.

Having expected Jonathan and the other men to return at any time, Alexandra smiled happily as she left the desk and hurried out of the room. She crossed the entry and went out the front door to the steps, her smile fading as she looked at the riders with the sheep and wagon. At any distance, she could see that neither of them was her son.

As the possibility of accidents and other calamities ran through her mind, a gnawing anxiety tugged at her. One of the men rode ahead at a fast canter, leaving the other man, the wagon, and the jackaroos with the rams behind. He disappeared into a dip in the track, then when he came into view again, she recognized the stocky form of Ruel Blake.

He rode up the hill, then up the tree-lined avenue to the house. Reining at the steps, he lifted his hat as he dismounted. "G'day, Mistress Kerrick. Mr. Jonathan stayed in Sydney to get wedded, and he'll be along directly. I expect he's less than a month behind us."

With an effort of will, Alexandra controlled her feelings as her general worry gave way to an instant of protective panic. Her son married to a woman she knew nothing about! She nodded in greeting. "Welcome home, Ruel. So Jonathan is married now, is he? Who is the young lady?"

"I don't know anything about her, mo'm," the man replied, untying oilskin packages from behind his saddle. "There's a letter from Mr. Jonathan about it in the mail here. This big package is your drawing thing from the printer in Sydney. All of your newspapers and books are in the wagon. I'll send them up as soon as it gets here."

Suppressing her demanding impulse to rip the mail open and read the letter from Jonathan, Alexandra tucked the packages under her arm. "Very well, Ruel. How are the rams?"

"They could use some feeding up, of course, but otherwise they're in fine shape. Not a sore hoof among them."

"That's good to hear. The flock in Witita Paddock has been the longest without an infusion of pure Merino, so have Corley and a jackaroo drive the rams down there. Take the new iron to the smithy and have some jackaroos help out there, because several horses are waiting to be shod. Mr. Kerrick and the head stockman are both out in the paddocks, and Kunmanara is building a new cattle pen. See if he needs any help with it."

Ruel touched his hat and mounted his horse, riding away.

Alexandra took the packages into the family parlor and sat down at her desk, hastily unwrapping the mail. Picking out the letter from Jonathan from among the others, she unfolded it and scanned it rapidly. More of a note than a letter, it contained only a few facts about his bride.

They were very favorable, however, and Alexandra's fears faded as she reminded herself that her son was a levelheaded man. A schoolteacher would be an intelligent woman, she reflected, with a world view that reached beyond babies and cooking. It also required a level of education that was extraordinary for an artisan's daughter, indicating that her parents had made sacrifices to give her every advantage in life. As to whether she would be happy in the outback, only time would tell.

The family name, Baxter, seemed remotely familiar to Alexandra, stirring the faintest of echoes from some place and time of years ago. Unable to isolate any memory associated with the name, she looked through the rest of the mail. Along with the usual assortment pertaining to the affairs of the station, there were letters from Sir Geoffrey Bodenham in London, Dierdre, and Creighton, but nothing from Morton, as usual.

As she read the letter from Dierdre, Alexandra smiled, every line reflecting her daughter's charming, energetic personality. She had agonized over sending Dierdre to England for her education, then had settled on Sydenham Academy as both the best choice and a much closer location. Drawing students from all over the world, its atmosphere was uniquely cosmopolitan.

It also offered an excellent curriculum and an opportunity for Dierdre to make friends who would benefit her throughout life.

Further on in the letter, Alexandra's smile faded as she read a full account of the relationship between Morton and Clara Tavish. Naively, Dierdre had included information that betrayed a personal knowledge of the woman. That perplexed Alexandra, but the news that Morton had a mistress deeply disturbed her and she hoped that it was only a temporary situation.

Creighton's letter included bad news about the firm, a familiar theme. In addition, his personal financial affairs had suffered serious reverses which also followed the pattern of the past few years. The letter stated that he knew little about Morton's private ventures, but there was evidence that they had mushroomed into a substantial fortune.

Ever since Adolarious had died, Alexandra had exchanged frequent letters with his brother, Sir Geoffrey, an official in the colonial office, and his letter reflected the increasingly personal and friendly tone of their correspondence. There was news about current developments in London and comments about his family. He was delighted over her plans for a book of etchings made from his brother's sketches and asked that he be provided with one hundred copies, whatever the cost, so he could present them to friends as gifts.

When she unwrapped the etching from the printer in Sydney and compared it with the sketch, she was very pleased. She had dreaded the possibility of sending the sketches to London to have the etchings made, and risk losing the priceless artwork. But the etching was superb, executed with masterly skill and faithfully duplicating the sketch.

Alexandra went through the mail concerning the station's affairs, then read the note from Jonathan again. After reflection, she was delighted that he had fallen in love and married, wanting him to be happy.

She also wanted grandchildren around her, and in addition, another generation would be forthcoming to assume the stewardship of Tibooburra Station. She put the note aside, the feeling of distant familiarity with the woman's family name still nagging at the back of her mind.

That evening, as she lay in bed and her thoughts were becoming murky with approaching sleep, something about the Baxter name emerged from the recesses of her memory. It slipped away again as she awoke, leaving only a vague impression of unpleasantness. Deciding that she was searching for problems, Alexandra firmly dismissed it and went to sleep.

On the day David returned, the first heavy rain of the season came. He rode up to Alexandra as she walked out of the supply warehouse, having checked the ceiling for leaks. Word of Jonathan's marriage had spread through the paddocks, and he was delighted about it. "From what I heard, Jonathan and his bride should be here shortly," he said happily.

"Yes, that's right," Alexandra replied. "According to what Ruel said, they should arrive fairly soon. Her family name, Baxter, seems familiar to me. Do you recall anything about any Baxters?"

David thought for a moment, the rain streaming from his hat and oilskins, then shook his head. "No, I certainly don't, Alexandra, but it's a fairly common name. I knew some Baxters in England, and you might have met some yourself at one time or another. Is that roof all right?"

"Yes, it's fine, and so is the one at the house. There are some leaks in the married stockmen's houses, and Kunmanara is seeing to them. We have mail at the house. I'll see you there in a few minutes."

He smiled and nodded, riding toward the barns as she went up the hill. At the house, she hung up her oilskins and hat, then tucked up wisps of her hair as she waited for David. He came in a few minutes later, at fifty still the strong, active man she had married.

Their marriage had aged like choice wine, the rich, mellow pleasure, of warmly familiar love having a deep overtone of passion as they embraced and kissed.

When he began reading the mail, she poured port for him and a sherry for herself. As she had anticipated, he spotted the implication in Dierdre's letter that she had personal knowledge about Clara Tavish. Also as she had anticipated, he was annoyed about it, but furiously angry that Morton had a mistress. He and Alexandra agreed that it was an unsatisfactory situation from both a moral and a practical standpoint, but they were powerless to do anything about it.

When he finished going through the mail, it was dinnertime. Alexandra looked forward to a pleasant, relaxing evening and the companionship of her husband for the next few days, but her hopes were dashed. Shortly after dinner, Silas, the head stockman, came to the house and said that a jackaroo had been sent from Boar Paddock with word that it was flooding. David left with Silas, riding off into the rainy night.

As the rain continued, the next few days were a familiar time of tension for Alexandra, and she slept lightly. In case urgent word came from Boar Paddock and other areas to the north that flooding had become critical, she remained ready to send riders for help from the high-lying paddocks to the south. In the meantime, she monitored the level of the creek below the hill, ready to move the families and Aborigines up to the house.

Then the threat passed when the rain ceased a few days later. The following day, the skies were clear and the mild autumn sun beamed down on a haze of fresh green that had replaced the sun-baked brown on the vast miles of rolling hills. David returned two days later, muddy and weary but content, no sheep having been drowned during the flash floods.

The next day, Alexandra was at her desk in the

family parlor when she heard David shouting her
name. She ran to the front door and outside as he rode
up to the house at a run. "Jonathan and his bride are
coming down the track!" he called elatedly, reining
his horse to a skidding stop and turning it. "I'm going
to ride out and meet them!"

Alexandra smiled and waved as David rode down
the tree-lined avenue at a run. Shading her eyes with
her hand, she looked at the track and saw two riders
with pack horses in the distance, one of them definitely Jonathan. As excited as her husband, Alexandra
had to stop for a moment and think of what to do first
as she reentered the house.

Hurrying into the kitchen to talk with Flora about
dinner, she decided upon the extravagance of stuffed
suckling pig. Then she rushed upstairs to make certain
that Jonathan's room was clean. Leaving his room,
she stopped in hers to touch up her hair, then went
downstairs and outside to wait on the house steps.

Any visitor was still a matter of lively interest, even
swagmen who passed through, but the arrival of the
Kerrick heir with his wife was an event of overriding
importance. Near the barns, the storekeeper, jackaroos, and stockmen had gathered to look, while the
families were in a cluster in front of the houses beside
the creek. The stable boy moved from side to side in
front of the steps, craning his neck to see.

When the horses were finally coming up the avenue,
Alexandra lifted her hand in response to her son's
happy wave, but her eyes were on his wife. She gasped
softly at Catherine's exceptional beauty, but she also
saw that Jonathan had chosen more than a pretty face.
The direct gaze from the green eyes was that of a
strong, self-reliant woman.

At a closer distance, Alexandra saw the depths in
Catherine's lovely eyes and the firm lines of her chin
and mouth that indicated a contained, tempestuous
nature. Utterly delighted, Alexandra went down the

steps to help Catherine dismount. Catherine smiled in response, climbing down from the saddle into Alexandra's arms.

"Welcome to your new home, Catherine," Alexandra said as they hugged and kissed. "I'm so pleased that you're here."

"I'm very pleased to be here, Mistress Kerrick. I had hoped that I would be welcome, and it's very gratifying to see that I am."

"Indeed you are, my dear. It would take a heart of stone and the mind of a dolt to do anything but welcome you with the greatest pleasure."

Alexandra turned to Jonathan and greeted him, then took Catherine inside as the men carried in the baggage. When their son and wife were in their room, Alexandra and David made preparations to have a holiday the following day, with a feast to celebrate the homecoming. David went to the barns to organize tasks for the men and jackaroos, while Alexandra did the same with the women in the houses beside the creek.

In her glow of happiness, the remainder of the day passed in a rush for Alexandra. Predictably, when dusk fell, the throbbing drone of didgeridoos, the clatter of rhythm sticks, and chanting voices came from the huts down the creek as the Aborigines marked the occasion in their own way. The sound carried into the house as Alexandra prepared for dinner. When her son and his wife came downstairs, her heart swelled with pride, the two of them the most handsome couple she had ever seen.

Dinner was another triumph for Flora. The tender, juicy pork was seasoned to perfection while the other dishes were equally delicious. Alexandra enjoyed the conversation with Catherine far more than the food, since the young woman was as interesting as she was beautiful. The lack of adequate education for the children at the home paddock having long troubled Alexandra, she was intensely pleased when Catherine expressed a wish to organize a school for them as soon as possible.

It was in the family parlor after dinner, when Catherine talked about her family, that Alexandra plunged from supreme happiness into an abyss of sorrow. Recalling conversations of decades before, she knew why the Baxter name had seemed familiar. She also knew why Catherine had such an excellent education. Her mother, possibly the only one knowing the dread secret, had believed that she would need every conceivable advantage in life.

Alexandra had to conceal her feelings only briefly because they all went upstairs to their bedrooms a few minutes later. When she and David were getting ready for bed, she knew that she would have to bear her burden of knowledge alone as she listened to him commenting happily about Catherine. Having forgotten their long-ago conversation that had revealed the entire story to her, David would also dismiss her fears as groundless. He still believed that the past could be left behind, but she believed differently, and now she knew that Auberta Baxter did as well.

In her gown and slippers, Alexandra picked up a candlestick. "I ate intemperately at dinner tonight, David," she told him. "I don't feel like going to bed yet, so I'll look at the sketches for a time."

"Very well, but don't stay up too late. You don't want to be too tired to enjoy the celebration tomorrow."

She nodded and kissed him, then left the room. As she followed the pool of light from the candlestick down the hall and stairs in the dark, quiet house, the sound of the didgeridoos, rhythm sticks, and chant still came from the huts. She wondered if in their mysterious way of knowing things, the Aborigines also knew what she did and the corroboree was an attempt to exorcise the ghosts of the past and send them back through the decades.

Sitting at her desk, she left the sketches untouched.

She looked into the darkness at the side of the room, recalling the conversation with the Underwoods at dinner in her father's home. They had talked about a maid named Auberta Mowbray who had married a shipwright named Hiram Baxter. Later, David had told her about Auberta Mowbray and her circumstances in Parramatta, which had explained the remaining details of the woman's situation.

Alexandra knew she would have to adjust to what had happened, never allowing it to affect her attitude toward Catherine even to the slightest degree. In her heart, she remained convinced that Jonathan had made a perfect choice for a companion in life. But when they had children, that corrupt, evil bloodline might be dominant with the stigma revealing itself.

As she sat in the dim, quiet room, that baneful, vindictive jeer still rang in her ears across the decades. He had said she would never be rid of him, and he had told the truth. That rotted hand continued to reach out from the grave, its putrid touch fouling her life and those of her loved ones. Her first child had been fathered by the depraved criminal, and now her second son was married to Enos Hinton's daughter.

Chapter Eighteen

"I concur with you," Morton said as he finished examining the balance sheet. "For all practical purposes, you're bankrupt." Sitting in the chair beside his uncle's desk, he handed the paper back to him. "Do you have any assets that you haven't listed there?"

"The house I inherited from my father," Creighton replied despondently. "It and the furnishings are worth a few hundred guineas. Other than that, I have a few land holdings and such that aren't producing any revenue. And my partnership in the firm of Hammond and Kerrick, of course."

"Well, that's hardly an asset. We agreed months ago that it is a charter entity only, because it has no holdings or revenues."

"Even so, it's been a firm of some standing for years and the name is well-known. The good will of the firm is intangible, but it's an asset."

"Good will!" Morton echoed scornfully. "All of the good will in the world, together with sixpence, will buy a sixpenneth of merchandise, and not a ha'penneth more. What has it got others these past months?"

Creighton somberly agreed since the previous months had been disastrous. Not only in Sydney, but in London and every other capital in the empire, many old, well-established firms had gone bankrupt. People at large had also suffered with money extremely scarce and commerce almost at a standstill. "But it hasn't seemed to affect you at all, Morton," Creighton mused.

"No, because I've accepted payments only in cash or in commodities or property with a stable value. I warned you to do the same, because it's been obvious from newspaper reports that there would be a currency crisis due to a shortage of government specie reserves. Now that crisis is here."

"Yes, you did tell me to do that, Morton. But I didn't understand what you meant then, and I'm still not sure I understand what happened."

"Manufactured goods are mostly traded within the empire, but many raw materials are bought from other countries. There has been a steady drain of specie, and the Bank of England is prohibited by law from issuing notes in excess of its gold and silver reserves. Most commerce is on the basis of debits and credits, of course, but once money became scarce, everyone began demanding cash. A crisis resulted, because there was too little money in circulation to support commercial activity at all levels."

His aged face drawn with fatigue and anxiety, Creighton nodded. "So for some time, you've been comparing the newspaper reports on the value of imports into the empire versus the exports, and saw there was a drain of specie. That was very astute, Morton. Not that it will help me, but I suppose the government will now take measures to procure more gold and silver."

"Yes, but it will take years to procure enough. The drain continues, and the world-wide specie reserves are limited. In the interim, to provide money for everyday business, joint-stock companies will be chartered to issue bank notes backed by the value of the company. I've been invited to attend a meeting on the formation of such a company here."

"One needn't ask why I wasn't invited," Creighton remarked bitterly. "Very shortly, I won't be able to provide food and other necessities for my family. I suppose I could go to Tibooburra Station with my wife. In the last letter I received from your mother, she made it very clear that Martha and I would be welcome to live there."

Morton knew about the invitation, having been responsible for it. Some months before, he had written a brief letter to his mother and advised her that her brother's finances were becoming critical. Creighton talked more about the situation, concerned mostly about his daughters whose opportunities would be severely limited in the isolation of the outback. He said that Dora and Leona could stay in Sydney with Melissa and Amanda, their married sisters, until they found either suitable work or husbands.

"Not that I want to make such arrangements," he added dejectedly, "but I have no alternative. This is a grievous thing to happen to a man at my time of life, Morton, and it will break my wife's heart."

"No doubt, but as you say, you can go with her to Tibooburra Station. There are many in your position who have no such recourse."

"That's quite true," Creighton agreed morosely. "As much as I detest being reduced to accepting charity, it is available to me. Everyone there seems to be very content, so life there must be pleasant. In her letter, Alexandra informed me that your brother's wife is expecting a child."

"So I understand. If you're going to the station, you should leave during early spring to avoid traveling in the summer heat."

"Yes, I will. There'll be expenses, and I must leave at least some money with Melissa and Amanda for their sisters' upkeep. Would you buy my house and its furnishings, Morton? It's among the finest houses in Sydney, and I think three hundred guineas would be a fair price."

Morton promptly agreed without bartering on the price, even though he had absolutely no desire to buy the house. He had been expecting to provide some financial help to his uncle, knowing his mother would want him to, and he hoped to recover the money when the monetary crisis eased. He talked with his uncle a few minutes longer, discussing details of the transaction, then went to his own office.

In contrast to those who had suffered losses, he had exploited the recent situation. Buying up the assets of bankrupt companies for pence on the guinea, he had laid the groundwork to become much more wealthy when the financial climate improved. Reading the papers on his desk, he again studied the invitation to participate in the formation of a joint-stock company that would be authorized to issue bank notes.

It had the promise of large profits, as well as something else he desired just as much. In at least some respects, it would place him on an equal level with other participants, most of whom were from the loftiest levels of exclusives in the colony. Along with recognition, a substantial position in the company would give him powerful influence.

The company's objective was to raise a minimum of twenty thousand guineas in specie as security to back the issue of bank notes. The voting stock would consist of three thousand shares at a nominal price of ten guineas a share, which had to be purchased with specie on deposit at the bank. Nonvoting stock was being offered at a lower price and could be purchased with either specie or liens on real property.

The newspapers had reported the chartering of similar companies in London and elsewhere, and

Morton had kept back a large cash reserve for such an opportunity. The meeting for the company's formation was scheduled for the next day, so he went over his accounts, figuring out how much he could invest, then he turned to other matters.

Along with the economic situation, other factors presented both opportunities for profits and hidden pitfalls. Parliament was debating the elimination of protective tariffs on grain imports in order to lower food prices, which would drastically reduce the value of wheat shipments from Sydney. Pondering that and other developments, Morton worked at his desk until late.

The next day, sleet and rain sweeping ahead of an icy, gusty August wind made the streets quiet as Morton went to the meeting. In the offices over the Bank of New South Wales, an apprentice took his coat and hat, then showed him into the room where the meeting would be held. At one end of the room, some fifteen people stood in front of the roaring flames in a large fireplace, and an apprentice served glasses of port.

One of them was an aged, wizened man named Farrel Ibbets, who had competed with Morton at various times and cooperated at others. "Don't anyone yawn," he warned jokingly. "This fellow here will have the gold out of your teeth before you can close your mouth."

The remark created a stir of amusement as Morton smiled weakly, exchanging nods with Ibbets and the other men. James Macarthur and Howard Montague, leading figures in the highest social level of the colony, spoke amiably to Morton in greeting. The managing director of the bank, Giles Newcomb, had been appointed by the governor to call the meeting. A portly man in his forties, he hurried toward Morton to greet him.

"I'm very pleased indeed that you accepted the invitation, Mr. Kerrick," he said with a brisk, practiced smile. "Come over to the fire and join the others. You know Mr. Osgood, the colonial treasurer, don't you? Yes, I'm sure you need no introductions to anyone here."

Morton declined the glass of port the apprentice offered, then warmed his hands at the fire as he exchanged comments about the weather and other general subjects with the men. A short time later, Giles Newcomb looked at his watch and announced that the meeting would begin. Moving across the room, the men took seats at a long table.

The meeting was opened by the colonial treasurer, who announced that he was speaking for the governor in stressing the importance of providing an adequate supply of currency for daily transactions within the colony. He appealed to the patriotism of those present, asking them to invest generously and capitalize the joint-stock company. While he was talking, apprentices handed around samples of the bank notes that had been ordered, which were similar to the currency issued by the Bank of England.

Newcomb took charge of the meeting, explaining that the company would be chartered for five years and would initially issue bank notes with a total face value of fifty percent over the capitalization. At the end of five years, if the Bank of England currency was still insufficient, the charter would be extended. During the charter, the bank would exchange available Bank of England currency for the bank notes on a one-for-one basis.

"Naturally," he added, "little will be available for a long time. The object is to have only our notes in circulation so as to increase confidence in them. If there are no questions, I'll open the sales of stock."

There were no questions, but the sales were slow. The nature of the investment was new and untried, and the men were reluctant to risk too much on it. Through tediously tracking the performance of similar companies in other places from scattered newspaper reports, Morton knew the profit potential was much greater than the risk, but he held back for the moment, waiting to see how much of the stock sold.

Ibbets and some of the other men produced property deeds as security for the cheaper nonvoting shares and signed bank drafts to buy small blocks of the voting stock. A few, including James Macarthur and Howard Montague, bought larger amounts of the voting stock, some ranging as high as four hundred shares. The apprentices scribbled in ledgers and handed out certificates, the sales of the voting stock climbing toward two thousand shares, then it stopped.

"Come, come, gentlemen," Newcomb called. "We're still a bit short of the twenty thousand we need for capitalization, and the company won't be chartered until we have it. Who'll buy more of the voting stock?" Silence fell around the table as the men shook their heads firmly. Giles Newcomb turned to Morton. "Won't you buy some of the voting stock, Mr. Kerrick?"

"Yes, I'll take a thousand shares."

The impasse broken, a collective sigh rose, along with comments about the huge investment. Newcomb beamed happily. "Very well," he said, "and it appears that I'll be working for you, because you have the controlling interest. But I'll be pleased to do so, Mr. Kerrick."

The company charter assured, more of the nonvoting stock was sold as Morton signed a bank draft and took his stock certificates. When the final details of the meeting were concluded, Montague, Macarthur, and others expressed their appreciation to Morton for his investment. The colonial secretary also thanked him gratefully, then left to inform the governor that the meeting had been successful and the company had been capitalized.

As the apprentices brought in more wine for the men to celebrate the occasion, Morton left. Newcomb left with him and helped him on with his coat, promising to keep in close contact. Walking out into the rain and sleet, Morton returned to his office to continue with his other affairs as he waited to see how his investment in the company fared.

The bank notes began circulating the next day, meeting with resistance among people to accept them. By the following day, a few shares in the company were being traded in the coffeehouses, selling at discounts up to thirty percent. Then, during the subsequent days, the bank notes began flowing on through the currency system, employers insisting that workers take them at face value, and then workers doing the same with merchants.

After the new currency had replaced the few Bank of England notes circulating in Sydney, the reluctance to accept them faded. Company stock being traded in the coffeehouses climbed in price, the discount diminishing to ten percent. Giles Newcomb gradually began releasing more of the bank notes, increasing the amount in circulation until the flow of money through the bank had returned to its normal level before the currency crisis.

When the bank director stopped releasing the notes, the total face value in circulation was several hundred percent of company capitalization. Rumors of that reached the coffeehouses, and trading in the stock immediately increased, the price of the shares climbing to a premium. On the day that his aunt and uncle left Sydney for Tibooburra Station, the value of Morton's shares had increased from ten to fifteen guineas each.

Creighton came to the office alone, explaining that his wife was too distressed even to make her farewells. "She'll feel better once we set out," he speculated hopefully, close to tears himself. "We have a comfortable wagon to travel in, with ample supplies and everything we need."

"The weather will soon be pleasant as well," Morton added. "There's no need for you to hurry, so it should be a pleasant journey, with new things to see on every side. Is there anything I can do for you?"

"No, buying the house was a great help, because I could have done nothing without that money." He handed Morton keys on a ring and a stack of papers. "Those are the keys to the house and deeds on a few holdings. None of them are producing any revenues, of course, but I've signed them over to you in the event you can get a few guineas from them."

"Very well, and thank you. I wish you the best of fortune, and please convey my regards to everyone at Tibooburra Station."

Nodding and replying in a choked voice, Creighton shook hands with Morton. He made his farewells to the office staff, and as the apprentices wept, he left. Morton gave the keys and papers to the head clerk, telling him to hire someone to watch over the house.

"I know of a gardener who is out of work, sir," the head clerk replied. "He's very reliable, and he'll be more than glad to live in the carriage house and watch over the place. What shall I do with these deeds?"

Turning toward his office, Morton shrugged and told him to file them. Sitting at his desk, he resumed studying a balance sheet on cargo profits that he had been reading when his uncle had arrived. When he was done, he thought about looking at the deeds his uncle had given him. Then he dismissed them, reaching for other papers on his desk.

During the following days, Morton missed his uncle and felt remorseful over what had happened. But his uncle had been out of step with the times and the inevitable had occurred. But Creighton had made the rounds of the coffeehouses daily, bringing back information he gleaned. Morton considered most of it useless, but wanting to maintain contact with developments in the town, he began spending an occasional hour or two in the coffeehouses.

When the first quarterly dividend was paid by the

joint-stock company, Morton received some twelve percent of his investment. The prospect of an annual return of about fifty percent more than satisfied him, but some of the investors wanted more. At a shareholders' meeting, they insisted that Giles Newcomb put more bank notes into circulation to increase the profits.

The bank director replied in technical terms that few understood and none wanted to hear, and the clamor continued. Morton interrupted, bluntly explaining that if the bank notes became too plentiful, people would lose confidence in them, their value would plummet, and the company stock would become worthless. That ended the debate, Newcomb and the others who had understood the situation nodding to Morton in thanks.

Later that same day, when Morton was in his office, the head clerk came in. He stopped in front of the desk, holding two papers, his diffident attitude indicating that they were controversial. "The man from the sheep station is here, sir," he said. "He brought these."

"Sheep station? A man from Tibooburra Station?"

"No, sir. The sheep station on the Murray River."

Morton thought for a moment, then recalled the sheep station that his uncle had financed. "What does that have to do with me?"

"You own it, sir," the head clerk replied uneasily. "The deed is among those that Mr. Hammond gave you and I filed away for you."

Morton frowned, reaching for the papers, then looked at them in disbelief. One was a bank draft in the amount of thirty-six guineas for wool, the other a bill for a little under two hundred guineas for transporting the wool. "Is this meant to be a jest?" he demanded.

"The man said that workers had to cut a track most of the way to get the wagon through," the head clerk explained hastily. "He said the transportation costs will be small next year, and the value of the wool should be much more. He's outside and wants to discuss it with you, sir."

Enraged, Morton snatched up the papers as he pushed his chair back and stood. He started to go out and order the man to get the people off the property, then send the deed to John Fitzroy for him to return ownership of the land to the colonial government. Then, as on each occasion when he lost his temper, a painful memory came to him from across the years.

It was his mother's voice, castigating him for allowing his anger to rule him, the memory so acute that he could almost hear her. He responded to it, controlling his rage. When he did, he recalled the box of stones that had been in his office closet for almost a year.

As he thought about the box, it occurred to him that if there were any mineral deposits on the land that could be of some future value, he might be able to sell the land instead of abandoning it. At least he would then recover the cost of transporting the wool. "Tell the man to come back tomorrow afternoon," he said, "and send an apprentice in here."

The head clerk left, and Morton wrote a note to the chemist, James Boland. He asked Boland to test the stones for minerals of any value, and provide the results by the next morning. The apprentice came in, as Morton finished writing the note telling the chemist that if he was unable to test the stones for minerals, to inform the youth and to discard the box.

The apprentice pocketed the note, then dragged the heavy box from the closet and lugged it out. Turning back to the papers on his desk, Morton noticed an invitation to join a group of investors who were forming a marine insurance company. In other places, the chartering of such companies had ended the common practice of shipping companies sharing risks through selling cargo shares, the major source of income for many investors. Always ready to change with the times, Morton studied the proposal closely.

Soon after, the apprentice stood in the doorway and tapped on the jamb. "Sir, the man told me to tell you that he could do it," he said. "He also said it won't be very accurate with the means he has at hand, but he'll do his best and let you know tomorrow morning what he finds."

Morton nodded, looking back down at the letter on the prospective insurance company and concentrating on it once more. Then he put it aside to study again later, and began looking through the other papers on his desk. At dusk, an apprentice came in to light the lamp on Morton's desk, the rest of the office staff leaving for the day. An hour later, the evening quiet was broken by the noise of the front door being hurriedly opened and then slammed closed.

Quick, heavy footsteps crossed the outer office, and the apprentice asked the person the nature of his business. James Boland stood in the doorway, the youth right behind him, trying to stop him. Surprised and puzzled, Morton motioned the apprentice away and told the chemist to come in.

The man's manner usually matched his studious appearance, but even in the dim light, he was obviously overwrought. Taking a rock from his pocket, he walked to the desk. "Gold," he said in a soft, trembling voice, placing the rock in front of Morton. "That is a piece of very rich gold ore, Mr. Kerrick."

Controlling his abrupt surge of excitement from the stunning revelation, Morton sat back in his chair, thinking clearly and logically. His first reaction was skepticism. Not the slightest hint of precious metals had ever been found in Australia. "Are you quite sure?" he asked.

"I'm positive!" Boland exclaimed in exhilaration, his face crimson and his eyes wild. "I'm telling you that it's—"

He broke off as Morton frowned, lifting his hand for silence, then pointing to the door. His feverish agitation changing to apprehension, the chemist tiptoed to the door and peered around the jamb at the apprentice in the outer office. Relaxing, he quietly walked back to the desk and sat in the chair beside it. "The boy heard nothing," he assured Morton softly, then he pointed to the rock. "There's no question that it's gold ore, Mr. Kerrick. I don't have the means for an accurate assay, but it's very rich."

"Were all of the rocks gold ore?"

"No, some contained a fair amount of silver, along with traces of tin, copper, and various other metals. There were four pieces of gold ore, and I crushed the other three to make the analysis. They contain traces of other metals, but a very high percentage of gold."

Boland continued in a tense, exultant whisper, explaining that he had made different tests to insure he was correct, each one having positive results. As he listened, Morton pondered the development in relation to his interests as a whole. Gold ore at the sheep station was obviously an opportunity for vast wealth, but it also presented him with a dilemma.

His shares in the joint-stock company now valued at twenty guineas each, he was looking forward to dividends of some five thousand guineas a year. However, at the first news of a gold strike, the currency crisis would immediately begin easing. Additionally, people preferred the solid feel of gold to paper. In the expectation of soon having gold, their confidence in the bank notes would fade, making them plunge in value.

When that happened, his stock certificates would become nothing more than a thousand pieces of worthless paper. He was unable to extricate himself from the situation because he was heavily invested in the company. If he began selling his shares in any considerable quantity, it would raise questions and cause the value of the stock to fall.

If the ore was present at the sheep station in a sufficient amount, the loss could be recovered, but that was too much of an assumption to risk such a large sum of money. Even attempting to find out how much there was would be too dangerous, the activity certain to start rumors flying. As he listened to the chemist, Morton decided to let the joint-stock company run its course, then investigate the potential of the gold ore.

"Only a few ounces of gold for each ton of ore may mean millions," Boland continued in a jubilant whisper. "This will produce several ounces from each ton. I presume that it came from Tibooburra Station."

Morton let the last comment stand, stroking his chin. "Unfortunately," he mused, "I don't own any part of Tibooburra Station. Making arrangements to exploit this will take time, perhaps several years."

Boland sat back, speechless for a moment in shock and disappointment. "Several years?" he gasped. "But why wait? I tell you, there's a fortune where this ore came from, Mr. Kerrick, and we could—"

"Listen to me very carefully," Morton interrupted. "I didn't become wealthy by dashing into things without preparation. The equipment required will be expensive, and I'm heavily invested at the moment. If I start selling off investments rapidly to buy the equipment, others will find out what we're doing. We must avoid having others rush in, or any legal problems. Have you told anyone about this? Your wife, for example?"

"No, sir," the chemist replied quietly. "I came straight here from my shop. No one else knows."

"Then keep your lips sealed. When I'm ready to proceed, I'll put you on a substantial retainer, with a legal agreement to share in the profits. You know how to mine and process this ore, don't you?"

"Absolutely, Mr. Kerrick. I'll need to brush up on details, but I'm familiar with mining and with processing various kinds of ore."

"Then you're the logical choice for the job, and you have my word that it's yours. You must remain absolutely silent on this, as well as wait for up to five years. But that will be much better than proceeding now and losing it to others or having it taken by legal means, won't it?"

Boland hesitated, then nodded emphatically. "Yes, of course, Mr. Kerrick," he agreed. "It would be insane to risk such enormous wealth. I'm fortunate to be involved in this with someone of your temperament and judgment rather than one who might be as rash as myself. I'll remain silent and I'll wait for as long as necessary."

Satisfied that Boland would do as he said, Morton again assured him that he would receive an ample share of the profits. They talked for a short time longer, then the chemist shook hands with Morton and left, just as happy if much less excited than he had been upon his arrival.

When Boland was gone, Morton thought about the danger that someone else would discover gold ore near the Murray River. Then he dismissed the possibility as very remote. The vast majority of land sales had been to the west and north of Sydney while the land Creighton had chosen was to the south. Because it was completely unsettled, it was much cheaper. The station was isolated for the foreseeable future, and there were no other stations within many miles of it.

Keeping it occupied was essential, however, and Morton decided to invest whatever was necessary in supplies and equipment to ensure that the people there remained content. He also decided to have them concentrate entirely on sheep and stop searching for other sources of revenue, because anyone who could recognize metal ores might become curious.

After pondering all the factors involved, he was confident that the situation would remain stable until he was ready to proceed. He looked at the stone on his desk, finding it difficult to restrain his hopes from soaring wildly. Instead of wealth that eventually rivaled any in the colony, he could in time have a fortune equal to any in the world.

At the same time, he might satisfy a yearning to achieve his goals, a longing that remained as strong as when he had first begun. Although he was wealthy and well-known in the town, he still felt as though success had eluded him. Something he was unable to define was still missing from his life. But if he could amass an immense fortune and world-wide fame, perhaps that inner need, whatever its nature, would be quenched.

Sitting in the family parlor with her husband, her son, and his wife, Alexandra listened to Creighton and Martha talking about the hardships of their journey. Now that they had rested, cleaned up and changed clothes, and eaten dinner, their appearance was much less dismaying to Alexandra. But the years and stress had taken a heavy toll since she had last seen her brother. Both he and his wife looked very old and feeble.

Even more than their physical condition, however, she was concerned about their mental and emotional state. They were very despondent, with a listless lack of concentration. Their attention wandering at times, they occasionally paused in conversation to think of a commonplace word, which made them seem even older. Alexandra knew it was a result of their upheaval and present lack of purpose in life, not age.

Creighton again thanked her and David for the warm welcome and unstinting hospitality they had extended. "Even though we were invited," he continued, "your kindness is exceptional. After such a long, harrowing journey, to have so cordial a reception is gratifying beyond words. Moreover, it makes dependence upon charity somewhat less bitter."

"Creighton," Kerrick said firmly, "that isn't a word to be used between us. You have a right to be here because you're family."

"Absolutely," Alexandra agreed. "Rather than being given anything, you're merely accepting what is rightfully due you. Please, let's put that to rest because we're grateful that you're here so we can enjoy your company. Now tell us about your family, and how they are."

Martha and Creighton talked about their children and grandchildren, becoming more animated on the subject of their loved ones. Their mood became sad again as they explained the arrangements they had made for their youngest daughters, then the conversation moved on to other things.

Catherine went to the sideboard for the brandy and cordial, then freshened the after-dinner drinks. As she poured more into Alexandra's glass, they exchanged a smile as they always did each time their eyes met. During the past months, the beautiful young woman had become like a loving and beloved daughter to Alexandra, and a deep affection had developed between them enriching both their lives. But during quiet, private moments, Alexandra was tormented by worry over the child that Catherine was carrying.

The Hammonds had brought the mail from the postal office in Sydney, which had contained letters to Catherine from her mother and father. That had pleased Alexandra as much as the letter she had received herself from Dierdre. Having visited the girl shortly before leaving Sydney, Martha said that she was still doing very well in school. Then Creighton mentioned that he had sold his house and furnishings to Morton.

"Does he live there now?" Alexandra asked.

Her brother hesitated, then shook his head, discomfited by the question. "No, he's still in lodgings, Alexandra."

A momentary, awkward silence fell. The Hammonds were embarrassed, and Alexandra was troubled by the implication that her son's living with his mistress was a permanent arrangement. Jonathan's poorly-concealed amusement drew a sharp glance from his father, who remained angry over the situation. Alexandra then asked her brother about Morton's business activities.

Creighton replied that he knew few details about Morton's ventures, but his financial success was evident. He mentioned several of Morton's investments, including a joint-stock company to issue bank notes. "Those involved in that company included a Macarthur, a Montague, and others such as that," Creighton continued. "Right there is clear evidence of Morton's great success, because those people do business with very few."

"Yes, that's true. Does he mix with them socially?"

"No, Morton has no social activities at all, as far as I know. He's at the office seven days a week, from early morning until after dark. While he has accumulated wealth, no one can say that he hasn't earned it."

He related in satisfaction how others tried to spy on Morton to take advantage of his business acumen. In contrast to her husband's attitude, Martha was silently moody, evidently believing that Morton could have done more to help them. Alexandra reserved judgment on that point, but she felt uneasy about what Morton was doing.

Over the years, she had been proud of her son's achievements and even more pleased that he had found his place in life. Now it appeared, however, that he had taken a wrong turn and was confused about his goals. Instead of working toward a prominent, respected position, which she knew was what he wanted, he was merely obsessively burrowing after wealth.

By the time the conversation had ended and everyone went to their rooms for the night, Alexandra had decided what she must do. She brought it up while she and David were getting ready for bed, and as she had anticipated, he objected strongly. "There's no need for that," he told her. "You can write Morton a letter and tell him what you have to say. Also, you can't leave when Catherine is going to have a child."

"A letter won't do, and Catherine's baby isn't due until the end of the summer. And there are other reasons why I must go."

"What reasons, Alexandra?"

"I haven't seen my daughter in over four years, David, and I'm losing the joy of her childhood. My explanatory notes on the sketches are finished, and I want to talk to the printer in person before work on the book begins. Martha can look after the household while Creighton attends to the station accounts, which will give them work to do while they settle in here. They both need some purpose, or they'll simply fade away."

David shook his head, pointing out alternative solutions to each of her reasons for going to Sydney. Some of them, such as bringing Dierdre to the station for a visit, were almost humorously impractical, and Alexandra knew he simply disliked their being parted for the three to four months it would take her to travel to the capitol and return. She shared his feelings, but her duty as a mother lay in Sydney.

The issue remaining unsettled that evening, Alexandra discussed it with David several times during the next few days. During one conversation, he suggested that they go together. Although she would have enjoyed that, Alexandra talked him out of it, because she knew he detested Sydney; it was part of his past which he thought he had put behind him.

Agreeing at last, as he always did on matters important to her, David selected an escort and began making arrangements for her journey. Creighton took over the station accounts and Martha the household while Alexandra packed clothes in trunks and saw to her other preparations.

On a late-spring morning in November, Alexandra set out. She rode with Ruel and Eulie in front of two wagons driven by jackaroos, others following with spare horses. As the procession reached the track, the home paddock turned out to bid her farewell. Family and employees gathered at the house and the barns. Women came out of the houses beside the creek, and Catherine brought the children from the small, adjacent schoolhouse. Everyone shouted and waved, and Alexandra waved in reply.

The everyday routine left behind, Alexandra had an expansive sense of freedom, enjoying the journey as she traveled south across the land she loved. On the second evening, however, her pleasure was marred when they stopped in Bushranger Paddock for the night. The camp beside the track was at the head of the valley reaching eastward from the hill where the battle with the bushrangers had taken place, the men buried at the foot of it.

The paddock itself, a part of the station, was as valuable to her as all the rest. But in the same way that the ghost of Enos Hinton was still a somber shadow on a vital part of her life, the bodies of the bushrangers at the foot of the hill tainted the land. Looking at the hill as the sun set behind it, she knew that having the skeletons dug up and scattered would be useless. Some physical remnants of Hinton would remain on the land, just like his odious specter that haunted her life.

That night, she dreamed she was attending Catherine in childbirth. The dream, having every sensation of absolute reality, became a nightmare when the child was born. Looking down at the baby in her arms, Alexandra saw a grotesque monster with huge, bloated male genitals. The ugly, birthmarked face was Enos Hinton's, jeering at her maliciously.

Drenched with sweat, Alexandra woke in time to stifle her scream of terror and anguish. Then, while she realized she had merely been dreaming, she still felt the weight of the baby in her arms. She moved her arms, unable to dispel the feeling. An aftermath of crushing depression following the nightmare seemed like a dread warning.

In the bright sunlight of the next day, and when Bushranger Paddock was left behind, she was able to shrug off her oppressive sense of foreboding. The memory of the dream, with its disquieting reality, gradually faded to the back of her mind. There it joined other harrowing memories and feelings that had lingered in those far recesses ever since the fateful day she had left Camden Park in search of Elizabeth Macarthur and her father.

Chapter Nineteen

"In short, Mistress Kerrick," Hermione Winthrop summed up, "Dierdre is an excellent student. As I've mentioned in my correspondence with you, she has an interest as well as talent in the arts. In time, perhaps she should pursue that by studying in England or Europe."

"Perhaps so, Headmistress," Alexandra replied doubtfully. "If she wishes to, I'll see that she has the opportunity to do so. As for my own preferences, however, I've already been separated from her too long, and I'm loath to encourage her to leave Australia."

The tall, thin headmistress of Sydenham Academy nodded in resigned acceptance of human weakness. With gray hair and eyes that matched the color of her meticulously neat, severely plain dress, she peered over her pince-nez as she continued discussing Dierdre with Alexandra. In charge of a large student body drawn from the far corners of the earth and ranging from ten to eighteen years old, all from affluent families that demanded a high standard from schools, she looked equal to her responsibilities.

While talking with the woman in her office, a portrait of the school's founder gazing down somberly from the paneled wall, Alexandra had learned that Dierdre had no problems that the staff knew about. Satisfied, she ended the conversation after a few more minutes. "It was very kind of you to receive me on such short notice, Headmistress," she said. "I've found our discussion enjoyable as well as informative."

"It's a distinct pleasure to receive you at any time, Mistress Kerrick. The games period should end momentarily. As soon as it does, I'll have your daughter sent to the visitors' parlor."

Alexandra thanked the headmistress, then left the office and went back downstairs. Having arrived in Sydney the previous night, she was taking care of her business in town, wearing a fashionable blue poplin dress with a pale blue brocade pattern on the bodice and a high, fitted neckline of pale blue lace. To go with it, she had put on a matching hat trimmed with pale blue tulle and blue kid gloves. Preferring the outback, she still remained completely at ease among the best circles that the capitol had to offer.

Sitting in the parlor, Alexandra waited with anticipation for Dierdre to arrive. A short time later, instead of the small child she had sent to the school, a tall, lovely girl in cricket whites entered the room, smiling excitedly. Dierdre gasped in delight, then she and Alexandra rushed to each other and embraced.

Tears of joy sprang to Alexandra's eyes as she clasped her daughter tightly and kissed her. Then they stepped back and looked at each other, Dierdre seeming vaguely and pleasantly surprised. "I didn't remember your being so absolutely beautiful, Mother," she blurted.

"I see that you've learned your social skills very well indeed," Alexandra teased her daughter, laughing merrily.

"No, I mean it," Dierdre insisted. "I've always thought of you as very attractive, of course, but . . ." Her voice fading, she searched for and was unable to find the words to describe her feelings.

Alexandra smiled wistfully, caressing her daughter's face. "I've always thought of you as the loveliest human being alive. The necessities of life can be so cruel. You must have an education, and yet I long to have you at my side every moment. I know that in your letters you've said that you're happy, but are you truly happy here, my dear?"

"Yes, I am, Mother. Like you, I'd prefer our being together. Failing that, it's very pleasant here. I have friends, and I enjoy my studies."

"Good. Come, let's sit down and talk, Dierdre."

They sat down on the couch and Alexandra held her daughter's hand. She let Dierdre talk, knowing she would have much to say, and she did. There was no hint of problems, and Alexandra searched behind the words for anything left unsaid. It was simply an outpouring of information about Dierdre's friends, amusing moments, and her school activities.

One of the friends she referred to several times was Alice Montague whose mother was the former Elizabeth Macarthur. Alexandra mentioned that Elizabeth was a close friend of hers from years ago, and Dierdre knew all about it. "Yes, Alice has told me that her mother speaks of you often," she said. "Also, her father is involved in business dealings with Morton."

"I understand he doesn't visit business associates, though."

"Morton?" Dierdre exclaimed, laughing. "No, if Morton accepted an invitation to dinner, he would take along one of his musty old ledgers to study over his soup. Business is his only interest, Mother."

Dierdre continued talking, and eventually got around to the subject of Clara Tavish. "I'm sure Auntie Martha told you about my conversation with the woman," she added, becoming apologetic. "I haven't seen her again. But if I do, I won't speak with her, of course."

"Why not? That would be most rude, Dierdre."

Her daughter was speechless for a moment in astonishment. "You mean you don't disapprove?" she asked, finding her tongue.

"I don't disapprove of your speaking with her, which isn't to say that you should make friends. As absurd as it can seem at times, one must consider one's reputation. But through knowing a poor woman who is on beam's ends in trying to provide for her children, perhaps you'll take greater care against the pitfalls of life." Alexandra laughed, shaking her head. "I do think, however, that you could have devised a more commonplace identity than Lady Dierdre Augusta Juliana Hanover, granddaughter of George III."

Dierdre smiled, studying Alexandra's face reflectively, then leaned over and kissed her. "Somehow I never realized before how wonderful you are, Mother. You're a very, very wonderful woman."

"No, I am merely one of God's creatures, Dierdre, with all of the imperfections to which human beings are heir. Now I must go and see your brother, but we'll have many talks while I'm here. Also, I'll arrange for us to have dinner several times with all of your cousins."

"It might be better if only you and I dined together. Melissa and her sisters aren't as warm as they once were because they're resentful toward Morton. They believe he could have done more for Uncle Creighton."

"Indeed?" Alexandra mused. "Yes, I should have foreseen that. Well, I'll attend to it, but the important point is that you and I will spend as much time as

possible together while I'm here. I must leave now and
visit your brother this afternoon, but I'll see you again
tomorrow."

"Could you also have high tea here at the school at
least once?" Dierdre asked eagerly. "Please do because I want all of my friends to meet you. I've always
been very proud of you, but I want my friends to see
just how extraordinarily wonderful you actually are,
Mother."

Crucially important to her, her daughter's regard
made Alexandra glow with pleasure. Hugging and
kissing the girl, she assured her that she would visit
with her and her school friends. Then they went to the
entrance together, exchanging farewells, and Alexandra left.

As Alexandra drove her buggy to her hotel, the
Sydney Arms, she realized that during the years since
she had last seen Sydney, it had expanded enormous-
ly, both in size and amenities to match its status as a
thriving colonial capitol. When she reached the end of
High Street, a short distance from the school, she
arrived at the hotel which was modeled on the Grand
Hotel in London. Alexandra had a large, luxuriously-
furnished room, overlooking the gardens at the rear,
while the stockmen and jackaroos were quartered at
an inn several streets away.

Alexandra eagerly entered the hotel for that morning, she had sent a jackaroo to deliver a request to call
on the Baxters, along with Catherine's letters to her
parents. At the front desk, she found an invitation
from Auberta Baxter to call at her convenience.
Alexandra had a leisurely lunch in the quiet, elegant
dining room, then went to see Morton.

The half-timbered building in the business district
where years before she had occasionally come to see
her brother while he had been at work was unchanged
and stirred fond memories. Inside, apprentices still
worked over ledgers and correspondence at tall desks,

OUTBACK STATION 421

just like then. But instead of Creighton, the man talking with a head clerk was her son.

Of medium height, his expensive, expertly-tailored clothes drew attention away from his paunchiness from too little physical activity. His face was somewhat fleshy and brooding, his blond hair and piercing, pale blue eyes his most arresting features. But to Alexandra, he was as beloved and no less striking than his tall, handsome brother.

Morton turned to her, the surprise on his face changing to a smile that made her heart warm with joy. Her intense love for him swelling within her, she yearned to take him in her arms, but he had always been undemonstrative, particularly when others were present. She forced herself to kiss him on the cheek as she greeted him, and Morton did the same.

After introducing her to his employees, he led her toward his office. "This is most unexpected," he commented. "What brings you to Sydney?"

Alexandra told him some of the reasons for her journey, sensing a change in his mood. His surprise and pleasure upon first seeing her became defensiveness, an all too common attitude of his. "Most of all, however," she said as she finished, "it's been far too long since I've seen you and Dierdre."

As he seated her in the chair beside the desk, she saw in his eyes the reserve that she knew so well and dreaded so much. "And you wish to condemn me about Clara Tavish, no doubt," he suggested, sitting in his chair.

"Condemn? That's a very harsh term, Morton."

"Perhaps, but it fits a great portion of our conversations over the years. When I was a boy, you censured me incessantly."

"I consider that too harsh a term as well, but let it stand. If you will, consider for a moment my purpose. I wanted to help you learn to control your unruly temper, help you find what you wanted in life, and then help you bring your energies to bear upon it. I believe I succeeded."

Morton looked away, pondering for a long moment, then slowly nodded. "Yes, you did," he acknowledged musingly. "I suppose I never realized all that before, but then you never told me about it, did you? If you had explained that, Mother, it would have been easier for both of us."

"I think not, Morton. You're a logical man, but as a boy, you were often unreasonable. Perhaps I was wrong because I'm only an ordinary human being, not a sage. If I was cruel, I earnestly beg you to forgive me." She reached out, taking his hand. "I've always had the most devoted love for you, and I could have never been deliberately cruel to you."

The reserve gone from his eyes, he shook his head as he squeezed her hand. "No, you weren't cruel, Mother, and I love you as well. And perhaps you aren't a sage, but I've never known anyone with more wisdom."

The frank exchange had resulted in a rapport that Alexandra had never been able to achieve with him when he had been younger. Their relationship seemed suddenly much closer and intensely pleased her. As they continued talking, she asked what had gone wrong with her brother's business affairs. Morton explained, giving examples of the misfortune and errors in judgment that had brought about Creighton's bankruptcy.

The subject changing to his business activities, Morton told Alexandra that he had recently added more apprentices to his staff and intended to move into the unused second floor of the building so he would have office space for an accountant and other employees. He added that one of the employees was his legal advisor, John Fitzroy. Astonished and amused, Alexandra explained that John had tried to court her years before, and Morton laughed heartily as he remarked that he was happy the man was not his father.

"Indeed," Alexandra agreed, smiling, then changed the subject. "It's always given me great pleasure to hear of your successes, Morton, and I'm delighted over how your affairs are proceeding." She pointed to a rock on his desk that he used as a paperweight. "But it appears you could afford a prettier ornament. Why do you have that stone?" As he frowned reticently, she quickly added, "Or would you rather not discuss it?"

Morton hesitated for a moment, then glanced at the doorway. "No, I'll tell you about it," he replied quietly. "It could affect my over-all financial situation in ways that you should know about. But I must ask for your absolute silence on the subject. You must tell no one else."

Puzzled and curious, Alexandra agreed. Morton then talked softly at length, explaining about the gold ore, and then why he had to wait instead of pursuing the opportunity immediately. While she was astounded over the discovery of gold, Alexandra's thoughts quickly moved past that.

Of far more importance to her was that his confiding in her meant that she had finally gained his unqualified trust. In addition—and paradoxically—she had a vague idea of how she could use the discovery to persuade him to widen the scope of his life beyond an obsessive pursuit of wealth.

"That is certainly most remarkable," she said when he finished. "You could teach patience to a cat watching a mouse's hole, Morton, but you would unquestionably risk too much if you proceeded immediately."

"Far too much," he agreed somberly. "If this turns out well, I intend to allocate a percentage to Uncle Creighton. Meantime, the chemist doesn't know where the ore came from, so only you and I know all the facts. I'm sure you understand the need for absolute silence on the subject."

"Yes, of course. I'm very pleased by your confidence in me, and you may be sure that I won't betray it. Also, I consider it very generous of you to allocate a share to Creighton. When you begin ordering equipment and other things, you must proceed with great care."

The change in subject was carefully chosen as Alexandra thought of a way to help him. Morton replied that he had been unable to think of how to order the necessary equipment from England without arousing at least some curiosity about what he was doing. Alexandra suggested that she order it for the station, then he could secretly take possession of it. Delighted with the idea, Morton enthusiastically accepted her offer.

The conversation proceeded until well into the afternoon. It brought great pleasure to Alexandra for the atmosphere between her and her son remained warmly harmonious. But he was still Morton, much quicker to take offense than her other children, and for the present she spoke of nothing that would be controversial.

Morton thoroughly enjoyed her visit, and was reluctant for her to leave as they went to the door. Promising that she would see him many times while in town, Alexandra held him and kissed him. For the first time, he hugged and kissed her with unrestrained affection. Then she drove toward the house that had once been her father's.

As the buggy moved through the late-afternoon traffic, Alexandra pondered another reason she had for wanting Morton to adopt a conventional lifestyle. For years, she had realized that when Dierdre finished school, her daughter would need an alternative to returning to the isolation of the sheep station on a permanent basis. One had been to live with Creighton's family, but events had eliminated that. However, Morton was easily able to afford a luxurious household where Dierdre could live.

At the house, the carriage gate was closed, with a

chain and lock on it. An old caretaker came down the drive as Alexandra stepped out of her buggy, then hastily unlocked and opened the gate when she identified herself. He gave her the keys to the house and brought her buggy through to the drive, and Alexandra went up the path toward the front door.

The house was musty, and the hem of her dress raised dust from the floor. In the dim light through the shuttered windows, the furnishings were bulky, formless masses under their canvas covers. Her footsteps stirred echoes that whispered back through the silent rooms. The house was like a tomb in more ways than one, and Alexandra felt the lingering presence of departed loved ones whom she had returned decades too late to see.

Going upstairs, she went into her old bedroom. She looked in the cabinet where she had kept her pistol, which could have changed the entire course of her life had she taken it with her on the day she had gone to Camden Park. On balance, however, she had no regrets. Even though Enos Hinton blighted her life, in all other respects it was boundlessly rich and rewarding, filled with purpose, joy, and love.

Alexandra opened the window, then took the canvas cover off a chair. Sitting at the window and looking out at the garden, she pondered how to proceed about what she had to do. Near sunset, when she closed the window to leave, she had decided. Previously, she had intended to remain in Sydney for only a short time, returning to the station well before Catherine had her baby, but now she realized she would have to stay longer.

During the next few days, she saw Morton and talked with him at least briefly each day in between attending to numerous other things. Their discussions continued to be pleasant and cordial, centering on his business affairs most of the time. Once he mentioned Clara Tavish again in a half-joking manner, apparently wanting to talk about her and dispose of the subject, but Alexandra turned the conversation to other topics.

In addition to her daily visits with her daughter, Alexandra went to the school one afternoon for high tea with Dierdre and her friends. An enjoyable occasion, it illustrated the cosmopolitan atmosphere at the school. Dierdre's friends included students from Britain and Australia, as well as a lovely Anglo-Indian girl from Bombay and a French girl whose father was a wealthy trader at Papeete, Tahiti.

Early one evening, Alexandra called on the Baxters, who received her with warm hospitality. While talking with them about Catherine, Alexandra stated the truth in telling them that her own family had been immeasurably enriched by having the young woman among them. When Alexandra left, taking with her the letters they had written to Catherine, the Baxters were happy and completely satisfied that their daughter had a good home.

Among her other activities, Alexandra had discussions with the printer about Adolarious's sketches and explanatory notes, and saw samples of the work done by the bookbinder who would finish off the volumes. In addition, she called on her niece, Melissa, whose courtesy had a cool overtone, but she invited Alexandra to visit on any Sunday, which her sisters and their families always spent together.

Then one afternoon, Alexandra called on Clara Tavish. Clara paled as she opened the door, recognizing Alexandra and fearing a confrontation. Leading the way into the parlor, Clara nervously commented that the situation was extremely awkward.

"Yes, it is," Alexandra agreed as she sat down. "But with good sense and good will, we should be able to overcome that."

Relieved at Alexandra's cordial manner, Clara smiled wanly. "Please let me explain my circumstances, Mistress Kerrick. When I met your son, I was recently widowed with three children. I was on the point of being evicted from my home, with no money or prospects for obtaining any."

"Yes, I'm aware of that. In the public gardens one day, you met a teen-age girl who represented herself to be Lady Dierdre Augusta Juliana Hanover. Well, she happens to be my daughter, Dierdre Kerrick."

"Your daughter?" Clara gasped, amazed. "Yes, I see the resemblance now, but I was sure she was who she said, Mistress Kerrick. She was so absolutely believable, and so utterly charming as well."

"Dierdre is a charming girl," Alexandra agreed. "And her imagination is exceeded only by her ability to be convincing. In any event, she told me about your circumstances, which she learned about from a school friend."

Clara sighed heavily, nodding. "Yes, there is nothing about my life that is secret, Mistress Kerrick."

"Indeed. Your children are fed and clothed, but your relationship with Morton will be greatly to their disadvantage as they grow older."

Clara promptly agreed, but pointed out that she had no alternative. As the conversation continued, Alexandra appraised Clara's personality. She decided that she could trust Clara to say nothing to Morton about the conversation. Then she explained that she intended to try persuading Morton that he should end his relationship with Clara.

"I've come to talk with you," Alexandra continued, "so you won't mistake my intentions and think that I would disregard your needs. If Morton agrees to do as I ask, I will see to it that he settles an amount on you that will be sufficient for you and your children's welfare."

Clara was thrilled, smiling joyously as she exclaimed that all of her problems would then be at an end. Alexandra cautioned her against saying anything to Morton about it, and Clara emphatically agreed to remain completely silent on the subject. Her purpose achieved, Alexandra talked a little longer with Clara, then left.

Prepared to talk with Morton about Clara, Alexandra knew it would be best if he brought up the subject himself, as he had before. When she saw him that same day, he said nothing about it, nor did he on the following day. As she waited for him to mention it, Alexandra continued visiting Dierdre daily and attending to business affairs.

In discussions with the broker who sold the wool from the station, the factor who shipped supplies each spring, and the head of the drayage company that transported the wool and supplies, Alexandra worked out ways to avoid minor difficulties that had developed from time to time. She wrote and dispatched a letter to Sir Geoffrey Bodenham in London, informing him that the book of etchings made from the sketches would soon be published, and telling him of the latest news concerning her family and Australia in general.

While she was looking at type faces for the book at the printer's office, the printer made an interesting offer. He said that there should be a ready market in England for a book about the outback, and he would share the costs of publication if she would undertake to write such a book. Having enjoyed working on the explanatory notes for the sketches, Alexandra replied that the idea intrigued her and she would give it full consideration.

When she talked with Morton again, Alexandra told him what the printer had said. He encouraged her to accept the offer, adding that he would subscribe for a substantial number of copies of the book. Then he finally mentioned Clara Tavish again and said he was sure that Alexandra disapproved of the situation.

"You're an adult, my dear," Alexandra pointed out. "What you do doesn't require my approval. However, you are taking unfair advantage of that poor woman's financial straits, which isn't worthy of you."

"Am I?" he mused. "I've never looked at it that way, Mother."

"You should, because others do. I presume that you intend to eventually marry for money or position, or preferably for both."

"Yes, do you disagree with that?"

"I would rather you married for love, but that's irrelevant. My role is to help you in whatever way I can to secure your objectives, not to make your decisions for you. To that end, I advise you that a woman who can bring you money, position, or both will be from a family that will take a very dim view of your situation with Mistress Tavish."

Morton frowned as he pondered, then nodded. "Yes, that's true," he agreed. "I'll have to give that some thought."

His tone suggested no intention of changing anything soon, but Alexandra knew she had said enough for the present. Reserving her most compelling argument until the subject came up again, she began talking about the poor state of affairs between Morton and his cousins. She pointed out that any prospective bride's family would regard his relationships with his own kin as a guide to how well they would get along with him.

"What would you have me do, Mother?" he asked. "As long as they treat me like a stranger, then I'll do the same."

"You should, my dear," she assured him, patting his hand. "And for my part, they can sulk forever. My only concern is the effect it might have on you, and it most definitely can, you know. Because of that, I'd like to smooth things over, if you have no objection."

"I have no particular objection," he replied grudgingly. "But I don't intend to make overtures to them."

"I don't think you should, Morton. But if they wish

to be cordial, you could be generous toward Melissa's and Amanda's husbands in their affairs as merchants in the town. If your cousins want to be on good terms with you, it would be easy enough for you to guide profitable business to Gilbert and Harrison, wouldn't it?"

Morton reluctantly agreed, and Alexandra was deeply gratified as another step in her plans fell into place. She was certain she could convince Melissa and her sisters to change their attitude. Then, if she could persuade Morton to establish a household, he would have relatives around him as well as four women to oversee social activities for him. Having accomplished more than enough for one day, Alexandra immediately turned to lighter subjects, leaving Morton in a cheerful mood when their conversation ended.

The following Sunday afternoon, Alexandra went to Melissa's home and met with the reception she had expected. All four of the sisters were there, as well as two of the sisters' husbands and children. In an atmosphere of forced courtesy, the setting was uncomfortable, the parlor crowded and noisy, and none of the adults making an effort to control the children.

The conversation was rife with innuendoes about Morton, as well as money in general. Weak tea the only refreshment, Melissa apologized and said she was unable to afford anything more. She also excused the noise that the children were making, remarking that her household allowance was insufficient to hire a nurse or a maid. As the hints continued, Alexandra smoldered and waited for the right opening.

It came when Leona, the most outspoken of the sisters, commented on the small amount that Morton had paid her father for the house. "How much should he have paid, Leona?" Alexandra asked mildly.

"Well, certainly more than he did," Leona replied indignantly, "considering that Father taught him his profession. If I had money for a dowry, I could have long since married the man of my choice."

"The transaction was the sale of a house, not the provision of a dowry for you, and Creighton taught Morton nothing. From the outset, Morton went his own way, in a more aggressive fashion than Creighton ever did."

"Aggressive?" Leona echoed, lifting an eyebrow. "From what I've heard, I think ruthless would be closer to the mark."

"Leona," Alexandra said in a soft, acid voice, "I will endure your impertinences, but I shall not listen to slander about my son."

Taken aback by Alexandra's tone and icy glare, the young woman flushed in confusion. "I beg your pardon, Aunt Alexandra," she apologized. "I meant no slander, and it's natural for you to defend Morton. However, it does seem that he could have done more to help Father."

When others agreed with her, Alexandra interrupted them, brusquely telling them that what had happened had been inevitable. "Most of Creighton's income was from investing in ship cargoes," she pointed out, "but that has now been eliminated by a marine insurance company in the town. Creighton would have refused if Morton had simply offered to give him money, and that would have been the only solution. And as all of you well know, Creighton is far from the only one who has gone bankrupt."

Except for the noise the children were making, an uncomfortable silence ensued, then Melissa spoke up, "Well, we love Father, and I think our view of what happened is understandable, Aunt Alexandra."

"None of you love your father a whit more than I love my brother, and your viewpoint is incomprehensible. You say you're in need, yet you've deliberately offended a wealthy relative. And if the firm of Hammond and Kerrick ever revitalizes, you'll be your father's heirs, you know." Alexandra turned to the two men. "Your conduct is the most illogical of all, because you must realize that Morton is in a position to help your businesses."

The men exchanged a startled glance, then Stephen admitted that he had made a mistake in not adequately demonstrating his fond regard for Morton. Harrison echoed the same sentiments, and the attitude among the four sisters also underwent an abrupt change. The parlor quieted when Dora herded the children outside to play, and the two men left hurriedly for the nearest inn, returning a few minutes later with a bottle of sherry.

The atmosphere became pleasant, the conversation warmly cordial over glasses of sherry. The sisters inquired about their mother and father, then with equal interest about the Kerricks. Alexandra left after another hour, everyone emphatically urging her to call on them again at her convenience.

Alexandra's visit produced immediate effects. Stephen and Harrison arrived at Morton's office the next morning to pay their respects. In addition, he happened upon Leona and Dora while he was going to the coffeehouses, and both of them were very amiable toward him. He told Alexandra about it when they talked later in the day, adding that he had made business arrangements that the two men would find very profitable as time went on.

The following day, Morton again brought up the subject of Clara Tavish. Alexandra had begun coming to his office in the early evenings, when only one apprentice remained and they could talk without interruptions. The offices were quiet, the summer dusk fading into night as Morton told her that he had decided to end his relationship with Clara.

When he stopped talking, Alexandra pointed out that he had an obligation to provide for Clara and her children after he left them. He thought about it, then agreed and said he would furnish whatever amount was necessary. His manner indicated a time in the indefinite future, and Alexandra told him he should do it soon, then broaden his interests beyond his business so he would have friends and the respect that was his due. Morton replied that he was already widely-respected in the town, with numerous friends who went out of their way to speak to him on the street.

"Those are business acquaintances, not friends," Alexandra explained. "And some fear you because you hold mortgages on their property, but that falls short of respect, Morton." She lifted a hand as he started to speak. "No, please hear me out, my dear. I believe you've strayed off the course from what you actually want, and now you're merely grubbing for money. When I lived here, Farrel Ibbets wasn't all that much older than you are now. I believe you're headed down the same road that he took."

"No, no," Morton objected. "He isn't even married, Mother. As we discussed, I intend to have a wife and family."

"Ibbets had the same intentions. He didn't find a wife and family in a ledger, and neither will you. You've become very successful in business, but you lack equal success as a man who is honored and respected. For that, you must be invited to all important social occasions, support charities, and be very generous toward your relatives and friends."

"But why should I do all that, Mother? I can find a wife from a good family without turning my entire life topsy-turvy."

"If you want her to be from a very well-placed family, you must change, Morton. And once you experience true respect from those around you, it will more than repay the effort." Leaning closer to him, she broached her final, most compelling argument. "Further, you must establish a reputation that is prerequisite to an honor reserved for very few."

"What do you mean, Mother?"

"I've mentioned Sir Geoffrey Bodenham to you. He's a high government official with whom I've formed a close acquaintance through our correspondence."

"Yes, I'm familiar with the name."

"When you're ready to pursue that," she continued, pointing to the rock on his desk, "first, send your chemist to find out how much there is. If it is a large amount, go to London and see Sir Geoffrey. Let him make political capital by announcing the discovery of gold, then he will become your sponsor. The gold will bring you immense wealth, but you'll also perform a great service to the crown by providing specie for the government. Such services are recognized with honors, Morton." Taking his hand between hers, she finished in a soft, urgent voice, "I refer to a knighthood."

He was silent for a long moment, stunned by what she had said, then he spoke quietly, "Is it possible, Mother?"

"I believe it is even probable," she replied, standing. She kissed him, then turned toward the door. "Think about it, Morton."

She left and drove to the hotel. After dinner in the dining room, Alexandra went upstairs to her room. As she prepared to go to bed, she was satisfied that she had done her best for Morton and could only await the outcome.

The next morning, as she was starting to dress, there was a knock on her door. Belting her gown, Alexandra answered it. Morton was in the hall, having slept little if at all. His eyes red and his face lined with fatigue, he said that he had decided to act upon her advice.

Her immense relief matching her joy, Alexandra told him that his cousins would have his belongings moved to the Hammond house and have it put in order for him that day. He exchanged a kiss with her, then left. Alexandra dressed, and when a maid brought up the breakfast tray, she asked the woman to have the manager send to the livery stable for a buggy.

On her way to Melissa's house, Alexandra stopped at the inn where the station employees were staying to send a jackaroo to Elizabeth Montague's house with a request to call.

At Melissa's home, she and Dora greeted Alexandra effusively. When she told them what Morton intended to do, Dora went to fetch her other two sisters as Melissa made tea. When they were all present, Alexandra told them what had to be done. The sisters knew of domestics who were seeking employment, and Melissa took charge, saying the house would be ready that evening. Confident that Morton's household was in thoroughly capable hands, Alexandra left.

At her hotel, she found a reply that Elizabeth had immediately given the jackaroo to bring back. Instead of an invitation, it was a humorously emphatic demand for Alexandra to call immediately. Pleased and amused, Alexandra got into her buggy.

At the large, expensive brick home set back in landscaped grounds, the butler started to open the door wider for Alexandra to enter. Elizabeth suddenly pushed past him, holding out her arms. She was still as slender and lovely as Alexandra remembered, with the same radiantly cheerful smile, and they laughed in pleasure as they embraced and kissed.

In a spacious, luxuriously-furnished drawing room, Alexandra and Elizabeth sat on a couch to talk, and a maid carried in tea and cakes. With a new generation having taken its place in the town, Elizabeth was one of the relatively few who readily recalled Alexandra's abduction a quarter of a century before. She mentioned it and her torment of fear until she had heard that Alexandra was well, then she brought up other matters.

Having much to discuss, they spent an hour in telling each other the major events in their lives during the past years. Alexandra then guided the conversation toward children in general and Morton in particular. Elizabeth said that she had met him only once, when she and her husband had happened to meet him on the street.

"As I'm sure you know," Elizabeth continued, "he and Howard are associates in several business ventures. Howard has invited Morton to dinner a number of times, but he never accepts. I'd be pleased to invite him to more formal occasions, but . . ." her voice trailed off, and she shrugged apologetically. "Well, he does have that rather unfortunate liaison, Alexandra."

"That's true," Alexandra replied, smiling blandly. "But one must wonder at our standards. If a woman consorts with her gardener or her husband has a mistress in the maid's quarters, they're admired for their impudence as long as they make no public issue of it. But let a man and woman live together openly and honestly, and they're disdained."

Elizabeth pursed her lips, annoyed momentarily, then she laughed. "Alexandra, I had quite forgotten that when you smile most sweetly, you may be baring your teeth to bite. I admire your loyalty to your son, but what would you have me do? Make myself a pariah?"

"First," Alexandra replied, taking her friend's hand, "I'll ask you to forgive my peevishness. Next, I'd like you to hear some news about Morton. He's now going to be living alone at my father's, and I've prevailed upon him to start accepting invitations."

Elizabeth shook her head, laughing. "You needn't apologize, because I truly enjoyed that spark of fire from you. And I'm pleased to hear that about Morton. We're having a garden reception on Sunday afternoon for the new judge advocate, and the governor and many others will be here. I'd be most happy to include you and Morton on the guest list."

Alexandra accepted the invitation and expressed her thanks, deeply gratified. After being a guest at a reception hosted by the Montagues, she knew that Morton would be picking and choosing among his invitations. She talked with her friend for a while longer, then ended the visit. Elizabeth went out to the buggy with her. As they embraced and kissed in farewell, they agreed to stay in contact with letters.

Alexandra drove back to the hotel, and after having lunch, she went to the inn and talked with Ruel. Giving him money to buy supplies, she told him to make preparations to leave at dawn the following Monday morning.

She then concluded her business in the town, filling the time until classes at the school ended for the day and she could visit with Dierdre. While everything around her was the same as before, inwardly she felt a transition as profound and distinct as a change in seasons. Her duty finished here, she had to return to Tibooburra Station and face the more menacing, insoluble problem of whether the foul taint of Enos Hinton would reach into the next generation of her family.

Later, during her conversation with Dierdre, Alexandra tried to find a way to warn her daughter against disasters such as the one whose enduring ill effects she was still confronting herself. Having to use the most general terms, because the keen-minded girl might guess the dread secret from any specifics, Alexandra succeeded only in confusing her.

"What do you mean, Mother?" she asked.

"I mean that you should always be cautious about how you go, Dierdre," Alexandra replied, still searching for words. "Always use good judgment in situations where you could be at risk."

"Yes, I do, Mother," Dierdre said, perplexed.

Alexandra hesitated, yearning for a way to provide her lovely daughter with armor against all injuries and weapons against all dangers. But she knew it was hopeless. It was impossible to foresee what Dierdre would encounter during her toiling climb up the steep road of life, and only fate could determine whether she would stumble. Smiling, Alexandra took Dierdre's hand and held it as she began talking with her about school.

Chapter Twenty

The westward journey, which began weeks later than Alexandra had originally intended, was plagued by delays from the outset. On the first day, they traveled only as far as Parramatta before a horse threw a shoe. The one blacksmith in the village was gone, searching for a horse that had strayed, and finally returned late that afternoon. By the time the horse was shod, it was too late to travel any farther that day.

The following day, the horses labored in the hot sunshine as they pulled the wagons up the steep eastern slopes of the Blue Mountains. After crossing the crest, the horses plodded leisurely ahead of the wagons as smoke boiled from the brakes and turned into steam. Two jackaroos dashed buckets of water on the leather pads to cool them. Then, when the youths were too slow with water for the front wagon, it went down a sharp incline, the leather bursting into flames from the intense friction.

The leather quickly burning through, the steel frame of the brake screeched against the wheel rim as the wagon picked up speed. The horses neighed in wild-eyed terror as the wagon veered and pushed them ahead of it. Ruel wheeled his horse around, racing back toward the wagon. Leaning down from the saddle, he snatched up a thick limb beside the road, then flung it into a front wheel on the wagon.

As the limb jammed the rapidly spinning wheel, the wooden spokes exploded into splinters. The wheel collapsed, and the front corner of the wagon slammed down on the axle. The horses slid and stumbled, and the heavy vehicle skidded in a cloud of dust and came to a stop bare inches from the edge of the road overlooking a precipice. The jackaroo driving the wagon looked down into the abyss, his eyes wide and his face blanched.

The other wagon and spare horses stopped, and Ruel dismounted in a fury at the jackaroos who had been cooling the brakes. "Get away from me!" he raged. "If you get within my reach, I'll throttle the pair of you!" The jackaroos ducked behind the wagon as he turned to the one on the seat. "I've told you that if your wagon gets out of control on a hill, drive it into the bank! Kill yourself if you wish, but these horses and this wagon are valuable! Now get down here and lend a hand with these horses!"

Her heart still in her throat from the near-disaster, Alexandra followed Eulie as he rode back and dismounted to assist in unhitching the team. She reined up beside the vehicle as the jackaroo led the horses away and Ruel knelt to examine the axle. He stood up, shaking his head grimly and telling Alexandra that the axle was damaged.

"That's nothing compared to what almost happened," she said. "Your quick action prevented a tragedy, Ruel."

"But not a broken axle," he replied wryly. "Our spare wheels will do us no good, Mistress Kerrick. We'll go to Bathurst and get you a room at an inn, then I and the other men will bring the wagon in."

"You know me too well to think that I'll sit at an inn while you and the men are out here working into the night, Ruel. Let's proceed with what must be done, and I'll rest when everyone else does."

He nodded, telling Eulie to unhitch the other team of horses. A few minutes later, with both teams harnessed to the disabled wagon, the animals strained and dragged the vehicle to the verge on the other side of the road. Then, leaving Eulie and a jackaroo to guard the damaged wagon, Alexandra and the other men traveled on toward Bathurst with the second wagon, the jackaroos keeping the brake on it drenched with water.

At the inn where they had stayed on their eastward journey, the landlord offered the use of an empty shed. Ruel and the jackaroos unloaded the wagon into the shed and locked it, then Alexandra went with them to a wainwright's shop. The owner, a toothless, ebulliently cheerful oldster, rummaged through wagon parts beside his shop and found a broken axle with an undamaged hub. He tossed the axle stub into the wagon and climbed in, then they set out.

When they reached the damaged wagon, the laborious task of moving cargo from it to the other vehicle began. The supplies and utensils were among the things, and Alexandra built a fire to cook dinner. After the cargo had been transferred, the men and jackaroos used thick limbs as levers to raise the front of the disabled wagon. The wainwright lashed the axle stub to the broken axle, then fitted a spare wheel onto the stub.

When the work was completed, everyone gathered around the fire and Alexandra served the food. After they ate and put away the utensils, they set out down the road in the thick darkness at a slow walk, the jackaroos carrying lanterns and watching the wheel. With frequent stops to tighten the lashings, they reached the wainwright's shop late that night.

They were stalled in Bathurst for two days as the old

wainwright painstakingly fitted a new axle to the
wagon. The stockmen and jackaroos helped him,
while Alexandra made preparatory notes for the book
about the outback, having decided to write it. She
found concentration difficult as she knew that the
time for Catherine to have her baby steadily drew
nearer. Finally, at dawn on the third day, they set out
down the track to the west.

Over the years, small sheep stations had spread
down the track. To the people at them, the giant
Tibooburra and Wayamba Stations far to the west
were legendary, their owners the royalty of the outback. As had happened on the eastward journey, word
spread ahead of Alexandra and her party that they
were passing. Late each afternoon, a station owner
would be waiting beside the track to offer dinner and
accommodations for the night.

Their arrival, a dramatic break in the stark loneliness and monotony at the small stations, always
created an upheaval of excitement. With homely
formality, Alexandra was introduced to wives and
families, and children happily vacated their room for
her. After large, hearty meals, she sat on verandas and
talked with owners and their wives, while the stockmen, jackaroos, and children gathered at the edge of
the light from the lanterns to listen.

Regarded at the small stations as a final authority
on wool prices, sheep husbandry, and station manage-
ment, Alexandra answered questions and gave advice.
Swagmen visiting the stations had described Tibooburra Station and told about events there, their tales
invariably more interesting and spectacular than the
facts. Alexandra and her husband had been known for
years among the small stations as figures larger than
life, and the people were always surprised to find that
she was only a youthful forty-three, her face without
lines and her hair still untouched with gray.

Alexandra enjoyed the visits, but all too frequently
their departure was held up while a piece of worn

harness, a broken trace chain, or a loose rim on a wagon wheel was repaired. Once they were on the track, their pace was tediously slow, the horses tiring quickly in the brutal heat of late January, and other things caused delays. One morning they found an ill swagman and spent most of the day in getting him to a station, while another day was lost in helping fight a grass fire at a small station.

Logically, it was a series of unrelated events, but it seemed like something more to Alexandra. During the long hours of riding down the track in the glaring sunshine, the horizon a blur of shimmering heat waves, she recalled other times when plans and schedules had become meaningless, meeting with the unforeseen on every side. Mysterious and impersonal, the outback seemed to have its moods, setting the rhythm and the pace at which events occurred. That inertia sometimes helped and at other times hindered, but struggling against it was futile, resulting only in frustration.

The last small station was finally left behind, and the track became a narrow path of human activity in the immense wilderness. The minor mishaps in this setting were even more difficult for Alexandra to accept as mere coincidence. The vast, harshly beautiful landscape would forever elude her full understanding, remaining a primeval, arcane place that harbored unknowns. She loved it, but only the Aborigines with their strange, inscrutable comprehension of events at a distance in time or space were completely adapted to it and a part of the remote land of the outback.

When thick dust clouds appeared on the horizon shortly after they set out one morning, they hastily turned off the track into a small, sheltered valley. The day turning dark, the wind rose rapidly in gusts that filled the air with choking dust as Alexandra and the men tethered the horses to the wagons. By the time they climbed into a wagon, the vehicle parked beside it was only a vague shadow through the dust.

The wind howled around the wagon and buffeted the canvas cover, and Alexandra and the men sat with blankets over their heads so they could breathe. Sweat trickled down her face, the heat under the blanket stifling, as she waited for the dust storm to end. Hours later, when the wind died, it was too late to set out again that day and a horse was missing.

Much of another day was lost in trying to find the horse. Ruel considered it a waste of time to look for the animal, but despite her urgency to reach the station, Alexandra insisted that they make some effort to keep it from dying of thirst or being killed by dingoes. At midday, after one of the jackaroos came perilously close to becoming lost while searching, she gave up and they set out down the track again.

Several days after the dust storm, they crossed the Darling River. West of the river, summer thunderstorms spawned by the torrid heat swept across the landscape. The dark, thick masses of clouds turned the days into twilight, bringing an occasional heavy downfall of rain or hail. More frequently, the clouds were accompanied only by displays of lightning that ignited grass fires and violent wind squalls that spread them.

The thunderstorms caused further delays, and Alexandra and the employees sheltered the horses in trees in the event bruising volleys of hail began falling. At night, angry red lines of grass fires were sometimes visible in the distance, and an ominous, thick odor of smoke was constantly in the air. Waves of kangaroos, emus, and other animals passed, fleeing in panic from the flames, but none of the grass fires approached the track. And despite the many hindrances, the journey finally began drawing to an end.

On the day they crossed Barren Mountain at the southern border of the station, Alexandra remembered the terrifying, appallingly realistic nightmare she had experienced in Bushranger Paddock on their way to Sidney. The practical side of her nature told her that associating the dream with the paddock was absurd, but the more empirical, introspective part of her personality pointed to the paddock as the direct cause of the nightmare.

Giving in to the latter, she told Ruel not to stop in that paddock for the night. The stockman adjusted the travelling pace, timing their overnight stops so they would pass completely through Bushranger Paddock in the daytime. They crossed the southern border of it early one day, with ample time to be well to the north of the paddock by sunset.

For the first time during the journey, something startled the spare horses and caused them to bolt, and an hour passed while the jackaroos tried to catch them. A few miles on up the track, the first wagon became mired in mud while passing a billabong. Both teams had to be hitched to the wagon to free it, which took almost another hour.

When they reached the place where they had camped on their earlier journey, midafternoon had arrived. It was oppressively hot, the air breathlessly still under dark clouds and thunder muttered in the distance. Passing the ashes where her campfire had been, Alexandra looked down the valley at the hill where the bushrangers were buried. Just then, there was a splintering crash from behind and the wagons stopped.

Muttering oaths under his breath, Ruel rode back with Eulie. Alexandra followed them, seeing that the left rear wheel on the first wagon had collapsed. "Look at that!" Ruel roared at the jackaroo driving the wagon. "Must you keep on causing trouble for everyone?"

"It wasn't my fault, Mr. Blake," the jackaroo objected plaintively. "That big rock just jumped up and broke the spokes. How was I to know it would do that? I can't drive around every rock on the track."

The two stockmen dismounted, looking at the wheel. Reining near the wagon, Alexandra saw that the wheel had apparently passed across the edge of a large, flat stone, which had snapped over with enough force to break the spokes. It had indeed been a freak accident, like many of the other mishaps that had occurred during the westward journey.

Ruel sighed in resignation, turning to Alexandra. "We'll have to put on a spare wheel, Mistress Kerrick," he told her, "which will take some time. We'll move the supplies from this wagon to the other one, then you can go on to the next paddock to camp. We'll catch up with you."

The stockmen and jackaroos were sagging in the sweltering heat, and Alexandra was unwilling to put them to so much extra work. "That's quite all right, Ruel," she said. "We'll camp here tonight."

"No, you want to camp in the next paddock, and that's what we'll do," he insisted. "It'll be late when we catch up, but we can—"

"Truly, it's quite all right," she interrupted, dismounting. "That was only a whimsy of mine, and we'll camp here."

The stockman merely nodded and accepted her change of mind, but the jackaroos looked relieved, having been spared the additional work. As the men and youths set to work on the wagon, Alexandra unsaddled and hobbled her horse. She released it to graze, then sat on a rock and looked down the valley, the flock in it moving slowly toward the fold on the hill.

She watched the sheep, keeping her gaze away from the hill, but she remained acutely aware of it. It stood like a huge monument above the grave containing the mortal remains that tainted the land, the spirit from those remains reaching deep into her life. Her acute melancholy was matched by the scene, the torridly hot day dark from the somber, black clouds and the thunder rumbling ominously miles away.

During late afternoon, when a spare wheel was on

the wagon, both of the vehicles were moved off the track and parked. As the jackaroos and stockmen attended to the horses and made camp, Alexandra took her things out of a wagon and built a fire. Having resolved not to sleep that night, she began cooking her meal, although she had no appetite.

Near sunset, when the flock was in the fold, Alexandra saw the stockman in the paddock riding up the valley. As he drew closer, she saw that he was Isaac Logan. He rode up to her fire, taking off his hat and greeting her. She replied and asked if he had recent news from the home paddock.

"Aye, only two days ago, mo'm," he said, "when Mr. Jonathan brought fresh supplies. His wife is well and expecting almost any day now. Mr. Kerrick and the head stockman are up at Coobar and Quandong Paddocks, where there have been some grass fires, but not bad ones. No sheep have been lost."

"Have you had any fires here?"

"No, mo'm, but I've had more than my share of trouble with dingoes. A whole pack of them moved in a few weeks ago, and I haven't been able to find their den. It's somewhere on the other side of that rise just beyond the hill where the fold is, but that's all I know about it."

"Have they killed any sheep?"

"No, mo'm, but they've kept me and my jackaroo busy a few times when the flock has been out of the fold. Mr. Jonathan said that as soon as there are some extra men at the home paddock, he'll send them down here to help me find that den and kill the dingoes."

"Very well. When I get to the home paddock, perhaps Ruel and Eulie can come back with the jackaroos there and help you."

The man nodded and spoke a word of farewell, then moved away. He tethered his horse and sat down at the other fire for a long chat, taking a dented, fire-blackened billy from his coat pocket. One of the jackaroos filled it with water to make tea for him as he and the other two stockmen talked, and Alexandra heard an occasional word of their conversation.

The good news about Catherine made her less depressed, and Alexandra was also pleased that there had been no severe grass fires. She ate and put the leftovers in a covered pan, then unrolled her blanket away from the fire. Still intending to stay awake, she lay down to rest as the stifling intensity of the heat diminished with nightfall.

At the other fire, the jackaroos lay on their blankets as the men talked. Just as Isaac said something about dingoes, Eulie leaned toward the fire to pick up his billy, the flames highlighting his distinctly Aborigine features. The combination of the words and the glimpse of Eulie's face stirred a memory in the back of Alexandra's mind.

For the most fleeting instant it barely nudged her conscious thoughts, then it was gone again into the murky depths of other memories. Very remote and from long ago, it had seemed more of a vague feeling of importance than a cohesive memory. She struggled to recall it, but failed.

The general impression of importance remaining, she wondered if it had been a momentary confusion of memories. She could think of no obvious correlation between her having heard Isaac say something and having seen Eulie's face at the same time. The possibility that the two could be associated with anything meaningful to her seemed very unlikely.

She continued thinking about it, events from her past having been summoned up by disassociated things before. After a time, Isaac left, and Ruel and Eulie went to sleep. With hours to pass while lying awake and waiting for dawn, Alexandra looked up into the thick darkness of the cloudy, nighttime sky and kept searching her memory.

She woke in Stygian darkness just before dawn,

realizing that she had fallen asleep despite her resolve to stay awake. The memory she had been trying to isolate was no longer buried in the recesses of her mind. At the very forefront of her thoughts, it completely possessed her.

More than important, it was paramount, of vital significance. It was a gleaming beacon of hope, offering a means to dispel the somber shadow that had lurked over her life and threatened her family for decades. At the same time, to the practical side of her nature, the train of thought keyed by the memory was utterly ridiculous, too pointless even to contemplate.

As the warring impulses seethed within her, the stockmen and jackaroos stirred, heating up their leftovers for breakfast and packing up to leave. Alexandra forced herself to eat, then saddled her horse. A short time later with another cloudy, torridly hot day beginning, they set out down the track.

The previous evening, Isaac's mention of dingoes and the glimpse of Eulie's face in the firelight had almost reminded Alexandra of her own conversation of years ago about dingoes with an Aborigine while sitting at a fire. The memory now clear in her mind, it had been on the night before her wedding, when she had talked with Mayrah Garrity.

Her English imperfect, Mayrah had searched for words to convey that dingoes purged the land, purifying it. Pat had overheard her and understood her to have said that they were scavengers, devouring noxious offal, but she had expressed a more profound thought. She had meant that dingoes consumed that which was malignant and rendered it benign.

From personal experience, Alexandra knew Aborigines had means of perception and other abilities that seemed inexplicable, but the practical aspect of her nature rejected the supernatural. Instead, she attributed it to folk wisdom and racial memory from their millennia in Australia that gave them heightened senses and a closer affinity with the land. Some of their beliefs, including that about the dingoes, seemed mere superstitions.

However, she wanted to believe what Mayrah had told her. Through her religious convictions, she accepted the existence of influences on a higher plane, and fate was a reality to her. She had also experienced moments while alone in the outback when she had felt a vital force about the land. With mysterious qualities beyond its physical characteristics, some things about it defied analysis from a practical standpoint.

Riding up the track beside the stockmen, Alexandra tried to reconcile her conflicting thoughts. There were no delays for once, and the horses knew they were near home, setting a pace that would cover most of the distance to the home paddock by sunset. Ruel and Eulie discussed the cloudy sky which heralded thunderstorms. At the end of the day, however, no storm had arrived, and Alexandra was still undecided.

When they set out the following morning, the home paddock only a few miles away, Alexandra remained in a turmoil. She finally resolved the conflict. Never passively accepting adversity, she was always ready to confront fate, preferring to do anything at all rather than nothing. The decision made, she then thought about how to put what Mayrah Garrity had said into practice. By the time the home paddock came into view, she had decided all the details, knowing precisely what she had to do. The jackaroos whooped in joy as Ruel and Eulie commented to each other in satisfaction. The long journey had ended.

Interrupting their remarks, she told Ruel what she wanted him and the other men to do. If the stockmen were disappointed, they concealed it completely, both of them always ready to follow orders with energy and dedication. "We'll leave immediately, then, Mistress Kerrick?" Ruel asked.

"Yes, as soon as we can get fresh horses and make ready. Let's take the wagon that has the supplies in it.

If we need more supplies for three or four days, get them out of the storeroom. We'll also need one of those large kettles that are used for rendering mutton tallow, as well as some mattocks and shovels. Leave the wagon that has my baggage in it and tell Kunmanara to take it up to the house for me."

"Aye, very well. What are we going to be doing, Mistress Kerrick?"

"I'll tell you when we get there."

Ruel nodded, turning and shouting at the jackaroos with the spare horses to ride forward. As the youths rode up past the wagons with the animals, Ruel told them to ride ahead to the pens and select fresh horses for everyone, as well as a team for the wagon.

Their hopes of resting after the long journey dashed, one of them exclaimed in dismay. "You shut your tucker hole!" Ruel shouted at him. "Now get those horses to the pens and pick out fresh ones!"

The jackaroos rode on down the track at a gallop, and Alexandra fully understood how they felt. The huge house at the end of the track was a haven of comfort, and she would have greatly preferred to stay instead of leaving again on what could very well be a foolish waste of effort. With the dark clouds thicker than ever overhead, she was sure her husband was still out in the paddocks watching for grass fires, which would eliminate her trying to explain to him what she was hard put to explain to herself.

At the foot of the hill, Alexandra took the mail out of a wagon and rode up to the house. Eulie followed her to take her horse to the pens for a fresh one. As she went inside, Martha came down the stairs and Creighton out of the family parlor. Greeting her happily, they looked much stronger and more content than when they had arrived at the station.

When she told them that she was leaving again, they were taken aback. "It's something I must do, but I'll return within three or four days," Alexandra explained, taking the letters to Catherine out of the mail and handing the rest to Creighton. "Melissa and her sisters are well and happy. Their letters to you are in that, and when I get back, I'll tell you all about what they've been doing recently. Where is Catherine?"

"In the garden at the side of the house," Martha replied. "But do you absolutely have to leave again so soon? You must be very tired."

Feeling exhausted in spirit as well as body, Alexandra repeated that she had to leave immediately. She made her farewells to the couple, then went down the hall to the garden door. As she stepped out, she saw Catherine reading a book on a bench in the conversation nook shaded by the rose bower. The profusion of late-summer roses made a perfect setting for her, now heavily pregnant and more bewitchingly beautiful than ever.

Crying out in delight as she saw Alexandra, she dropped her book and started to get up. Alexandra rushed to her, putting a hand on her shoulder and sitting beside her, then they embraced and kissed. "I'm ever so pleased that you're back, Mistress Kerrick," Catherine said blissfully. "The days have been so long while I've waited for you to return."

Alexandra sighed regretfully, kissing her daughter-in-law again, then sat back and held her hand. "Catherine, I'm dreadfully sorry, but I must attend to something immediately, and I'll be gone for three or four days. But I'll come back as soon as I possibly can, then I'll stay."

Her joy changed to disappointment, then Catherine nodded in resignation. "I know you wouldn't go if you didn't have to, Mistress Kerrick. Please do hurry back as soon as possible." She smiled wryly, placing a hand on her stomach. "I'll try to prevail upon your grandchild to wait."

"Please do," Alexandra said, laughing. "In the meantime, here are letters from your parents. They and the rest of your family are well and happy, and I spent a very pleasant evening with them. I'll tell you all about it when I get back, my dear.''

Catherine thanked her for the letters as they hugged and kissed again, then Alexandra left and went around the path to the front of the house. There she met Jonathan, who had just returned from taking supplies to a paddock. He was more troubled than any of the others that she was leaving, wanting her to stay with Catherine, but he never questioned her decisions.

A jackaroo rode up to the house, leading Alexandra's fresh horse, and Jonathan helped her up into the saddle. As she rode down the hill with the youth, the wagon was moving away from the pens and buildings, the stockmen riding ahead of it and jackaroos following with spare horses. Alexandra took her place beside the men, turning onto the track.

After the normal, solidly rational surroundings of the house, what Alexandra intended to do seemed more of a fool's errand than ever to her, and she wanted to be done with it. The horses were well-rested and spirited, and she and the stockmen rode up the track at a fast canter, the wagon and spare horses pacing them. When darkness fell, they carried lanterns to light the way, continuing on up the track until late into the night.

At dawn the next morning, they set out again after having rested for a few hours. The threat of thunderstorms during the past few days was drawing to a climax, as unbroken black clouds hovered overhead and thunder steadily drummed in the near distance. It was insufferably hot, the breathlessly still air tense with enormous forces that had gathered to a trembling peak, poised on the brink of erupting in a violent cataclysm.

When they reached the center of Bushranger Paddock shortly after noon, Isaac Logan and his jackaroo were driving their flock back to the fold because of the ominous weather. Alexandra and the stockmen turned off the track into the valley, and the wagon lurched over stones and ruts under the deep grass as it followed them. Down the valley, the dense clouds seemed to brush the top of the hill overlooking the grave.

In the supercharged atmosphere, St. Elmo's fire flickered among copses and on the isolated trees scattered about, fiery jets dancing on the uppermost limbs. Frightening the sheep, it made them hard to control as Isaac and his jackaroo hurried them up the hill toward the fold. The dogs raced about and turned back sheep that tried to break away from the flock.

A large ball of the luminous electrical discharge rolled from around the hill near the grave and moved up the valley, dancing across the top of the grass. Eerily bright in the dim light under the murky clouds, it disintegrated into a mass of glowing coils as it swept toward Alexandra and the men, terrifying the horses. They neighed and plunged in panic, and Alexandra controlled hers by whipping it into a gallop toward the hill. The others followed suit, and the wagon bounced wildly behind.

The flock in the fold, Isaac and the jackaroo rode down the hill as Alexandra and the men reined up at the foot of it. "I didn't expect to see you back here, Mistress Kerrick," Isaac called curiously.

"Well, here I am, Isaac," she replied. "Have your jackaroo put these horses in the pen with yours so they can't bolt, then both of you lend a hand. We have more work to do than time in which to get it done."

A few minutes later, the team unhitched from the wagon, the youth led them and the saddle horses up to the pen beside the fold. The stockmen tossed the mattocks and shovels out of the wagon, and two jackaroos dragged out the large, heavy kettle. They put a pole through the bail on it, hoisting it to their shoulders. The other men, carrying shovels, went around the hill toward the grave as Alexandra climbed up the slope.

Standing near the hut below the fold, she tried to recall where David had dug the grave. The memory, decades old and vague from her confusion on that day, was further muddled by new trees that had grown. Flickers of lightning and the boom of thunder steadily marched closer, and St. Elmo's fire swirled about as she shouted and pointed. The stockmen and jackaroos dug furiously, but the first and then the second attempt were unsuccessful.

At the third place she pointed out, Ruel stopped digging after a few minutes and shouted up the slope over the roar of the thunder, "We've found bones here, Mistress Kerrick!"

The brush tugging at her clothes, Alexandra raced down the hill. She pushed through the stockmen and jackaroos gathered around the deep hole and jumped down into it, seeing the white gleam of bones. Kneeling and scraping at the dirt with her hands, she uncovered a rotted boot, then the cavernous eyes and grotesque, fiendish grin of a skull.

"Ruel, keep two jackaroos here to help you, and put all of those bones in the kettle," she told him, climbing out of the hole. "And I mean each and every one of them. I don't want a single, solitary knucklebone, tooth, or the smallest bone from a finger left in the ground here."

He beckoned two of the youths, who took the heavy lid off the kettle as they moved it to the hole. Alexandra told Isaac to take a jackaroo to help him gather a cord of firewood, pointing out an exposed shoulder of the hill below the hut where she wanted the wood brought. As he left with a youth, Alexandra went up the hill toward the spot with Eulie and the other jackaroos who carried mattocks and shovels.

The lightning and thunder drew closer, and the air stirred ahead of the storm. St. Elmo's fire danced on the brush rustling in the torridly hot breeze as Alexandra climbed the hill with Eulie, telling him that she intended to make an earth furnace. "The kind that Mr. Kerrick made to bake clay pipe and bricks," she explained. "If you recall, he used a very large, funnel-like contrivance made of poles and bark to gather the wind and force air into the furnace. I want you to make one of those, Eulie."

The stockmen had long since ceased wondering what she was doing and were merely following orders in their usual prompt, determined way. As he looked around at the brush moving in the breeze, however, Eulie offered an opinion. "In a very short time, you're going to have plenty of wind for a furnace without anything to help it, Mistress Kerrick."

"Perhaps, but I want the inside of the furnace to be as hot as the shores of the nether world, Eulie. Make that thing low and wide, and cut posts to support it so the wind won't blow it over."

He beckoned a jackaroo and turned toward a stand of eucalyptus trees to gather slabs of bark as Alexandra went up to the grassy shoulder of the hill with the other youths. Taking a shovel, she marked off a large rectangle on the ground and had the jackaroos dig up the sod in squares. When they were stacked at one side, Alexandra drew lines on the bare earth, leaving ledges to support the sod as a roof for the furnace. Setting to work again, the youths dug a deep trench inside the lines.

As the trench deepened, Isaac and his helper carried heavy loads of wood and piled it nearby. On the exposed flank of the hill, St. Elmo's fire occasionally brushed around Alexandra and the youths with a tingling sensation. When it happened to the jackaroos, they laughed and joked in bravado, their young faces pale and tense with fright of the strange phenomenon, as well as of the violent storm bearing down.

The breeze became muggy, and Alexandra was

relieved as she turned to look at the storm. Now only a few miles away, dark curtains of rain trailing down from the black thunderheads extinguished any fires ignited by the lightning. Isaac noticed it when he brought another load of firewood, commenting happily about it to Alexandra.

Ruel also observed it as he came up the hill, viewing it from a different perspective. The jackaroos followed him with the kettle hanging from a pole between them. First he assured Alexandra that he had found all of the bones, then he pointed to the storm. "When that's upon us," he said, "you'd best get into shelter, Mistress Kerrick. There's ample room in Isaac's hut, or you could go to the wagon if you wish."

"No, I want to stay here, Ruel. When everything is finished, though, I'd prefer for you and the men to go to the hut or wagon."

He frowned, starting to object, then changed his mind and went down the hill to the wagon. Presently, he returned with her oilskins, blanket, and a square of canvas. He and the jackaroos drove poles into the ground and made a tent out of the canvas, pegging the edges down firmly against the coming wind, and Ruel put her oilskins and blanket inside.

When the trench was deep enough, the men put firewood into it, wedging the sticks and logs tightly into a solid mass until the long hole was half full. Alexandra looked in the kettle, wanting to see the jumble of bones, and replaced the lid. The men set it on the wood, then packed firewood on and around it, filling the trench to the edge.

Eulie and his helper had finished making a large air scoop, using tough strands of spinifex grass to tie slabs of bark over a framework of poles. The jackaroos went to help them drag it up the hill as Ruel and Isaac covered the trench with the sod. Leaving an opening on the downwind side for an exhaust vent, they placed the thick blocks of soil tightly together up the opposite end where they left another opening for an air intake.

The storm closed in rapidly, and the twilight was broken by brilliant flashes of lightning, followed closely by roaring peals of thunder that made conversation difficult. When the air scoop was beside the trench, the men helped Eulie drive in posts to hold it firmly in place as Alexandra gathered dry grass and pushed it down into the earth furnace.

The grass burned rapidly and ignited the wood when she touched a phosphorus match to it, the rising wind making a draft through the furnace. The men put the air scoop into place, the wide end facing into the wind and the small one over the air intake. The draft through the furnace became a concentrated blast of air, and the smoke lazily billowing from the exhaust vent turned into a tall, thick plume reaching high above the ground.

The wind suddenly gusted to a gale, and the storm swept down in a raging fury of crackling lightning and shattering thunderclaps. As he and the other two men lashed the air scoop to the posts, Ruel shouted to the jackaroos and pointed to the hut. They thankfully fled, seeming to move jerkily in the stroboscopic effect of the landscape alternating rapidly between twilight and blinding brilliance from the lightning.

A jagged bolt crackled down from the clouds to a solitary eucalyptus a hundred yards away. The tree split open in a shower of smoldering bark, and a crash of thunder was so loud it had the impact of a physical blow. The bark fell into the grass and ignited it, the fire spreading rapidly ahead of the howling wind. Finished with the air scoop, the men looked at the fire in dismay, then heavy raindrops began falling and thickened into a downpour.

The men laughed in relief, and Isaac and Eulie ran toward the hut through the rain as Alexandra put on her oilskins. Ruel hesitated, turning to her. "Perhaps I'd best stay here, Mistress Kerrick," he offered.

"No, I'll be all right, Ruel. Go to the hut with the others."

He touched his hat and walked away, and Alexandra sat down inside the tent. As the fire worked its way through the tightly-packed wood in the furnace, flames appeared at the base of the smoke gushing from the exhaust vent. They gradually emerged higher and higher into the smoke until a beacon of roaring fire was spewing from the vent, whipping in the wind.

At nightfall, the initial fury of the storm passed, the lightning becoming distant flickers. The furnace, rumbling from the tempest rushing through it, radiated searing heat. Rain falling on it instantly boiled away into steam, the pillar of fire shooting out of the exhaust vent illuminating the vapor as it whirled and billowed in the wind.

Watching the steam fraying into wisps and floating away into the darkness, Alexandra was highly satisfied. In the fiery heart of the furnace, the mortal remains of the bushrangers were meeting the end that they had earned for their souls in the eternal fires of hell. It gave her a sense of finally reaching out across the decades in revenge.

A jackaroo emerged from the rain and darkness, bringing tea in a billy and a plate of food protected from the rain by another tin plate. Alexandra ate, then covered herself with her blanket. The purpose that had infused her with driving energy now near an end, she allowed the fatigue, like a heavy weight, to bear down on her, and the patter of the rain made her drowsy. Soon, the glare of the flames from the exhaust vent of the furnace was only a glow through her closed eyelids.

Shortly before dawn, the wind moaned low and plaintively as it rushed through the furnace. Alexandra woke to the mournful wail and to a cloud of diffused, eerie light in the rainy darkness, the steam billowing over the oven illuminated from within by a nimbus from the white-hot coals shining through the exhaust vent.

Pulling her oilskins around her, Alexandra walked

out of the tent. She loosened the lashings on the posts holding the air scoop in place, then dragged it to one side so the furnace would begin cooling. As the thick darkness started to lift a few minutes later, a jackaroo brought her a plate of porridge and tea in a billy.

After she ate, the light brightened into a gray, wet dawn, and the men and jackaroos set to work. Taking the air scoop apart, they used the poles as levers to prise the sod off the furnace. The blocks of soil had baked as hard as stone, the grass on them shriveled to brittle stalks. While the others uncovered the furnace, Eulie cut down and trimmed a tall sapling that had a stout branch low on its trunk.

Squinting against the scorching heat of the glowing coals, the men slid the sapling down into the trench and hooked the bail on the kettle with the stub of the branch, then lifted it. Rain hissed and turned to steam as it touched the hot metal. Everyone stayed well away from the large, black vessel as the men set it down beside the trench.

The sheep were bleating with hunger in the fold at the top of the hill, and Isaac told Alexandra that he had to take them and the horses to graze. "As soon as they're settled," he added, "I'll leave my jackaroo to look after them and come back here to help."

"Very well," Alexandra said. "When you let the flock out, leave one wether in the fold." She turned to the other men. "Eulie, take a jackaroo to help you butcher that wether, then bring it here. Ruel, you can have the tent taken down, and have someone collect the knives. I want that wether boned out, then the mutton chopped up in this kettle."

The men and youths turned away, going about their tasks. Alexandra gingerly touched the kettle, as the rain started to trickle down it instead of turning to steam. When the lid was cool enough to grasp, she lifted it and looked inside. The bones had been reduced to fine dust by the heat. Nodding in satisfaction, she replaced the lid.

A rumble of hoofs came from the other side of the hill as the sheep and horses were taken to graze. A short time later, Eulie and a jackaroo carried a skinned sheep carcass down the hill, and Ruel and the other youths sharpened the knives. They worked on the carcass, tossing bones into the trench and mutton into the kettle. Alexandra stirred the meat and dust in the kettle with a pole, mixing them thoroughly.

Isaac returned as the place was being tidied up, the mutton in the kettle and the jackaroos shoveling the last of the dirt back into the trench. As the day before, he and the other men had simply followed orders without wondering about their purpose. When Alexandra told him to point out where he had seen the dingoes, only one of the group revealed any reaction. That was Eulie, a thoughtful expression on his Aborigine face.

Ruel and Eulie carried the heavy kettle on a thick pole as Isaac led the way across a rise west of the hill and down into a brushy, rocky ravine. With the kettle placed in an open spot, Alexandra removed the lid and set it aside, then went up the slope overlooking the ravine and sat under a tree. The men and youths grouped under a tree a few yards away, talking quietly among themselves.

As the rain pattered on the foliage overhead, Alexandra watched the kettle and listened to the conversation among the employees. After a few minutes, the scent of the raw meat wafted through the ravine, and she glimpsed a tawny form slinking through the brush near the kettle.

Isaac also saw it, pointing it out to the others. "I asked for help in killing dingoes," he commented wryly. "I can feed them mutton by myself, but that's what I've been trying to keep from doing."

The men and youths laughed, with the exception of Eulie. Other wild dogs moved furtively about in the brush around the kettle, then one that was hungrier or braver than the rest ventured into the open. As soon as it snatched a bite of meat from the kettle without coming to harm, others swarmed out of concealment and joined it.

The kettle became hidden under a mass of squirming, hairy forms, as the dingoes snapped and snarled at each other while gulping the mutton. Some leaped into the midst of the others, trying to force their way through to the meat, while pairs tumbled out of the cluster and rolled on the ground, locked in raging fights. Within a few minutes, it was all over, the wild dogs disappearing into the brush once again.

As she went back down the slope into the ravine, the employees following her, Alexandra noticed that the rain had stopped and took off her oilskins. The dingoes had licked the kettle clean, the inside of it looking as though it had been scrubbed and polished.

"Let's get ready and leave, Ruel," she told him, then glanced at him and the others. "From now on, this is Dingo Paddock. Spread the word about, and I'll do the same and change the map at the house. I want everyone to know, and I don't want to hear this paddock called anything else."

The employees nodded and replied in understanding, then Ruel began giving orders. Two jackaroos raced away to get the horses, two more running toward the wagon to get the harness ready. Others carried the kettle, following Alexandra and the rest of the employees to the wagon.

During the next hour of hurried preparations to leave, Alexandra was too busy to wonder about the possible effects of what she had done. Then, when she and the others left the valley for the track, it occurred to her that there should be some detectable result, unless she had merely performed a meaningless ritual. However, nothing apparent had happened, no changes of any sort had taken place.

She was, she realized, much happier than before, but there were obvious reasons for it. The clouds had broken, revealing the sky, and the rain that had ended a short time before had been a godsend. A break in the dry season that would renew the pastures for the sheep also ended the danger of grass fires for the year. In addition, she had finally finished what she had wanted to do and was going home.

After starting out late in the day, they had reached only the northern part of the paddock when they stopped for the night. Alexandra noticed that her previous dislike of staying in that particular paddock was gone. In her mind, it was now Dingo Paddock, much the same as all the others and simply a part of the land she loved.

Later, waiting for sleep, she let her thoughts wander at random, a fold of her blanket wound tightly around her ankles. The sensation summoned up memories of when she had been a captive, lying on a blanket at night with her hands and feet tied. Before, she would have kicked frantically to loosen the blanket, but for some reason, she was now indifferent to it.

She suddenly realized that she felt a tranquillity about that period in her life that was the opposite of her previous feelings. Before, she had always avoided thinking about the torment the bushrangers had inflicted upon her, the memory too painful. Now, with a sense of having reached out to destroy the cause of her suffering, she regarded that time and its events as merely an unfortunate episode in her life, and felt no pain.

As she pondered her change in attitude, she thought of a rational explanation. Among primitive people, as well as many who considered themselves anything but that, rituals produced results simply because they were considered effective. The actual agent of change was the mind, with its capacity to perceive what it believed. Through convincing herself that she had exorcised the bushrangers from her life, she could have done just that.

At the same time, however, she was unable to dismiss at least the possibility that she had done more.

After decades, she had never quite adjusted to celebrating Christmas in the sweltering heat that December brought in the outback. She knew that there were vastly more significant but subtle ways in which she had failed to adapt, aspects of the outback that she would never comprehend because she had yet to realize that they even existed.

The next morning, while she was saddling her horse, Eulie was also attending to his. Ruel and the jackaroos were several feet away. The stockman quietly referred to what she had done. "It appears," he continued, "that you know something of Aborigine conjuring, Mistress Kerrick."

"A bit, perhaps. I'm sure you know more."

"No, I'm like Kunmanara," he replied, chuckling. "I've been eating mutton and damper too long to know anything of Aborigine ways. However, what you did put me in mind of things my ma used to do."

"What was that, Eulie?"

"Well, she believed that if you needed to get rid of something completely, you had to get a dingo to eat it. When one of us kids was poorly, she would have us spit on something that dingoes liked, then put it out for them to eat. That was supposed to get shot of the illness."

"Did it do as your mother believed it would?"

Eulie hesitated, then shrugged. "I think it did sometimes, but there were times when it certainly didn't. When that happened, though, my ma always said that a bird or something had got the food before a dingo found it." He laughed heartily. "Now there's a handy excuse for you."

Alexandra laughed, agreeing with him. She mounted her horse as the others prepared to leave. A few minutes later, they rode down the track.

Her mood was even more lighthearted than the previous day, but her surroundings made it difficult to be anything less than cheerful. A few fleecy clouds floated in the sky, and the sun beamed down on a landscape that appeared bright and freshly-scrubbed after the rain. The foliage had reacted quickly to the moisture, the sun-baked brown of the spinifex already lightened with a haze of green, while the trees were a rich emerald.

The sweltering heat had ended, and the day was pleasantly warm with a refreshing breeze. There was a hint of approaching autumn in the air, an ineffable feeling that gave rise to poignantly nostalgic reflections about the swift passage of the years. The coming change in season around her also gave her a sense of contact with the cycles of the land she loved so much, the only place on earth that she would ever regard as her home.

As the track led past pleasant, shady groves of giant trees and across lush grasslands, kangaroos and wallabies sprang out of brush and bounded away. Koalas stared down haughtily from high limbs as they munched eucalyptus leaves, while wombats, emus, brush-tailed possums, and other animals scurried away from the horses. Like always, the birds made the scene come alive in their staggering variety and multitudes. Flocks of colorful galahs, lyrebirds, currawongs, pipits, and numerous other species chattered and swarmed about.

The hours passed swiftly, Alexandra looking around in enjoyment as she rode down the track beside the stockmen. But in the back of her mind, there was a gnawing anxiety about Catherine's baby. Her terrifying nightmare of months before about the baby had been as real as life, too much like an ominous portent for her to dismiss.

Late in the day, the home paddock came into view. The sun low in the west, the light had a warm hue, tinting the clouds and the landscape with rich, golden shades. The huge stone mansion in its gardens on the hill had never been more beautiful to her, the shadows long around it. Towering over the complex of station buildings and pens at one side of the hill, and the married stockmen's houses and Aborigine huts on the other side, it was her castle as well as her home, the center of her domain.

Only a moment after her first glimpse of the home paddock, Alexandra saw that the track was being watched for her and her party. A rider left the barns at a gallop, and she knew it was either her husband or Jonathan, the two of them identical from a distance. Leaning forward on her saddle, she nudged her horse with her heel and urged it into a gallop, leaving the others behind.

Her horse tried to run, eager to reach the pens, but Alexandra kept the reins tight and held it to a gallop. The wind brushing her face, she balanced herself lightly on the saddle and looked at the rider as the distance closed. Then, she saw that he was her husband.

Glancing over the paddock again, she noticed smoke rising from the Aborigine huts. It was a corroboree, undoubtedly because Catherine was in labor. Releasing the pressure on her reins, she let her horse run.

At the same instant, David urged his horse into a run, and Alexandra knew the reason. It was one she shared, because their months apart had also been very long for her. A few minutes later, they reined up beside each other on the track, their horses panting. A wide smile of delight on his tanned, handsome face, David leaned over to kiss her.

His warm, fresh scent and the feel of his muscular arm around her awakened a yearning need. She clung to him and kissed him eagerly. Then, almost losing her balance on her saddle as their horses pranced about, she pulled away as he sat back on his saddle.

"God, I've missed you," he said with sober intensity, then he smiled again. "But why did you leave again so suddenly, love? What was so important that it couldn't wait?"

"I'll explain later," she replied, pointing toward the

huts. "Are the Aborigines having a corroboree because Catherine is giving birth?"

"Yes, she began this morning. Martha is with her, as well as Isaac Logan's wife, Mandy. Amy is there also, looking forward to being nursemaid to another baby, and Emma is helping the others. She has plenty of women with her, love."

Alexandra sighed in regret, turning her horse toward the house. "I knew she would have, David, but I did so want to be with her myself when it began. That can't be helped, but I can go to her now."

David nodded as her horse moved away, then he laughed and called out after her, "You'd better not leave again! If you do, this is the last time I'll let you out of my sight!"

Alexandra laughed as she replied, promising to stay, then she let her horse run again. A short time later, she heard the corroboree over the wind past her ears and the pounding of her horse's hoofs. The mournful groaning of didgeridoos, along with the clattering rhythm sticks and voices harmonizing in a chant, evoked memories of when her own children had been born, as well as other events the Aborigines had considered important.

At the foot of the hill, her horse tried to turn toward the barns and pens. Tugging a rein, she rode straight up the slope. When she reached the tree-lined avenue leading back to the house, she saw Jonathan sitting on the wide steps. He came down the steps, then reached up to help Alexandra down from her saddle as she reined up.

"I've been waiting here all day, Mother," he said worriedly as she dismounted, "and no one has told me anything. Would you either come and tell me or send word about how Catherine is doing?"

"I'm certain she's fine, Jonathan," Alexandra assured him. "What she's doing is very natural, and I had three babies myself, remember."

"Please, Mother," he insisted. "I must know."

"Very well," she replied in amused resignation. "If it's going to be much longer, I'll let you know."

He smiled in gratitude, squeezing her hand affectionately and kissing her, then Alexandra entered the house. As she crossed the entry and climbed the stairs, the house seemed too quiet to her. There were none of the sounds of pain and effort that accompanied bringing a new life into the world. Then, going down the hall, she heard a baby crying. She paused outside the door, breathing a silent prayer, then opened it.

The four women were at the washstand, bathing the wailing baby, and Catherine's beautiful face was lined with fatigue and the aftermath of pain as she lay in the bed. The women's faces revealed nothing, all of them tired after the day of tension and rushing about. Just as Alexandra started toward the washstand, Catherine saw her and lifted a hand toward her. Alexandra rushed to her daughter-in-law, taking her hand.

Bending over the bed, Alexandra kissed the young woman. "Catherine, I'm very, very sorry that I wasn't here," she told her. "I came back just as quickly as I could, but obviously it wasn't soon enough."

"You couldn't have had the baby for me," Catherine replied, smiling wanly. "And I'm very pleased that you're here now."

Alexandra smiled, pushing Catherine's raven hair back from her face. "No more than I am to be here with you, my dear. How do you feel?"

"Well enough, but weary. May I see my baby, please?"

"Yes, I'll fetch it for you, then I'll tell Jonathan that he can come up for a few minutes. After that, you must rest."

Catherine nodded, smiling drowsily. Alexandra kissed her again, then turned toward the washstand where Martha was wrapping the baby in a soft blanket. Both apprehensive and eager, Alexandra crossed the room, and Martha held out the baby to her.

When she took it, Alexandra experienced an instant of terror, the feel of the baby in her arms identical to the sensation she remembered from her nightmare. Forcing herself to look down at it, she opened the blanket. It was a beautiful baby girl, with no sign of a birthmark. On its head was a haze of black hair, similar to Catherine's, and the small, lovely features were very reminiscent of Jonathan's as a newborn.

Weak with relief and sheer bliss, Alexandra took the baby to the bed. She placed it beside Catherine and looked down at them, the young woman and her child exquisitely beautiful together. Then, as Martha and the other women put the room in order, Alexandra left to get Jonathan and to spread the good news about her granddaughter.

Alone in the hall, she gave in for a moment to her joy, as tears of happiness streamed down her face. She remained unsure if what she had done had changed anything at all. But she did know that after decades, the last vestige of Enos Hinton's evil presence was gone from her life. Even more important, the stigma of his corrupt bloodline was no longer a threat, having failed to appear in the next generation.

The future was now bright with promise, free of his malignant influence. Her happy, productive life with her husband and family would now be more rewarding than ever. But she and her husband were mortal, and an end would come to their stewardship of the sheep station they had established in the outback. Then it would be time for Jonathan and Catherine to accept the responsibility of protecting it for the next generation.

The first of that next generation had now been born, and continuity was assured. Some of the Kerricks would seek other paths, as Morton had, but some would remain at Tibooburra Station and maintain it as a family seat for generations to come. That gave ultimate meaning to what she and her husband had done, making their lives a triumph. They were the founders, the ones who had established a dynasty and its heritage in the outback.

The coming generations would fight grass fires, floods, droughts, and other perils as they labored up the steep, winding road of life. They would also be faced with more insidious dangers, as she had been in battling against the ghost of Enos Hinton, but Alexandra was certain that they would prevail and Tibooburra Station would endure. Rapturously happy, she dried her eyes as she went down the hall and the stairs to her son.